THE WILDERNESS NATIVITY

THE WILDERNESS NATIVITY

A STORY OF CHRISTMAS

BY GLEN BOWMAN

EDITED BY JEFF SCHMITZ

Greetings from the Church with the Red Door in the town of Mere D'Osia.

Enjoy the story.

Glen Bowman

iUniverse, Inc.
New York Lincoln Shanghai

THE WILDERNESS NATIVITY
A STORY OF CHRISTMAS

All Rights Reserved © 2004 by Glen E. Bowman

No part of this book may be reproduced or transmitted in any form or by any means, graphic, electronic, or mechanical, including photocopying, recording, taping, or by any information storage retrieval system, without the written permission of the publisher.

iUniverse, Inc.

For information address:
iUniverse, Inc.
2021 Pine Lake Road, Suite 100
Lincoln, NE 68512
www.iuniverse.com

ISBN: 0-595-32137-2

Printed in the United States of America

Contents

Chapter 1:	PRELUDE TO WORSHIP	1
Chapter 2:	THE KYRIE	4
Chapter 3:	CONFESSION	29
Chapter 4:	THE LESSONS	83
Chapter 5:	THE GOSPEL	171
Chapter 6:	THE SERMON	225
Chapter 7:	AN OFFERING	240
Chapter 8:	COMMUNION	244
Chapter 9:	THE BENEDICITON	249
ABOUT THE AUTHOR		251

Chapter 1

▼

PRELUDE TO WORSHIP

"You goin' to tryout for the Nativity, huh?" Amy said in the sarcastic tone young girls use to bait each other.

"Yeh." Jody replied nodding her head. One could barely hear her voice, as she stood slightly chilled in the late autumn sun shining on the narrow sidewalk of a small Illinois town.

"Might as well not waste your time." Amy said emphatically. Jody just looked at the cracks in the concrete as ants burrowed into their little domes of sand. Absently she wondered when the little creatures would call it quits and retire for the winter.

"I'm talking to you, Missy!" Amy nudged Jody lightly to get a response. Jody knew that there would be no fight today. She had already been down that road. Jody had a few pounds on Amy and Amy now realized she could not win when things got down and dirty as adolescent scraps sometimes do. That was the problem in a nutshell Jody thought to herself. Amy was the pretty one and everyone knew it. Also, it didn't hurt that Amy's father was the bank president. It was a done deal that Amy would get the best part in the annual Christmas pageant. Jody thought to herself that life could be so unfair. Still she knew that Amy would not let her be until she said something.

"I can try, can't I? Dad says it's a free country!" Jody's voice raised an octave in her obvious frustration.

"My Dad says there's nothin' free in the world and I believe him. You gotta have connections." Amy sounded as if she was parroting what she had heard at home.

"Mom says the point of the Nativity is not who plays what part. It's all the stuff that's give for the poor." Jody was beginning to get argumentative.

"Your Mom would say that 'cause she knows you don't stand a chance in getting a good part. Face it. You ain't got connections, Missy." Amy flaunted her superiority but kept her distance. She still remembered the black eye from her first argument with Jody.

"I'm still goin' to the Parish Hall for tryouts. You can walk with me or not. Your choice, girlie!" Jody emphasized the "girlie" word. She figured two could play at name-calling and she wasn't willing to risk the penalty for slapping Amy up side the head.

"We'll just see what happens." Amy moved off down the street scuffing her toe through the anthills Jody had been observing. It was her only way of getting back at Jody. Jody felt a brief twinge of sympathetic pain for the poor creatures. They covered the remaining two blocks to the Parish Hall of the Lutheran Church in silence.

Laughter and a buzz of voices greeted them at the door. The warm yellow glow of the ancient incandescent lights compensated for the nip of winter in the air. The two girls got in line to wait their turn to audition. As such things usually do, the line moved exceedingly slow.

"I wish they would hurry up!" Amy tapped her foot as Jody tried to do some homework while she waited. "It ain't like they've got a choice, or anything." Jody shrugged her shoulders with evident disgust.

"Give 'em a chance, would you, Amy? We all gotta have our chance." Jody said.

"Yeah, and you still believe in Santy Claus too, I bet." Amy gave it her best whiny voice.

"Even if we can't all get the lead parts, there's still the shepherds and the extras. They are all important, too. 'Sides, that ain't the point." Jody was quickly frustrated.

"And just what is the point?" Amy glared at Jody with her hands on her hips as if she didn't already know the answer.

Jody was about to reply when their Sunday school teacher who was helping with the auditions interrupted them.

"You know the point, Amy. You have been in Sunday school like everyone else. Christmas is a time for giving, not getting." The teacher lectured them sternly.

"Yeah and its my turn this year to get. I'm finally old enough to be Mary and that's what I'll be."

"Oh, Amy! You think you know everything." Another child in the line stepped in to help Jody who seemed to have been harassed long enough.

"Hush, Amy and take your turn, or I'll see you don't get to tryout." The woman overseeing the tryouts was becoming impatient.

"Like that will happen." Amy turned to face the front and became quiet. She had decided not to push it.

John Bent, the organizer for the annual Wilderness Nativity Pageant, overheard this interchange in frustration. John was under too much stress. It wasn't enough that he would lose his farm if the auction didn't raise enough money to pay an overdue note at the bank. He had to endure this endless bickering. It's the same thing every year he thought to himself. The politics of the whole deal were becoming unbearable to him. Amy was right that certain kids got the best parts. John could not afford to step on the toes of those who helped finance the event. For several years now John had justified this by trying to convince himself that the greater good was what was important. Indeed, the Wilderness Nativity brought in food, clothes, gifts and money for many needy people of the area. Still, he felt guilty about compromising his values. There had to be some other way, or his days as pageant director were numbered.

Chapter 2

THE KYRIE

The late October day in Western Illinois near the town of Meredosia was crisp and somber. It was certainly unusual for this time of year. The brooding, gunmetal gray clouds held a definite hint of snow, though the locals said that could not happen for it was way too early in the season. This did not portent well as the local farmers and townsfolk gathered at the Bent farm for the auction scheduled that day.

The price of corn and beans, the staple crops of the Midwest, were fickle on the commodity market of the 1970s. For the past several years a glut of corn and beans on the market had sent prices plummeting. The price went so low that it spelled doom to the farmer who wasn't able to make wise business decisions. Many farms that had been in the same family for generations were hitting the auction block to pay the debt incurred from trying to feed and shelter a family on such meager profits. Farming was not what it used to be. No, sir! It was no longer sufficient to be in tune with the land. One had to be shrewd at business as well. Just because you were born to farming didn't make you skilled in a business that was becoming high tech.

Today, the Bent family farm, one that had been in the family for generations, was on the brink of disaster. If this auction of extra equipment and precious household items did not raise enough cash to buy the family some months of breathing room for one last crop, the land itself would have to be sold to cover overdue bank loans. The Bent family was clinging to tradition and a way of life by a mere thread.

The two boys who watched the gathering of potential buyers from the neat red Dutch-style barn loft were well aware of their situation. Fourteen years on a working farm made them a serious contributor to the family business. Even though their parents had tried to shelter them from the harsh realities of life, the late night discussions between mother and father coupled with the worried frown on their father's brow hinted something was amiss. This had been going on for several months now. Although unsettling, this tension was becoming a burden that must be endured. The true terror of the situation was not fully realized until the family was gathered to formally discuss the prospect of selling their treasured heirlooms.

An antique is a valuable commodity. A farm with generations of history usually contained an attic full of this dusty treasure. Oak and walnut furniture including cupboards, beds, dressers, and bookcases brought high prices at auction. The Bent family had a house and barn full of these items. Their ancestors could be termed as pack rats never willing to discard serviceable items. These items were viewed more as a part of a heritage than just possessions. To the Bent's this auction would mean selling a part of their soul. It would be like a radical surgery removing things from the collective family body that could never be replaced. But to retain these precious articles would surely signal the death of their way of life.

Each member of the Bent family felt the pain of parting with something they valued. Ida, the mother, silently mourned parting with furniture her great-grandmother had brought with her from the family homestead in Vermont. Greta, her nine-year-old daughter, was losing a porcelain-faced doll dressed in turn-of-the-century frills. Her doll's wardrobe included a miniature trunk stuffed full of embroidered dresses and other garments. Destined to accompany the doll on the auction block was a white wicker baby carriage sure to bring a good price. John, the father, was losing several antique pieces including a threshing machine, a fully restored compliment of horse drawn equipment, and a like-new General-Purpose John Deere tractor that his grandfather had bought new in 1928 to keep up with the trend toward farm mechanization.

The two boys who sat in the barn loft shivering against the brisk north wind on that unseasonably cool October day were also losing precious things. Sure, they were losing the old furniture they had grown up with, but they were unable to appreciate the craftsmanship that went into each piece of furniture. Several rifles and guns that dated back to the early 1900's would also be gone. No longer would they be able to shoot rabbits with the old 1890 pump .22 caliber Winchester rifle given to their grandfather as a Christmas present. Nor would they be able to hunt quail with the Model 41 .410 gauge Winchester shotgun. This would be a deep wound but they knew it would heal.

The loss that would cause the boys the most pain was a collection of Indian artifacts the family had accumulated over several generations. This collection from bird points to lance heads and effigies had been found in the area by the boys and their ancestors as they went about working and playing on the family farm. The boys had played with these rocks for years. When they finally realized their value, they had lovingly researched and cataloged each piece. Well over one thousand artifacts from this collection would be sold at auction on this day.

And of all these Indian trinkets, the loss of one item in particular would cause immense pain. Elvin Bent, the younger brother, had found this prize personally in the back timber above the creek. Perhaps it was luck, but the boy felt it was the hand of God that guided him that special day to retrieve the most exquisite war lance that had ever been discovered in this part of the state.

On that spring day several years ago, Elvin and his brother Lawrence had been playing near the old cemetery hidden in a small wooded corner of the farm. The boys often came to this special spot because of the happy feelings the quiet meadow gave them. To be sure, there was a graveyard close by. One would immediately assume that this would conjure up uneasy feelings in young boys still prone to fantasy. Yet, the aura of this special spot suggested a deep serenity rather than terror. It was as if God's faithful were resting in a blissful sleep nearby. Those sleeping saints offered the boys nothing to dread. The peaceful glade had an almost mystical quality.

Given this beautiful location on a sunny spring day, should one not expect a memorable event to occur? Elvin had just passed by the sleepy cemetery and was headed under the barbed-wire fence that meandered through the trees. Avoiding the four pronged barbs he wiggled under the fence.

"Wow! I can't believe it!" Elvin exclaimed as his attention was immediately drawn to the lush grass cluttered with jack-in-the-pulpits and May apples that grew along the fence line. A sparkle of sunlight reflected on something partially hidden in the grass.

"Oh no you don't," said Lawrence as he jumped in the grass trying to be the first to the treasure. He wasn't in the mood to hunt rocks on such a glorious day. He only wanted to have a romp. Lawrence was the comedian of this duo.

"You hush now and back off." Elvin spoke seriously trying not to smile. He was the elder brother and wanted to maintain his decorum even if no one could see them. Not expecting anything special, Elvin slowly moved toward the source of the reflection. Kicking the dirt, as boys are want to do, a large, stony article rolled out from under a pile of soil. There on the ground, still covered by the moist, black dirt of the Illinois woodland, lay the most perfectly shaped lance-head the boy had ever seen. Its size alone was several inches longer than most.

"Got it," Elvin said as he quickly seized the object. "You can look but don't touch. I'm not giving this up for anyone."

Elvin held in his hand a black spear point approximately 10 inches in length. Two things were immediately discerned as making it different from the usual spear point found around this area. First, the point was cold black with a highly polished, shiny surface. This was what had reflected the sunlight and caught the boy's eye. Flint rock, the raw material used by the natives to make their weapons, was always white, tan, or, occasionally red, but never black. This trait alone would make the point valuable. But, the second characteristic of the point served to make it unique. The lance was superbly shaped to resemble a crucifix. Its graceful lines suggested the design of a fleur-de-lis, the crest of the French explorers. Where had this thing been crafted and for what purpose? Was it Native American, or European? To be sure, it was a discovery that would keep the boys and eventually the people of the area talking for a long time.

The local rock hunter club was especially enamored with the discovery. There was much speculation about the story behind this artifact. The point was surely black obsidian, the product of a quickly cooled outpouring of volcanic lava. Obsidian was not native to Illinois. Historians came from several local colleges to document the rock and speculate on its origin. An attractive offer had even been tendered for the relic. But Elvin's father firmly believed that this artifact belonged to his son. It was up to his son to decide what to do with it. The boy had held on to it despite the money. Elvin knew it was his destiny to find it. Destiny would guide him in his choice of what to do with the spear.

On this gloomy auction day, Elvin knew that the lance had to be sold. The treasures of each family member were being relinquished to serve a greater good. Elvin knew he could not be so selfish as to hoard this article for his personal pleasure, and it made him feel good to contribute something of substantial value to help save the way of life he had come to love so dearly. The Bent boys shivered in the drafty barn loft door from anticipation as much as the cold as they waited for the sale to begin.

Friends and neighbors were coming up the lane to take part in this country ritual. Farm auctions were usually social gatherings celebrating retirements from a long, rewarding life spent tilling the soil. This sale was unusual in that it had a more depressing purpose. Sorrow and happiness lay in the balance today. Would the proceeds of the sale save this family and their precious way of life? The usual festive air was stifled as friends pondered the possibilities.

Many strangers could be discerned among the crowd that was growing by the minute. They came to view the collectibles and have a chance at taking a treasure home. Collectors from the nearby cities of Quincy and Springfield appeared ready to bid. Antique dealers were in abundance looking for a bargain. Given the variety of people at the sale, it would surely take an unusual person to stand out in a crowd. Yet, there he came, driving up the lane in a rented car. The car itself was not unusual, but the driver was another matter. As he emerged from the vehicle and began walking toward the auctioneer's booth everything seem to grow quiet.

This man was very nondescript to be causing such a reaction. He was not of a stature that would draw attention. Certainly not! Rather, he was small-framed and dark. So what was so extraordinary about him? Some would probably say it was his way of walking for his stride was that of a commander proceeding to review his troops. The stranger moved with dignity and sense of purpose. This aloofness undoubtedly separated him from the crowd.

But, it was the stranger's speech that betrayed him as a foreigner. His English was impeccable. That, in itself, gave him away. He had reason to say, "Pardon me!" as he moved toward the hayrack wagon after obtaining his bid number. This was immediately after he had caused quite a commotion with the sale clerk as he wrote down his name and address. Soon the crowd was whispering the rumor that the stranger had presented a large bank letter of credit. He could well afford to purchase anything that he might fancy, and apparently he was interested in the Indian artifact collection.

"I bet he will buy your spear," Lawrence whispered to his brother. He spoke solemnly with the innocence of youth.

"Shush up," said Elvin with irritation. He tried to hide a small tear.

The Bent boys had watched the stranger's arrival from their lofty perch in the barn's hayloft. Since the rocks were their personal property, they had watched closely for signs of anyone who might show interest in their treasures. After all, even inanimate objects deserve an owner who could appreciate their value.

It was obvious to anyone in attendance that the artifacts held the attention of the stranger. He smiled as he beheld the collection. Elvin Bent thought he actually saw the stranger beaming as he first laid eyes on the exotic spear point. The stranger had respectfully asked the sales attendant to inspect the point. It was with seemingly deep reverence that the stranger took the point in his hands. What motive could this stranger possibly have in singling out this article from such a large collection? Elvin knew that the stranger would purchase the lance even before the sale began. He almost felt jealously as he thought about having to part with his prized possession.

The auctioneer gave a brief speech about the terms of the sale and the quality of the items being offered. Following established tradition, the auctioneer then asked John Bent if he had anything further to add before the sale began. With eyes on the ground, John quickly declined the privilege. Elvin thought he saw a tear in the corner of his father's eye.

The sing song voice of the auctioneer and the buzz of the crowd began to blur as treasure after treasure fell under the gavel. The collection of guns was quickly dispersed. A substantial price was realized from each one. Antique furniture also sold in a frenzy of heated bidding. Likewise, the extra farm machinery brought a reasonable price. The Bents knew it would take a miracle to let them stay on their beloved farm another season.

Soon the only items remaining to be sold were the Indian artifacts. The stranger had not moved from his position in front of this collection. What was it he prized so much? The native artifacts were well organized and displayed. Size and type segregated them. Miniature bird points were sold first in groups of five or more. Some were framed in sets. The frames were the old, weathered boards from a barn that had stood in the back pasture. Very few of these points were blemished and the collectors recognized quality when they saw it. Some of the initial sets sold well above one hundred dollars. Several knowledgeable friends of the family had told the boys that their collection was valuable, but these early bids still came as a welcome surprise. Maybe there was just a chance that they could actually remain on the farm after all!

Ax-heads and effigies were presented next on the auction block. Several bidders showed no hesitation to push the bid higher and higher. Who would have guessed that these crude rocks unearthed by the moldboard of a plow in past years would generate such enthusiasm? Viewed as oddities and conversations pieces by the family, this collection of stone assumed a new importance. Maybe the miracle the Bent family had been praying for was now materializing before their very eyes. God, indeed, works in mysterious ways.

Finally, it came time to sell the larger points everyone was sure would bring a respectable price. The unusual obsidian lance was included in this group. Now the auctioneer was selling one piece at a time in hopes of getting the best price. Time seemed to drag as no item in this group sold quickly. Just when you thought everyone was done bidding someone's hand would go up and the exchange of bids would start again.

To this point John Bent had been keeping a general tally of the proceeds of his sale to see if there was any hope of saving his farm. He needed to clear over thirty thousand dollars to meet the bank foreclosure notice. Even though things had been selling well, John knew they only had around twenty five thousand dollars and the auctioneer's fee had to come off the top. The final few Indian rocks would have to bring nearly ten thousand dollars, a seemingly impossible task. The bidding was very competitive, but you needed at least two bidders willing to pay an exorbitant price to have any hope at all. Unknown to anyone at the sale just such a circumstance was developing. It seems a local college professor in charge of obtaining rare artifacts for the campus archives was in attendance. He intended to purchase the black obsidian lance that might prove to be a historical break through. For years there had been speculation among the intellectual community that Indian trading routes were well established in North America as early as the 17th century, possibly before. The theory was that different sections of North America provided material unique to its geographic region. Obsidian was a rock that provided a base for crafting excellent weapons and jewelry. Could Western Indians have brought this material to the Midwest and Eastern tribes in exchange for some other product they valued as much? No one knew for, sure since to date, there was no proof to substantiate the theory. Yet this particular lance found in the Illinois woodland might be the proof that was required to support a revolutionary historical theory. Given his voluminous research and a little luck, Professor Shadwick knew that he could make a name for himself in the halls of academia. He was in the right place at the right time and he had been authorized to pay top dollar for the right piece. The professor smiled for he knew that surely the rock would be his when the bidding stopped. Fame might be just around the corner.

The stage was set for a round of heated bidding that would be talked about in the area for years to come. Realizing what hopes rested on this single artifact, the auctioneer did his best to build interest before he started the bidding.

"What am I bid for this showpiece of the Bent family collection?" The auctioneer sang out in a hearty voice.

"Surely, you experts out there know its worth better than any of us here and the Bents truly hate to part with it. So let's make it worthwhile for everyone. How about two thousand dollars? Come on, don't be shy!"

The crowd seemed to gasp at huge starting bid. But most experienced bidders knew the auctioneer was just fishing. It was an obvious play in hopes of catching an eager bidder off guard, and, as usual, it didn't work.

"I'll give two fifty to start," said a local farmer standing quietly in the background.

"Thank you, Bob!" said the auctioneer as he began calling out the familiar cadence of numbers. Before anyone knew it the current bid was at one thousand. The auctioneer smiled because he knew that at that price he had done his best for the Bent family. For a seemingly interminable time the bid was stuck there. The auctioneer spent more time than usual trying to cajole or beg at least one more bid. He figured the current high bidder, the college professor, was willing to spend more if he had to. All he needed now was a passionate fellow to keep the whole deal going. Some unscrupulous auctioneers would have been prepared for this situation with a plant in the audience. At predetermined signal to his conspirator the auctioneer could easily move on to a higher figure. The only danger would be that he might be stuck with the item should he misread the enthusiasm of the other bidder. However, the auctioneer handling this sale was a personal friend of the Bents. The auctioneer was as honest as the day was long. He simply would never contemplate a dishonest dealing. As a result, the auctioneer was nearly prepared to end the sale at that very moment.

"Going once, going twice," he sang out content in the knowledge he had done his best for his friends.

Suddenly a bid card shot up in the crowd. The dark stranger standing on the front row next to the hayrack wagon seemed to wake up from his slumber. Until now he had remained in the background. That is not to say he had not been keenly observing the bidding on this final item, the black obsidian lance. Maybe his apparent foreign demeanor made him unfamiliar with the protocol of American auctions. Whatever the reason, he had almost waited too long. In the knick of time the auctioneer stopped from making the current bid final.

"Please to accept my bid for this item," said the stranger with a distinct foreign accent. The auctioneer had the word "sold" on the tip of his tongue when his assistant grabbed the sleeve of his heavy, worn Carhart coat and pointed to the stranger.

"I'm bid eleven hundred dollars," sang out the smiling auctioneer in a loud voice as he breathed an obvious sigh of relief.

"Thank you very much!" The auctioneer said, thinking that someone's prayer had been answered.

The college professor was caught off guard. He had felt assured that the unique artifact was his. He had been in reverie of the fact that he had saved the college a tidy sum by obtaining the item so cheaply. Now he must regroup his thoughts and evaluate his competition. Like any veteran bidder, Professor Shadwick now proceeded to determine if his adversary was willing to go higher. Or, on the other hand, was this bid just the last gasp of someone who hated to see the item sold, yet had no bankbook for a higher figure.

Professor Shadwick let the bid linger on eleven hundred while he performed his mental assessment of the situation. What he saw in the stranger's eyes led him to believe, even now, that he had lost his chance to advance his career. For the stranger's disposition reflected a resolve to purchase the item regardless of price. Still, on the hope he might be mistaken, the professor pushed the ante to fifteen hundred dollars. He reasoned that such a jump would surely reveal the stranger's perseverance.

"Two thousand," countered the stranger without hesitation. The auctioneer, sensing the competition between the two men, decided to take advantage of the situation. This veteran of many sales knew that once a bidding frenzy began, often the sky was the limit.

"I've got two. Who'll give two five?" The crowd murmured.

"Come on now," the auctioneer continued. "We all know what Indian rocks are worth nowadays and so far I must say that this is a steal." The bid cards began raising with regularity so there was no reason for conversation. The atmosphere was electrifying and the crowd loved it.

The exchange of bids between these two adversaries now came fast and furious. Apparently, each wanted to demonstrate to the other that they were not ready to stop any time soon. Before anyone knew it the professor had bid five thousand dollars and the action slowed. The crowd thought that surely the end was now in sight. Who would have guessed anyone would be prepared to pay such an exorbitant price for a rock?

Neither the lofty bid, nor the response of the crowd seemed to daunt the stranger. He had experience enough to know that, given the recent pace of bidding, the auctioneer would give him ample time to consider his next offer. In his mind the stranger reviewed his options as he carefully eyed the artifact. There was no doubt that Providence had brought him to this Mid-western farm. The lance, down to the last minute detail, was exactly what he had prayed to find. God had also blessed him with the means to acquire this almost religious artifact. He could not allow it fall into the hands of some academic who would only use it for their own personal advancement. No, he was not about to stop bidding at such a reasonable price. But the professor couldn't accept the fact that he had already lost the battle.

Professor Shadwick breathed a sigh of relief when the stranger stopped advancing the bid with a quick wave of his black gloved hand. Surely this was the successful end to the game, he thought to himself, as he looked into the eyes of the stranger. Five thousand dollars was a heavy price to bring before the College Board, but intuitively he felt it was justifiable. With a little luck and this exquisite artifact he could put his college on the map as a leader in North American native historical research. Why the publicity alone could be worth a gold mine. As the professor was becoming complacent in his reverie, the stranger's hand went up to advance the bid.

"I bid ten thousand dollars." The stranger spoke almost matter-of-factly. As the auctioneer leaned forward with his hand to his ear, assuming that he was imagining what he heard, the stranger repeated the bid so there could be no mistaking what he had said.

John Bent, astonished by this event, swayed and nearly fell against one of his friends. He was so taken aback by what he had heard that he feared he was daydreaming. This large amount would guarantee his family safely fed and clothed through the coming winter, as well as giving him some breathing space with his creditors. Everyone in the crowd was on their toes waiting to see what would happen next. A hush fell on the crowd and only the distant sounds of the barnyard livestock could be heard.

The professor could not believe his ears either. Had this madman just doubled his bid? When reason finally returned, Professor Shadwick halfheartedly considered going forward. Then, realizing the futility in this situation, the professor merely shook his head as the auctioneer looked for his response. He cast his eyes dejectedly to the ground as the auctioneer went through the motions of soliciting a higher bid. But there was no response from the crowd and soon the gavel fell completing the final transaction of a most remarkable farm sale. Everyone began to move toward their vehicles or to have a final word with friends. What could have been a grievous situation had a happy ending!

In the excitement of the sale everyone had forgotten about the weather. Big, fluffy snowflakes began to fall from the steel gray sky. Had the auction ended on a sour note this would have been a fitting punctuation to a distressing day. Somehow though there was a joyful lightness in this weather that portended a sparkling winter. The hearts of the Bent family and the community were as light as the slowly descending flakes of snow.

The Bent boys made their way from the perch in the hayloft of the old rusty-red barn to the barnyard below. The crowd was quickly dispersing. Successful bidders were carrying off their treasures smiling as they went. Neighbors were saying their good-byes as farmers' left to do afternoon chores before the snow got too deep and the dark of night closed in. Elvin and Lawrence quietly went to stand by their father as he joked with some friends.

Observing their father as he laughed heartily, the boys could see that a great burden had been lifted from his narrow shoulders. This was the old Dad that they had known so well, but had been absent from their lives for the past year, or so. Farming as an occupation could be very rewarding, but it could also be extremely stressful. It took a special person to live with the trials and tribulations of such a life. For, indeed, it was more than an occupation. To till the soil was to live a life in harmony with nature. Farming required commitment and dedication for the round-the-clock work and worry. Even if you could leave the land for a few days, you still carried the cares with you. No one who receives a 40-hour paycheck can ever understand this life. No farm job was ever finished. When the crops were harvested, plans for the next spring had to be made. Once a crop of cattle or hogs was shipped to market, preparation for the birth of new livestock must begin. The stress was endless. Many develop stomach problems and ulcers. Yet, John Bent now seemed truly relieved. John knew he had a tomorrow to worry about again. When put in this perspective, his life had suddenly become a great joy.

The dark stranger who had helped to grant John Bent his reprieve to continue the life he loved so much had moved over to the concession stand for a hot cup of coffee. Feeling gratitude toward this unlikely benefactor, John hollered to the clerk that it was his treat. He quickly walked over to the stranger to introduce himself and the two boys followed.

The stranger smiled benignly as he began to sip the warming liquid.

"You must have traveled very far to be with us today." John broke the silence. John smiled a big Midwest farmer's smile that showed his sincerity.

The stranger had been unsure of how welcome he was in this foreign place. This was the first bit of conversation he had had since leaving his hotel twenty miles away in Jacksonville that morning. Until now he had been feeling like an outcast and had an urge to leave as quickly as possible. Still, he knew there were many questions that he wanted to ask. The artifact now in his possession was a welcome surprise. It verified a hunch he had for quite sometime. Surely, his brethren back in France would be overjoyed at this extraordinary stroke of luck. While some questions were answered, the exquisite rock he now held in his hand suggested that much more research needed to be done before he could realize its full story. Perhaps these farmers held the key to answering several centuries of questions.

"You cannot imagine how far, Monsieur," said the stranger in careful, precise English. "It is a journey both in time and space," he added rather cryptically. He smiled at the idea of finally finding a friendly person in this large expanse of land called America. The stranger thought fleetingly that this lack of hospitality he was experiencing might well explain why his ancestors did not stay to call it home.

"And you can't imagine how glad the Bents are that you made the long trip," said John, trying to break the icy conversation. "I hope the coffee is thawing you out a bit. Blasted weather around these parts can't be predicted. The weather people have even given up. It changes almost daily."

The stranger nodded as he clutched the thermal cup between his cold hands and tried to absorb some of its dissipating heat.

"Know what they say about Illinois weather?" John asked rhetorically. "If you don't like the weather right now, just stick around." John chuckled half-heartedly at the well-worn joke wondering if he should get with his chores.

"Too be sure, Monsieur. I have read that weather of the North American continent can be most unpredictable. Merci, beaucoup for the warm drink. You are very kind," said the stranger. Not wanting to seem aloof he continued, "Are these fine young men your sons?"

"You know it!" laughed John slapping the boys on the back. "They are a man's blessing in an uncertain world—more precious than gold." John's sincerity was obvious. He had wanted to tell another joke to make the stranger feel welcome, but he was feeling very thankful just now and this comment came straight from his heart. The boys seemed rather embarrassed at this praise. They shuffled their feet nervously in the grass that was already caked with snow.

After looking directly into John's eyes, the stranger said, "You are seem a man who knows what is important in this life. You are religious, no?"

"Have you ever met a farmer who wasn't?" John replied, uncomfortable at letting the conversation descend into such a solemn subject. He remembered his mother saying that religion and politics hardly ever lead to anything but arguments.

"French farmers hold a deep reverence for the creator of all their earthly bounty. But of course basic truths transcend nationality," replied the stranger as if he had long ago arrived at this conclusion.

"So you're from France," said John sheepishly, trying to return the conversation to a happier topic.

"Oui, I am from Alsace near the German border. You have visited my country?" The stranger was reluctant to become too involved in a long discussion lest he miss an opportunity to further research the history of his artifact. He hoped this farmer could shed some light on its origins. At the very least, he wished to know how this farm family had come to possess this exquisite lance. The stranger reluctantly proceeded with amenities, waiting for the first opportunity to ask his questions.

"Me? To Europe?" said John raising his arms and taking one step back with feigned surprise. "No, sir!" he stated. "I don't think I have been over three hundred miles from this farm in my whole life. A farmer's work doesn't allow time off, what with the livestock, crops, and everything else."

Just then John's wife, Ida, came over to the group and put her arms around her boys with obvious affection.

"John, why haven't you asked our friend to come in and get warm before he freezes himself absolutely too death." She was radiating warmth on this cold day as she spoke with evident hospitality. "The least you could do is introduce us!"

The stranger responded before John could utter a word. "I'm afraid I've been remiss. Please, I beg your pardon." He said, reaching quickly for her hand and nearly spilling his coffee.

"I'm Father Jacob Reneau of St. Theresa Parish in eastern France. It is a distinct pleasure and honor to meet each one of you." Father Jacob smiled as he vigorously shook Ida's hand. Ida proceeded by introducing her family knowing full well how John hated formal introductions. Just then the wind picked up and it began to snow in earnest.

After shaking the Priest's hand, John raised the collar of his sheepskin coat and commented, "Boys, we really need to get busy with our chores before it gets dark. Feels like the temperature has dropped ten degrees since we've been here talking with Father Jacob."

Turning to Ida, John said, "Honey, why don't you take our new friend over to the house and serve him some of your famous mulled cider to warm him up?"

Ida gave a short laugh as she expelled her breath mockingly. She took Jacob's arm and led him away.

"John's been looking for an excuse for me to make some of his favorite cider for weeks and I guess you're it!"

The boys hustled off to feed the chickens and gather the few eggs the hens would have managed to lay on such a cool day. John started the Allis-Chalmers tractor that was sitting near the barnyard fence. After parking tractor and wagon under the open barn loft door, he proceeded to toss small bales into the wagon.

Rather than helter-skelter, the bales fell rather regularly into a sort of stack. This was obviously the result of years of practice. As if on cue, the cows awoke from their malaise instinctively sensing it was their feeding time. As the cattle began to bawl for their supper and move toward the wagon, John yelled to Ida over all the cacophony.

"Don't you be asking Father Jacob too many questions. He'll have to repeat everything when I get in!" John chuckled as he continued. "'Sides, I'll be bawling louder than these cows if you don't have supper ready. Hungry men gotta be fed on time."

Ida just shrugged since she had learned long ago she could never get in the last word with her husband no matter how hard she might try. Soon John and the tractor were out of sight, engulfed by hungry cows and swirling clouds of fluffy, white snow. Ida stomped the snow from her unfeminine black chore boots as she opened the door to the back porch. The soft glow of the lamp light in the windows of the sturdy two-story wood framed farmhouse made a welcome winter scene against the background of an approaching storm front on a cold night.

"Come right on in Sir, and don't be bashful. You must be near catch'n your death in that light jacket!" Before Father Jacob could reply Ida continued, "Of course you must stay for supper, and the way that storm looks, possibly the night as well." Father Jacob was so overwhelmed by the hospitality that he could only nod.

Ida took their coats and hung them on an ancient looking rack on the back of the enclosed porch. Jacob with his history background thought it looked turn-of-the-century with its beveled oblong glass and brass fixtures. Ida ushered the Father into her living room and soon had him drinking a warm cup of deliciously spiced apple cider in an easy chair beside a Franklin stove.

"Make yourself at home," Ida said as she turned on the radio before going into the kitchen. "Maybe we can get a weather forecast that will tell us what to expect. I doubt you'll be going anywhere but our house tonight. The snow is starting to pile up high already." Ida nodded toward the powdery accumulation on the windowsill.

"Just rest. I'll have your supper in no time." Ida said with a kindly smile. "You don't have a problem with farm cooking, do you?" She said as an after thought, not really expecting a reply. "I'm afraid I'm not a cosmopolitan cook and don't have a French cookbook."

"I'm sure anything you prepare will be delicious, Mrs. Bent," said Father Jacob as she disappeared into the kitchen.

"I enjoy new dishes." Father Jacob continued, trying to keep the conversation going. He was left alone in the living room in a threadbare but very comfortable recliner. The room had a much-lived in look, typical of most farmhouses. Wood was stacked near the hearth for easy access on a cold night. The blazing yellow-gold fire in the stove made a lively crackling sound. Jacob began to feel sleepy in the warmth after the long hours outside in the cold.

There were several pictures on the white plaster walls. Quail peered out at him from underneath a white pine tree in a stunning print by some artist named Owen Gromme. A calendar with a wildlife advertisement on top suggested that someone in the family enjoyed hunting. Another framed photograph in particular drew his attention. The picture must have been taken many years ago because the horses and an elderly bearded gentleman by the barn looked from another era. The lady next to the gentleman was dressed in a long pleated dress typical of the fashion many years out of style. Her hair was perched severely clasped in a neat bun on the top of her head. Jacob suspected that it was a portrait of the Bent farm as it appeared in the early years of the century. He thought to himself that indeed, the roots of this family were deeply planted in Illinois soil.

"I'll turn on the TV and see if we can get a more detailed forecast. The radio has too much static for my liking." Mrs. Bent said as she stepped through the doorway to hit the power switch. Just as quickly she was back in the kitchen and soon a wonderful aroma was permeating the living room. Jacob must have been tired because the warmth of the stove coupled with the drone of the TV program caused him to doze. In what seemed only a moment Jacob was startled awake by the slamming of a porch storm door and an icy blast of wind. The boys and John were talking loudly as they removed their boots and chore clothes on the nearby porch. Jacob looked at the gingerbread clock on the mantle and saw the time was after six o'clock. He realized over an hour had passed since he had assumed this comfortable position by the warm fire. Jacob felt hungry and wondered what type of American cuisine he would be enjoying for supper. He could hardly wait for he guessed Mrs. Bent was probably a great cook for all her modesty.

"Getting nasty out there," John said loudly to his guest as he ushered his boys through the open porch door.

"I was afraid the boys might freeze the way that wind has come up howl'n. Thank the Lord that we got the chores done for another day. Hope the calves can stand this type of weather."

John's face was beet red from the cold, but his wrinkled brow showed deep concern for his animals. The boy's faces were also cold and red. But the weather obviously did not dampen John's spirits. After all, he had so much to be thankful for on this particular day. The Lord had seen fit to save his beloved farm, for the time being. They had food on the table, warm and dry shelter, and their health. What more can a body ask for thought John?

Ida appeared from the kitchen to welcome everyone inside and make sure all was well. She had a bread knife in her hand, which would account for the sweet smell of fresh baked bread in the air.

"Hope you all are hungry!" she exclaimed with a wide grin. Apparently the cold weather had improved everyone's appetite because the family moved in mass toward the neatly prepared kitchen table.

"Come on Father Jacob," John motioned graciously toward the kitchen door, "or the way my boys eat you'll be left hungry."

A young girl quietly appeared on the spiral staircase leading upstairs. She could not be more than ten. Obviously shy, she had brown hair with bright blue eyes. She had the slight build that apparently ran in the Bent family.

"Have you met our daughter, Father?" John said as he lovingly put his arm around the girl and stroked her long hair.

"Ada, meet Father Jacob Reneau." John continued with the introductions. "He is visiting from France, Alsace I believe. No doubt he will have some interesting things to talk about after supper. Perhaps we will have our own personal travelogue."

Father Jacob grasped the tiny, delicate hand of the girl and was surprised at the hearty handshake she supplied.

"Our daughter is fascinated with Europe," said John. "She's quiet now, but get her started on a subject that she's interested in and she will talk your leg off."

"I am very pleased to meet you, Mademoiselle." Father Jacob said with his distinctly French accent surfacing. Apparently, he had been trying to hide it before. Or was it that he was becoming comfortable in the company of this friendly and loving farm family?

"You are a very pretty young lady." Jacob continued. "Obviously you take after your mother." He smiled to show he meant the compliment sincerely. Both ladies blushed, being unaccustomed to such chivalric behavior.

"For that you get an extra piece of pie," said Ida jokingly as she fairly glowed. "John," she said turning to her husband and patting him on the shoulder, "you could learn a thing or two about manners from this man. Let's hope he won't be a stranger."

"I'm sure Jacob don't have the years it would take to get your manners straight," retorted Elvin quickly. Everyone laughed at his wit and proceeded to sit down around the supper table.

"Please sit here Father," Ida gestured to the obvious place of honor at the end of the long oak table directly opposite her husband John's seat.

"I'm sorry we aren't dining in the dining room, but it would take a month of Sundays to find the table what with the books and other junk piled in there." Ida continued. "We rarely have the honor of entertaining guests and the children have taken over that room as their personal library."

Ida smiled as Father Jacob held her chair out for her to be seated. He waited for both Ada and Ida to sit before moving to his chair. Ida thought to herself that she could easily become accustomed to such manners. But then again this formality would simply not suit her men. Ida sighed noticeably as she bowed her head for the blessing.

"Father, would you do us the honor," John softly said to his guest.

"Of course, my son." Father Jacob nodded and folded his hands in pray.

"Our most heavenly Father, please bless this bountiful table as we dine with new found friends. Keep us safe and protect us from all evil as we journey along life's way. If it be thy will, help this family to continue in the life of their ancestors. Continue to aid me now on my quest as you have aided me in the past. Above all, let thy will not my will be done. We ask all of this in the name of our Lord, Jesus Christ. Amen."

There was a pause as everyone contemplated the meaning of the good Father's prayer. Ida then let out a sigh of happiness and proceeded to pass the mashed potatoes to her guest.

The harvest table was steaming with bowls of meat and vegetables. Everyone began to take the bowl nearest to them and ladled out a helping before passing it to their left. The menu consisted of pork chops, mashed potatoes, pickled red beets, green beans, coleslaw, and freshly baked bread topped with real butter. The butter had been churned by Ida and formed in an ancient round wooden butter mold. The picture of a cow was stamped on the top of the golden yellow mound. The fare was typical of an old-fashioned farm family living off the fruit of their labor. The past season's garden had been very bountiful. Naturally a freshly baked apple pie peeked out at them from the counter of an old Hoosier cabinet. The cabinet was a cherished family heirloom that Ida could not bring herself to sacrifice on the sale bill. She held it in reserve for a more needful time. The wonderfully golden pie waited to complete the perfect meal for a cold and stormy winter's eve on an Illinois prairie farm.

For a time all was quiet but for the clanking of the tablespoons on the bowls as the "family style" meal proceeded. The guest had served to dampen the usually dinner conversation. John took a sip of the hot, black coffee as he pondered what subject to begin discussing.

"What do you think of our country, Father?" Ida said nervously, attempting to break the uncomfortable silence.

"America is very enchanting," Father Jacob said without a pause. His quick and smooth reply made everyone feel at ease.

"Your, what you say," Jacob grasped for the appropriate English words, "Midwest, especially is most hospitable. Everyone has been most gracious, and your gesture of taking in this humble stranger on a cold and lonely night is simply amazing." As the Father spoke everyone became aware that he had chosen the correct profession. The priest fairly exuded warmth and sincerity in both his words and gestures. One could sense immediately that he truly cared for his fellow man.

"Why are you so far from home?" Lawrence blurted out the question that was on the mind of every person at the table. There was genuine relief on the faces of the family as they began to eat the delicious meal and awaited the Father's response.

"Son, that's prying into another man's business. It is considered to be impolite." John mildly rebuked his son as his manners compelled him to do.

"It's the logical question to ask, Monsieur Bent, so please don't be hard on him. I really don't mind answering." Father Jacob grinned and all in the room were quickly put at ease.

"Son, I'm a historical scholar interested in my ancestors and their apparent link to your country several centuries ago." Jacob turned to address Lawrence as he placed a savory bit of pork in his mouth and began to chew.

"Have they taught in your school about the French exploration of the New World?" the priest asked seriously.

"Yes Sir," replied Lawrence politely. He was quite happy to be included in the adult conversation. "Not too much though about the French, Sir. They've taught more about the Spanish. I guess the French were not as important." Lawrence qualified his statement.

"About the only French names I can remember are La Salle and Champlain. I only know that a lake was named after one or the other and I have no idea why," continued Lawrence. He did not want to look stupid in the eyes of a learned man.

"Don't feel ashamed at not knowing the details of the French participation in the exploration and settlement of your nation and your state called Illinois." Father Jacob smiled and patted the boy's arm to reassure him.

"I've found that your schools view the French role as quite mercenary. If mentioned at all, we French are often portrayed as men in pursuit of selfish personal gain with little regard for anything else." The good Father waxed philosophical. "My research has come to show the French explorers in quite a different light."

"So your trip to Illinois is some sort of fact finding mission," John picked up the conversation, not wanting it to get too serious because he felt he detected the subject was dear to the heart of his French guest.

"Oui, you see I am convinced that the French motives for coming to North America were just as noble as our English counterparts. Various aspects of religion were very influential to our migration as they were to the English. My research seems to prove that. As a historian, I hope I can prove that my countrymen deserve better treatment in retrospect."

"And did your research bring you specifically to Illinois?" Ida questioned.

"To Meredosia, in fact," replied Father Jacob in a matter of fact manner.

"How so?" said John, thinking that the conversation was becoming fascinating.

"For instance, do you know the origins of the name of your hometown, Meredosia?" Jacob smiled as he continued eating. The others were eating also, but slowly as they pondered all that was said.

"As a matter of fact I do," replied John. "I'm something of an historian myself and I read the book on our town's history published by our local historical society a few years ago. I'm sure you already know that it is of French origin. Roughly translated it means something like willow swamp. As a native Frenchman can you confirm that?"

"I'm impressed, Mr. Bent, that you know so much about the origins of your village," Jacob continued the casual conversation of the winter evening meal. "I'm sure you know the work of the French missionaries among the natives of this area between the great rivers, Mississippi and Illinois."

"Only vaguely," said John. "If you're here to do research about the early Indian tribes and French settlements, I'm afraid you are not going to find much." John didn't want to discourage his new friend but the words slipped from his lips before he thought better of it.

"Actually, I'm more interested in local traditions that might shed some light on my research." If Jacob was discouraged by John's comment he gave no indication.

"I can't think of anything like that that around here and I was born and raised by this river," said Ida in passing. "Unless, of course, you want to hear about the annual Christmas production our church sponsors," she said as an after thought.

"John has become a real authority on that tradition." Ida winked at John playfully as they both grinned at their private joke.

"Please continue," Father Jacob said, obviously very interested. "I've found even seemingly trivial circumstances can have a profound meaning."

"Well, let's have our desert and coffee in the living room. Once John gets started talking, we may all need a comfortable place to snooze." Ida continued her joke. The children quickly cleared away the dishes and the apple pie was sliced and served. Soon everyone was in front of the wood stove ready for a good winter's eve conversation.

"You have my undivided attention, Monsieur Bent." Jacob worked to restart their discussion on local traditions. "I'm sure your project is a worthy one."

"Well, yes, actually it is." John spoke, half-embarrassed and not really knowing why. Perhaps he was feeling slightly guilty for making light of a project that did so much good each year in the community.

"As a council person of St. John's Lutheran Church, Meredosia Parish, I have the responsibility of organizing the annual Rural Nativity festival." John noticed Father Jacob's eyes widen and he seemed to gasp for breath as John spoke the last few words. John paused as he waited for the Frenchman to regain his composure. He was about to continue when the good Father interrupted almost desperately.

"Pardon, did you say Rural Nativity, or Wilderness Nativity?" Jacob asked in an extremely animated manner. These few words had struck a passionate chord in the mild-mannered priest. John didn't quite know what to make of this sudden interest.

"I said Rural Nativity, but I recall reading somewhere that the festival had been called the Wilderness Nativity some years back," John replied.

"Rural and wilderness are words somewhat akin," John continued, "although rural seems more befitting to our modern world. God knows this part of Illinois hasn't been a wilderness by any stretch of the imagination for over a century." John chuckled. "The last Native American was forced across the Mississippi in the 1850's, if I remember my history correctly."

"You speak of tradition and allude to a distant past," Father Jacob began his quest for facts. "Just how old do you believe your annual festival to be?"

"I have no idea exactly, but I can certainly speculate." John looked into the priest's eyes and saw they were begging for answers.

"Nearly two centuries. Definitely as long as the white man has settled this land and possibly years before. As a historian, you know the word old is a relative term when applied to America. Obviously old is not the same here as in Europe."

"Ah-ha!" exclaimed Father Jacob. "That is precisely what I had hoped you would say. I would guess that the festival is staged on Christmas Eve. You most probably solicit young children to stage the manger scene. Residents bring what gifts they can spare, especially basic items like food and clothing, to present to the Christ child. Later that night these gifts are distributed to the poor and needy throughout the area. As one of the organizers, I'm sure you feel quite blessed when this good work is accomplished."

John was taken aback at this outburst of enthusiasm as was his entire family. They had been near slumber listening to the droning conversation so near after supper. Now things were becoming exciting. It was as if Father Jacob had discovered a treasure. They couldn't wait to discover what was so important to him.

"Before we go any further, Father," said John, raising his hands as if trying to slow the sudden tempo, "I want to ask you a question."

"Please proceed, my son." Father Jacob spoke in a quiet tone, again assuming a more priestly composure.

"How is it that you know so much about our little annual ritual when you are a complete stranger to these parts and I have not given you any details of the celebration? It's as if you are a past resident of our town recently returned from a long journey, although I know you have never been here before in your life." John mused and Ida nodded in agreement.

"I'm truly sorry for my lack of decorum when you mentioned your local celebration. Things are not always as they seem. Perhaps I assumed too much." Father Jacob spoke slowly, as if carefully deciding how to proceed.

"The reason for my joy is that your rural festival sounds so much like a custom practiced for centuries in my Alsatian homeland." The Father continued, "I may be reading too much into the similarity of the festival's name."

"So that is why you asked about wilderness as opposed to rural," Ida said and the priest nodded.

"Please describe your annual festival. Perhaps there is little similarity beyond the name." Jacob stated this with a hint of disappointment in his voice.

"John will be glad to, won't you honey?" Ida said quickly, wishing to cheer her guest up.

"Not much to tell really," said John smiling. "You pretty well hit the nail on the head with you previous comments. You must have a crystal ball to know all of that."

"The idea of giving gifts on Christmas Eve is not novel. I could have easily guessed the details. But it is the name of the festival that makes its similarity to ours in France so unusual." The priest wanted to ask more questions.

"It is too much work for sure for a small congregation like as ours, Father." John shrugged. "Just not enough people interested in helping the needy in our town these days. Why is the world turning so selfish Father?"

"My son, each generation is afflicted with similar doubts and misgivings. Such thoughts are the Devil's work meant to discourage God's faithful from good works. We must not let ourselves be troubled, but rather endeavor to do what is right in the eyes of God." Father Jacob responded with heartfelt sincerity. "What, in fact, is your rural nativity, my son?"

"Much like you described, it's like an annual Christmas pageant meant to collect food and clothes for the poor and needy." John began to explain. "Each year the pageant director—"

"That would be John," interjected Ida with obvious pride.

"Yes, that's me," said John lowering his countenance as if carrying a heavy burden, "I must prepare, cast, organize, and direct this celebration which culminates on Christmas Eve with the best children of our town acting out the Nativity of our Lord. As these costumed kids gather in a stable in a local barn dressed as Mary, Joseph, shepherds, and the Magi, the rest of the town brings their offerings. This abundance will be distributed later that night to the less fortunate. That's it in a nutshell." John slapped his hands on his knees and stood up to get a cup of coffee. This movement did little to disturb the children who were by now fast asleep, so tired from the work of an exciting day.

"It appears that you are not entirely enamored with your noble cause, Mon ami," said Jacob wanting John to continue what he feared was finished.

"Well, the rewards can be great, but the path treacherous." Ida took up where John had left off. "What with all the jealousy and bickering, one can lose sight of the ultimate goal." She shook her head wearily lowering her gaze.

"Human nature dictates that the way will not always be easy in these matters." Father Jacob continued his sermonizing. "But good will always prevail and the ultimate reward is in heaven, not here on earth. Truly it is worth the grief one is forced to endure."

"We have always found that to be true," John said, sipping his hot coffee carefully, "but that still doesn't make it easy to repeat the months of preparation each year. Also, in the past, the responsibility could be passed around a bit. But lately there are so few to rely on. I swear I make more enemies over petty things! Every child can't be Joseph or Mary. Everyone in the town is always second guessing the decisions of myself and the pageant committee."

"Are you a praying man, John?" Father Jacob posed the simple question so sincerely and directly it took John by surprise.

"Not as much as I should be, Father." John gave a humble reply.

"Therein lays your strength and consolation." Father Jacob said with absolute conviction of a very wise and holy man.

"Does our celebration sound familiar then to you, Father?" Ida sensed the conversation was degrading into a confession. She wanted to get some answers rather than listen to a sermon.

"Oui, very much so Mrs. Bent." Jacob slid back and relaxed in the overstuffed recliner by the fire.

"The similarities seem striking although you have not given me much detail. Our Alsatian celebration is an annual event much like yours I assume. It probably dates from the early 18th century, or even before. My research on the matter is certainly not conclusive. That is why I continue my search where ever it leads me." Jacob assumed the conversational style of an historian discoursing on a favorite subject.

"Would you say the basic intent of both celebrations is to provide for the less fortunate in our society? Both affairs seem to encourage mass participation and have a distinct religious flavor." Jacob paused as Ida nodded her head in agreement with what he had said.

"There is one puzzling thing about all of this though." John seemed to be thinking out loud. "I assume your celebration is Catholic sponsored while ours is Lutheran. Do you have any thoughts on this?"

"It is simply a reflection of the surrounding cultural mix. France continues to be predominately Catholic with that religion providing the societal glue for all the rural areas. Here in Illinois you Lutherans obviously assume the role that was once Catholic. The type of religious faith is secondary to the good that is perpetuated in such a tradition. Besides, Catholics and Lutherans are not that far apart ideologically. Would you not agree, Jon?" Jacob concluded.

There was silence for several minutes as John considered what to say. He was not sure if this was the time or the place to state his true feelings.

"But you cannot imagine the depth to which petty human jealousy descends in our small town," said John. "I'm sure you French do a better job in maintaining the ritual as the noble cause it truly is." John shook his head and gazed at the floor.

"Remember, my son, you are speaking to a member of the clergy. I have many years of experience in dealing with these things. Frailty of human nature knows no ethnic or cultural bounds. All of God's children experience less than flattering times. It is enough that good can result from seemingly unpleasant details." Father Jacob replied in sympathy.

"It is not a complete coincidence that a stranger from Europe should suddenly appear in a town with a French name and attend a farm auction to buy some Indian relics." Ida speculated, wishing to revive the interesting conversation.

"You must have quite a story to tell, Father. Let's wake the children and pop some corn. Tomorrow we will be snowed in any way so they can sleep late if they want. I'm sure we all want to hear what you have to say." Ida hurried off to prepare the snack while John bribed his children awake with a promise of soda pop.

Outside the fluffy snowflakes were swirling in the utility light on the pole near the barn. Already several inches of the white stuff had accumulated on the back porch. The barn was completely obscured and the snow mixed with the darkness gave the sense of friendly isolation. The cares of the world seemed far away to John at that moment. The warmth of the farmhouse provided a welcome contrast to the blizzard conditions outside. All of the Bent family got comfortable as they prepared to listen to what would prove to be a most extraordinary tale. Father Jacob was a parish priest of some experience and a noted historical lecturer at university. He was just the person to spin all the knowledge he had gathered about the French explorers in Illinois, the native inhabitants of this area, and the coincidence of two similar traditions into an exciting story. This would certainly be a welcome change from the usual television fare.

"I want to know why you paid so much for that black spear point we found a couple of years back." Lawrence in an obviously excited state urged the priest to proceed.

"My research into the tradition of the wilderness nativity in my village in Alsace has revealed some interesting facts that may be associated to that piece of rock." Father Jacob began.

"I believe that I can prove a link between this very stone and a tradition that has been practice for centuries in both France and Illinois. If this proves to be true, the lance assumes a very deep meaning."

"How can a rock buried for years in Illinois have anything to do with events in France today?" Lawrence, the young Bent son, was skeptical. The rest of the family eagerly awaited Father Jacob's response.

"I believe I can prove that the founder of the tradition known as the wilderness, or rural, nativity spent time both here in Illinois and in France. This legacy of good was somehow perpetuated for centuries on two continents. It is a mystery of God that with his grace may now be revealed to his faithful. I'm sure that my discovery will bear wondrous fruits to all in ways only God alone can now know." Father Jacob paused.

"In my historical research in France I discovered that the tradition of the rural nativity is the legacy of a local monastery founded by two Catholic priests. These priests are renowned for their exploits as missionaries in Europe, the Middle East, and North America. Before retiring to this monastery in their old age, these priests worked hard to bring Christianity to the heathens of newly discovered lands. They had a noble cause that was in direct contrast to the modern portrayal of the French explorer as purely mercenary.

"Before I begin my tale, fact or fiction, I must admit it can be very tedious at times," Father Jacob continued. "May I humbly request another favor of my gracious hosts?"

"Oh, just ask Father," Ida quickly interjected. "Don't be so humble with us common country folk." She smiled warmly, eager to hear the story.

"I would be so very grateful if you could show me the precise spot where the stone was found," Father Jacob said softly. "I feel that site may hold tremendous religious significance for me." His voice seemed to tremble.

"If you're willin' to brave the cold and snow tomorrow, then it would be the least we could do considering you helped save the family farm." John beamed at being able to grant such a simple request.

"Now get on with the story. The night is not getting any younger." John settled in his easy chair, turning his full attention to the priest. The whole Bent family was filled with anticipation.

Father Jacob began his story in the easy conversational style that marked an accomplished speaker and an experienced storyteller. Soon his audience was oblivious of everything but his wonderfully descriptive words that immediately transported them to another land in another time.

Chapter 3

CONFESSION

In the year of our Lord 1675, French interest in the colonization of the New World was increasing. Until that time, French exploration was limited to the adventurous few who wished to shed the conventions of the time and strike out on their own. These were mostly outdoorsmen who saw the opportunity to escape from civilization and gain a fortune in the bargain. Animal furs were plentiful, the scenery was beautiful, and there was always a chance of stumbling onto a cache of gold. If they were very lucky, some of these explorers could return to France with enough money to live like kings.

Word had recently been received in the court of Louis XIV concerning the exploits of Joliet and Father Marquette. Their adventures had allowed France to lay claim to a sizeable portion of the North American continent. King Louis was well aware of how the resources of this New World contributed to the power of his rivals, King Leopold of Spain and King James of England. Louis hoped that his claim to the Mississippi valley and the Illinois territory would fill his royal treasury as well. To realize this, Louis saw the establishment of a successful French colony in the Illinois territory as a necessity to keep his realm in Europe safe and his throne secure. Louis needed a bold explorer to implement his policy of colonization. Robert Cavelier, Sieur de la Salle, was the perfect choice to assume this royal commission. He would begin his adventure in less than one year.

Meanwhile, officials of the French Catholic Church were also discussing how they might take advantage of the treasures of the New World. The Catholic Church was still a temporal power to be reckoned with even in 17th century Renaissance Europe. Although ethnic identity had already established a sense of nationalism adding to the power of the French throne, King Louis was still unwilling to antagonize the Pope, Christ's representative on earth. However, French Church leaders recognized their power was waning. The wealth of the Americas—silver from Peru and gold from Mexico—continued to make the leaders of the Catholic Church in Spain wealthy. Maybe gold from the New World could revive Catholic fortunes in France. King Louis continued to give the French Catholic Churchmen great latitude. Bishop Jean Colbert, the Pope's emissary in France and successor to the great Cardinal Mazarin, believed he might use this influence to entrench his power as well.

When Bishop Colbert expressed his interest in exploiting the resources of the New World for personal gain his advisers listened. Knowing the penalty for not carrying out the Bishop's wishes, a plan was quickly drawn up to beat the King to the treasure. Priests would be immediately dispatched to the Illinois territory to find and send back any form of wealth they could discover. Spanish priests had the good fortune to find gold and silver. Why couldn't the French priests be just as lucky? Of course, the priests would live among the heathen Illinois Indians and convert them to Christianity. This would add a sense of propriety to this mission and disguise the true reasons for the French Church endeavors. Indeed, the propaganda specialists could portray this as a great crusade, which would gain the support of the entire French population. The Bishop would be a hero and increase his wealth simultaneously.

Like King Louis, Bishop Colbert needed an intrepid explorer to pursue his policy in North America. Father Marquette was the logical choice, but the trials of his recent expedition had left him physically and mentally exhausted. It would be necessary to entrust the fortunes of the French Church in the New World to a team of unknowns. A list of possible candidates was solicited from every parish in France. Unfortunately, the skill to survive in the outdoors was not part of the average French Churchman's experience. The list of those who had even a remote chance of succeeding was indeed short.

On the list of possible candidates to lead the French Church expedition into North America was two men qualified by their lengthy pilgrimage to the Holy Land. Father Bertrand and Father Constance had only recently returned from a two-year journey to Jerusalem and North Africa. Although such journeys were commonplace to churchmen centuries before, the pilgrimage had fallen from fashion in the 17th century. It was a time to remain in ones own backyard and to maintain the home fires. However, Fathers Bertrand and Constance seemed destined to wander. Their trip to the Holy Land was a delicate mission to recover a holy relic for the Church in Paris. The mission required a physical hardiness to endure the trials of thousands of miles of dirt paths and unfriendly people. Further, it required a delicacy of diplomacy and a commitment to see the lengthy job through. The good Fathers learned about the evil side of mankind the hard way. Untold hardships were their standard fare. They accepted them without protest. Their dedication to the task earned them a reputation that had preceded them to Paris. Father Bertrand and Father Constance were the obvious choice to go to the Illinois territory.

It was a rainy spring day when the good Fathers were granted audience to His Holiness, Bishop Colbert, at his palace in Paris. The splendor of the building endeavored to overcome the mood of the two men as they were admitted into the Bishop's audience chamber. There was an obvious Laurel-and-Hardy comparison to the appearance of the priests although the simile definitely ended there. Father Constance was the rotund member of the duo with a suggestion of joviality in his demeanor. This dark featured man had the soft features associated with a kind and generous person. While Constance was certainly no comedian he usually had a smile on his face and approached life in a positive manner. His counterpart, Father Bertrand, was the tall, lean, no-nonsense part of the team. His sharp angled face beneath a tonsured head suggested a practical approach to life. Bertrand was always asking questions and weighing options. On first impression one would guess him a stern man. However, his soft brown eyes conveyed a deep sense of compassion for his fellow man. It was certain that Constance and Bertrand complemented each other in their priestly mission.

"Welcome Father Bertrand, Father Constance. I appreciate your quick response to my summons," said the Bishop with an air of aloofness. The Bishop was the standard cliché' for opulence. His magnificent white robes trimmed in ermine served as a perfect backdrop for his exquisite jewelry.

The Fathers entered through huge oak double doors shoulder-to-shoulder as equals, bowing low in deference to His Holy Eminence. Never had they been in the presence of a high church official. They had been dispatched to the Holy Land by one of the Bishop's representatives. Both were in awe of the situation so they remained in a contrite position until the Bishop spoke.

"Please, stand up and approach me, my dear brothers. Your reputation as devoted churchmen preceded you. Considering your dedication to our Lord, it is

I who should be bowing to you," said the Bishop. His voice held the tone a person experienced in the arts of diplomacy and persuasion.

"Your Eminence, you are too kind! We are but two lowly parish priests doing as our Lord bids us," said Father Bertrand. Both priests rose and kissed his jewel-encrusted hand, but their eyes remained to the floor.

"No, no," the Bishop quickly replied. "I know you are men of impeccable honor. It is I who am graced by your presence. Do you know why I summoned you dear brothers?"

"Of course, we have heard rumors—but we will not bore you with repeating them," Father Constance took his turn to reply.

"We can only assume you wish us to do the work of God," said Bertrand.

"That is our mission on this earth. We each wait for his bidding and pray we will have the courage and strength to succeed," said the Bishop in a courtly voice.

"I wish you to do me a personal favor that no one else in my realm is qualified to do," continued the Bishop.

"You have only to ask, your Eminence," said Bertrand. The two priests still did not meet the Bishop's gaze directly.

"I expected you would feel that way," said the Bishop. Was there a smirk or merely a smile on his angular face?

"I require you to lead an expedition to the New World. No doubt you have read of the exploits of your brother, Father Marquette. He has identified a peaceful people in the land called Illinois who long for the word of our Lord. They long for our instruction. Can we ignore our Lord's call on their behalf?" continued the Bishop.

"We are but recently returned from a long journey to Jerusalem which has tired us so. But, if it be our Lord's will to begin another journey, then we are ready to proceed." Constance spoke with resigned dedication.

"I had hoped you would feel this way, dear brothers. As we speak, your ship is being outfitted at our port in Le Harve. Provision, trade goods, and the latest maps will see you safely on your way. I hope you can leave within the week," Bishop Colbert said.

Father Constance replied, "We will strive to do as you request. Do you have more explicit directions? How long do you wish us to stay?"

"All of the specifics will be answered by my appointed representative, Monsieur Geoff, who will accompany you and attempt to maintain communications with me," said the Bishop.

"Bon chance and may God see you safely on his mission of salvation."

"Merci, Your Eminence," replied both priests in unison as they backed out into the corridor of the Bishop's splendid palace. They both walked quickly out into the street happy to be away from the uncomfortable atmosphere of the gilded court.

* * * *

The good Fathers retired to their favorite tavern to discuss the recent events. They had many affairs to attend to with only a short time to accomplish them. Historians have written volumes concerning the ulterior motives that caused Christ's word to be carried to the ends of the globe. But, more often than not, the priestly missionaries were very sincere in their commitment to carrying out their Lord's commission. If they had to take the bad in order to accomplish the good then so be it. This was part of the conversation that unfolded between Father Bertrand and Father Constance as they feasted on wine and cheese.

"I'm so glad that our pompous meeting is over and done with. I know I should be flattered to have an audience with one of the most powerful men in Europe. But, I can only feel a sense of relief and hope it won't be repeated too often," said Father Constance in a shaky voice. He was not the strong one of the two. Constance depended on Father Bertrand for encouragement.

"This is more than we could have hoped for. We have a new adventure in a new land doing God's work. What more can we need in our earthly existence?" said Father Bertrand.

"A little peace to recuperate before running to the ends of the earth would have been nice," stated Constance indignantly with a frown.

"Would you rather be stuck in one of these poor rural parishes in our beloved France while someone else saw the marvels of the New World? I think we have been truly blessed," said Bertrand with some frustration over a familiar argument.

In a deeply serious tone, Bertrand continued, "We both know that it is more than conversion of the savages that our dear Bishop's wishes. Still, I believe with care we can satisfy him and still do the work of the Lord. There was treachery every step of the way to the Holy Land. Why should this trip be any different?"

"I agree that we must endure evil to see any good out of the Bishop's plan," replied Constance. The waitress interrupted with a new bottle of wine. Two bottles were excessive on a priest's wages. Still that was the furthest from either ones mind. "God knows there is no gold in the Mississippi valley, but this seems to be a fact our dear Bishop cannot accept."

"Our mission should always be to carry God's word to those who are willing to accept it. How can the Bishop condone the exploitation of people less fortunate than us? Does he not realize that all the gold of this world will not assure him peace and heaven?" said Bertrand.

"That raises the question of what is to become of us when we can't send any gold back to France. The Bishop will be angry and his anger often knows no bounds. The catacombs of Paris are full of those who displeased his Eminence," said Constance, his eyes glazed in fear. Bertrand gave a sigh and shrugged.

"The pious Bishop can't touch us so many miles across the sea. Monsieur Geoff will doubtless relieve us of the job of hunting gold. He will surely leave us alone, if he understands that we want no part of it," Constance continued. Geoff was the special emissary of Bishop Colbert that always accompanied the good fathers to look out for the special interest of the Catholic Church. In this instance, it was to find treasure.

Bertrand laughed nervously. "Yes, but his assassins are dedicated. At best, we will return to France old and broken. At worse, we will never see our beloved France again."

"It is God's will. If we pray, God will provide and his will be done. For what more can we hope?" said Constance. Constance had the faith for two while Bertrand's strength was in seeing to the details. The Fathers complimented one another and acted as one. God's hand was in their being together.

"Well, Bertrand, see that our ship is completely outfitted for our voyage. The Bishop will spare no expense since we give meaning to his evil excess. I'm looking forward to eating well on this voyage. Let Monsieur not cut corners. Oui?" said Constance, slapping his friend on the back.

"We will need people loyal to us. Shall I try to recruit some?" stated Bertrand.

"Oui! Trust and loyalty may be the only virtues that save us on this adventure. Contact our English friend, Monsieur Stuart. His knowledge of the wilds served us well through Europe. It will doubtless apply in this New World as well," said Constance.

"Monsieur Stuart will not work cheap, but the Bishop's friend may have some discretionary funds available. At any rate, Stuart is an adventurer. How can he turn down a free trip to the Americas?" laughed Bertrand.

"God will provide, dear friend. Arrange our affairs quickly. Say your farewells to those you love. We may not see them anytime soon." Constance and Bertrand toasted their wineglasses one last time.

The two Fathers walked out into the damp streets of Paris. The sun's rays were breaking through the clouds of a recent storm. This could only be a sign that God was smiling upon this new adventure.

*   *   *   *

Major Jon Stuart was dining alone in a fancy French café not far from the royal residence in Paris. The Major was a man of the world who knew how to take advantage of what life offered. When off in the wilderness Stuart was resourceful enough to get by quite handily on what nature had to offer. Conversely, when in the midst of luxury the Major liked to indulge his passion for good food and good company. Impeccably dressed in the attire of a true gentleman, the middle-aged Englishman slowly ate his dinner of roast lamb and vegetables. Save for his Scottish accent, Stuart blended well with the crowd. No one took notice of him.

Unfortunately, an Englishman in 17th century France was not likely to attract interesting acquaintances given the political climate that existed between the French and his homeland. Often he had to endure snide comments and insults concerning his lineage. Sometimes a conceited Frenchman would attempt to physically force Stuart to defend his honor. Since his return from the Holy Land with the good Fathers, Constance and Bertrand, the Major had become somewhat of a celebrity in Paris. Rumors of his skill with a blade and pistol seemed enough to discourage anyone wishing to teach the Englishman a lesson. Some were brave enough to approach him to hear his tales of adventure abroad. At first the Major was willing to recount these tales with gusto. After a few days he developed a demeanor that discouraged friendly advances. Currently, he was relishing solitude.

For his own safety Major Stuart always had a keen sense of his surroundings. This defense had been developed and honed by his many years in the military. He never let it down, even in a seemingly innocent cafe' in the middle of civilized Paris. That is why he had already noticed two inconspicuous French gentlemen who had followed him into the cafe' and positioned themselves close to his table. Stuart was pretty sure he had recognized at least one of them on the street hours earlier. Could they be following him? Stuart was sure of that, but he could only guess they were just some more Frenchmen looking for an opportunity to harass a foreigner. Stuart continued to enjoy his meal knowing he could handle whatever developed later.

Stuart noticed that one of the two had made a sojourn to the kitchen prior to the delivery of his meal's final course. A less observant person would have been oblivious to this detail. Yet, the Major had survived many years by paying attention to such triviality. He sensed these men meant him harm. Stuart would not give them an easy opportunity.

The smell of the berries and cream was somehow odd. After several glasses of wine, most men would not have noticed this. Had it not been for the uneasy composure of the two Frenchman at the adjacent table, Stuart might have discounted the smell as well. At this juncture he was not about to eat another item delivered from the kitchen. Stuart quickly called for his check and glanced to see the reaction of his assumed enemies. Not surprising they had disappeared from their table. Where they had gone Stuart could only guess.

"My compliments to the cook", laughed Stuart as the waitress picked the money off the table. "I should go back to give him a carving lesson, though. The lamb slices were quite thick. And God knows what he did with the berries. Perhaps he would taste them for me—or maybe you could identify this odd smell, Madame."

"Oh, no, Monsieur!" said the waitress raising her voice and spilling the dessert as she gather up the dishes. "Please leave or I shall be forced to summon the King's guard. We are a respectable establishment. Your uncouth behavior is not welcome."

Stuart knew what happened to foreigners detained by the King's guard. The prisons were dark, smelly and full of rats. One might spend months there before managing to bribe his way out. Stuart had to be at the docks in Le Havre in three days. He had no time to avenge this attempt on his life. Poison was a popular weapon of this era. It was quiet, effective, readily available, and hard to prove any crime given the medicine technology of the day. Stuart had seen men die horrible deaths from poison. He was glad he had paid attention tonight.

Major Stuart stepped boldly out into the dark and narrow streets of 17th century Paris. His hand grasped the hilt of his sword tightly as he set a quick pace back to his abode to gather his bags for the trip to Le Havre. Given the recent events Stuart dared not spend another night in Paris.

The two men from the cafe' loomed out of the darkness ahead of him. The streets were unusually deserted for this time of night. There would be no witnesses to the coming events. It was all so convenient. Obviously, someone didn't want him to make his appointment with the good Fathers.

"Hold, Englishman. We are the King's agents. We wish to discuss your travel plans," said one Frenchman in a measured voice. "There is no need to fear us. Please accompany us back to our barracks."

"I have no time for this. Why should you be interested in my travel, anyway? It is no business of yours," replied the Major. "Beside, you'll be unhappy to know that I could not eat the berries. They seemed tainted."

Obviously, the Frenchmen realized that Stuart was aware that they meant to kill him. Knowing they could not lull him into a false sense of security, the man on the right raised his pistol to fire. A matchlock takes full seconds to ignite the charge. Stuart already guessed that harm was coming his way. The dagger from Stuart's belt found its way swiftly to the man's throat. The pistol was discharged harmlessly into the cobblestones.

The other Frenchman advanced quickly with pistol in one hand and sword in the other. Stuart could not deal with him until he handled the man who was approaching from his rear. Stuart's short bladed sword neatly cleaved his enemy from throat to skull before any damage was done.

Stuart turned to face his remaining opponent. The Major had sword in one hand and cutlass in another. The last Frenchman had lunged before Stuart could turn inflicting a minor wound in the muscle below his rib. The Frenchman was obviously a good swordsman. He seemed confident of the outcome. Taking advantage of the moment Stuart tried to learn the reason behind the attack.

"Why do you attempt to murder a loyal subject of both Church and State who recently returned your sacred relic from the Holy Land?" Stuart said, breathing easily.

"You maybe a hero to the Church, but my master thinks otherwise," said the Frenchman, lunging with his sword. "We cannot allow you to be successful twice."

The two men traded slashes and insults for several more seconds. Soon the Frenchman became quiet and eventually desperate as he realized that the Major was toying with him to learn more. Stuart tired of the game when he found that his opponent would offer no further information.

With no defense for the cutlass, the Frenchman took his last breath. Stuart moved on down the street as the moon appeared from behind a cloud. The King's guard would surely be looking for him as soon as they discovered their three comrades. Stuart felt he would be safe once he was under the protection of Father Constance and Bertrand. He must get to Le Havre as soon as possible.

* * * *

The corsair hired by the Cardinal bobbed like a cork at the end of a fishing line as the travelers gathered to embark on their mission. Was it to bring Christianity to the savages or fill the Cardinal's treasury? Well, no matter, for go they must. The die had been cast. Their destiny and possibly the destiny of many generations to come would ride in that speedy ship.

The corsair was a beautiful piece of craftsmanship. The massive beams were made of solid oak cut in the forests in the foothills of the Pyrenees Mountains. Each beam was hand hewn and drawn by experienced carpenters. To be sure, the English were not the only nationality to be skillful enough to master the art of sailing. The French fleet was equal in grace and quality, if not quantity. Since the English ruled the waves, the French were forced to defer to this superiority, but every Frenchman was proud of the naval prowess of his sailors. The corsair's brilliantly colored pennants fluttered proudly in the wind beckoning the Church entourage to come on board.

The sun shone brilliantly against a sky of blue as highflying cumulus clouds floated randomly by. The green tinted ocean stretched endlessly toward the horizon enticing the adventurers on the dock at Le Havre to come explore its mysteries. Behind the ocean's gay facade was a subtle hint of the doom that could descend on those ill prepared for the trip to the New World.

Fathers Bertrand and Constance were well prepared for what lay before them. Their experience in southern Europe and North Africa served them well. First, they gathered around them men and women they could trust. These people had proven their loyalty with year of service. When the road got tough, these friends would not flee in the face of adversity. They were all brave, hardy, and willing to do their duty to advance God's cause.

Chief among those loyal to the Fathers was Major Jon Stuart, an honorable veteran of His Majesty's, the King of England, infantry forces. A chance encounter, or according to Father Constance, God's purpose had led Stuart to rescue the good Fathers in Italy when they had found themselves in a deadly predicament. Thieves were preparing to rob Father Constance and Bertrand of money and baggage in Venice when Jon Stuart arrived to thwart them. His sharp cutlass and matchlock, along with impressive bravado, served to chase away or kill at least five scoundrels. While reserved on the surface Jon Stuart had proven to possess a heart of gold. He felt compassion for the Fathers and refused to let them out of his sight until he saw them safe to the Holy Land and back. Both Bertrand and

Constance know their mission would not have been successful without the intervention of Major Stuart. And now he was answering their call again.

Major Stuart, a dark middle-aged warrior, stood smiling broadly as Father Constance and Bertrand hastened to greet him on the dock. A man of impeccable dress, Stuart's manner hinted of years devoted to duty and honor. His military demeanor reassured them that he could control every situation. Everyone close to him felt safe and secure in his presence. No doubt this served to attract the Fathers to him.

Father Bertrand had spent nearly one week preparing for the journey. The ship's store was supplied with food, water, clothing, tents and trade goods. Everything necessary for the trek to the Illinois territory was aboard. Father Joliet's experience and that of Major Stuart would serve them in good stead.

Prior to boarding their ship, Le Voyageur, His Eminence, the Bishop arrived to give final instruction to his adventurers and offer a solemn blessing. The Bishop was very happy since recent information from court indicated that the King was still having trouble recruiting a leader for his own expedition to the New World. Rumor held that Robert Cavelier, Sieur de la Salle, might be enticed if he could tear himself from the family estates. There seemed little hope of that happening this year since the crops were ripening and time was short to assemble a company before the stormy autumn season. It looked as if the Bishop's party would have no competition in North America for at least a year. The Bishop knew much could be accomplished in that amount of time. Monsieur Geoff had received extensive instructions. God had apparently blessed this endeavor.

Le Voyageur caught wind to sail and tacked out of the harbor. Friend and relatives of the party waved tearfully as the ship moved out of sight. For some unknown reason, a squadron of the King's Guard had arrived to see them off, too. As they aligned their forces at the entrance to the narrow dock, there was obvious antagonism between the Guard and the church retinue. Father Constance and Father Bertrand stood on deck gazing back at their homeland with Major Stuart by their side. The bandage and blood on Stuart's cloak gave the Fathers cause for concern about his welfare. Specifically, they wanted to know why Stuart had remained on board ship since his arrival late the night before. Could it have something to do with the untimely arrival of the King's men? At any rate, these questions could wait until after they were safe at sea.

The ship's captain, Monsieur Grendel, made polite conversation about the good weather and how he wished it would remain so. Monsieur Geoff had made himself scarce below deck. The Fathers were not truly happy venturing into the unknown, but they took comfort in the idea that they were doing God's will.

Prayers were said often during that trip across the Atlantic. Even though a summer passage on the North Atlantic was relatively safe, the ocean could be extremely unpredictable.

Except for one squall that made the party test their sea legs, they came quite easily to the shores of North America in record time. About midway through the passage the fury of the ocean almost claimed some of the church party. It began quite peacefully one morning when their anxious Captain Grendel was pacing the deck. Father Bertrand, being the one who paid attention to detail, asked if there was a problem.

"A red sky in the morning is a bad omen even for land lovers," barked the Captain.

"I'm sure I don't understand what you mean," said Bertrand, rather perplexed.

"The weather, man, the weather!" The Captain was nervous and irritable. "More often than not we will sail into a terrible storm by nightfall."

"Prepare for the worst tonight, men. And let the good Fathers pray I'm wrong this time," Grendel shouted to his crew.

The weather remained balmy all day. The warm sun lulled the passengers into a sense of security. Even with the early warning they were quite unprepared for the bank of clouds that seemed to appear out of nowhere that dark evening to batter the ship for several hours.

The Fathers and their group had been instructed by the ship's officers to remain below deck and ride out the storm. Unfortunately, the storm struck so suddenly that Constance and Bertrand were aft when the first terrible wave struck the side of the ship. Le Voyageur paused, shuddered, and lunged like a bucking horse. The Fathers were thrown against the railing. Before they could get their breath and regain their composure, the second mammoth wave struck the ship broadside. With the deck being very slick it seemed inevitable that they would be washed away.

In the nick of time, their earthly guardian angel, Jon Stuart, reached out his hand and snatched Bertrand from the swirling vortex that the Atlantic had become. Constance was already clinging for dear life on a cask lashed to the deck. There was no time to retreat to the hold of the ship. Luckily, the wise Stuart had brought a strong length of rope. With this he securely bound himself and his two wards to a mast of the ship. From this unique position, they were able to witness firsthand the fury of a North Atlantic storm. Many times they felt the ship would capsize under the weight of the tremendous waves that washed over them. They were barely able to breathe between onslaughts of water. What a ride that was, as the night seemed to go on for an eternity, but the Fathers were very brave. Pray they did, but not for God to save them. They only asked that they be delivered from the tempest if it were God's will. This was the courage displayed by these brave adventurers.

Eventually they fell asleep from fatigue slumping in the ropes only to wake to a beautifully refreshing morning. The Fathers owed much to Jon Stuart. Again his friendship had saved their lives. Their mission was proceeding as planned. No one said it would be easy, but with God's grace the trip would be successful. This brush with death only made them all appreciate the sweetness of life more. After the storm, time seemed to pass quickly. Before they knew it, the New World was shining fair on the horizon.

* * * *

Nova Scotia was the name of the forested land that first appeared on the horizon to the good Fathers. They had gazed off toward the horizon where water meets sky for so many days that the sight of land seemed like a dream when it finally appeared. The constant pitch and roll of the ocean had contributed to the weak stomachs of many. Some never found relief until the voyage was over. What a price that was for making such a journey, but finally their prayers were answered. God had seen them safely across the ocean with little difficulty. Bertrand and Constance only hoped the inland portion of the trek would be as uneventful.

The route to the interior country known as Illinois would be an endless series of rivers and lakes with difficult portages in between. Father Joliet, their predecessor, had kept detailed notes of his trip. For God's work he had been eager to supply Father Bertrand with anything he had. As Father Bertrand and Major Stuart review the surprisingly detailed maps of their journey, they silently wondered how they could cover this great distance before the hard winter common to North America settled in. Hunting and the bounty of the land would be their only salvation if they were lucky enough to find the Illinois and Mississippi rivers before the snow fell.

The party's baggage was unloaded on the desolate shore that was the mouth of the St. Lawrence River. They had sailed between shores that were ever narrowing for many days. Finally, it was time to begin the long canoe trip. They had no time to waste. Tarrying too long in one place could prove disastrous considering stories of warlike native and wild animals.

Captain Grendel had decided to spend sometime along that coast to repair his ship. It seems the terrible squall they had endured had cracked a supporting beam of Le Voyageur. This beam must be shored up for the return trip. Otherwise, they might not survive another storm. Fortunately, each French crew in these days had shipwrights skilled in the construction of ships. They could fashion what they needed from the plentiful timber along the coastline. In no time Le Voyageur would be as good as new, and the Captain knew the crew would appreciate sampling the good hunting of the New World for awhile before they began the long return.

Therefore, a great feast was prepared on shore before the Churchmen left for the interior. Game proved to be very plentiful. Hunters brought back a variety of meats for the campfire chefs. Geese, duck, deer, squirrel, rabbit and fish made for a veritable smorgasbord to feast from. The French cooks proved very artistic in their preparation of this bounty. The ship's store of liquor was brought forth to add to the festivities. Needless to say, the adventurers were reluctant to take their leave.

Farewells were said quietly one morning. The Churchmen's canoes vanished into the misty dawn of the river. All said a silent prayer for these brothers who were braving the unknown to bring God's word to his children.

* * * *

The trip to the Illinois country led southwest along a succession of pristine lakes and rivers. The weather was cool, crisp and sunny. The waters were deep and the current swift. The journey would be long, but certainly not boring. 17th century North America was fresh and, for the most part, untouched by human hands. There was a breathtaking vista to behold around every bend of the river. The glory of God's work reflected in every nuance of nature. The travelers absorbed the beauty of forest and stream with the appreciation of a blind man suddenly given his sight. Being far away from the intrigues of the French court further contributed to their joy. Needless to say, these days of relaxation passed quickly.

Unfortunately, they were traveling through country controlled by the Five Nations of the Iroquois. The Iroquois were a fierce race of people who practiced war with fervor reminiscent of the Mongol hordes. They showed no mercy to those travelers unfortunate enough to cross their path. The Iroquois recognized few friends. Fathers Bertrand and Constance were well aware of the Iroquois torture of Jesuit missionaries. The Iroquois had martyred a fellow priest, Father Lalemaut, in the year 1625. Being worshippers of the sun, the Mohawk clan of the Iroquois had taken extreme exception to the idea of only one God. Father

Lalemaut was tortured most hideously. Undoubtedly, Lalemaut had been a sacrifice to Iroquois spirits of the forest. Woe be unto anyone unfortunate enough to stumble upon an unfriendly Iroquois clan.

The French travelers encountered spectacular scenery on their trip along the St. Lawrence River. Water so clean and clear was a thing of beauty to the Frenchmen who were accustomed to the slow, muddy brown waters of their homeland rivers. One would have to travel into the Pyrenees or the Alps to find similar splendor. A counterpoint to the blue river was the spectacular colors of the cathedral-like forest. God's immediate presence could be felt surrounding the clergy. The beauty of the countryside dazzled the senses. To match the myriad colors, were the damp, earthy smells. It gave the impression that the whole of North America was fresh and new. The travelers could hardly describe the freshly scented smells they encountered at every stop along the river.

Then there was the intense sounds of the river and forest as a complement to the sights and smells. The wildlife was abundant. Deer, bear, raccoon, and wolf oblivious to the presence of humans paused to drink in the riffles of water as it flowed over smooth worn rock. The blue sky with billowy clouds seemed always full of beautiful birds. The piercing cry of the eagle could be heard as he circled high above the river gorges. The occasional booming of a thunderstorm added melodic counterpoint to the skimming of the canoe paddles in the swift flowing river.

Early in the journey the party came upon a small French settlement known as Quebec. To be friendly, Father Bertrand urged that they stop to refresh themselves since evening was nigh. The party readily disembarked their canoes being fatigued from the day's paddling. They proceeded to the heart of the village to greet the settlement's governor. They passed through an Iroquois encampment by the river's edge. The long houses, crudely constructed due to a lack of permanence, clearly exhibited Iroquois craftsmanship. Built of nature's material, the structures had a stately air about them. Jesuit brothers ran to greet Bertrand and Constance like long lost kin.

"We wish to greet you, holy fathers, and wish you success in your heavenly mission", said one Jesuit with a deep, commanding voice. He was obviously the leader of the group.

"I am Father Louis Hennepin and this is Father Augustus," said Hennepin gesturing to the slight figure beside him dressed entirely in black. With friendly smiles, the brothers in Christ embraced.

"We are so glad to see new faces. Indians and trappers can be tiring after awhile. The conversation becomes boring unless, of course, one is interested in the size of deer, or how many pelts an area can yield. Oh, to be able to converse with educated scholars about politics or religion. But this is the drudgery of a missionary. Simple things bring simple joy," said Hennepin.

"Thank you for the hospitable welcome, brothers," said Constance. "How do you survive among the fierce Iroquois? Marquette warned us of these hellish warriors and suggested we avoid them at all cost."

"Dear friends, these are Iroquois to be sure; of the Five Nations no less. But they are Cayuga and we have come to trust them with our lives." Father Augustus continued, "As you become familiar with our red brothers, you will learn that each Iroquois Nation exhibits a personality of their own. The Cayuga are probably the least warlike. In many of their villages they have readily accepted our missions."

"We pray that we can be as trusting of the native as you apparently are," said Constance. "Our destiny is in God's hands. He will surely bless our mission." At these words, all the clergy present made the sign of the cross.

"Still, I'm haunted by the story of the martyrdom of our dear brother, Lalemaut. The path Christ chose for him was not an easy one to bear." Bertrand lowered his gaze to the ground.

"And Lalemaut's cries continue to float in the wind on a bleak winter's eve to haunt our babies," said a female Iroquois with a forthright voice that belied her stature.

The French travelers were astonished to hear such exquisite French from a local heathen. The woman seemed to smirk as she realized the impression she had made on these naive visitors.

"Let me introduce Kateri Tekawetha to you, my friends," Louis Hennepin quickly responded as the Iroquois woman moved from the periphery of the crowd. As previously noted, her stature was petite, yet sophisticated. Kateri was distinctly beautiful, but her beauty was of a wild type that no man could hope to contain.

"She is one of our greatest successes," Father Hennepin explained. "Mademoiselle Tekawetha is, even now, in route to Montreal for her own safety having stood fast for Christ in the face of death threats from her own people."

"How do you know of Father Lalemaut?" asked Constance, astonished to find a native of the New World so well versed in Church missionary history. "He died in this savage new land many years before you were even born."

"I know the story from my grandmother who once told ghost stories at our long house fire to help pass the cold, winter nights," said Kateri in perfect French.

"It is told that Lalemaut came to our village one summer day speaking of one God, the father of everyone. He wanted us to believe as he did. Lalemaut was so peaceful and harmless that the clan council let him stay. Many days passed quietly. Unfortunately, our brothers in the council of the Five Nations were warning against the white man's influence. They sent emissaries to our village to question Lalemaut's intentions. When Lalemaut would not acknowledge that the spirits of the forest existed his end was swift." Kateri shook her head as grief began to overcome her stoic expression.

"My grandmother said Lalemaut never did an unkind deed. He never spoke ill of his accusers. Like our Savior, Jesus the Christ, he forgave those who despised him. One night in late autumn when the leaves were falling and spirits are said to roam the forest, the Council Shaman came for him. First, they made him run a gauntlet naked. He was flogged unmercifully. Next, they skinned him alive. Lalemaut only whimpered as blood ran from every pore. Last, they strapped his quivering body to a crossed tree and burned him. He who had preached of one man dying for all was forced to suffer in a like manner." Kateri was sobbing by now as she continued to describe the brutality of her own people.

"My grandmother said no cries crossed his lips until the very end. Our Shamen say that he recanted his rejection of the Iroquois spirits. But my grandmother insists he said, "Pe're, forgive them!" over and over. The story is meant to scare little Iroquois children to behave and to go to sleep. But, I find the howl of the winter wind comforting. It reminds me how great Lalemaut's love was for my people. How much greater can Christ's love be? His God is surely our salvation." Kateri finished as she wept openly.

There was silence for several minutes in the late afternoon, which was very unusual for the bustling village of Quebec. Not even a dog barked. Father Hennepin was the first to break the silence.

"Kateri is a sister in Christ, having been baptized by Jacques de Lamberville some years ago. She has worked with us diligently to pacify and convert her brothers, the Cayuga. She has been most successful."

"Too successful!" Augustus interjected. "The Council of the Five Nations see Kateri as a threat to their way of life. They feel they can't desert the old ways for this foreign God. They worship the sun. They feel the sun must be avenged for her heresy."

"That's why Kateri is traveling to Montreal," continued Father Louis. "There have been threats and attempts on her life. She is no longer safe among her people. Kateri does not know whom to trust."

Constance was surprised that she could hope to be safe in Montreal. "Can she trust Governor Frontenac? Joliet told us that Frontenac wishes to maintain peace with the Iroquois at all cost. This is the only way to further his plans for French colonization of North America. You know as well as I that Frontenac has no love for the Church."

Augustus nodded his head in agreement. "We have no choice. We are not men-at-arms. A priest can offer her no protection. We can only pray that Frontenac will not give her over to her enemies. God's will has brought you here to escort her on to Montreal. We assume that is your destination. We must trust in his will."

"And if I must die, let me die like Father Lalemaut, in Christ's name I pray. Amen!" Kateri shouted with gusto. Her tears were dry and she was smiling again. The strength of her character was obvious to all assembled. Impressed by her courage, her "Amen" was repeated loudly by all.

"Now let us escort you to meet the military authorities of Quebec. Then we will return to supper here. Our Iroquois brothers are good hunters and fisherman. I know you will not be disappointed," said Father Louis as they walked toward the palisades of the enclosed town. The talk of torture and ghosts made the fortress town look ominous indeed. The early joys of exploring a New World had suddenly been dampened with a feeling of deep despair. Hopefully this did not portend the future of their holy mission.

* * * *

The French fortification of Quebec resembled those already established throughout the New World. The walls of hewn logs sat high on a hilltop that overlooked the St. Lawrence River valley. The logs were at least 25' high forming a protective shield on three sides of the settlement. The fourth side was natural rock against which the village was nestled. This rocky cliff extended straight up to the top of the river bluff. This side was seemingly impenetrable to attack. The engineers had done their job well in locating the fortress in one of the most defensible locations in the area. The vegetation had been stripped away at least 100 yd. in all directions so that any enemy would have to expose themselves to the defenders' field of fire as they approached. This area was aptly termed the "killing field" by the French garrison. Slits were hewn into the wooden walls at even intervals to allow musket fire without exposing the defenders. There was a depression resembling a moat immediately adjacent to the walls with the expressed purpose of further hindering an enemy advance. The wooden poles forming the wall were spiked to discourage any attempt to scale the walls.

Only one entry, a huge double gate, gave access to the garrison inside the fortifications. The churchmen walked through this open portal toward the neatly kept building on the opposite interior wall up against the rocky cliff. The French flag with its proud fleur-de-lis fluttered bravely in the breeze. A garden of colorful flowers stood in stark contrast to the military nature of the surroundings. Even as the party approached the garrison headquarters no officials appeared to greet them. Soldiers in their white uniforms with blue great coats drilled on the commons. Apparently, close order drill was a regular occurrence as evidenced by the bleak area of dirt where no grass could possibly survive. Several cannon were mounted into the wall and ready for action. Obviously, the garrison was in a state of military preparedness. In minutes the gates could be closed if any alarm was given. Everyone the travelers met seemed polite, but nervous. Major Stuart wondered how trustworthy the Mohawk and Cayuga were given this state of readiness. Apparently death could strike the unwary like a summer thunderstorm in this savage country.

Major Stuart had remained in the background thus far into the journey. He was being paid well by Bishop Colbert to protect the missionaries. Stuart was well prepared for any eventuality. He could afford to remain silent. Stuart's calculating military mind was always looking ahead. This was part of his success. He was a survivor and the good Fathers were very lucky to count him as a friend.

Monsieur Geoff also remained quietly in the background. The spy had reason to be discreet as well. To succeed on his mission of keeping the King informed of the real purpose of this church expedition, he must bide his time. Though Geoff knew several in the group suspected he was a spy, he was no threat to them. He was being paid well to tag along. Geoff felt if he could be of service, his rewards would be great when he returned to France. The church already wielded too much power. If his actions on this mission could help reduce the Church influence in the government of France, then he would be performing a patriotic duty as well. Geoff looked to the future with optimism. This mission to the convert the heathen natives of the Mississippi valley was only a facade covering a deeper church intrigue to improve its power base at home.

The ornately carved door of the Quebec regimental headquarters creaked loudly as it open. Out stepped two officers outfitted in the uniform of the French infantry. A third person in neat civilian dress accompanied them as they approached the visitors. The immaculate French uniforms looked oddly out of place in this primitive surrounding.

"Welcome, gentlemen. I'm Captain Valmont and this is Lt. Bende, my adjutant. Also, let me introduce you to the mayor of the small colony, Monsieur Hallet. It is always a pleasure to greet fellow countrymen. The news from France travels slowly. We look forward to pleasant conversation concerning the situation at home over a fine glass of wine." Captain Valmont smiled cordially.

Louis Hennepin introduced the travelers to the Quebec officials. Everyone was greeted with warmth and courtesy. Captain Valmont was eager to receive news from his homeland. He felt his career was stagnating in this backwater garrison away from the intrigue of the court. He continued the conversation.

"I trust your journey was without mishap. Couriers from the English settlements toward the ocean say the local tribes have resumed hostilities. Farms are being burned and Englishmen murdered. This would be good news to a military man since the English are our ancestral enemies. Unfortunately, these red savages can't always distinguish us French from the English dogs. Did you encounter any natives on your journey from the coast?" This statement was a direct affront to the Englishman, Major Stuart, but Valmont was unaware that an Englishman was in the party. Major Stuart's countenance remained nondescript. If the comment irritated him, he gave no noticeable indication.

"No. Our journey inland was quite peaceful and relaxing. Your scenery is quite magnificent and pristine." Father Constance, being the leader of the French travelers, addressed the question.

"Did you notice any distant smoke while camping in the morning or evening?" Lt. Bende joined into the conversation. "Often, Iroquois war parties will shadow their unsuspecting prey waiting for an opportune time to attack."

"On one occasion, I came across a cold fire," replied Major Stuart since he was the acknowledged security officer of the visitors. "Close investigation revealed a hunting party of four or five. I followed their trail several kilometers away from the river until I was sure they were no threat to us."

Father Constance was surprised to hear this news. Major Stuart had not mentioned this distressing detail, but it only served to reinforce his trust in his English protector. Their security was in good hands.

"Forgive me, Father Constance," interjected Captain Valmont, "but how can you trust a paid mercenary of English descent with your very life? A man who sells his services to the highest bidder surely knows no loyalty." Major Stuart remained icily calm, but his red knuckles grasping his sword belied his true feelings.

Monsieur Geoff nodded his head in assent to the Captain's comment, but he was too timid to express his feelings. Major Stuart long ago realized he had an enemy in his entourage. Ultimately, Stuart would have to deal with this problem. He was willing to wait for a more opportune time.

"We have no fear of the Major's loyalty. We owe him our very lives. He has saved us from death countless times and on two continents," said Father Constance, speaking out in defense of his good friend.

"Reaching the Illinois country alive may well depend on how observant you are. Death in this wilderness can be very swift," said Lt. Bende. "This is no place for amateurs."

"How goes the hostilities in the Low Countries?" asked Valmont. "Is our sovereign, King Louis, still supreme on the continent?" This comment was meant to disturb any self-respecting Englishman who supported a balance to French power.

"It is beyond lowly churchmen to know the intrigue of European politics," said Father Bertrand hastily trying to diffuse a tense situation. "Suffice to say, our King, God's Anointed, has been very successful in waging war. Holland will soon fall to Conde' and our navy is on the verge of mounting a challenge for control of the seas."

"And the poor pay for his success in taxes they cannot afford while their children cry without food." Constance shook his head in sadness. "Death visits my countrymen in the form of either a musket ball or empty stomach. Our misery pays for his beautiful palace at Versailles."

"I believe our Sun King even fancies himself a God," said Bertrand. "Such blasphemy will surely not go unpunished." Geoff squirmed at this affront to his beloved majesty.

"Who are you, Fathers, to criticize our master?" Lt. Bende snarled. "Surely, Versailles is no more excessive than the Vatican or some of our Grande French cathedrals."

The conversation was quickly turning into a political disagreement. Apparently, Frontenac, the French Governor of North America, had schooled his military subordinates well. The animosity between church and state was very evident even at this remote French outpost. Constance and Bertrand could expect no help from the French government in this New World. They could only pray that their countrymen would not actively seek their demise.

"Forgive us brothers if our rash comments offend your politics," responded Father Constance in a kindly tone. "We of the Jesuit order have taken vows to defend the poor, the helpless, and the unfortunate. We wish only peace for our countrymen. War means pestilence, starvation and horrible death to many Frenchmen. This is contrary to the precepts of our faith."

Father Bertrand signaled his fellow travelers to open their packs. In short order several bottles of the finest French wine from the Loire valley were produced.

"Please join us in a toast to His Royal Majesty, King Louis XIV. May his reign bring glory and peace to our beloved France," said Bertrand in a loud voice with a smile beaming from ear to ear. The genuineness of this toast touched the heart of all. The antagonism, so evident before the toast, melted as quickly as a passing summer thundershower as glasses were raised. Conversation continued in small groups for many of the town's people and even a few Indians joined in. Topics included news from France, the affairs of the colony, and mutual friends back home.

Major Stuart took this opportunity to question Lt. Bende concerning the status of relations with the local indigenous population. He wanted to be prepared for any eventuality as they planned to proceed up river on the morrow.

"Regardless of your personal feelings for me, you must understand that I take the security of these good Fathers very seriously. For your countrymen's sake, I trust you will not withhold important information that might impact our journey," said Stuart, referring to the centuries of animosity that flowed between French and English.

Lt. Bende smiled genuinely and seemed to open up.

"You see that matters remain very tense here in Quebec. French farmers have been slaughtered and their farms pillaged and burned. The situation is getting desperate. Our colonists demand retaliation by the military. However, Governor Frontenac has ordered us to remain cautious for the present. The Governor wishes to win the friendship of the Five Nations of the Iroquois. That would be impossible if we acted irrationally. Still, I am very sympathetic to our people's plight."

"Do you know for sure that the Iroquois are responsible?"

"There lies the problem, Major. It is impossible for the layman unfamiliar with aboriginal political intrigue to distinguish the deadly workings of a Mohawk from that of a more reticent Cayuga. Though separate tribes, they often act as one through their central council. How do we know which Iroquois camped at our very gates has blood on their hands, and which one does not?" Lt. Bende gave a shrug of frustration.

"I can see your dilemma," replied Stuart. "Is there no way to identify friend from foe?"

"Frontenac has been successful in winning over the Mohawk and the Cayuga. They have both responded to our missionaries, some more so than others, as is to be expected. Their leaders either support us or, at least remain neutral when the

Council of the Five Nations meets. But the old religion is very strong. Many Iroquois hate us for threatening the religion of their ancestors. Isn't it ironic that our King Louis is called the Sun King and the Iroquois worship the sun god?" Bende spoke as if he had the lives of all the colonists resting on his shoulders. He obviously took his commission to protect the civilian population very seriously. Major Stuart, being an experienced military man, well understood his position.

"So, we can trust both Mohawk and Cayuga," said Stuart thinking out loud and trying to make sense of this information."

"No!" Lt. Bende replied. "For the sake of the lives of those in your charge learn to trust no native. Just know that the Mohawk and the Cayuga won't always be openly hostile. The noble red man can be very cunning. He can smile at you with the blood of your kindred on his hands. Although docile, they can prove to be an enemy to be feared. Skilled in deceit they will kill silently when the campfires burn low," said Bende recalling the story of one French family who entertained a Mohawk at supper only to have their throats slit later that same night.

"Surely once we are well inland we won't have to worry about Iroquois," said the Major. "They can't hold sway over such a vast amount of territory. There will be natives in Illinois less hostile."

"Though small in number, the Iroquois are ferocious warriors. They command a region as far as their canoes can carry them. Their slaves number many different tribes from lands far to the west. Their skill at war is well known on this continent," Lt. Bende answered. "I'm told the Illinois tribes are peaceful and very receptive to our missionaries. You should find fertile ground for your Christian teachings, but you must know that the Iroquois consider the land between the two great rivers, the Mississippi and Ohio, their own. Should they decide to plunder that land of plenty; no Illinois tribe will be strong enough to shield you from their onslaught. Your small number of muskets cannot slow them down. Flight will be your only salvation."

"Thanks for the advice, Lieutenant," said Stuart. He continued, seeking clarification on come points that concerned him. "What about the Cayuga woman, Kateri? In your opinion, is it safe to travel with her in our company?"

"This is a question that I cannot honestly answer. Depending on the circumstance, she may either be a great asset, or a tremendous liability. Some say she is a saint. Since you have met her, you can understand her powerful presence. Kateri has worked miracles, this much I know. Even the skeptics like me have been convinced. Once she walked through a bonfire to save Father Lamberville, her mentor, from being roasted alive by her own kind. Likewise, she has interceded for

Iroquois ready to be massacred by the French. Kateri has the power to overcome tragic situations. She might be salvation for your party should the wrong native cross your trail." Bende was obviously sincere.

"But Kateri has enemies who would stop at nothing to remove her as a factor for peace between the French and the Iroquois. If you take her to Montreal you will be doing us a great service. As long as she camps at our gates, she invites trouble. Only you can decide if it is prudent to be near her. I suggest you trust God to help you make the correct choice." Lt. Bende smiled and rose to leave. "You are a gentleman, Major Stuart. You are a worthy adversary. As one soldier to another, I truly wish you well."

"Thanks for speaking candidly, Lieutenant. I'm sure that our dedicated Fathers have already made the decision concerning Mademoiselle Tekawetha. I will have to make the best of it." Stuart moved across the parade ground toward the main gate of the palisade. Indians milled around the entrance, but never tried to enter. It was as if there was a hidden barrier they could not penetrate. The Major could not help but feel the tension in the early evening air.

The feast prepared by Father Louis Hennepin was sumptuous to say the least. The Cayuga and Mohawk were superb hunters, fishermen, and, much to Major Stuart's surprise, farmers. The bounty of this New World was spread out on blankets around the campfire for the travelers to enjoy. There was blackened fish cooked over an open fire, along with deer roast and stewed rabbit. Fowl including dove, quail and goose was cooked tenderly in clay pots. The bounty of the fields complimented the abundance of meats. Corn, beans and squash rounded out their menu. The harvest season was bountiful and the Iroquois were good stewards of their land.

The travelers, including Father Constance, Father Bertrand, Major Stuart, Monsieur Geoff, the clerics, the men-at-arms, and the few colonists looking for a fresh start in a new land, enjoyed the food and conversation. The natives accepted them with hospitality and treated them like brothers. At no time did they feel the tension that had existed at the garrison earlier that day. Major Stuart thought to himself that if this was the deceit of the red man then they were very good at it. This intrigued him and so at the first opportunity he asked Louis Hennepin why.

"Simply stated, our French brothers have failed to learn that not all natives are evil, just as not all Frenchmen are good. When you distrust every native, you must learn to accept similar treatment in return. If you expect the worst, too often it will come to pass," said Louis.

"But Governor Frontenac wishes peace with all the tribes. Do they not realize that their mistrust will make peace impossible?" Major Stuart sighed.

"They have witnessed too many deaths first hand to ever let down their guard. Never take the red man for granted. His friendship must be cultivated. Their ways are not ours. An innocent mistake on our part can cause tempers to flare. They are quick to anger. They do not take affronts to their customs lightly."

This was not news to the Major. In his worldly travels he had often encountered primitive societies. He assumed these New World natives would act no differently. The Major's trust was not freely given, nor his respect. Unfortunately, his wards, Constance and Bertrand, did not always recognize the realities of life.

"Thank you for your words of warning, Father Louis. They will serve me well as we continue our journey." Stuart shook the clergyman's hand firmly.

"I hope you will not be offended by the decision of Father Constance to escort Mademoiselle Tekawetha to Montreal. I realize it is a great burden, but Kateri has tremendous influence on her people for good. She can help insure the success of our missions in this new land." Father Hennepin searched Stuart's face for a reaction.

"If assassins find her they will not spare anyone in our party," the Major replied with a stone-faced expression.

"On the other hand, she may assure you safe passage given her reputation with the Cayuga and Mohawk," Hennepin argued. "At any rate, you stand little chance of encountering Iroquois until after you pass Montreal. Their primary encampments are near the large lakes that you must cross farther inland."

"We will surely need a guide," said Stuart tersely.

"A native will serve you well. I'm sure Kateri will provide you with one you can trust," replied Hennepin.

"We cannot linger here many days. Any hope for our continued safety depends upon constant traveling. Our journey will be long," Stuart continued.

"Father Constance informed me that he plans to leave at sunrise. Even now Kateri's party prepares for the journey," Hennepin said with a grin. To make light of the situation served to ease the strain. They both shook hands and smiled.

"May Our Lord bless you and see you safely to your destination," Father Louis made the sign of the cross.

"Thank you and good night." Major Stuart said as he moved over toward the sand dune overlooking the campfire. He spread his blanket to sleep. Always a cautious man, Stuart decided to trust Louis, Augustus and Kateri. He reasoned this might be the last good night's sleep for him for quite sometime to come. He would try to make the most of the opportunity. The Major quickly fell asleep lulled by the murmur of voices in friendly conversation and the trickle of river water flowing over rocks in the shallows.

* * * *

Major Stuart was up at the break of day to oversee the systematic packing of the canoes. The orange ball of a sun rising over the distant purple hills was a sight to behold. The optical distortion made the sun look tremendously large. Its vivid orange hue coupled with the splash of color from the surrounding hills gave an impression of an artist's palette thrown in disarray among the works of a disorganized studio. The outline of common things like trees, rocks, and clouds were quite indistinct. Amid this blaze of colors the Frenchmen transported their loads oblivious to the scenery around them. There was little joy as the travelers contemplated the long, arduous trek that lay ahead.

Mist was rising from the deep blue waters of the St. Lawrence River as the party, including four canoes filled with Kateri and her Cayuga kinsmen, glided silently into the main channel. It was easy to distinguish the Iroquois' canoes from those of the French. Each had bright symbols representing what appeared to be the sun emblazoned upon the bow. These colors overshadowed the gray birch bark from which the canoes were constructed. This gave a festive impression of royalty setting out for a leisurely time on the river. Yet, it still did not overshadow the dark foreboding felt in the heart of each traveler.

Montreal was nearly 250 kilometers away beyond a wide part of the St. Lawrence River known as Lake St. Peter. This was still an easy part of the trip to the Illinois territory. Portages between streams would make travel more difficult later in their trek if the information Joliet had provided was accurate. Stuart wondered how his party would stand up to carry their canoes and baggage over these stretches of nearly impenetrable wilderness. He was sure the mercenaries were prepared, but he had some concern for the strength and endurance of the churchmen. It would be a true test of their faith and resolve to bring religion to the heathens of the interior. Stuart only hoped this trip was worth all the pain and sorrow that might lie ahead.

The trip of several days was rather uneventful except for an encounter one night along the shores of Lake St. Peter that would haunt them for months to come. The party had beached their canoes several hours before sunset in order to prepare their meal in daylight and establish a secure perimeter for the night ahead. Even though no threat was evident, Stuart wanted to protect his party from any eventuality. He was quite strict when it came to proper military procedure.

Once the base camp had been established and firewood gathered for the night, Stuart allowed no one to venture any great distance from his protection. Yet, on this particular night, the Bishop's spy, Monsieur Geoff, wandered off into the forest away from the beach. Apparently, he was bored and felt a solitary stroll would improve his constitution. The primeval forest untouched by civilization held allure, which was almost magical.

As he walked along in the dimming light of a beautiful sunset flashing through the tall trees, Geoff came to a natural clearing. In this clearing was a recently cut oak tree. As he moved toward the center of the clearing, Geoff saw a man in deep meditation wearing a rough-hewn mask. Tobacco was laid neatly on what appeared to be a sacrificial altar in front of the fallen oak. Wisps of smoke ascended in spirals toward the darkening sky. There was an eerie silence befitting an area dedicated to religious ceremonies.

So quickly had Geoff come upon the scene that the individual with the mask was not disturbed. Rather, he sat in deep meditation oblivious of his surroundings. The person was an imposing figure of native stock. His muscular frame was sparsely clothed, as was the custom of the natives in this particular season. His features were completely hidden by the wooden mask.

The wooden mask was a true work of art. The colors painted upon it were of vivid hues prepared from the natural condiments available in this wild land. The artist's lines were bold and distinct giving the mask an expression of tremendous power. The facial expression was that of anger, love, war and peace all rolled into one. Different angles of view presented new emotions not noticed a moment before. The impact of this mask was of such primitive force that Geoff was frozen in his tracks. Minutes passed before he could recover enough from the initial surprise to obtain coherent thought. He realized he was witnessing a ritual not meant for the eyes of another human being. Suddenly shaking all over from the danger he was in, Geoff slowly started backing toward the edge of the forest.

One step. Another. And another. Geoff was surprise at how silent he could be given the circumstances. Things seemed to move in slow motion. He calmed his nerves as he began to believe he might be lucky enough to escape unnoticed.

Then it happened! Geoff forgot about the branch he had stepped over upon entering the clearing. As his heel became entangled in the brush and the leaves, he tumbled backward with an astonished cry of surprise. He did not remain down for long though. In a split second, Geoff was on his feet and running for the protection of the sandy beach by the river and his fellow French protectors. Needless to say, he didn't waste any time to look back. He knew pursuit would be swift.

The blinding speed brought on by extreme fright, the fear of one's very life, made him move like a man possessed.

The figure with the mask was slow to respond. This probably saved the unlucky traveler's life. The native moved slowly as if aroused from a deep slumber. The majestic mask fell to the ground revealing another facial expression, this one of untold anger. Anger over another human witnessing that solemn communion meant only for one man and his God. Not only another human being, but also a white man alien to the ways of nature had defiled the sanctity of this religious rite.

Luckily for Geoff the native had been in very deep meditation. The red man had been so engrossed in his ritual that he was unaware of his surroundings. In this vast expanse of wilderness that was North America of the 17th century it was not unusual to go weeks without seeing another human. The native had felt completely safe in his solitude. Therefore, it took him full minutes to return to consciousness. His response was slow, much like a locomotive starting to pull a train from a stationary position. First, the native took slow, deliberate steps. By the time he reached the low bushes at the edge of the clearing he was finally at a dead run. The distance between him and his quarry began to quickly diminish.

Fleetness of foot was a common trait of an Iroquois. Unlike their western kinsmen who were accustomed to the horse as a mode of transportation, the Iroquois practiced to become endurance runners. Often the ability to run swiftly and for many miles meant the difference between success or failure, from eating or going hungry, or from taking slaves and plunder in war or returning to camp in disgrace. This particular Iroquois was a swift warrior indeed. Years of practice had honed this skill to a fine edge. With a loud war whoop, the native brandished his spiked war club above his head as he plunged into the dense brush.

Geoff had been blessed with a good head start back to the riverbank. Though short of stature, his frightened state moved him at a tremendous pace. Geoff knew his fate if he failed to win this foot race. That type of motivation can work miracles in the face of overwhelming odds.

When Geoff felt the sand of the riverbank under his feet, he sensed the Iroquois extremely close behind. The hairs on the back of his neck stood up and he swore he could feel his pursuer's hot breath on his clammy, sweating skin. He knew that his time was at hand unless something or someone intervened soon. Out of the corner of his eye, Geoff saw the flash of a musket lock and heard the delayed report. The red man grasped at his arm as the war club jumped in the air. He then staggered and fell. Major Stuart had come to Geoff's rescue. For that accurate shot, he would be eternally grateful.

Earlier that evening Major Stuart had taken a head count of his party. He had realized Geoff was missing. Although Stuart was inclined to let Geoff fend for himself, Father Constance had insisted a search be undertaken. Stuart had just picked up his matchlock and was about to head toward the forest when he heard the war cry.

A beautiful attendant to Kateri had been near to Stuart and Father Constance when this commotion started. In fluent French she made the comment that she prayed none of her people would die that night. She had had a premonition and her prayer had saved the warrior from death. Also, Stuart was an excellent marksman, his skill well known on the European continent. When danger threatened his patrons, as a mercenary he was inclined to resolve the problem quickly. Momentarily impressed by the plea of this attractive Indian woman, Stuart took a course of action contrary to his best judgment. Consequently, the warrior lived. Stuart fervently hoped he would not live to regret this decision.

Armed French troops surrounded the red man where he lay in a small, sandy depression at the edge of the river. Dazed from the close proximity of the musket ball, the Indian held his hand over a wound from which blood flowed. He was quickly disarmed and brought over to face Father Constance who was standing by the blazing campfire. Geoff had already collapsed at Father Constance's feet, shaking uncontrollably from his deadly ordeal. Obviously, Geoff realized he had narrowly cheated death. Stuart and the remainder of the party came over to question their Indian prisoner.

"Why do you try to harm one of our party? The French are not your mortal enemy." Father Bertrand asked in French.

The native continued to look at the ground, his hands held behind his back by armed French guards. He did not acknowledge a word that was spoken. Kateri, the saintly priestess, said something in Iroquois. The Indian grunted and spit at her feet.

"He has no respect for a cross bearing shaman. He is a disciple of the old gods. As such, he cannot be trusted," Kateri smirked in disdain. For a saint, there was a distinct lack of compassion in her response. This was probably a result of the fact that kinsmen were ready to kill her on sight should they be presented with the opportunity.

Kateri and the prisoner exchanged more words in her native tongue.

"He knows who I am. Though he won't admit it, I'm sure he would rather see me dead." Kateri spoke in a weary voice, her face down cast.

Major Stuart decided to take charge of the situation. Poor judgment in handling this could mean disaster later in the long journey ahead of them.

"Kateri, did he tell you his name, or which tribe he is associated with?" Stuart paused awaiting a reply. The Iroquois woman didn't answer for several moments weighing her response. Obviously, she knew much about the warrior. Would she confide everything she knew, or leave out a detail that might spell disaster? Stuart hated to be in such a position, left to the mercy of a potential enemy.

"His name is To-Ko-Wan and he is an Oneida war chief. I have seen him at the council fires of the Five Nations many times. He is no friend of mine. His devotion to the old gods is well known." Kateri's voice softened as her Christian nature of mercy gained ascendancy.

"But, why would a wise war chief blunder into an armed French party? That was definitely stupid from a military point of view." Stuart searched her face awaiting a reply.

"It seems your friend here," Kateri pointed to Geoff, still lying panting on the sand, "disturbed a solemn ritual between a shaman and his gods. To-Ko-Wan was in the process of requesting that a tree spirit make a gift of a spirit mask to him. The spirit mask commands great respect among our tribesmen. He who possesses the mask is a person who carries great weight at our council fires. Only a warrior and the spirits can observe this ceremony. It is a bad omen to disturb this ritual. To-Ko-Wan is greatly offended." Kateri tried to explain the situation so the foreigners would understand the seriousness of the matter.

"So he determined to dispatch poor Geoff regardless of personal cost?" Stuart answered his own question.

"Pray, are there more of his kind lurking in the forest surrounding us?" Bertrand grimaced at the thought of more savages bursting from the dark, foreboding landscape. Spending the night in this particular spot suddenly didn't seem so tranquil and inviting.

"Acquiring a spirit mask is a long, solitary journey of faith fraught with many hardships. The spirits are said to lead the warrior on a difficult trail of pain and self-discovery. It is an experience that cannot be shared with others. It is extremely personal. To-Ko-Wan is alone on his quest, that I assure you." Kateri spoke with grim confidence.

Father Constance's countenance brightened.

"No harm done, then." he said. "We must release him to go about his personal business. What harm can one man do against our formidable weapons?"

Kateri wilted at these words, nearly buckling at the knees. Her attractive escort, Sha-Na, spoke quickly.

"To-Ko-Won is my lady's sworn enemy. You cannot protect us should he go free. Please do not be hasty in your decision."

Father Constance replied in a flustered voice, "Surely he cannot believe he is a match for fifteen armed Frenchmen. Major Stuart's men are veteran mercenaries of several continental wars. Such action on his part would be suicide."

Sha-Na shook her head. Her eyes blazed with defiance uncommon to their usual Christian demeanor. "He only knows that the men of the cross preach peace and love. Those he has come into contact with are not warriors. They do not defend themselves. Therefore, To-Ko-Wan believes we are easy prey."

"Then our only recourse is to escort him to Montreal. Governor Frontenac wants to be friends to all the Iroquois. We will let him deal with this problem." Major Stuart replied decisively. "Shackle him and, Sha-Na, make it clear to him that, as French warriors, we will not be averse to taking his life should we be given no other choice. Were it not for you, he would be lying dead on the sand already."

Sha-Na exchanged a few words with the Iroquois. Surprisingly, the proud Oneida chief was asking for something, judging from the tone of their conversation. Kateri and Sha-Na whispered for a few moments before addressing the Major.

"To-Ko-Wan wants to return to the forest to retrieve his mask. It would be dishonorable to leave the mask after it has been blessed with nature's power. He would rather die this very minute than leave his mission incomplete."

"We must be tolerant of the heathen's beliefs," interrupted Father Constance, even as the Major considered granting the native's request by summary execution.

"We can surely make some sort of accommodation to preserve human life and dignity," Constance continued.

Stuart's lieutenant, Ramon Hallet, who had been silent for most of the trip, spoke up. "We cannot let that happen, Sir. If the native were to escape, we may suffer a grievous disaster."

Sha-Na replied to this statement, "To-Ko-Wan has given his word he will not flee. An Iroquois' word is a sacred bond. You can trust that completely with you very life."

Against his better judgment, Major Stuart agreed. He was obviously struck by the beauty of Sha-Na. She was of slight build, but her features were finely etched. Her dark eyes suggested wisdom. Her hair was majestic in its ebony beauty. Sha-Na's smile was captivating and sincere. She was truly a statuesque beauty.

Sha-Na was obviously pleased, as Major Stuart ordered an escort into the forest to retrieve the mask. She insisted on going along. Stuart, suddenly feeling protective of her, accompanied them. The party of seven marched quickly back into the wilderness. The shadows were very long and the small amount of light shining from the treetops had a golden glow. The massive trunks of the centuries old deciduous trees suggested giant guards standing watch over a pagan fortress. The party was in awe of their imposing surroundings. Soon they arrived at the sacred clearing; the repository of the native's Holy Grail. The clearing had an air of magic that the white men were noticeably reluctant to intrude upon.

"Remove his bonds and let him proceed alone. His word is his bond. To-Ko-Wan would rather die than flee." Sha-Na restrained Major Stuart with a gentle hand on his arm as he sought to grab the red man's shackles.

In any other situation, Stuart would have considered this suggestion ludicrous. Somehow though, at this particular moment, this course of action seemed perfectly logical. The French soldiers seemed reluctant, yet they obeyed the Major without a word. The soldier's duty is to completely obey a superior officer without question.

The late evening air was heavy and moist. There was electricity in the air and thunder rumbled from an approaching thunderstorm. The glow of the golden sunset produced an eerie shine on the foliage in the clearing. The effect was positively dazzling. Sha-Na strongly suggested that the French not observe her kinsman's actions in the clearing. He would not forgive further intrusion. But, the yearning to look upon the forbidden was as strong as a child's urge to spy on Santa Claus at Christmas. It could not be ignored. To their credit, the French cast their eyes aside, only looking when they knew To-Ko-Wan was totally engrossed in his work.

The Iroquois bowed before the oak tree from which he had carved the ceremonial war mask. He spent several minutes in solemn meditation. The offerings to the spirit, the tobacco and a small carved rock effigy, were left at the makeshift altar. The smoldering fire was quickly doused.

The magnificent mask seemed to glow on the ground where it had been discarded when the footrace with Mr. Geoff began. The Frenchmen were definitely not prepared for its impact. The colors of the mask were striking. The natural hues of red, gold and green screamed in their silence demanding attention. The carved lines were simple, yet intricate. Viewed from different angles, the mask actually changed expression. Ferocious, comical, spiritual, and sober all described its appearance. The magic was evident even to the uninitiated. To-Ko-Wan delicately wrapped his prize in his long cloak of skins. Even covered from sight, the mask's image remained indelibly etched in the memories of the French. They would be able to describe its features in detail years later. Although covered, the very presence of the mask made them somehow nervous and slightly on edge.

This was very disquieting to devout Catholics. How could a primitive trophy have such an effect?

To-Ko-Wan joined them at the clearing edge. They marched back to the river's edge as the evening thunderstorm dumped torrents of water on them for several minutes. Yet, as quickly as the storm started it stopped. Even the rain could not dampen the effect of the mask. Actually, this fury of nature emphasized the mask's power even more.

Supper was awaiting their return. The aroma of salt pork and beans cooking in the open kettles was welcome indeed given their encounter. After the ordeal of the day, somehow the warmth of the fire offered welcome solace. To-Ko-Wan remained docile and everyone slept well, except of course for the sentry staring into the night. The spirits were definitely abroad that night. Thank God for the peace of the campfire!

The boats were loaded at sunrise and the journey to the Montreal settlement continued without incident.

*   *   *   *

To-Ko-Wan prayed that night to his new spirit guide, the guide of the mask, before sleeping. He realized that this encounter with the Christian shaman, Kateri, was his destiny. The Iroquois believed that the spirit of the forest embodied in the wooden mask would lead them to their life's work. It was not coincidence that the French party stumbled upon To-Ko-Wan's ritual in the middle of the vast North American forest. There was a purpose to all these events. He was resigned to bide his time and see where the path chosen for him would lead. To-Ko-Wan was positive that he was destined to fulfill Kateri's desire for martyrdom. He reflected that it was surely a strange god who prized disciples that willingly surrendered their lives like cowards. How could these sheep not raise a hand even to save themselves? Weakness was not in the Iroquois tradition. Survival of the fittest had always reigned supreme as a dogma of the Iroquois tribe. The Iroquois were determined to be the fittest. Kateri's influence over her people must come to an end.

As for Monsieur Geoff, To-Ko-Wan would make him pay the price for his intrusion on the sacred ceremony of the forest. Retribution would be swift and unmerciful. And for the rest of the French, they had treated him with respect. Therefore, he would not hate them, but as warriors they would die if he had the opportunity. To-Ko-Wan slept well knowing that he was on a mission of the gods of his people. He knew his destiny was to be the salvation of the Iroquois from this foreign god.

As the days on the river passed, the romance between Sha-Na and Jon Stuart blossomed. Beyond Montreal lay Lake Ontario and the heart of the Five Nations. To make their way safely through this dangerous land, the French party would need an experienced guide. Who better than a native Iroquois to fulfill this need? Maybe the couple would not have to say farewell at Montreal after all.

Major Stuart made it a point to remain close to his charges, the good Fathers Constance and Bertrand. The Major and Constance were often in the same canoe discussing the future journey. After the problem on the shores of Lake St. Peter, Jon Stuart insisted on Sha-Na riding with them. The long days of travel were spent learning more about the lands between Montreal and the Illinois country. It was amazing how a young Iroquois woman could know so much about this vast land. Evidently, information was freely shared between the Iroquois during the long winter nights around the campfire. Although Sha-Na had never seen the Illinois country firsthand, the second hand stories would prove to be a valuable resource in the future.

Sha-Na was an Iroquois maid of the Oneida clan. She was about the same age as Kateri. Other women her age were busy raising families. However, the fact that Sha-Na had given her life to the white man's god made her unattractive for marriage. Kateri's entourage of women was doomed to a solitary life of devotion to their new religion.

The beauty of the native Indian women captivated Major Stuart and the others in the French party. Sha-Na was one of the most striking of the group. She stood approximately 5 ft. 4 in., tall by European women standards of the period. Her dark features made her seem mysterious and intriguing. Her long hair of glistening ebony further contributed to her allure. Sha-Na's eyes were almond brown like muddy pools hiding fascinating details in their depths. The Iroquois had a habit of staring focused and unblinking on the subject they were scrutinizing. Their direct and unembarrassed gaze could pierce the heart of an ordinary man. Sha-Na exercised this ability quite often. This expressionless stare made her thoughts unfathomable. While most of the French viewed this as unfriendly, Major Stuart recognized this manner as a peculiarity of the race. Therefore, he didn't take offense. On the contrary, he believed this made Sha-Na very attractive.

Each Iroquois was prone to not react openly to anything that might happen. This stoicism served them well in this wilderness where everyday events could bring new hardship and little joy. Stuart learned from Sha-Na that the Christian view of joy and love is what attracted her to the faith. While the daily life of an Indian often brought pain and sorrow to be accepted without emotion, Christ taught us to find joy in small blessings. Indian religion was basically pessimistic in that only the strong would survive and the weak should be shunned. Yet, Christianity gave hope for the weak and the less fortunate. They were of value to society also. Catholicism was a faith of optimism foreign to the Indian mentality, which is probably why there were so few initial Indian converts. But Kateri, Sha-Na and the others in their group embraced this new faith with enthusiasm.

Little by little, Sha-Na opened up to Jon Stuart and Father Constance. As the canoes glided along the blue, unspoiled water of the St. Lawrence River they all joined in the conversations of life, home and love. The trip to Montreal seemed to blur. By the time the smoke plumes of Montreal's fires were sighted on the horizon, the disparate group began to feel much like old friends. A true friendship had been cultivated. Everyone hated to see this leg of the journey end.

* * * *

Cannons boomed from the steep heights along the river as the boat party of French and Iroquois approached Montreal. The cannon smoke blossomed high in the air and mingled with the billowy white clouds. It was obvious Montreal was built for defense. It would take a large army of siege, or deceit to sack this town. Montreal in the year of our Lord 1675 was as near to civilization as a Frenchman could get in the northern reaches of the New World. Following the success of Spanish explorers finding riches in the Americas, many French believed that they could make a fortune there also. Increasing numbers ventured across the Atlantic to seek their fortune. Many were ill prepared for the hardships encountered in the vast, untamed wilderness. After brief exposure to these dangers, they were drawn to what little civilization this new land had to offer. Montreal was a natural attraction. It offered music, culture, artisans and a refinement that was welcomed after months of "roughing it". Everything about Montreal reminded the Frenchman of home. The streets had names and cobblestones, rather than dust, or knee-deep mud. Bells chimed from more than one church. Soldiers drilled on a green, manicured parade field. Yes, Montreal offered refuge to the weary adventurer, and so Montreal welcomed our travelers with open arms. It even beckoned them to stay.

The riverside docks were crude by European standards, yet a marked improvement over those of Quebec. Rough-hewn logs had been buried vertically in the water and mud to support a lattice of board and railing. Steps appealing to the eye beckoned the visitor to climb approximately 10 ft. up to a broad causeway leading toward the distant settlement. Systematically placed along this causeway were poles supporting oil lamps. Some of these poles were even festooned with cloth banners depicting reminders of the French homeland. These colorful flags flapping in the breeze gave the river entrance to Montreal a decidedly metropolitan flavor. For a moment, this sign of civilization helped the traveler to forget that he was lost in the middle of a virtually unexplored and inhospitable continent. No wonder the few French settlers and explorers treasured memories of their visit to this French provincial outpost.

These French cosmopolitan airs successfully camouflaged the reality of the river dock. Actually, during periods of low water the docks were barely functional. To approach boats moored at the dock during arid times required the use of ladders below the serviceable stairs. This made embarkation and disembarkation quite inconvenient, to say the least, and down right tedious if goods had to be unloaded. Conversely, during periods of torrential rain the structure barely withstood the rushing current of the St. Lawrence River. Often many sections were actually swept away. This forced seemingly continual construction on the dock to keep it functional. In spite of this, the imposing structure of the Montreal docks gave the visitor an impression of security. This refuge beckoned them to stay and enjoy. The Fathers realized it would be hard to proceed into the wilderness if they stayed here too long.

Several large ships with mastheads and sails were moored along the docks. At least one of these ships appeared seaworthy. Their presence completed the cosmopolitan flavor. Several languages were heard spoken by the various groups mingling by the ships and wandering up and down the docks. An argument was being carried on in Spanish, which threatened to get ugly. The booming laughter and accent of the Dutch could be heard. The various dialects of the Native Americans added mystery to the mix. This was definitely an era of exploration and colonization. Each adventurous group was represented here. It was an inspiring time to be alive. Major Stuart bathed in the excitement of this place in time. The bustle made the French fathers, Constance and Bertrand, feel at home in the wilderness.

Being close to midday, the dockside taverns were quiet. Signs with crude paintings advertising ale and wine creaked softly in the breeze. Each tavern had a quaint name that suggested the clientele that frequented the place. If one was from Spain, he might enjoy the "El Toro". "The Boars Head" had a decidedly British flavor. This might not be a safe tavern to frequent given the enmity between the British and French. Obviously, the French bistros were the best represented. Any traveler, regardless of his ancestry, could find a tavern to make him feel at home for a few brief hours. Some drunks experiencing the effects of too many brews from the previous night snored against the dock rails. Even the heat of the midday sun could not disturb their slumbers.

The travelers were struck by the contrast between this settlement and their visit to Quebec. At Quebec they had been the center of attention. A delegation of city officials had greeted them. All had been eager for any news from the old country. On the contrary in Montreal they were just faces in the crowd, another group of adventurers out to seek their fortune. No one paid particular attention as they left their canoes and moved away from the docks toward the village common.

On the other hand, the group of Iroquois that had accompanied the travelers created quite a stir among their native brethren. Apparently, Kateri had a reputation among other Iroquois and even the French voyageurs. Everyone had heard about the Catholic woman convert who was near canonization. Kateri was known for her compassion and kindness toward all—regardless of ancestry. Many on the docks flocked to get a glimpse of this Iroquois priestess. Her entourage of women screened her from the crowd. They accepted this notoriety as a common occurrence. Kateri smiled and talked in the manner of a queen holding court. All were in awe of her luminescence. Yet, she was very approachable. Like a flame, she drew the moths unto her. Like all celebrities, Kateri repeated the timeless ritual of administering to her admirers.

Jon Stuart reflected on this gathering of the adored and adoring. From what he had been told previously in Quebec, he expected enemies to be among the crowd that sought after her in Montreal. However, Stuart failed to see a scowling face that could be construed to be an enemy. There was nothing but smiles from most of the admirers. It must be noted that smiling is generally foreign to the Native Americans. Their hard life does not lend to joviality. Therefore, it is hard for one to construe if the Iroquois is happy, sad, distraught, or at peace. Still, no expression on the faces of Kateri's brethren gave an indication of displeasure. Actually, the gathering assumed a definitely festive air. Stuart noted that there were few white men present. Maybe her fellow Iroquois was not Kateri's true threat.

Down by the traveler's canoes another small crowd was gathering. Apparently, some Iroquois on the dock had recognized the Iroquois clan chief, To-Ko-Wan. To-Ko-Wan sat on the riverbank chewing a piece of dried venison the French had supplied. He was reflecting upon his eventual fate. He was not physically restrained, but the French guards of Major Stuart kept a close watch.

To-Ko-Wan felt he could easily escape into the crowd of his brother Iroquois, but he was not about to leave without his spirit mask. His fate was intertwined with that forest sprite. But, the time was not opportune to try to retrieve it now. To-Ko-Wan would bide his time waiting for an opportunity. He believed the Iroquois forest spirits had placed him with the French party for a purpose. Kateri was a traitor to her Iroquois heritage. To-Ko-Wan might possibly be the appointed one to administer retribution for Kateri's heresy.

Jon Stuart, Father Constance, Father Bertrand, and Monsieur Geoff left the docks behind and moved into Montreal. The settlement was built into and on top of a hillside overlooking the St. Lawrence River. The town site had been chosen initially for ease of fortification. With the competition between European powers for colonies throughout the world, fortification was necessary to militarily control and lay claim to the surrounding countryside. Protection from the natives was also a prerequisite since opposing powers often bribed them to harass and discourage the settlers. Montreal with its French garrison was a refuge from the terrors of the red man. Though the natives were allowed to walk the streets, squads of blue-coated French infantry that regularly marched through the town closely monitored their activities. There was a sense of security unknown to the French in other parts of the upper great lake region.

As a French squad marched past the travelers, their lieutenant sang cadence and their boots stomped regularly on the cobblestone street. Montreal storefronts exhibited wares for sale. Magnificent rifles, finely wrought silver jewelry, earthen glazed pottery, aromatic tobacco, all the trappings of civilization, beckoned to the travelers. All was available if one could afford the price.

The one difference between Montreal and other French towns of similar size was the fur trade. Furs were readily accepted in lieu of currency for anything from food to jewelry. Plush beaver, glistening otter, and soft muskrat pelts were piled at street corners and hanging in store windows. It was evident that the French had found something of value in the New World that could be a substitute for gold or silver. European demand for fashions cut from animal pelts like beaver and otter kept prices for fur very lucrative. A young Frenchman could invest a few years in the wilderness trapping and return to France a wealthy man. The fur business was as good as a gold mine. A shrewd trader could amass a fortune in fur by trading with the natives and never stepping foot in the wilderness. The advantage to this was you didn't have to spend cold winters along a lonely creek working in solitude. One could live in Montreal and trade with Indians who willingly trapped, skinned and dried pelts for some of the trinkets of civilization.

The travelers followed the cobblestone streets toward the government houses of Montreal. They passed many people of various ancestries. A lamplighter was busy preparing his lamps for the evening. Stuart, Constance and Bertrand stopped to ask directions.

"Where might we find Governor Frontenac, monsieur?" said Constance in a jovial voice. The civilized atmosphere of Montreal had lifted his spirits from the depressing contemplation of the arduous trip that lay ahead.

"Who wishes to see his eminence?" roared the lamplighter in a deep voice seemingly uncharacteristic of his slight build. He was an older man and the years had not been kind. Indeed, the only thing intimidating about him was his voice. He eyed Major Stuart with suspicion. The lamplighter recognized the demeanor of an Englishman. Assassination was a common tool of political intrigue in 17th century society. He feared for his beloved leader, Frontenac.

"It is Father Constance, Father Bertrand and their bodyguard, Major Stuart. Finance Minister Jean Colbert has sent us on a mission. We have important business to discuss," said Constance. Anger was beginning to flare due to this shabby treatment from a fellow countryman.

"Forgive me, good Father!" the lamplighter immediately kneeled and kissed the priest's hand when he noticed the Roman collar. "The Governor's quarters are straight ahead. It is the two-story white masonry building of imposing stature at the end of the street," he said gesturing toward the distant buildings. "You will know the one I mean. Pardon my insolence, good Father." The lamplighter lowered his eyes and went about his work of refueling the lamps.

Father Bertrand said a blessing as the group moved on down the wide street. Major Stuart continued to attract glares from other French on the street now that his nationality had been exposed. The English and French had been mortal enemies for centuries. This was a common occurrence and Major Stuart had long ago learned to accept it.

They soon found the building. It was an imposing structure for these wilderness surroundings. Obviously, it was designed to house a dignitary of some importance. An alert sentry demanded they halt and state their business. Mention of Colbert's name always seemed to produce immediate results and this time was no exception. An usher was summoned to greet them and soon the party was standing in a spacious first floor parlor with a huge fireplace and rustic furniture. The warmth of a crackling fire seemed to portend good fortune for them. An audience was granted quickly suggesting that their arrival had been expected. In a short time Louis de Bade de Frontenac came strutting into the room with a broad smile and greetings for all. His sincerity made a deep impression on everyone.

Louis de Bade, commonly known as Frontenac, was a tall, imposing figure. Well over six-foot in height, he was a giant compared to the average man of the seventeenth century. His dark hair had more than a few streaks of gray indicating age and wisdom from years of experience. Louis' blue eyes twinkled with a crafty genius that had been feared by European military field commanders for years. Success in battles fought for his native France gave him an air of confidence that set him apart from other men of similar position. Yet, politeness, manners, and evident strength of character made all in the room feel comfortable in his presence. Frontenac was a man people could trust. It was apparent why those under his command would follow him anywhere—even to the jaws of death!

Major Stuart knew the reputation of this great man, Frontenac. He welcomed this unusual opportunity to meet and evaluate a one-time mortal enemy. Stuart knew the stories of Frontenac's valor in battle. Were they true, or merely embellishment born of cowards? One thing stood out as unique. Even though Frontenac was aware of the Englishman's presence, he still treated him with courtesy. Stuart even sensed an element of rudimentary respect. This was unlike the common Frenchman on the street. Perhaps Stuart's exploits while protecting the church fathers were better known than he suspected. Stuart felt that for all their differences, Frontenac was still a man he could admire and respect—possibly, even befriend.

"Welcome travelers to Montreal! I trust your journey from France has not been too arduous." Frontenac's voice was warm and sincere. If the stories were true that he disliked the clergy and anyone associated with the church, Frontenac certainly disguised his feelings well. Frontenac was a well-known champion of nationalism. This put him at odds with the ruling establishment, which included both the church and the monarchy.

"Except for some minor difficulties, our trip has been very pleasurable thus far. This continent has spectacular scenery rivaling anything I've experienced in my worldly travels." Constance assumed the role of the spokesman. "Let me introduce you to my friends and fellow travelers."

Constance introduced the group one-by-one. Frontenac took each one by the hand firmly and shook it warmly. All were made to feel very welcome indeed.

After the amenities were dispensed, Frontenac directly broached the subject of why they were in Montreal. Obviously, he had not time to waste on political intrigue. "How might I be of service to you, my countrymen?"

Constance was surprised at this candor. He had expected a more circuitous route by Frontenac to learn their mission. Constance explained in detail their mission to the Illinois country. Though many felt they were here to find a pot of gold for the church, nothing could be further from the truth. He directly expressed this to Frontenac. Constance spoke with evident passion concerning their desire to bring religion to the native of the interior.

"Your idealism is to be commended," said Frontenac after listening intently to each and every word. "but you must learn to deal with the red man to assure your safety. Not all are as innocent as they would seem. They would lull you into a sense of security from which you may not awake. If you do not know their culture, you may make a grave mistake and pay with your life."

"That is why were hoping you could recommend a guide to help us through our difficulty." Constance spoke with trust in his voice. He did not view this military man as an enemy.

"I understand you are traveling with an Iroquois who is somewhat of a celebrity. Surely Mademoiselle Kateri and her friends can provide what you require for a safe journey to the Illinois country," replied Frontenac unconcerned.

"But Monsieur, you misunderstand. Mademoiselle Kateri and her friends are only traveling companions. They only come as far as Montreal. We let them travel with us as a favor to our Quebec friends. This is their final destination. Now Kateri is under your protection," said Constance noncommittally.

"Gentlemen, you must understand that politically her presence here poses somewhat of a dilemma. Animosity is building between the natives converted to Christianity and those that cling to the old ways. The French must remain friends to all natives regardless of their religious persuasion. As Governor of New France, I cannot be perceived to take sides in this matter of religion. There are lives of colonist at stake. I take this responsibility very seriously." Frontenac spoke sincerely, unlike the politician the group had expected.

"If you cannot see fit to protect her, at least, do not openly persecute her!" Constance's anger flared and he began to raise his voice. Constance, Bertrand, and Major Stuart had heard the rumors that Frontenac had no love for the Catholic clergy, white or native. Maybe his true motive was being revealed.

Frontenac responded calmly, giving no indication of detecting anger in Constance's voice. "You misunderstand me, my dear friends. Mademoiselle Kateri is welcome to stay in Montreal as long as she wishes. I simply wish for you to understand my position. I, as Governor, cannot guarantee her safety. Such action might jeopardize my attempts to make this new land safe for all French colonists."

"We sympathize with your position and pray Kateri's presence doesn't jeopardize the lives of any of our fellow countrymen," Constance said coolly, his reason restored.

"My sources tell me Kateri should fear her own people more than me. She is no threat to me where ever she chooses to reside," Frontenac said tersely, but with honesty.

Constance continued, ignoring the remark.

"Major Stuart has made arrangements to allow two of our militia to remain as Kateri's bodyguards. They will be no trouble to you. They are very trustworthy and loyal to France. I hope you have no objection."

"Of course not," said Frontenac, apparently relieved that the safety of such a controversial figure would not be his by default. He went on to address the problem of a guide.

"Gentlemen, you are in luck! A French voyageur of some reputation and countless years of experience in this trackless wilderness has recently arrived in Montreal to sell furs and obtain provisions. His name is Pierre Radisson. Perhaps you have heard of him? Pierre is a personal friend of mine. He has direct experience with these natives. I'm sure I can persuade him to accompany you to the Illinois country. Pierre has spent several years exploring the wilderness just north of that region. He knows first hand many of the native tribes of that region. Pierre knows well the Iroquois temperament." Frontenac chuckled, making reference to Radisson's years of Iroquois captivity.

The joke was lost on our travelers who were unfamiliar with the intrigues of the New World. All of their knowledge and experience was centered on Europe. They were unaware that one Iroquois clan, the Oneida had held Radisson captive, for several years. At first they had tortured him unmercifully. Being a very brave young man, Radisson had remained defiant, his spirit unbroken. Over time he had gained the respect and even somewhat of a reputation among the Spartan Iroquois. One had to be strong indeed to gain their admiration. There was no one better to guide them through this wilderness than Monsieur Radisson.

"We appreciate your consideration in this matter," said Constance, warming as to a friend. The gossip he had heard about Frontenac hating all clergy may have been incorrect. Frontenac was a leader of men who genuinely cared for his charges. Kateri would have nothing to fear from him. The travelers would be in good hands with Monsieur Radisson.

"We have one other favor to ask," Bertrand interjected, taking over for Father Constance. "We have an Iroquois clan chief detained due to his obvious animosity towards some in our group. It seems we inadvertently interrupted the native's sacred religious ceremony. Something about a spirit mask. I'm sure you know more about the implications of this than we do."

"Another delicate problem to address, heh?" said Frontenac, showing no emotion while quickly evaluating the situation.

"We wish him no harm, you must know," continued Bertrand. "Maybe you could detain him for a few days to give us a head start on our journey. Then you can return the obscene mask to him and set him free. We can only pray he will not follow."

Frontenac made no response for several minutes. He silently wondered if these "babes in the woods" understood how serious this situation could become for everyone. When he began to speak, all were aware of the gravity.

"It will be a hard choice for this Iroquois chief, revenge on the heretic Kateri, or revenge on you. Who can guess which he will choose? Pray no one has to deal with his wrath. The Iroquois warrior can pursue a mission with deadly purpose. It could take all your wiles and luck to survive." Frontenac shook his head and continued.

"Still, I'm sure we can manage to restrain him for awhile. I will make the necessary arrangements. Meanwhile, please join me at dinner. We have prepared a sumptuous feast in your honor." Frontenac's mood lightened and he motioned for the door that led to the banquet room.

The group retired to a large room with another huge fireplace and long table heaping with culinary delights of the wilderness. Golden oak hewn timbers reflected the warm glow of the oil lamps. The flames in these lamps danced merrily, casting alternate shadows on the walls. A string quartet provided a jaunty melody that gave the meal a festive mood. Who would expect such amenities of civilization? Wine from their native France topped off an evening of delightful conversation. All this made the travelers yearn for home. Farewells were said after Frontenac promised to act at first light on the morrow upon the matters they had discussed. They walked the few blocks back to the river docks in the cool night air reflecting on this turn of events. The fathers had a new appreciation for the burden of political office. They resolved to pray daily for their new friend, Louis de Bade de Frontenac. The travelers knew the events of this night would help to seal the success of their missionary endeavor into the interior of this wilderness.

*   *   *   *

Arrangements for the next leg of their journey were quickly made. Pierre Radisson heartily agreed to guide them on their inland trek. He was an easy person to get to know and conversed extensively about his exploration of the inland wilderness. Radisson had made at least one trip to the region known today as

Minnesota. Given his knowledge of the intertwined lakes, more like inland seas, Radisson was convinced that a northwest passage existed linking the Atlantic Ocean to the far eastern ocean commonly known as the Pacific. If he could but locate this passage, he could open up a lucrative trade route to the Far East that would position France as a major player in world trade. This would undoubtedly make him a wealthy man and earn him a reputation for exploration to rival the Spaniards like Magellan and Columbus. Radisson had planned on another journey as soon as possible in an attempt to locate his passage to the Pacific. These missionaries fit well into this plan. They would provide welcome companionship on the initial leg of his long journey west.

A first impression of Monsieur Radisson did not suggest an indomitable explorer. On the contrary, Radisson was short of stature and of dark complexion. Pierre undoubtedly descended from the Basque people that inhabited the south of France. He had inherited their spirit of independence and adventure. Pierre was tough as nails. What he lacked in size and physical strength he more than made up for in determination and perseverance. He was a man of congenial high spirits when associating with close friends, but woe unto his enemies. Only death could stop Radisson from anything he set his mind to.

Indeed, the Iroquois knew from experience this inner strength that Radisson possessed. He had earned their grudging respect having spent several years in their captivity. Around 1651 Radisson had the misfortune to be with some companions trapping in interior New York. The French voyageurs were always in search of abundant furs. They had been very successful in obtaining many pelts in this land of plenty. Unfortunately, in their greed they had trespassed on Iroquois territory. Coveting the furs the French party had accumulated, an Iroquois war party had fallen upon Radisson and his friends. In the ensuing battle the entire party was killed save Pierre. He should have also died from his many and grievance wounds for he put up a tremendous fight. Unconsciousness before a mortal blow could be dealt and luck worked in tandem to save him.

The Iroquois were not wanton killers. Indeed, they valued able-bodied slaves quite highly. One Iroquois warrior recognized the value of Radisson as a slave thus sparing his life. Consequently, this warrior had his mate nurse Pierre back to health. Though he lived the life of a dog in an Indian village, Pierre survived all that the Iroquois could give. First, there was torture for many months. Many times Pierre was forced to run the gauntlet. The whole Iroquois village turned out eager for the opportunity to pummel and bruise Pierre's white body. Somehow Pierre was able to run the length of this tortuous path before collapsing. He well knew they would beat him to death should he ever stumble. Having survived this merciless sport, Radisson was then worked into the ground performing the most menial tasks of the clan. Ironically, his strength seemed to grow as he survived each terrible beating. It was as if he drew power from these ordeals. Eventually, he was able to slip out of camp one night when his captors let down their guard for a few minutes. Pierre made his way back to civilization looking the worse for wear, but immensely wiser in the ways of the red man. It was surely a stroke of fortune that allowed Bertrand and Constance to travel into the North American interior with such a man.

Radisson and Major Stuart spent several hours becoming acquainted. Radisson explained in detail the obstacles along the route that lay ahead of them. Leaving Montreal they would travel southwest on the St. Lawrence River to a large lake the Iroquois call "Ontario". In their language, this meant "beautiful lake". Portaging around an immense waterfall they would eventually arrive at another inland-sea later to be named Lake Erie. Radisson spent some time explaining to Stuart the nature of these bodies of water. Although described as lakes, these waters were small oceans. The water was deep and the currents, at times, treacherous. The seasons of late autumn, winter, and early spring were not a time for the traveler to be out in the open waters of these lakes. Consequently, they would follow the shoreline as it wound westward toward their ultimate destination, Illinois.

Radisson also explained that the leg of their journey from Montreal and well into Lake Erie took them through the heart of Iroquois country. The travelers would need to be alert constantly lest they come across unfriendly natives looking for plunder and slaves. Radisson was determined never to fall into the clutches of the Iroquois again. When Stuart commented that he was told that not all Iroquois were enemies, Radisson became irritated and asked how to tell friend from foe. He made the point that by the time you obtained enough information to make the judgment, it was then too late. Radisson made it clear that he wished to complete this leg of the trip as quickly as possible. In this manner they could shorten the time when disaster might strike them unaware.

The second leg of the journey would be more difficult. Portage would be necessary if the wished to take the most direct route to Illinois country. Travel would be easier if they stayed with the inland seas, but that route would take them many miles out of their way and farther north. Given the lateness of the season, Radisson stressed that they could not afford the extra time. Also, the lakes could turn treacherous if winter threatened to come early. By sticking to rivers and short portages, the travelers would go through country inhabited by natives of Algonquian stock. These tribes included the Miami, Peoria, Cahokia, Michigainea, and the Tamaroa. Basically, they were peaceful people. In fact, their lack of success at war was the reason they had been pushed west by the Iroquois. Most of the Algonkins were mortal enemies of the Iroquois and loyal to the French. These natives were fertile grounds for missionaries. Radisson explained that the chance of having ones throat slit at night was lessened by taking the route he suggested.

After this conversation regarding the route their journey would take, Radisson and Stuart discussed the preparation that needed to be completed before they left. Radisson was a robust man with much nervous energy. He wanted to leave as early as possible. They agreed to assemble two days hence prepared to continue the journey down the St. Lawrence River. Radisson set off to purchase his supplies for the long winter ahead. Stuart resolved to acquaint Bertrand and Constance with some of the details he had learned. Also, he must make his good-byes to the Iroquois maids that had accompanied them from Quebec. Stuart was also eager to get back on the trail.

* * * *

Monsieur Geoff, the little ferret of a man who was Colbert's planted spy, was very attentive to the voyageur Radisson. Geoff had heard comments from the locals alluding to the reputation of Monsieur Radisson. Apparently, Radisson knew from experience the interior of North America. Who would better know if a fortune in gold and silver might exist farther west in the primeval forests of this New World? The Spanish had discovered riches beyond man's wildest dreams farther south. Didn't it seem plausible that similar riches could be found in North America as well? Colbert was counting on just such luck. Such a discovery would allow France to challenge Spain for ascendancy in Europe. If a treasure could be located, Geoff's master, Colbert, would be very pleased indeed. Geoff stood to profit handsomely in both wealth and position back in France if he could somehow fulfill his secret mission.

It was obvious to Geoff that Constance and Bertrand cared little for secular wealth. Though he admired their dedication to converting the heathen natives, Geoff viewed their disdain for worldly pleasures as monumental stupidity. The good fathers would be no competition to his claim of the wealth should they be fortunate enough to locate any. Conversely, since the Father's priorities obviously didn't include active prospecting for gold, they would be of little help in accomplishing his mission. Perhaps Monsieur Radisson, given his robust, adventurous nature might prove a welcome ally. Radisson, with his apparent knowledge of the Iroquois, might also be able to suggest how Geoff could avoid the anger of

To-Ko-Wan, Iroquois medicine man. As Radisson moved to leave the docks following his conference with Major Stuart, Geoff seized the opportunity to ask a few questions.

"Monsieur Radisson, if you please," called Geoff in a low voice attempting to be as discreet as possible, "might I have a moment of your precious time?"

Radisson in his usual jovial manner began to answer Geoff's direct questions. Obviously, Radisson was a man who never met a stranger. Also, this popularity with the new travelers made him feel somewhat of a celebrity. He could never pass up an opportunity to brag about his exploits. Besides, Geoff looked like he could afford a few mugs of ale, or possible a precious glass of wine, in return for some information. Radisson put his arm around Geoff's shoulders and they retired to a nearby tavern along the docks.

As Radisson tipped his second mug of ale, Geoff came directly to the point.

"In your travels into the western wilderness, have you ever seen any hint of mineral wealth? You are surely aware that the Aztecs farther south had their storerooms overflowing with gold and silver. Do their northern cousins have similar wealth?"

Radisson, eager to continue the free drinks, looked directly at Geoff and paused a few moments before he answered. He suppressed his immediate inclination to roar with laughter. Obviously, a search for treasure was one of the reasons this party of Frenchman wanted to travel to the Illinois country. Radisson wondered if he should encourage this folly. Radisson answered quietly.

"Tales of wealth in the lands north of New Spain abound. Coronado lost his life pursuing the fabled seven cities of Cibola. De Soto undoubtedly hoped to find a treasure cache as he ventured up the great inland river prior to his untimely death. You have surely heard of them or you would not be here. The gold fever spread fast and far. Indeed, these stories may have some basis in fact." Radisson could not resist the temptation to string this naive traveler along.

Geoff's gaze dropped to the table unhappy with this oblique response.

"I don't want to listen to fairy tales!" Geoff slammed his fist on the table to make his point. "I asked you, as an explorer who has seen the interior of this country firsthand. Is there any hope that gold will be discovered there?"

Radisson quickly decided there was no reason to encourage such obviously soft, ill prepared adventurers to chase a dream into this harsh country. They would not be prepared for the hazards they might have to face.

"Otter and muskrat pelts are the only gold I know to exist in this wilderness," Radisson winked. "One can't expect poor people like these red men who live in stick and mud huts to have a secret cache of gold. Magnificence is not a word in these native's vocabulary.

"In your experience then, one of the seven cities of Cibola could not exist in the Illinois country?" Geoff's question was rhetorical, since Radisson's answer was obvious. Geoff suddenly grew depressed at the thought of a long winter spent in primitive conditions with no hope of success. His shoulders sagged as if an immense weight had been place on him. How could he possibly handle Colbert's wrath once he learned such news? Geoff was truly glad an immense ocean separated him from his master.

Radisson sensed Geoff's despair and tried to lighten the moment.

"My dear Monsieur Geoff, I must say I have never ventured as far south as you intend to go. The Illinois country is blessed with rivers making it more easily accessible from the south and New Spain. The weather is more temperate as well. Perhaps the Illinois red man is different from these Iroquois pigs, eh?"

Geoff took a long drink from his mug. "Your words provide me little encouragement," he said, shaking his head.

Radisson laughed, pressing his point to cheer his fellow Frenchman who had been so liberal with the refreshment.

"De Soto, the Spanish dog, traveled up the large river called Mississippi searching for the wealth you describe. His faith in the truth of the Indian fable should serve as some encouragement to you!"

"I hope my search does not end like Monsieur De Soto's," said Geoff referring to the notable explorer's death in the New World. "This reminds me of my problem with To-Ko-Wan, the Iroquois shaman." Geoff proceeded to relate his encounter with To-Ko-Wan and the war mask along the banks of the St. Lawrence River. As the tale progressed, the usually happy Radisson became sullen.

"Do you have any advice on how I might avoid the wrath of this heathen?" Geoff asked when finished with his tale.

For once Radisson was lacking for words.

"Unfortunately, my dear friend, you have been given an irrevocable death sentence. To-Ko-Wan will personally execute you at his first opportunity. Your only hope is that he will count revenge on mistress Kateri more sweetly that dealing with you. It is probably a toss up since both of you have committed sacrilege to his ancient religion. I suggest you return to France as soon as practicable."

The weight on Geoff's slumping shoulders was unbearable after Radisson's candid opinion. He felt as if he were a walking dead man bereft of all hope.

Radisson ordered another round of ale hoping to take Geoff's mind off his troubles. The ale was certainly improving his spirits!

"I'm on a mission for Cardinal Colbert," said Geoff. "My return to France is out of the question. Colbert deals as coldly with failures as my friend To-Ko-Wan deals with religious transgressors."

"Then you must proceed to the Illinois country with the missionary fathers," said Radisson patting Geoff on the back. Four mugs of ale had succeeded in getting him slightly inebriated. Soon his words would slur.

"If it is any consolation", continued Radisson, "the Iroquois do not inhabit the land south of the big inland seas and between the rivers. The Iroquois do in fact claim that land as their own, but their war parties seldom venture there. There are too many other weak tribes closer to their home from which to take slaves and women."

"Although I may be safe there in the short term," responded Geoff, "I fear there is little hope for my life in the long term. Unless there is gold to fill Colbert's coffers, I can never return to France. Assassins will make short work of me."

"Take heart," laughed a near drunk Radisson, "Major Stuart and his soldiers seem very capable of protecting you."

Monsieur Geoff failed to respond positively to these words meant for his encouragement. Geoff knew that his party viewed him as a spy of the King's court. With no hope for a future he proceeded to drown his sorrow in the primitive ale that Pierre Radisson was all too happy to share. Geoff would have to live one day at a time. He was beginning to understand that friends could be more valuable than gold in this heathen country. Too bad he had little prospect of being rich in either.

As the night wore on, Radisson finally passed out and laid his drunken head on the planked wooden table in a drunken stupor. Geoff had drunk nearly as much ale but stress and worry seemed to keep him alert. He decided to make his way back to his traveling companions and try to get some much-needed sleep.

The fresh smell of the night air hit him full force as he opened the tavern door and served to awaken his senses even more as he stepped out on the rough-hewn dock. Being unfamiliar with wilderness ways Geoff could not know the danger he was in yet, somehow, he sensed that things were not right with the world. Suddenly, the soft whizzing of a swift arrow split the silence of the quiet night. This messenger of death was so silent that had Geoff not been so keyed up with worry he might have missed it all together. In that split second where death and life are balanced for a man, Geoff also heard the sound of his salvation. The gleam of a short sword flashed in the pale lantern light as it deflected the primitive arrow into the nearby dock rail. Another flash of the awful blade and a native Iroquois lay dead on the street. It took Geoff several more seconds to figure out what had happened. From the rustle of bare feet he realized that other enemies of his life were quickly retiring lest they suffer the same fate of their kinsman. Apparently, someone had stepped out of the darkness to save him from a horrible death. Before he could reconstruct the events of the past few seconds, he heard a clear voice speak his name.

"Monsieur Geoff, are you in good health this fine evening?" The voice was clean and commanding. He recognized his savior as Major Stuart. Even in the shadows Geoff could see an abundance of blood. More than one Indian had taken grievous wounds. He hoped some of the blood was not Stuart's.

"It is I who should be asking that question of you." Geoff's voice wavered from the tension of the night and the near death experience. Silently, Geoff wondered if he had been wrong in judging Stuart as a military man who would let him die with no remorse.

Stuart dipped the blade of his short sword in a nearby puddle of rainwater and cleaned it on the leather clothing of the dead native. Stuart seemed to be weighing his response, as it was some time before he replied.

"It seems your life is in extreme danger, Monsieur Geoff. You should not venture out alone at night given the current situation. Please allow me to escort you back to our quarters."

"How did you happen to be here at the right moment, Major?" Geoff voice echoed his sincere appreciation.

"Divine Providence, Monsieur. God must be watching over you." The Major replied in a calm voice. Death had no effect upon this veteran of many skirmishes. Relief and a sense of security descended on Geoff as they walked down the quiet street in the pale light of the oil lamps. With this superb swordsman beside him, surely no one could threaten his life now.

* * * *

The supper fire still glowed amber and red in the lodge of Kateri Tekawetha as Sha-Na helped her Iroquois sisters prepare to retire. Thick, soft furs of deer and bear were spread on the ground near the warm fire. Their warmth beckoned the weary from the cares of the long day. Many chores were necessary before these women could rest. Water had to be carried for cooking and bathing tomorrow. Clay dinner pots from supper had to be cleaned. Sha-Na went about this routine in a daze while she thought about the gallant Major Stuart and their impending separation.

Major Stuart had somehow managed to become a very special person to Sha-Na. This was very unusual since she had learned early in her life that most men were boisterous and egotistical. They were not sincere in their feelings and never showed any compassion for a woman. Her attraction to the Major upset her very much for she had vowed to follow Kateri and the Christ she had come to love. A relationship with any man, let alone a foreigner from across the great sea, was simply out of the question.

Sha-Na had prayed to her new God asking for a solution to this great dilemma. However, she found that the more she prayed, the more distress she felt. Sha-Na was deeply attracted to the Major. Yet, in her mind she could not believe this was for the best.

Mistress Kateri had been involved in her daily prayers and meditation when she first sensed the distress that Sha-Na was feeling. Kateri had a deep devotion for this kind, devout woman. They were almost like sisters. Kateri remembered them playing La Crosse as children. At times in their youth they had been nearly inseparable.

Although women hold a place of respect in the Iroquois nation, the independent, often outspoken nature of Kateri caused her to be shunned by many in her clan. Kateri did not follow tradition. For this, she was viewed as strange and unclean. Still, Sha-Na had remained a loyal friend. When Kateri embraced the foreign God, Sha-Na did not criticize or question. Sha-Na had taken Kateri's vision and made it her own. For this faith and trust, Sha-Na had commanded Kateri's absolute and undying love. It distressed Kateri to see her friend so upset.

"Love should never be a problem, only a wonderful solution," Kateri remarked simply when, at last, only she and Sha-Na remained awake in the lodge.

Sha-Na was suddenly awakened from her unconscious revere.

"I cannot speak of something I have but limited knowledge," Sha-Na said noncommittally.

"Brother Paul speaks of love in our Christian book. Love is everything. It is a reason to exist. Turmoil and distress should not be associated with love," replied Kateri. "Love has not troubled you before. Why does it upset you so now?"

"Love doesn't enter into it at all," said Sha-Na defensively as the tone of her voice rose. "I'm merely concerned with the safety of Father Constance and Bertrand as they venture west to convert our brothers," Sha-Na assumed a mask of stoicism to hide her true feelings.

"The love of a woman for a man is something you have not experienced, yet I believe that is what you are feeling now," said Kateri.

"I am not attracted to either Father Constance or Bertrand," said Sha-Na trying to be difficult. "I'm astonished that you can suggest such a thing."

Kateri calmly sat by the flickering fire in silence for several minutes. Sha-Na nearly came to believe that their conversation had ended before anything had been resolved. She was beginning to feel quite disappointed. She so hoped for a cure for this strange ache in her heart. To be sure, they were not the giddy, naïve' girls they once had been. Years ago they could have openly discussed anything that came to mind, but now Kateri was viewed as nearly a saint. With the position comes required decorum. Sha-Na understood Kateri must remain aloof even to her closest confidantes. How Sha-Na wished that just this once Kateri would open up to a deep emotional discussion like the ones they had when they were younger. She desperately needed that now. With a small tear in her eye, Sha-Na prepared her furs near the fire for sleep. Surprisingly, Kateri broke the silence of the peaceful wilderness night.

"My friend, you know I'm not referring to the good fathers. Even the blind can see your infatuation for the gallant white warrior. How can you deny your true feelings to one who knows you so well?"

With these welcome words Sha-Na broke down in tears as she fell into her friend's beckoning arms. Like a mother lovingly consoles a child in distress, Kateri caressed Sha-Na's raven black hair and murmured words of consolation.

"There, there, my child. These emotions you are having must be very serious to upset you so. This foreigner has surely stolen your heart." Kateri's face showed more emotion at that moment than Sha-Na had seen in her friend in years.

"How can I know if it is truly love when I have no experience with such things?" Sha-Na sobbed barely controlling herself. "Love is supposed to be a sweet thing. If this I'm feeling is truly love, why am I in so much pain?"

"Love, my dear friend, is so splendid that it heightens our senses. It's as if we were dead before love came along. Suddenly, we see everything from a new perspective. The moonlight is brighter. The morning dew on the wild flowers fills up our senses. If we knew color before, their vividness is ten times as bright. Each common thing in our world takes on a new meaning that we were blind to before. And, yes, even pain becomes more excruciating."

"You describe exactly how I feel my friend," said an astonished Sha-Na, "but how can one as devout as you know of worldly pleasures?"

"I may be reborn, my child, but I'm a mortal woman with mortal thoughts. I cannot deny what God has wrought. Everything our God has made is good and serves some useful purpose. This is what I strongly believe. I'm sure my mortal weakness in the ways of love can be of service to our Lord in some way." Kateri spoke like the old friend Sha-Na once knew.

"I too have been in love," Kateri continued in a manner she hoped would console her friend. "You smile in disbelief, but it is so very true. Several years ago, when we were in our youth, I was attracted to a young hunter of our clan. No one knew, not even you. We used to meet when the campfires burned low and everyone was asleep. Oh, how I longed for his gentle touch. When we were together, it was as if my life took on new meaning. We were as one. And, oh, the awful pain when we would have to part."

"Why did you not tell me? You surely knew I could be trusted with a secret," Sha-Na interjected, somewhat dazed by this revelation.

"I was on the verge of doing just that. My hunter was preparing to ask my father for my hand in marriage. And then…." Kateri's words trailed off. Her eyes glazed and her mouth tensed as if some unseen hands had struck her. The pain of her memory was evident in her face as she recalled long suppressed emotions.

Sha-Na feared her friend could not proceed. "Pray do not continue if it is too painful." She sensed Kateri's pain was nearly as great as was her own.

"He went out with a hunting party to supply our village with meat for the long winter. The game was more abundant to the south in the forest of our enemies. He did not return." Kateri's said these words with finality. There was a long pause and the horrible meaning had its impact on Sha-Na.

"I know the pain of a love lost," Kateri continued stoically. "It is more terrible when it cannot be shared with those who care and can make the burden lighter."

"So you actually believe I'm in love with this Major Stuart?" Sha-Na replied quickly trying to distract her friend from all the painful memories.

"I know this to be so, my dear sad friend," said Kateri simply. "For your own happiness you must not deny it. Rather you must act so as not to lose this precious gift."

"Even if what you say is true," Sha-Na began impatiently, "I could never desert you and renounce my vows to our God." Sha-Na's face was contorted in obvious distress as she realized the true nature of her futile dilemma. To her it was as if she were being pulled in two directions at once. Each was a greater force than she could hope to overcome. She feared ultimately she would be torn apart.

"I will not keep you from your love and your destiny," said Kateri with deep affection for her troubled friend. "If you value our friendship, you will pursue your love. Fate chose to deny me the happiness of earthly love. I cannot let this tragedy happen to you. You must go to the Illinois country." The stoic look on Kateri's face led Sha-Na to realize that arguing was futile.

Kateri continued, "Radisson knows the territory you will be traveling and you know the people. Together you can assure that Father Constance and Bertrand will arrive safely in the Illinois country to do the work that our God has ordained. It is God's will you should go. All the more opportune that you can be with the man you love as well." Sha-Na began to sob both with joy for the resolution to her dilemma and sorrow that she must leave her beloved friend.

"Remember, child, it is not our will but God's will that must be done in all matters. I will tell the Fathers tomorrow that I have instructed you to accompany them as my representative. We must praise our God for this opportunity to be instruments for his purpose," Kateri said with finality.

Kateri then removed a necklace from around her neck and placed it around Sha-Na's. The black obsidian crucifix hanging at the end of leather thong was a prized gift that would bond their friendship forever. The onyx talisman glistened in the flickering firelight. The trinket was elongated to a point much like that of a lance head. Its appearance suggested that it could serve in war as well as peace.

"Let this cross protect you on your long journey of faith and love. May the Lord see fit to bring you back safely to your loved ones. Amen!" Kateri became silent as this prayer faded into the silent night.

Sha-Na was in reverie as she prepared to sleep. She felt as if a tremendous burden had been lifted. Now she could follow her heart without feeling a responsibility to always sacrifice herself for someone else. The long distance to the interior beckoned her with mystery and adventure. Sha-Na was so full of anticipation that she could hardly rest.

Chapter 4

▼

THE LESSONS

IN SEARCH OF TREASURE: EARTHLY AND HEAVENLY

To-Ko-Wan, the captive Iroquois war-chief, sat brooding in the log stockade by the Montreal boat docks that served as his jail. He must plan his escape carefully. Then he would have to decide which of his enemies to pursue first. Would it be Kateri, the heretic who dared to question the God of her ancestors, or Geoff, that ferret of a Frenchman who had angered the ancient forest spirits?

To-Ko-Wan already knew the destination of the French missionaries. Friends of the Iroquois were everywhere in this remote French colonial outpost. Anyone who had ears knew it was Illinois country. The boisterous Radisson made no secret of the fact as he went about his work of assuring the party was properly outfitted for their journey. Did these stupid French think they could survive in the wilderness interior that was acknowledged as part of the Iroquois domain? Or, were they so sure that their God would protect them that they had nothing to fear? Brave or stupid, it did not really matter. To-Ko-Wan knew that every oar stroke the missionaries made on their journey inland drew them closer to their doom.

In the back of his mind, To-Ko-Wan made a mental note not to underestimate his adversaries. He may have to pay a dear price to seal the missionaries' fate. Already, one of his warriors had died and one had been severely wounded in a failed attempt at revenge on the thief of his spirit mask. The report was that the leader of the French military contingent fought with an uncanny wit and a nerve of steel as the Iroquois assassins fell upon Monsieur Geoff. To-Ko-Wan still did not believe the reported swiftness of Major Stuart's blades. This Major Stuart had earned the Iroquois warrior's respect. To-Ko-Wan realized that the French mission's success in the Illinois country counted heavily upon the abilities of Major Stuart. He knew he must end Stuart's life as quickly as possible. How hard could that be, he reasoned? The French were but a handful and the Iroquois were many. If the Christian God could save these few from great odds, then that God, indeed, would be worthy of his reverence.

As To-Ko-Wan pondered his next move regarding the blasphemous Iroquois maiden, Kateri, and the French missionaries to Illinois, Radisson finished loading supplies into the sturdy birch-bark canoes moored at the foot of the Montreal docks. Within an hour after sunrise, strong Ottawa and Huron warriors guided these canoes out into the swift current of the St. Lawrence River. The French missionaries and their military entourage had the pleasure of enjoying the scenery seemingly everywhere along the riverbank. Unlike their initial journey to Montreal when they were forced to laboriously propel boats upriver, the French now relinquished this work to Indians hired by Radisson. These natives skillfully moved their oars in unison through the rippling river water with seemingly little effort. Without the past experience in reaching Montreal, the French could never have appreciated the effort expended by their Indian allies.

Indeed, ally was a good term to describe these fellow native travelers. Both Radisson and Kateri assured the missionaries that they were not to be feared. For neither the Ottawa or the Huron held an abiding love for the Iroquois. These men in particular felt a deep hatred for they had been slaves to the Iroquois. As youths they had been captured during a particularly bloody Iroquois raid on their villages. Radisson had purchased their services from their Iroquois masters. In effect, Radisson had bought their freedom. Once their service with Radisson on his journey to the interior was complete, Radisson would set them free to return to their homeland. Meanwhile, in the short months of work they would remain devoted allies of the French. It was the duty of these noble savages to fulfill their verbal contract. If nothing else, these heathens were men of honor.

The French missionaries were blessed to have an experienced man like Pierre Radisson in their service. He knew only too well the habits of the North American Indian. Radisson had lived among them as well as traveled by their side. Pierre had journeyed this way several years earlier during his exploration of what would eventually be called Minnesota. His capture and slavery at the hands of the

Iroquois made him an authority on their native habits. The unspeakable torture and humiliation that Pierre was forced to endure had scarred him for life. The Huron and Ottawa that accompanied the travelers were aware of Radisson's experience. They held deep respect for his experience with their native culture.

Upon learning the depth of animosity held by Radisson and his native companions for the Iroquois, Father Constance questioned the safety of Kateri's Iroquois brethren traveling with them. Radisson explained that there were Five Nations of the Iroquois. These included the Seneca, Mohawk, Cayuga, Oneida, and the Onondaga. Luckily, the Seneca occupied the land directly adjacent to their river route. The Seneca, though fierce warriors, were less openly hostile to foreigners. The Seneca were more often exposed to sojourners through their territory due to their river location. As a result, they had developed a "thicker skin," so to speak, than their Iroquois cousins of the North American interior. Besides, Sha-Na and her friends were blood Iroquois. Even though they gave allegiance to a foreign God, the Iroquois would still respect their blood relatives. If by chance they encountered a Seneca hunting party while camped along the river at night, the travelers would undoubtedly be safe. To be sure, as Radisson explained they must pass by Seneca and Algonquin villages as they paddled up the St. Lawrence River. They hoped that by remaining silent and passing swiftly there would be little danger.

At the request of Major Stuart, who was interested in the logistics of their journey from the aspect of providing security, Radisson outlined the route they would take to Lake Erie. It was approximately 240 kilometers from Montreal to the mouth of the first inland sea. Radisson explained that sea was the appropriate term for the body of water because of the size and temperament of this geographical feature. The word "lake" simply didn't describe its grandeur. There were at least five of these large bodies of water in the North American interior. These seas had their own surf and were very deep having been carved out by glaciers during the Ice Age. These seas could be as tranquil as the surface of a mirror in the best of weather. However, tempests to rival any on the great ocean called the Atlantic could suddenly engulf the unwary traveler. Woe to the person who had to travel these inland seas during late autumn, winter, or early spring. Radisson noted that the natives would rather trek along their coast during uncertain weather. He hoped everyone would pay heed to these words lest they become irretrievably lost.

Continuing his travel narrative, Radisson explained that they would then travel on an inland sea known in the native tongue of the Seneca Iroquois as "Ontario", or beautiful lake. They would remain on this lake for perhaps 120 kilometers traveling as far away from the south shore so as to remain inconspicuous to any Seneca villages. While the Seneca were not unreasonably hostile, Radisson reasoned that one should travel the safest path whenever possible. With some luck they should not encounter any native whatsoever. It was best that their presence, even to friendly natives, remain unknown lest the news spread to possible enemies.

Eventually, the travelers must locate a river called the Genesse by the local inhabitants. They would then leave the lake called Ontario for this river's mouth and proceed generally south and west. By traveling some of the lesser tributaries of the Genesse River known specifically to Radisson, they should arrive at another inland sea. At that point they could remain on this lake called "Erie" for nearly 450 kilometers. An Ottawa village that had been friendly to Radisson should provide a brief respite for recuperation before they would embark on the more difficult leg of the journey into the interior.

Sha-Na asked why they did not stay on the Ontario Sea all the way to the inlet river of Erie. Radisson explained that there was a huge falls on the river that made this route very treacherous. This course would require a portage around the gigantic falls to the calmer waters below the falls. Radisson said that his route might allow them to avoid any portage. He feared that a trek of many miles carrying provisions and their heavy canoes through hostile territory would be much too dangerous to attempt. Sha-Na nodded her approval of his plan realizing that a very experienced explorer was leading their party. The falls, which Radisson referred to, was a true wonder of nature that would leave the French in awe. Still, Sha-Na knew much valuable travel time could be lost on the difficult trek around it.

Time was passing quickly and they were already many miles along the river called St. Lawrence. Around every bend the French marveled at the abundant wildlife. Ducks and geese of many different species were busy gathering their daily sustenance upon the water. Fish of all types and sizes flopped beside their canoes. Indeed, the natives had taken to hand fishing for their supper each evening with great success! The quick reflex of the oarsmen in snatching the bounty from the river was another wonder for the French to behold. This bounty tended to make the evening meal very exotic. Frogs croaked their baritone song as the canoes slipped near the shore. Birds, including the majestic white headed eagle, soared high in the clear blue sky overhead as their canoes glided silently through the swift waters below. This was nature in the height of her glory!

The travelers did not stop for a midday repast, instead wishing to put as many miles as possible behind them before nightfall. They ate a snack of smoked, dry meat and washed this down with clear, cold water from the river. The natives feasted on fish they had caught both by hand and with hooks. These fish had been deftly cleaned and filleted with sharp trade knives obviously obtained in some past barter session. The natives including Sha-Na and her companions ate this uncooked fish with great relish. They could not understand why the French would decline this staple of their diet. Major Stuart told Sha-Na he would rather wait to cook his fish on an open fire later that evening. And so with an abundance of scenery, food, and camaraderie the travelers passed their first day on the journey to the Illinois country.

Soon the sun hung low in the western sky and they pulled their canoes up on a sandbar to prepare for a peaceful night of rest. The French were impressed at how the natives could labor with the oars tirelessly all day. Radisson explained that for the native there was a time for everything. There was a time to work, to eat, to hunt, and to sleep. This point was made clear when it finally came time for sleep. The natives were asleep in the blink of an eye. The hard, rocky shore did not deter them for a deep noisy sleep punctuated by loud snores. The French military contingent under Major Stuart assumed the security duties of the night watch. Sentries were posted and relieved at two-hour intervals. In this manner, each member of the party shared in the responsibilities of the trip equally.

Each day the French missionaries had further opportunity to hear interesting tales concerning the natives of this territory through which they were passing. Radisson had spent several years learning the ways of the red man. He had the sort of jovial temperament that enjoyed both hearing and telling a good story. As a storyteller there was few that could equal Radisson, although one was often forced to wonder how much was the truth. The hours of their long journey passed quickly as they all were mesmerized by Radisson's fascinating tales.

On one subsequent day of travel, Radisson got on the subject of the fierce, warlike nature of the Iroquois. He explained that tribal lore suggested this fierceness was not always the case. The Iroquois had at one time been peaceful farmers. In reality, the Iroquois were not very skilled at hunting and were forced to rely on their neighbors, the Algonkins, for the supply of meat. Each autumn the Iroquois would trade part of the grain and vegetables they had grown for meat, which was an important part of their winter diet. The Iroquois dried this meat and stored it with their reserve of grain to see them through the winter. Not being inclined to hunt, fresh meat was seldom available in the winter and the season could often be very harsh for the Iroquois.

Sha-Na interrupted Radisson to explain that her people, the Five Nations of the Iroquois, had once been vassals to the Algonkins. It was assumed that since the Iroquois were peaceful farmers, they were an inferior tribe. The Algonkins considered hunting a bold and manly trait. Farming was for women. This sense of superiority made the Algonkins quite aggressive. The Iroquois remained humble in their relations with the Algonkins, wishing to maintain the status quo of friendly trading partners. Sha-Na explained that treachery on the part of the Algonkins changed the Iroquois forever.

Radisson could not keep quiet any longer.

"I was just coming to that part of the story when I was so rudely interrupted." Radisson laughed jovially and resumed his tale. Sha-Na meekly submitted to his rousing oratory. With gestures that relatively shook their large canoe, he related the following tale to explain the drastic transition in Iroquois temperament.

One winter many seasons ago an Algonkin tribe invited an Iroquois village to spend the winter with them and share their provisions. The Iroquois readily accepted this offer since a fresh supply of meat was preferable to their dried provisions. When the time came to hunt in order to replenish the meat stores, the Algonkins proceed to teach the inferior Iroquois a lesson in hunting. Unfortunately, several hunting parties came back empty-handed. It seemed the skill, or luck to kill the elk was lacking and the hunting parties returned meekly to camp.

The Iroquois who had accompanied the Algonkins had quietly observed the misfortune of the hunting expedition. They were determined to supply the village and humbly suggested that the Iroquois might try one more time. This brought hoots of laughter from the conceited Algonkin hunters. After all, if the superior prowess of the Algonkins had failed, what could the lowly Iroquois farmers hope to accomplish. So, without the blessing of tribal leaders, a small part of Iroquois hunters left the village after dark one night. When their absence was discovered the Algonkins dispatched other hunters to find them. Meanwhile, the Iroquois were very successful in applying the hunting techniques taught by the Algonkins. Eventually the Algonkin hunters came upon the band of proud Iroquois hunters skinning several large elk they had killed. At this point, the pride of the conceited Algonkins forced them down a treacherous path for which their descendant would continue to pay dearly.

No one knows if the Iroquois were boastful of their accomplishment. At any rate, it was impossible for the proud Algonkins to accept that these lowly Iroquois had bested them in hunting. In a fit of rage, the Algonkins turned their weapons upon their Iroquois neighbors and killed them all. To disguise the murders, the Algonkins placed the Iroquois bodies under snowdrifts, for it was now early winter and the snows had come.

The treacherous Algonkin hunters returned to camp with the meat harvested by the slain Iroquois. They shamefully boasted of their hunting prowess to anyone who would listen. When the Iroquois in the winter camp asked the fate of their brothers, the Algonkins made up a story about how the weak Iroquois hunters had the misfortune to fall through the thin ice of a nearby stream. In this terrible tragedy all were drowned and their bodies lost. The remainder of the winter passed quietly with no further problems.

Unfortunately, the coming of spring and the melting snows revealed a grisly sight. The bodies of the misfortunate Iroquois hunting party displayed wounds that revealed to the village what had really happened. The actions of the defensive Algonkins left no doubt as to their guilt. Consequently, when the Iroquois in the camp demanded justice tempers flared as the pleas of the Algonkin tribal elders were ignored. Drastic action was taken when the Algonkins decided they must cover up their crime. Iroquois witnesses could not be allowed to remain alive to tell the tale to their brothers. Being outnumbered these unfortunates were savagely massacred, down to the last man, woman, and child.

As fate would have it, several Iroquois managed to escape into the woods during the confusion of the carnage. With the weather turning warmer survival was easier. These few made their way to a neighboring Iroquois tribal village. News of the heinous crime spread like a prairie fire among the whole Iroquois nation. They were determined to seek revenge. The Iroquois trait of loyalty to their brothers and sisters united them in their mission of retribution.

In the ensuing war, the Algonkins seemed to have the advantage. They outnumbered the Iroquois. They were skilled hunters while the Iroquois were basically farmers, but the Algonkins could never agree on a united plan to defeat the Iroquois. As a result, each tribal leader followed a separate plan. The Iroquois were able to essentially divide and conquer their enemies. Apparently, the burning desire for revenge was a great motivator and catalyst. The Iroquois quickly learned the art of warfare and became very adept. Their latent talent for ferocity ultimately sealed the fate of the poor Algonkins.

Algonkin clans were massacred savagely one by one. Those lucky enough to escape the carnage fled north across the St. Lawrence River. They would never be able to return to their homeland. The tables had turned and the Iroquois learned that warfare had its own rewards as well. Other tribes such as the Huron also came to feel the Iroquois ferocity. Soon the Iroquois began their march west and south as they expanded their tribal dominance of the northeastern region. Radisson noted that the Iroquois even claimed the Illinois region to which they were bound.

Sha-Na, the Iroquois maiden and Christian missionary, had listened intently to the story Radisson told. When he appeared to have finished his latest discourse, she boldly entered the conversation.

"Monsieur Radisson, you portray my people as no better than wild beasts of prey. You do us a serious injustice. Although we have a deserved reputation for brutality toward our enemies, we have proved we can live quite peacefully when not provoked."

Radisson was surprised at the tone of Sha-Na's scolding voice. Radisson understood that he may have been too critical of the Iroquois, but he had good reason to dislike that particular race of natives. Radisson wondered if now was an appropriate time to let everyone know the reason for his obvious emotions.

"Perhaps Mademoiselle is not aware that I have a firsthand knowledge of her tribal brothers and sisters." Radisson spoke with a smirk on his face and dreadful seriousness in his eyes.

"Have you ever been dragged through the wilderness for days with your hands tied behind your back and a leather thong around your neck? If you stumble, the leather cuts your throat and shuts off your breath." Radisson pulled open the collar of his fringed deer-hide jacket to reveal deep scars encircling his neck.

"Woe unto the one who falls for he is beat severely and made to run again before he can catch his breath. One learns quickly not to fall for he may never get up again. Only the strong willed can survive." Radisson grimaced and his whole body seemed to shudder as he recalled the brutality that he was forced to endure.

"You take offense at my comparison of an Iroquois to a wild beast," Radisson continued, "but you have never been tethered like a dog outside a long house and forced to fight with dogs for scraps to eat."

"For you see, Mademoiselle, I have been a slave to you Iroquois for many months. I have been beaten, forced to work endless hours without food or rest, and even pissed upon for the slightest offense. What would you call something that treats his fellow man in such a despicable manner? Animal is a kind term, for even an animal will give some compassion to its own species."

Radisson had fire in his eyes now as he recalled the indignities that the Iroquois had heaped upon him. He seemed in a different world as he gazed toward the tree lined blue horizon.

Sensing a severe disagreement that could ultimately threaten the success of their journey, Father Constance interceded with a firm, but gentle voice.

"Monsieur Radisson, please forgive us for we had no idea of the severe misfortune you apparently suffered at the hands of the natives." Constance made a sweeping gesture as if to include everyone who had been listening. "We will pray that a loving and just God will absolve you of all your hate. God will help you forget your pain as surely as he will deal with those who have mistreated you."

This action on the part of the good Father seemed to diffuse the volatile situation. Sha-Na withdrew from the direct sight of Radisson as Major Stuart placed his arm around her. They began speaking in soft whispers as Radisson turned his attention to the journey that lay ahead. Father Constance decided that the time had come to discuss his need to minister to the natives along their route rather than silently passing them by.

"Father Bertrand and I have decided that we must stop at the next native encampment we encounter so that we may preach the gospel of our Lord regardless of the danger. God has sent us many kilometers to this wilderness for this very purpose. Therefore, God in his infinite mercy will protect us from all harm as we do his will."

Father Constance spoke these words with such decisiveness that argument seemed futile. As a result, there was a long, interminable silence as each traveler sat idly watching the passing landscape. The native oarsmen made the only sound as they smoothly parted the river waves.

Radisson, again resuming his boisterous nature, was the first to reply to the comment of the revered priest.

"Possibly I should have been more graphic in my description of the savage nature with which these natives treat their enemies. All of us, both men and women, stand to suffer cruelly if the natives so choose. I vowed that, once free of Iroquois captivity, I would never allow myself to be put in jeopardy again. I must humbly beseech you to not engage in this folly." Radisson lowered his gaze to the bottom of the canoe as he shook his head in grief.

"You must trust in God, my son, for he will protect us on his special mission." Father Constance spoke with assurance that calmed the fears of many despite Radisson's graphically gruesome story.

Radisson looked for an ally to aid him in his argument against seemingly foolish action. Somehow the expression on the face of both Major Stuart and Sha-Na suggested he may have them as unlikely supporters. Radisson quickly addressed Major Stuart.

"Major, as security officer for the good Fathers, do you not have misgivings with this proposal?" There was pleading in Radisson's voice as he spoke. The Major was slow to speak as he carefully chose his words.

"Realistically it seems we are tempting fate by placing ourselves in the midst of an overwhelming number of natives whose motives are questionable. But I have had the privilege of serving Father Constance and Father Bertrand for many years in similar situations. Their faith has seen us safe before. It will surely protect us again!" Stuart's reply closed the door to his support of Radisson's position.

Radisson's futile glance fell upon Sha-Na as his only hope to avert this probable course of doom. Given her obvious dislike for him Radisson guessed there was no hope for avoiding disaster. Just when Radisson was ready to accept the will of the majority, Sha-Na spoke up.

"Father Constance," said Sha-Na turning to address the priest, "Sister Kateri sent me along on this journey to see you safe to the land of the mighty rivers. I'm blood relative to the natives, as you call them, which inhabit the southern shore of this beautiful water. As a result I can travel this land with impunity. Likewise, I may be able to intercede for you and gain you safe passage. Still, I would be remiss should I fail to warn you of the possibility of danger. Recently many Iroquois are demonstrating fierce loyalty to the old ways. Some encampments may be unfriendly to my God and his white emissaries."

Sha-Na did not speak passionately against the Father's proposed missionary purpose. Rather she only wished to prudently warn of potential trouble.

"We are convinced that God is guiding us on this journey." Father Bertrand replied in a compassionate voice half-smiling as he spoke. "Yet, we respect your wisdom in these matters. Please pray upon this matter tonight and seek heavenly guidance. I'm sure God will allay all your fears and convince you that our course of action is necessary. We will discuss this with you further tomorrow."

Radisson breathed a sigh of relief at this welcome reprieve from a course he considered sheer madness. Since the sun was riding low on the western horizon, the party began to search for a cove along the lake to spend the night. The light of day was nearly gone as the canoes were pulled with a crunch on to the beach and provisions unloaded. After the supper of stew and rye bread had been prepared and eaten, Major Stuart took an opportunity to spend some time alone with Sha-Na, the beautiful Iroquois maiden.

By this time, the relationship between the Major and the maiden had become very close indeed. The long hours together in the birch bark canoe had revealed to Sha-Na the softer side of the veteran military man. They had confided intimate details of their lives to each other that only a very close friend would know. Sha-Na remembered her conversation with her mentor and close friend, Kateri, just prior to their departure from Montreal. Sha-Na recalled Kateri's evident regret and sorrow with her lost love. It was only her strong sense of duty to assist the Fathers on their journey to the interior that kept Sha-Na from sharing so much more with the kind Major Stuart. Sha-Na's deep dedication to the white man's God created a tremendous turmoil within as she wrestled with the question of pursuing religion over love. Sha-Na sat alone by one of the campfires along the glistening beach that was bathed in the pale light of the rising moon while here maids washed the cooking pots and eating utensils at the lake. The sky had turned from a brilliant red to a deep purple as the last rays of the sun surrendered to a brilliant silvery night. Sprays of glowing golden embers illuminated the twilight as Sha-Na poked absently at the fire with a dead cottonwood branch. All was quiet as the military contingent prepared to post the sentries before evening prayers. Jon Stuart approached the beautiful dark maiden quietly as she sat staring into the flames.

"What is in you thoughts, Mademoiselle?" Stuart asked in a sincere, obviously caring voice. He could see from the lines on her brow that some worldly care weighed heavily on her mind. At first Sha-Na did not answer. Stuart was about to turn away and leave the maiden in peace when Sha-Na finally whispered in a subdued voice.

"You know I cannot guarantee our safety in any Iroquois village." Sha-Na's voice was filled with emotion. Her voice quavered suggesting that she was near to tears. In these few words Sha-Na verified all of Stuart's fears. But before he could think of a reply, Sha-Na continued.

"Even though I'm Iroquois, I cannot even save myself if the clan's Shaman decides to actively oppose our missionary activities."

Stuart thought he heard her try to repress a sob.

"The Seneca, our western brothers, can be very hostile. They have been very active in pushing the Huron and Algonkins farther west. Being on the western marches of Iroquois territory the Seneca must be constantly prepared for the sporadic war parties sent by their unfriendly neighbors. This constant need for vigilance makes the Seneca very nervous and impatient. No one can guess how they might receive white men in canoes rowed by their mortal enemies. I am very worried!"

Sha-Na's shoulders slumped as if she had shed a heavy burden. The mere discussion of her misgivings with a trusted companion was having a therapeutic effect.

Realizing the emotional state of his friend, Major Stuart chose his words carefully before attempting a reply.

"I have been in far worse situations with Father Constance and Bertrand in the years I have been in their service." His words were strong and reassuring. The experience of a veteran of many conflicts rose to the surface.

"God is with us so who can prevail against us? Your apparently deep religious commitment should help to reassure you." Though tears were still evident in

Sha-Na's eyes, she attempted a smile as she felt the confidence in Jon Stuart's words. As the emotional atmosphere relaxed, Stuart continued in a soothing, even voice.

"While we cannot know exactly how we will be received in any encampment, we can prepare for most eventualities by careful military planning. In order to do this I must use your knowledge of your people's customs. For instance, what is the average size of an Iroquois village and how many armed warriors will meet us?"

Sha-Na thought carefully before she answered. Evidently she had regained her stoic composure.

"Your question is impossible to answer with certainty. I can only speak in generalities. Several hundred people make up an average clan including men, women, and children. If you hoped for men to be absent on extended hunts that will not be the case. This is what we call the bountiful season. The Iroquois still practice farming and will be engaged in tending and harvesting crops. On a positive note, and abundance of food tends to make for a festive spirit and relaxed atmosphere. Winter and the potential for famine are far from everyone's thoughts. Traditionally, this is a time for relaxation and games. Depending upon our time of arrival, many may be immersed in the competitive nature of the games." Sha-Na's attention seemed far away as she recalled fonder times as a child.

"My people approach games much like war. They put their heart and soul in their play. Likely they will be playing hard or exhausted from these endeavors. Either way they will probably not notice our arrival until later. If we can convince the limited reception party that we are friendly and pose no threat, our safety will be assured but..." Sha-Na's voice trailed off as she imagined another possible scenario.

Before attempting to discover Sha-Na's threatening alternative, Stuart asked, "What is the chance of our arrival happening in the peaceful manner you describe?"

"Oh, very good. I would expect it to happen no other way." Sha-Na replied as if her own words would allay her worst fears.

"And what is the worst possibility you can imagine?" Major Stuart wanted to anticipate any possibility. He had learned form experience that surprise can often be ones worst enemy.

"At the recent tribal assembly of my people, my mistress Kateri Tekawetha brought our Catholic religion before the tribal council for their consideration." Sha-Na spoke softly as if reliving some recent event.

"As you can imagine, this was a very bold move even though a woman's point of view is well respected by the Iroquois. In truth you must understand that women hold a position of reverence with my people."

"If all Iroquois women are as intelligent and forthright as you, I cannot doubt your words." Stuart's comment made Sha-Na blush momentarily before she continued.

"Though given due time for consideration, it was obvious that the old religion was still very strong among my people. A younger group of radical shaman dedicated to the ways of our ancestors prevailed and the elders of the Five Nations treated Kateri's religion with silent indifference. Though the radicals pushed for open hostility, calm prevailed and Kateri's contingent quickly left for Montreal. We feared for our lives lest some of the radicals intercept us on our long journey."

"I assume To-Ko-Wan was one of this radical group?" Jon Stuart questioned the obvious.

"Oui. Your chance encounter with him and his ancient ceremony in the forest made him your eternal enemy." Sha-Na referred to Stuart's tale about Monsieur Geoff's foot race through the wilderness with To-Ko-Wan.

"The radical medicine men dispersed from the assembly of the Five Nations to rally the support of all Iroquois villages in a religious war against all French missionaries and their God."

"And you fear one of these radical shamans will be at the next village to receive us?" Jon Stuart finished Sha-Na's thought.

"The chance is remote given our distance inland, but possible," said Sha-Na. "The location of a village along the lake shore makes it readily accessible to those wanting to contact supporters quickly."

"If this would come to pass, can my small military contingent hope to prevail?" The Major asked pragmatically with no show of emotion for he already knew her answer.

"I have no knowledge of the power of your weapons, but I can say you will be outnumbered at least ten to one." Sha-Na's words had no obvious effect on the Major.

"You mentioned the warriors might be weary from too much frivolity." Stuart searched for an advantage.

"Oui, but I would not give this much weight. The Iroquois men are known for their stamina and skill with weapons. I fear you would have little hope." Sha-Na replied dejectedly.

"Well, it is late and we must rest," Stuart said positively, trying to be encouraging.

"As I said before," he continued with a lighter tone in his voice immediately dissipating the clouds of gloom, "God has always protected these holy priests and their associates. It will be no different on the morrow. At any rate, be sure to pray heartily for us tonight." The Major marched off to prepare his contingency plan if a fight should come. Sha-Na spent a long time gazing into the glittery, silver night sky praying for deliverance. She fell asleep reassured that the spirit of her new God was at her side.

* * * *

To-Ko-Wan remained in his small, dark cell in the wooden prison stockade on the docks of Montreal. His blood hit the dirt floor in small drops only to be quickly engulfed by the thick layer of dust at his feet. The Iroquois shaman sneezed involuntarily. His whole body trembled and he felt momentarily dizzy. To-Ko-Wan was sure the loss of blood by self-inflicted wounds would soon accomplish his purpose. Just then he heard the clanking of keys and the approach of a guard. A crude wooden tray was shoved under the iron door that stood between him and freedom. On the tray sat a tiny tarnished metal cup and a pottery bowl with a gruel-like mixture of hard bread, milk, and boiled grain. To-Ko-Wan promptly kicked this back out in the hall half in anger and half amused. His weakness from loss of blood and starvation was diluting his ability to reason.

"You savage son-of-a-serpent!" roared the guard in frustration. For the past eight days the prisoner had treated his single solitary daily meal with the same disgusting response.

"You must at least drink, crazy son-of-a-savage-whore, or you will surely die. Then I will have to go to the trouble of burying your worthless carcass." The rotund French guard chuckled at his private joke as he continued.

"Personally I do not care if you ever eat or drink again. You would do me a service by dying today for I would no longer have to waste my time serving you tomorrow." Although very plump, the guard was quite muscular. He was definitely equipped to handle even the most ruthless prisoner and he spoke as if he had years of experience to back it up. The guard dipped another cup of water from the squat oaken bucket that sat in the corner of the jail corridor. He had no sooner pushed the half-full cup of water under the latticed door when he received it back squarely in his face.

"You pig!" he screamed savagely. "I would kill you now myself with these bare hands just for the pleasure it would give me were it not for your special status.

Unfortunately I must notify Lord Frontenac of your failure to cooperate. It would surely go harshly with me if you were to die on my watch." The guard sneered and then spat squarely in the Indian's face.

"I have no idea how Frontenac expects to keep you alive if you will not eat. But I want him to know that I did not assist you with your suicidal tendencies."

The guard turned and stomped down the hall of the stockade with his keys clanking against his armor. He slammed the door forcefully and again all was quiet. It was now day and all the drunks had already been released into the harsh light of day. To-Ko-Wan felt he was the only inmate remaining in the jail. He should have enough time to accomplish his purpose before any visitor interrupted him.

To-Ko-Wan's plan was to escape the confinement of his tiny prison cell, but not physically. He was fasting and inflicting pain in order to break his corporeal bonds and ascend to the spirit world for in this other world lay the answer to his current dilemma. To-Ko-Wan was convinced his ancestral gods had a sacred purpose for his life. He was in a position to stop the spread of the foreign religion in his native land. He must not waiver in his dedication. After days of suffering To-Ko-Wan felt he was finally on the threshold of an unearthly journey toward enlightenment.

The Iroquois warrior pulled the thin splinter of wood from its place of concealment under a small mound of dirt. He had torn his hands many times and bled profusely before this splinter had finally separated from the upright pole of his wooden cell. To-Ko-Wan proceeded to jam the thin piece of wood carefully into his side. Even in his dazed state, the shaman knew the exact placement of the weapon to induce bleeding while doing no mortal harm. One last thrust and To-Ko-Wan swooned at the paralyzing feeling of intense pain. A crimson flood gushed from his side as he rolled on his shoulder. Momentarily To-Ko-Wan had collapsed in the moist puddle of dirt created by his own life's blood.

Initially To-Ko-Wan had no concept of time. Now all was dark and silent. His senses were so dull that subconsciously he feared that this time he may have actually committed suicide. At the same time his experience in this ritual reassured him that all was going as he had planned. Suddenly a million points of light exploded in his mind and he found himself soaring like a bird into a brilliant blue cloud-spattered sky. The immediate sense of falling was so intense that the shaman feared he might not catch a breath. Then the journey became slow motion and he was able to savor every part of this exquisite experience. To-Ko-Wan was at once one with his vision. Past experience in other spirit reveries allowed him to somehow control the events.

Momentarily To-Ko-Wan realized that he had feathers protruding from his arms. Gazing down at the forest and blue waters below he reasoned he was actually an eagle flying westward. This in itself did not amaze him for he had realized at the time he achieved manhood that the eagle was his spirit mentor. For the time being To-Ko-Wan's senses were submerged in the exhilaration of the seemingly endless flight.

Below To-Ko-Wan could see an intense battle materializing. As he swooped lower toward the treetops he saw two adversarial groups engaged in mortal combat. To-Ko-Wan intuitively knew that his brother Iroquois warriors had their enemies surrounded. The opponents of the Iroquois were falling before the fierce onslaught of arrows and war clubs. From his perspective in the clouds To-Ko-Wan could see that the enemy was fighting for their very survival.

At this point in his vision To-Ko-Wan sensed that he clutched an object in his talon hand. Looking down at his clenched fist To-Ko-Wan could barely make out an intricately etched ebony stone blade. As he glided lower toward the battle To-Ko-Wan could hear the cool moist wind howling by his ears. To-Ko-Wan was completely engulfed with a sense of purpose to deliver the talisman he possessed to a participant in the foray. He sensed the glory and decisiveness in his mission. All other cares and emotion in his life paled to insignificance as the eagle struggled to do the bidding of his creator. As the blade was released it was as if he followed its spiraling path downward to the outstretched hand of a preordained recipient.

All at once To-Ko-Wan was jerked back to reality by a kick to the sole of his bare foot. Struggling weakly to regain consciousness, he realized that he was back on the floor of his dismal little jail cell. The contrast between this world and the one he had left was so poignant that his body was racked with pitiful sobs. For seconds that seemed like hours the shaman gasped for a breath. It was as if he had been plunged into a frigid lake of reality and his physical being rebelled against the sudden return.

To-Ko-Wan eventually realized that there was a distinguished man towering above him dressed in a brilliant white tunic embroidered with golden thread. Fleetingly he thought it might be his guiding spirit appearing in human form. Vaguely To-Ko-Wan could see the man's lips were moving, but he could not distinguish any sound.

The reverie of soaring among the clouds in the form of the majestic eagle coupled with the reassurance of his ultimate victory against the foreign transgressors made To-Ko-Wan want to return to the shelter of his vision. While he would normally respond to severe treatment from his captors with retaliatory blows, at this moment his recent insight only made him complacent and even smug. It was certain that physically To-Ko-Wan did not have the strength in his current incapacitated state to respond effectively anyway. Unfortunately, his failure to pay attention to the rough treatment of the guards only compelled them to use more force. The guards were nervous that their prisoner could remain so unaffected in the presence an eminent personage like Lord Frontenac. Seldom did the supreme officer in command of the French forces in the New World condescend to visit the squalor of the Montreal military prison. Even though Frontenac must know that the army prison garrison was not the model of discipline by any means, the guards still felt that they must force some measure of respect from their wards.

To-Ko-Wan was being rebellious, as he had always been. Maybe now was the time to teach him a lesson he would never forget. The leather thong with the leaded tips called the cat-o-nine-tails bit deeply into the muscular flesh on the Iroquois' back. The blood began to flow freely as the guard began his dreadful work. Louis Frontenac grabbed the guard's arm quickly to restrain him for he had some measure of respect for this shaman. Frontenac certainly did not come to torture his prisoner. He only paid this visit to determine To-Ko-Wan's mood and guess at his future plans with regard to the French missionaries.

To-Ko-Wan groaned in pain as he rolled on his back and looked up at the commander. Even in this pitiful state the Indian remained in a peaceful serene mood.

Turning his attention to the prisoner after pushing the guard out of the cell Lord Frontenac spoke.

"Mon Dieu, Monsieur! How can you accept this savage treatment with such obvious indifference?"

Only now had the Iroquois shaman regained consciousness enough to hear the Frenchman's words. Although he knew enough French to understand what was said, To-Ko-Wan toyed with the idea of feigning ignorance. Realizing, however, that this response may cause the guard to renew his blows with that appalling weapon, the Iroquois decided that it was to his advantage, considering his weakened state, to answer. To-Ko-Wan's uncaring attitude signaled to him that his body was hurt drastically. More abuse might ultimately result in his death. At this point death was a very attractive option, but To-Ko-Wan knew from his recent revelation that he had not yet fulfilled his earthly destiny. The spirits had given him a mission and he was now resolved to see it through.

"Is this how the French treat their enemies across the great water?" To-Ko-Wan spoke with a sneer even though this small token of rebellion took a grievous toll of his remaining strength.

"I truly apologize, Monsieur, for the actions of my subordinates. They are under strict orders to make your stay here as comfortable as possible until I can allow your release." Frontenac assumed a military bearing as he came to attention and turned his gaze to the guards huddled in the shadows of the jail cell.

"They will be duly punished for their obvious failure to follow my orders!" Frontenac's words were so forceful that the two guards withdrew from the cell to the hallway and cowered in the shadows. Frontenac was left alone with the weakened native. Now his words assumed a benevolent, almost fatherly tone.

"You have done nothing to deserve such harsh treatment. It has been my mission to improve cooperation between our peoples. I hope you will not let these events cloud your perception of what is best for both the French and the Five Nations of the Iroquois."

As Frontenac spoke, To-Ko-Wan looked stoically into the Frenchman's eyes. He thought the foreigner spoke with a sincere voice. To-Ko-Wan felt he could believe him, yet another side of his consciousness told him that friendship between them was wrong. Enemies of the Iroquois would construe peace with the French as weakness. It would encourage the Huron and Algonkin to challenge them for supremacy both to the west and south. More French missionaries would also come to preach the despicable message of their foreign God. The Iroquois would slowly forget the old ways. To-Ko-Wan could not condone the turmoil that would result should he accept this French warrior's gesture of friendship.

To-Ko-Wan rolled his head to the side and spit blood on to the dusty dirt floor of the jail cell. He would have spit in the Frenchman's face had he been able to summon the strength to do so. In his present weakened condition To-Ko-Wan feared he could not even defend himself should the guards decide to resume their lesson with the whip. He decided to be content to listen to what Frontenac had to say. Perhaps if he bided his time, his captors would actually be foolish enough to release him.

"We truly respect your position as a leader of the Iroquois and wish you to understand that you are being detained to assure the safety of the travelers that brought you to Montreal." Frontenac continued speaking not expecting conversation from his prisoner. The general sensed that he was speaking to one of the radical Iroquois element that could not accept peaceful coexistence with the French. Since his words of peace were wasted, Frontenac wanted to only ensure that the prisoner was not mistreated. He still must deal with his prison garrison's obvious dereliction of duty.

"I know your true feelings on this matter of peace. Therefore, I won't waste time in argument to change your mind." Frontenac spoke quickly.

There was still no response from the prisoner, not even a blink of an eye. Frontenac visually examined the Iroquois' wounds and wondered if the man would survive to see his release. Shaking his head in pity he continued to speak.

"You will be relieved to know that you shall be released in due time, Monsieur. If it were up to me I should be reticent to allow such a thing knowing your radical inclination. However, my oath to the Reverend Fathers will not allow me to do otherwise. Meanwhile, you will receive good food and medical treatment by the company physician."

Sensing there was no need for further speech, Frontenac turned quickly and was gone down the hall of the prison.

"Corporal-of-the-Guard!" Frontenac yelled with the absolute authority of a man experienced in command.

"Secure this jail cell and summon your subordinates. I must impress upon you how I intend for you to treat this prisoner from now until his release. Oh yes, someone will pay for what I have seen here today!" The general's words faded in the distance as the clank of chain and locks signaled to To-Ko-Wan that he was again alone with his thoughts.

With the sure knowledge of his ultimate release, To-Ko-Wan could now plan his revenge upon both the French missionaries and Kateri Tekawetha, the traitor Iroquois maiden. He knew from his spirit vision that he must ultimately lead a war party to the distance western land called Illinois by the French. To-Ko-Wan knew from his spies in Montreal that Kateri was under the personal protection of General Frontenac. As a result, she was heavily guarded round the clock. As a native Catholic soon to be sainted, Kateri had protectors high in the Catholic Church hierarchy. It was rumored that Bishop Colbert himself had ordered her protection as a matter of political expediency. Kateri was the nominal leader of the conversion of the warlike Iroquois. She was the key to blunting the native threat to French colonists. If the New France frontier could be pacified French farmers and artisans would be encouraged to immigrate to North America. These people would establish a stable French presence and solidify the French claim to the St. Lawrence River and lake region. In the European power struggle, France could become competitive with the English again. England had a distinct head start with colonies already secure immediately to the south.

The English encroachment was already beginning to threaten French interests by 1675. While To-Ko-Wan had no understanding of the intrigue of European court politics, he sensed Kateri Tekewetha's value to the French in maintaining their precarious foothold in the New World. The English were no viable ally to the Iroquois since they were as much a threat to the Iroquois culture as the

French. To-Ko-Wan realized that Kateri must be assassinated to halt the more immediate threat of French expansion. With this successfully accomplished, To-Ko-Wan could then turn his attention to destroying the English settlements.

At this moment To-Ko-Wan decided that his ultimate goal should be to eliminate Kateri Tekawetha and her followers. Due to the security provided by the French military, To-Ko-Wan reasoned that stealth might be an avenue to accomplish this task. It was a fact that Iroquois women working in the French garrison mess kitchen had access to the food supply. His spies had already explored the possibility of poisoning the Iroquois traitor and her entourage. To-Ko-Wan had hoped his plans could be accomplished easily and soon.

Unfortunately, To-Ko-Wan's contacts had explained the peculiar method employed by the French to negate the threat of poison. Just as the King of France had a royal taster responsible for assuring the wholesomeness of all things contacting his royal lips, Frontenac had taken similar precautions with his own food supply. As a ward within his protection, Kateri enjoyed the same security. Early in his tenure in the New World, Frontenac had realized the deceitful nature of the Native American aborigine. Total trust was not an option when dealing with a foreign population whose loyalty was questionable.

While Tekawetha's security was certainly not impregnable, To-Ko-Wan was not inclined at this time to take desperate measures. He was so confident of his eventual success, mainly as a result of his transcending spirit vision, that he was content to take his time. To-Ko-Wan's spirit guide would provide the opportunity to resolve the situation in due time. In this case patience was a virtue and To-Ko-Wan was willing to wait for the proper time.

Days passed and the Iroquois shaman began to regain his strength. Immediately after Lord Frontenac's visit to his cell, a foreign shaman had visited the jail and ministered to the Iroquois' wounds. Although inclined not to allow this, To-Ko-Wan remained passive as the bandages and salve were applied. He drew the line though when the doctor attempted to administer a parasite to induce bleeding. Try as he might, To-Ko-Wan could not understand the logic behind this peculiar foreign practice of weakening the body through loss of blood when attempting to restore strength. Ironically, barbaric acts were being practiced by the supposedly superior civilized society. To-Ko-Wan reasoned that such actions justified the superior attitude he had assumed in dealing with the French. As soon as the military doctor departed, the bandages were off and To-Ko-Wan was busy applying a herbal concoction a brother had passed through the bars of his cell window the previous night.

Other improvements in To-Ko-Wan's captivity were realized by order of Lord Frontenac as well. Meat and vegetables began to accompany his daily fare of bread and milk. Since To-Ko-Wan had successfully experienced his vision through fasting, he was now consciously working to restore his strength. When he was to be released, To-Ko-Wan wanted to be prepared to travel to quickly assemble his war party.

The treatment of the guards in the prison had definitely improved. New faces had replaced those with whips and clubs. To-Ko-Wan's spies had indicated that the military justice administered by Lord Frontenac had been both swift and severe. Five guards, including the corporal, had been publicly flogged on the military parade ground the day following Frontenac's visit. They remained chained to a wall without food or water on public display for five full days. These guards lost their rank and were reduced to menial duties. These duties included maintenance of the camp latrines. Obviously, Frontenac was experienced at dealing harshly with dereliction of duty. The example was designed to make an impression upon the entire Montreal garrison.

Within a week, To-Ko-Wan's carefully constructed plan was beginning to occur. He had already dispatched a warrior westward to locate the French missionaries and Sha-Na, their Iroquois maiden guide. This spy was to follow them to their ultimate destination and report back on the missionary's success or failure. It was distinctly possible that the French missionaries would become victims of the wilderness. Such an event would save To-Ko-Wan the trouble of pursuit although he knew he must journey to the Illinois region. Clearly his spirit vision had resolved that point of his destiny beyond any doubt.

To-Ko-Wan had decided that the path to Kateri's destruction lay through Sha-Na, her Christian disciple and handmaiden. Kateri would likely sacrifice her own safety, even her life, for her close friend. After all, wasn't personal sacrificing the Christian ideal? To-Ko-Wan could not fathom the logic in a religion that glorified weakness instead of strength. The Iroquois spirits were strong and would ultimately prevail over this weak God.

As soon as To-Ko-Wan was released, he planned to assemble powerful warriors who held absolute allegiance to the old ways. Their commitment to his plan would be total. To-Ko-Wan could depend upon these warriors to fulfill his spirit vision and ultimate destiny. If the French missionaries survived the journey westward and the subsequent winter in the heart of the continent, To-Ko-Wan's war party would deal them a final fatal blow. This would effectively end the French God's presence in that part of the Iroquois domain.

Two of To-Ko-Wan's primary goals would be accomplished by his raid into the western French territory eventually to be called Illinois. First, the raid would reassert Iroquois power and dominance in this western march. The weak clans in this area had become complacent to Iroquois rule due to their extreme distance from the heart of Iroquois power. A wake up call for these simpering cowards was long overdue. The long held terror of the Iroquois needed to be reemphasized and slaves was always needed to attend to the menial tasks in Iroquois' long houses. Captives that could survive the long forced march back from Illinois would be sturdy workers.

Second, the Iroquois war party would capture Sha-Na, the close friend and confidant of the blasphemer Kateri. To-Ko-Wan reasoned that Sha-Na would provide the key to vulnerability. Only Sha-Na could draw Kateri from her bastion of safety in the military fortifications of Montreal. Thus exposed, Kateri would be at To-Ko-Wan's mercy. Once under his control, To-Ko-Wan would torture this Iroquois traitor and kill her in front of a convocation of the Five Iroquois Nations. By this sacred act, all would know the strength of the old ways. The French plan for colonization would be in shambles. Things could then be as they were. The Iroquois shaman was full of self-satisfaction in knowing that his vision of the future would surely come to pass. Little did he realize that things were not always as they seemed.

* * * *

The lean, muscular Iroquois warrior glistened with perspiration as he ran along the deer trails that led west through the pristine deciduous forest southwest of Montreal. He was bare to the waist except for the amulet he wore around his neck for protection. The warrior's legs moved swiftly and easily as he strove to put distance under his moccasin feet. Below the waist, he was clothed only by a breechcloth and a beaded leather belt carrying a hunting knife made of the foreigner's polished rock. He did not expect trouble so his weapons had been left behind for the sake of speed. The knife was meant only to forage for food along the way west. Roots, berries, and grubs would be his meager fare for the next few days, yet it would be plenty to see his tempered body through the arduous trek. Determination shone in his stoic expression and the rock hard features of his face.

From his outward appearance one could not have guessed his mission. The Iroquois warrior ran so quietly that even the wildlife seemed to miss his passing. Years of physical activity had made his movements like that of a perpetual machine. The warrior had learned to totally divorce his mind from the physical stress he exerted on his body. Consequently, he felt no pain, no hunger, no thirst, and no exhaustion. The mind was free from the distractions of reality, which allowed him to weigh the alternatives available to accomplish his solemn mission.

This warrior was named Kor-Oh-Tin, blood brother to the Iroquois shaman To-Ko-Wan, defender of the old ways. Kor-Oh-Tin had been sent west to locate the French missionaries recently departed from Montreal. This should be simple for one steeped in the ways of tracking, since the French were obviously new to the wilderness of native North America. Kor-Oh-Tin had been informed that the voyageur Radisson had been engaged as their guide to the interior. Radisson would advise them well for he had direct experience with the savage habit of the Iroquois. However, the size of the French party would preclude them from moving westward quietly. Kor-Oh-Tin had no doubt that his quarry would be easy to locate.

Once Kor-Oh-Tin had located the French missionaries, he had been instructed to shadow their movements and, eventually report back their final destination to To-Ko-Wan. Kor-Oh-Tin was told not to make his intentions known to the French. It was best the French missionaries were not aware that their progress into the interior was being monitored. Kor-Oh-Tin knew that his mission would take a long time since the territory known as Illinois to the French had been mentioned. He could not expect to return to his clan for quite sometime. Luckily, this did not bother him much since he was at home in the forest. Kor-Oh-Tin was one with nature. He was comfortable to sleep on the bare, moist soil and eat only roots and grubs dug from the ground. It would not be difficult to successfully complete his mission.

Surprisingly, To-Ko-Wan had even told Kor-Oh-Tin to make the journey of the French as easy for them as possible. He was to even intervene with his tribal brothers if the way of the French missionaries was impeded. Why would the great Iroquois shaman, champion of the forest spirits, want to help the infidel French in any way? This simply did not make any logical sense to the Iroquois warrior. Personally, Kor-Oh-Tin with his deep respect for the ancient religion would rather murder the French now and put an end to their blasphemy. To let them pass safely, yeah, even help them on their way, was revolting to Kor-Oh-Tin's soul. Obviously To-Ko-Wan had a purpose for pursuing this course of action. Kor-Oh-Tin would have much to consider as he crossed the endless miles toward the mighty waters splitting the center of the North American continent.

* * * *

As the French missionaries and their contingent traveled west along the south shore of the lake to be known in the future as Ontario in the early dawn, Father Constance began to question Radisson, their experienced guide, about their ultimate destination. Father Constance was aware that the territory where they were destined to start a mission was called Illinois. Father Marquette named the Illinois region for the tribal confederation living there. Father Marquette had even started a mission there, which was assumed to still exist. He had personally reported to Father Constance when they met at the Bishop's residence back in Paris that the Illinois natives were peaceful, gentle, and very eager for the gospel of Christ. Indeed, it had been Father Marquette's encouragement that was partially responsible for this current missionary expedition. Because of Constance and Bertrand's preeminent success among the savages in remote regions of both Asia and Africa, Father Marquette believed that the New World was fertile ground for an experienced ministry.

But Father Constance wanted to make sure that their final destination was the land described in such beautiful detail by Father Marquette before their departure from Calais. The New World was an expansive region. Most cartographers conjectured that it might even be a continent larger than all of Europe. In this uncharted region, it would surely be quite easy to lose one's way. Major Stuart paid particular attention to this conversation for he was concerned that they might not arrive safely in Illinois and be settled before the first snow. He had heard that the interior winter could be very harsh. Stuart would not allow the party's safety to be compromised in any way.

Radisson reassured the travelers that he knew the land called Illinois by Father Marquette quite well. Apparently, Radisson had spent several seasons trapping beaver and muskrat along the rivers and streams that interlaced the region. When Father Constance referred to the mighty river that Father Marquette had traveled with his partner, Louis Joliet, Radisson's eyes twinkled and he became particularly verbose.

"The Illini natives call this particular river the father of waters. They named it so because they believe it is the very wellspring of life. To be sure this river is one of the main transportation links north to south in the interior. Though I have only traveled the river a few kilometers, I believe one could easily use this river to reach the warmer regions to the south, but those devil Spaniards control that land so we must be careful." Radisson shook his head and continued.

"Good Fathers! You cannot imagine the abundance and diversity of the wildlife along these interior rivers. Although the region we pass through is impressive, this all pales in comparison to the interior region." Radisson's countenance displayed obvious awe and wonder as he recalled in his mind this bountiful land.

"I cannot imagine game more plentiful than this." Stuart spoke only to encourage Radisson into continuing his story.

"Ah, Monsieur, the flocks of duck and geese are so numerous that when they rise they literally blot out the sun! Deer and elk are always in close proximity. Hunting is not a sport in Illinois since the game is so easy to acquire. The natives have become quite lazy and complacent. No wonder they do not have the reputation of the Iroquois for being fierce warriors."

"Are we to assume there is no poverty and famine to administer to in the native population?" Father Bertrand actually sounded distressed that the natives might not need his help.

"Oh no, Blessed Father," Radisson quickly answered. "They are an ignorant lot depending upon hunting more than farming. The Illini do not always store sufficient supplies for the winter. Thus their life is one of seasonal feast or famine. They know both gluttony and starvation. The natives can surely benefit from your wise counsel and benevolent ministry." Radisson spoke like an eloquent politician.

"Monsieur Radisson, do the Illinois tribes possess agricultural skills, or are they basically hunters and gathers?" Father Constance wanted to become more familiar with the people among which he would be living.

"Oui. They do cultivate some root crops while they remain encamped for a longer time during the summer. The women of the tribe are quite adept in farming. The vegetables they raise do contribute to a healthy diet. Also, like the squirrel, most natives have learned to store food for the winter season. They either bury the food in tightly woven baskets, or store it in the caves that frequent the bluffs along the larger streams. It is quite amazing that these natives can find their caches many months later for they tend to wander quite extensively from season to season." Radisson spoke with authority for he had some years of experience living with these interior natives while he trapped furs to sell.

"How can our mission be successful if the natives never remain in one place for any length of time?" Father Bertrand shook his head in dismay.

"That should be no problem, Father." Radisson smiled and continued. "As I said, the food is relatively plentiful and many will remain at one location if there is a good social reason to do it. For instance, many natives will stay close to one of our trading posts. They seem to enjoy the social activity and there are always travelers passing by. This variety is an attractive alternative to the mundane life they are forced to experience in the wilderness. I'm sure you will have many permanent residents at your mission, Father Bertrand."

"But how can we hope to supply them? Is the wildlife really plentiful enough to sustain such numbers without an efficient farming system?" Major Stuart asked the question many of the others listening to the conversation were thinking.

"Oh, oui, oui!" Radisson replied. "As I said, the wildlife, especially the aqueous species along the rivers and streams are innumerable. Also, I have failed to mention one unusual animal that can feed many people for weeks if the meat is properly prepared and preserved."

"What animal in God's creation, other than possibly a elk, could possibly feed so many?" The Major asked curiously.

"Alas, I'm at a loss in giving you a name for the animal since I'm sure that even with all your travels you have never seen such a creature." Radisson shook his head obviously enjoying this chance to have the absolute attention of everyone.

"Go on, Mon ami!" Stuart said, perturbed with the slow progress of the conversation. "Surely you can provide some idea using words we understand."

"I'm afraid you will not believe that such an unusual animal exists." Then Radisson launched into his usual embellished description.

"These creatures resemble cattle although they are much larger. Their heads are very massive with thick horns and a thick, curly mat of hair. Their lower jaws are elongated giving the impression of a beard being attached. Their head is definitely one trait that sets them apart from all animals you would be familiar with." Radisson gazed into the distance tree line seemingly oblivious to his present surroundings. Everyone sensed that Radisson's first sight of these creatures had left quite an impression.

"Now imagine if you will a massive head and front torso attached to a hump similar to that of a Dromedary camel." Radisson again paused.

"Are you saying this creature is like a camel?" Stuart interjected anxiously trying to keep the description of this curious creature flowing.

"Oui and non! It is incomprehensible how God fashioned this animal." Radisson had become introspective and his words dragged.

"Please, please proceed with your story. As you see, you have our undivided attention," Mr. Geoff said with a smirk on his face. He found the idea of a cross between a cow and a camel quite difficult to imagine, let alone believe.

"Oh, you unbelievers!" Radisson exclaimed in disgust. "You, Good Fathers, of all people, who believe in our risen Savior even though you have not seen him in the flesh, should give me some credibility. For all your travels, are you saying you have never encountered an exotic beast that has left you completely speechless?" Radisson now fell silent.

"Please excuse our skepticism, Monsieur." Father Constance quickly interjected, always playing the peacemaker. "Given the extreme abundance of wildlife in this new land, I must surely believe that it could produce the magnificent beast that you have described. It is just that we all are numbed by the sheer diversity."

"Apology accepted, Father." Radisson grinned and returned to his jovial self.

"Why have we not encountered these beasts as yet, since we have already traveled several hundred kilometers into the interior?" Major Stuart continued to question Radisson, obviously intrigued that this novel beast could actually exist.

"I cannot say for sure, Major, since I'm not a learned scholar." Radisson answered solemnly. "However, I have noticed in my wanderings that the beast seems to have a definite eastern limit. Perhaps it has something to do with habitat and climate. While the beast likes to cool itself in the muddy swamps near rapid streams, it tends to shun the deep forest. The animal definitely prefers a grassy meadow as is natural for a possible relative to the bovine. These dark woods do not supply abundant sustenance for such an animal. And the forests we have encountered until now grow down to the edge of the water."

"Then Illinois is a different type of land?" Major Stuart continued the line of reasoning hinted at by Radisson.

"Oui and non again, Monsieur." Radisson replied, happy to be involved in any type of intellectual discussion.

"The landscape does open up, if you will as we travel west." Radisson continued. "The forests remain dark and impenetrable near the waterways, but the conifer does not retain its dominance farther west. You will note that deciduous trees will become more plentiful."

"What is it like as one moves away from the river?" Father Bertrand asked intent on learning as much as he could about the land in which he was to establish a mission. This would surely help him plan for its success.

"I have not much to tell you, for I, like the natives, stay away from these areas. I can tell you that the prairie is vast indeed." Radisson shook his head sorry that he could not be of more help.

"My livelihood comes from the furs to be trapped along the waters edge while the lands grazed by the great humped beasts offer no enticement."

"Surely you can tell us something," Major Stuart asked seriously.

"Oh, oui. I would tell you to avoid the prairie as if it were infested by the plague."

"Why so, good Sir?" Monsieur Geoff reentered the conversation.

"Well, the prairie has plants taller than a man and they are of nearly impenetrable thickness. Travel through this mass of dense foliage is impossibly slow and tiring. Only small game like rabbits and birds are available for sustenance. And the incessant buzz of insects will drive one insane in short order," Radisson paused.

"And the natives will tell you it is quite easy to get lost in this vast ocean of tall, wavy grass."

"How are the natives successful at locating and killing the great humped beast then?" Stuart was trying to make sense of this new land.

"Of course the beast must come to the streams or lakes to drink. They love to wallow in the swamp mud next to these waters, as it is very soothing and cooling to them. The mud provides respite from the biting insects. Engaged in such leisure, the beasts are easy targets for the cunning natives who are very skilled in hunting."

"This sounds like a source of sustenance through the cold interior winter," said Stuart storing these facts for future reference. "Our flintlock rifles should make it easy to fill our winter cache. But now what about our intended destination?"

Everyone waited for Radisson to supply some detail about his or her future residence.

"What would you say to a place called by my fellow voyageurs as Mere D'osiers?" Radisson paused and smiled as he waited for the reaction he knew to be forthcoming.

"Mere D'osiers, Mere D'osiers, Willow Lake?" Father Constance repeated incredulously shaking his head. "You would have us spend our days in a disease infested swamp? Is this your idea of meeting your obligation to Frontenac when you promised to watch out for our welfare?" Past missions in nearly uninhabitable regions of the earth passed through the priest's mind. He wondered how they could possibly make life better for the heathens when they may themselves suffer immediately from unhealthy living conditions. A willow lake was possibly a polite term for a muddy swamp. Surely in this land of abundance as this there was a better site for their mission of comfort and peace. The rest of the party was silently contemplating months of extreme hardship.

"Isn't it humorous how just the name can conjure up some abominable picture of hell on earth?" Radisson replied apparently enjoying his personal joke.

"Even the natives respond negatively to the name. But, I can assure you that it is more accommodating than it sounds."

"That is preposterous!" said Father Bertrand, ready to reject the site before Radisson had a chance to explain.

"Now, now, Pe're," said Major Stuart, raising his hand to ask for calm. "Let us give Monsieur Radisson a chance."

"Merci, Major." Radisson replied. "You might be interested to know that Father Marquette adored the place."

"Non, non, it cannot be that you actually met Marquette," said Father Constance. "I find that hard to believe for he was in this vast region for only a brief time."

"Oui, but I had the opportunity to speak with him in Montreal prior to his return to France." Radisson spoke as if no one could doubt him.

"It was an extreme coincidence to be sure," said Radisson, "that I should have intimate knowledge of the very region through which Marquette and Joliet had passed. At any rate, we discussed the tribes of Algonkin origin that inhabit the region known as Illinois. There is also a large population of Cahokia, Kaskaskia, Michigamea, and Tamoroa in the area. I know that these natives all like to trade at the tiny French post called Mere D'osiers. Father Marquette knew the name of the settlement very well. We laughed and shared a glass of wine over the providence of God that should have two distinct opposites follow the same path in such a vast region. Father Marquette had commented to me that Mere D'osiers would be the perfect place to establish a mission. With a large native population in close proximity I naturally assumed you would agree."

Radisson looked rather coquettish knowing full well that Father Bertrand and Father Constance would be hard pressed to disagree with the venerable Father Marquette. Both priests were obviously in awe of Marquette's reputation.

"Surely there must be a more hospitable site for our encampment than a soggy swamp?" Major Stuart was not constrained by a similar respect for Father Marquette's opinions. His duty was to assure the security of his party and make their journey as comfortable as possible. Stuart wanted to explore his options.

"But non Monsieur. You have the wrong impression." Radisson was willing to defend his choice for the mission. "The site is quite well drained making it unlike any swamp you could imagine. It is naturally sheltered from the weather. Most importantly, Mere D'osiers is strategically located on a major waterway that provides quick access to all points of the compass. This is a fact that you should appreciate, Major Stuart, given your obvious military background."

While Stuart stared with a blank expression indicative of a man carefully weighing the information, Radisson continued.

"At any rate I believe that the name for our destination may be only a monumental coincidence."

"What can you possibly mean?" said Father Constance, unsure of where this was all leading.

"To be sure there is an inlet along the bend in the river that could be termed a lake. And the willow trees grow in great profusion in the sandy soil surrounding the site; hence the name "lake of the willows." Radisson spoke softly.

"Go on, monsieur!" Stuart was becoming inpatient to end the conversation.

"A native with whom I trapped one winter did say the trading post was named after the first French priest to stay in the vicinity. His name happened to be Antoine, Antoine D'Osia. The name for the place is likely a combination of this man's name and the lake located close by." Radisson said with finality.

At this very moment the travelers were awakened to the reality of their current situation. They would soon test the hospitality of an Iroquois village for as their lead canoe rounded a bend they could see on the distant shore many Seneca long houses. Smoke curled from dying campfires into the blue cloud splattered sky. Dogs barked as they sensed the strangers' approach even before the villagers became aware of the fact. Stuart and his military contingent clasped the hilts of their swords as they mentally prepared for a possible skirmish. The major prayed that Sha-Na could intercede with her Iroquois kinsmen before an arrow was unleashed that could not be withdrawn. The French canoes approached the village head on deliberately intending to show no fear. Major Stuart had learned long ago that bold action often led to a peaceful resolution of a hostile encounter. He could see natives gathering along the shore. Several Iroquois canoes filled with stout, muscular warriors cast off to meet the French party. Soon enough the French would know how they were to be received by the Seneca village.

Sha-Na and her sister Iroquois maids were conspicuously positioned at the bow of the lead French canoe. They were attired in typical Iroquois dress of deerskins with ceremonial beadwork. The approaching Seneca war canoes would know immediately that the French entourage encroaching upon their village was likely friendly. This was part of Major Stuart's plan. He hoped that Sha-Na would be able to gain them safe passage. The French could not afford the casualties that would surely result if they were forced to fight.

In this moment of imminent military action Stuart found himself worrying about the safety of the Iroquois maiden, Sha-Na. He shuddered mentally as if trying to concentrate on the situation at hand. This was quite unlike the Major to be preoccupied with the safety of one lone individual when the safety and success of his troops were in the balance. He knew he must stay focused or this encounter could be a disaster. Yet, mentally he continued to devise ways that could guarantee Sha-Na's safety in the event of hostilities. How could he even contemplate saving a lone individual, a foreigner no less, at the expense of his own comrades? This was certainly a new problem for which he was totally unprepared.

Each French soldier displayed discipline and courage as they met the hostile war canoes head on. Their flintlock muskets were primed and cocked. Any overt aggression on the part of the Seneca warriors in the approaching canoes would unleash a volley of leaded musket balls. This would effectively end that threat and give the French time to flee to the far shore. Stuart, ever the military tactician, knew that they stood little chance in a battle with the Seneca upon the water. On the shore they could quickly assemble fortifications by stacking their canoes, equipment, and provisions. On the shore they would hold the position of strength. The Seneca would be hard pressed to attack headlong across the water. They would be forced into a flanking movement that could take considerable time. Stuart reasoned the resulting stalemate would give him time to implement other strategies. His military experience gave him several options that could be employed quite effectively. Stuart prayed he would not have to use them.

As Stuart prepared for the worst from the approaching grim-faced Seneca warriors, he was pleasantly surprised when one of them actually grinned. This simply astounded the French and almost left them defenseless. Sha-Na's countenance was beaming and her hand was waving expansively in greeting. Apparently, the Seneca's had recognized her as Iroquois kin. The Seneca canoes swiftly flanked the French as they turned about and headed back for the village. The once threatening war canoes became an escort of honor. Suddenly there seemed to be a hint of festival in the air. The entire French entourage breathed a sigh of relief at this unexpected change of fortune.

*   *   *   *

Back on the continent the French King Louis XIV anxiously awaited news of further French success in the New World. Louis Bade de Frontenac, the French military hero, had recently reported success in establishing fledgling French settlements. Also, Frontenac was demonstrating to rival nations on the continent that France could maintain a position of strength and pacify its minions in North America. Indeed, French fortunes worldwide were looking up. All that was needed was the discovery of a new treasure to fund French expansion. In this era of mercantilism, colonies were meant to provide the mother country with a return on investment, as well as a profitable trading partner. Colonial holdings had made Spain and England preeminent powers. With a little luck King Louis reasoned that France could use her claims in the New World to bolster his fortune and power as well. It made no difference whether an expedition of the King or the Catholic Church found the treasure. If La Salle, the King's representative, did not actually find wealth, he could still commandeer it from the Church's expedition. Both represented France and, therefore, it was his to claim.

Like King Louis, Bishop Colbert daily anticipated word of the success of his mission into the continental interior of North America. Colbert had heard the Spanish stories of the Seven Cities of Cibola. Father Marquette and Monsieur Joliet had personally reported on the expansive waterways that crisscrossed the New World. They had seen with their own eyes the great inland lakes that some said rivaled the interior seas of continental Europe. Surely such terrain would be the site of a grand and wealthy civilization. Such colonial wealth could restore the fortunes of the Catholic Church and stop the constant encroachment of the King's political power. Bishop Colbert wished to implement the dream of his mentor, Cardinal Mazarin, to reestablish the transcendent power of the Church in Europe. Conquest of a wealthy civilization similar to the Aztecs or Incas could make this dream a reality. Much of the French army was still loyal to the Church. Bishop Colbert felt he could still wield the power behind the French throne, but he knew the Church power was on the wane. Something had to happen and happen soon. Colbert prayed that God would see fit to restore his Church to the grandeur of old.

The two most powerful men in France sat contemplating their fate. Colbert was sure that God had given him a mission in history to keep the Church strong. Louis also believed God was on his side. But, in contrast, he felt he was destined to claim power for the people and end the endless corruption and prostitution of the Church. Louis was convinced that he was God's anointed. God would assure his success in the New World.

The two men had one thing in common and that was the pursuit of personal power. Power is a special gift God bestows on special people. Joan of Arc knew that power and proclaimed its true source until the end. Power has another face, too. Power is granted by the devil to those who are so conceited as to believe their personal goals have divine origin. Noble ideals often have roots that are themselves corrupt. Therefore, the harvest is bitter. Good can come from evil. Both Louis and Colbert would see the truth in these words.

* * * *

As the French travelers stepped onto the sandy beach near the Seneca village, only a few Iroquois greeted them. From the shouts and drum beats coming from the center of the village, the French could tell that some type of celebration was being held. In particular, one Iroquois man sought out Sha-Na and they talked in hushed whispers for several minutes. Again Major Stuart encountered another emotion that was very foreign to him. As he watched the friendly conversation between the Iroquois man and Sha-Na, Stuart found himself experiencing the stirrings of jealousy. He feared that the man was a long lost paramour of the Iroquois maiden. Stuart knew that encounter might spell the end to their special relationship. Being a soldier, he was used to seizing the offensive, unfortunately there was no obvious way to approach this event and Stuart had the supreme misfortune of feeling totally defenseless. He realized he was infatuated with the maiden and completely at her mercy. What if she did not feel the same about him? After all, he was obviously years older than her. Stuart wondered how he could hope to cope with such emotional destruction.

Father Constance abruptly awakened Stuart from his mental malaise by a tap on his shoulder. The good father was motioning him to follow the Seneca greeters to the festivities. To his surprise, Sha-Na and the Iroquois stranger came over to walk beside him. Sha-Na introduced the stranger as Kor-Oh-Tin, a kinsman from the Oneida tribe to the east. Little did she know that he was a spy and possibly an assassin. She explained that Kor-Oh-Tin was also a visitor to the village on his trek west. The stranger had indicated a desire to travel with them and they could discuss this further after they had eaten.

Before Stuart could properly address this request, the sight that greeted them when they arrived at the center of the Seneca village further overwhelmed him and the other Frenchmen. On a stump near a large communal fire sat a native gazing off into space. He sat deathly still with his arms folded at his chest. The Indian resembled a king surveying his vassals with an aloofness that transcended the cares of this world. Around the man was piled all types of offering from food to weapons and clothing, which emphasized the suggestion of monarchy. The Seneca villagers formed a line that passed in front of this stately individual. Each in turn laid a gift at his feet. Still the native did not move to acknowledge the kindness. There was a surreal atmosphere around this entire scene that served to make Major Stuart uncomfortable.

As Stuart turned to question Sha-Na in order to satisfy his curiosity, he realized that she and the other Iroquois in their party had joined the line paying homage to the native. Stuart watched as Sha-Na removed an intricately beaded necklace from around her neck and placed it at the man's feet. Kor-Oh-Tin and the Iroquois maidens followed suite. Stuart noticed that most had little in the way of possessions to offer, but each one was able to find an offering somehow. This ritual simply astounded Stuart. He found himself carefully scrutinizing the native chief in an attempt to solve the riddle.

After a time, Stuart could not guess how long, he was startled from his trance by the light touch of Sha-Na on his forearm. She smiled shyly and asked if he would join the line passing in review. Sha-Na said that such a gesture by the French would do much to earn the respect of her Seneca kinfolk. Major Stuart fell into line without thinking and his entourage followed suit. When his turn came, Stuart found himself offering some glittering coins, the only thing he could find on this short notice. As Stuart respectfully bowed while passing, he secretly looked up in an attempt to see if the native would acknowledge his unusual present. To Stuart's surprise, he recognized that the Seneca warrior had the pallid color of death. Why were there so many lavish gifts for a dead man? Stuart could not wait to ask Sha-Na the purpose of the ritual.

Later the entire French party was introduced to the elders of the village. They were treated to a lavish feast consisting of all manner of fowl, fish, and fruit. All were impressed that barely civilized hunters-and-gathers could afford such lavish feasting. To the dismay of Father Constance and Father Bertrand, Sha-Na explained that, indeed, the poor Seneca could not afford it.

Sha-Na told them that it was the tradition of her people to give their best in honor of the deceased. The Iroquois are a proud people that tried to take care of a family at their time of loss. To meet this responsibility, many Iroquois often gave what they could not afford to give. By offering their best, they often left themselves with little to survive. With the autumn approaching, there would be children going hungry as a result of this ritual.

To further complicate the situation, Sha-Na made the point that her people were very competitive. Their pride would not allow themselves to hold back anything. The Iroquois always wanted to win, whether in the hunt, a game, or in war. Consequently, when a villager passed away each Iroquois family unit willingly gave up their treasures and, when nothing else was available, necessities in order to win the unnamed competition between each other. To fail to be generous in the death ritual was a point of shame for any Iroquois. Sha-Na explained that years of toil to build up some measure of wealth in this harsh land could be needlessly squandered in observation of the death ritual. Sha-Na hoped that her work as a Christian missionary could stop this insanity. The dead man's family often became very wealthy in native terms as a result of the death. Much suffering among her people could be avoided by simply stopping such a pointless tradition. Sha-Na privately wondered why people continue to cling with tenacity to traditions that are obviously illogical. She feared that this insanity would continue to plague her people for years to come. Sha-Na in her wisdom would probably not have been surprised to learn that irrationality regarding traditions was not limited to her culture.

As the feasting continued around blazing bonfires that spit glowing embers into the starlit night, Sha-Na, Major Stuart, and the stranger, Kor-Oh-Tin, finally had the opportunity to gather to discuss the continuing journey.

"Our arrival today was most fortunate," Sha-Na said in near perfect French. Kor-Oh-Tin nodded quiet assent at this observation.

"The village was quite preoccupied with my people's death ritual. Although usually ready to fight at the least provocation, this tradition is taken quite seriously. Only a major threat would have distracted the attention of the village in the middle of a feast. Our Christian God must truly be smiling upon this missionary journey." Sha-Na spoke with finality.

"It is unlike the Great Hare to let people committed to a foreign god walk into his domain unmolested," Kor-Oh-Tin mumbled.

"Quite so, brother. The Great Hare, if he exists, never did me a favor as long as I have lived. I can't imagine him starting now. Non, it must be a greater power than he."

Kor-Oh-Tin merely gazed into the fire after hearing Sha-Na's view upon his native religion in noncommittal and bemused silence. He was not about to become involved in a theological discussion at this point. He needed the friendship of the French to accomplish his mission. The Iroquois could not afford to invoke their enmity.

"I gather you are far from home. What brings you to this village?" Major Stuart asked. He was obviously suspicious of the stranger's coincidental appearance. Stuart wanted some assurance that he was no threat.

Kor-Oh-Tin did not immediately respond. He just sat gazing off into the night as if in another world. Such an interminable time passed that the Major was about to repeat the question when the stranger finally uttered a response.

"Why do your people leave the comfort of home?"

Stuart immediately confirmed his dislike for the stranger with that reply. His military background cried for a concise response. He had no use for those who answer questions with questions. Stuart had already noted in his dealings with the native inhabitants of New France their penchant for stoicism and inscrutability. He realized that he must control his temper if he was to gather any information from this man.

"We have a variety of reasons including curiosity, fortune, political necessity, and religion. That is precisely why I asked your motivation. Are the reasons your people travel so different from mine?"

"We all have purpose on this earth. Things are not always as they seem." This cryptic comment showed that the Iroquois stranger chose his words carefully.

"You have not answered my initial question." Stuart said calmly realizing that this stranger was quite intelligent.

Sha-Na sat quietly. Women were respected in the Iroquois society so she knew that she could contribute to the conversation at any time. However, like Stuart, Sha-Na had an uneasy feeling about this stranger. She wanted to be reassured before openly accepting him as a fellow traveler. It was definitely time for some answers.

"My motivation, as you call it, for traveling west is wealth," Kor-Oh-Tin replied in an open and friendly manner meant to persuade. He realized he could not afford to upset the French. Kor-Oh-Tin's mission would be much more easily accomplished if he could be accepted as a friend and trusted traveling companion. His conversation with Sha-Na earlier during the ritual had seemed to win her respect. But Kor-Oh-Tin saw that Sha-Na had great respect for this foreigner as well. Perhaps there was an even deeper relationship between Sha-Na and Stuart than anyone realized. Kor-Oh-Tin instinctively knew that Sha-Na would not accept him if Stuart had any reservations. He must choose his answers wisely.

"And what type of treasure would cause an Iroquois warrior to venture such great distance from his home fire?" Major Stuart was relieved that the conversation was not dragging. He hoped he could get enough information to determine if the stranger was friend or foe.

"Wealth among my people can be accumulated by hard work. Game is abundant in the land toward the setting sun. In a few short seasons many pelts can be gathered. I will return to my village as a respected hunter." Kor-Oh-Tin failed to mention that wealth among the Iroquois was also counted in slaves. The lands to the west had always been a prime source of slaves for aggressive Iroquois war parties.

"I hold great respect for anyone unafraid of hard work," Stuart commented offhandedly. He waited to see if the stranger would offer further information about his purpose.

"Are you French not venturing toward the setting sun for the same reason as I? Monsieur Radisson has nothing to hide. Pursuit of wealth is his life." Again the Iroquois stranger was probing for information, but this time Stuart did not seem upset.

"Au, contraire!" Stuart answered decisively. "Our mission is benevolent. You must by now know that Father Bertrand and Father Constance are holy men among my people. They have no desire for wealth. Their avowed purpose is only to bring comfort to those in need. We understand from past French voyageurs that the natives of the interior yearn for our ministry."

"They also have many furs to trade," Kor-Oh-Tin replied with no inflection in his voice. "Maybe some in your party get rich as well, eh?"

"If you are referring to Monsieur Radisson, it is no concern of mine what he does. He is responsible for guiding us to our destination. Even you mentioned that Radisson was acquainted with your land. Who better to show us the way?"

"My people know that even a brother is not always the best council. Trust must be earned. How long you know Radisson?" Kor-Oh-Tin was skilled at keeping the topic of the conversation away from him.

"Did I say I trusted the man?"

"You must to follow him blindly into a wilderness."

"And whom do you think I should follow? You?" Stuart tried to assume command of the discussion.

"You could do worse."

"Do you wish that I dismiss Radisson and employ you as a guide?"

Sensing the conversation could become antagonistic, Sha-Na decided to give her opinion.

"My kinsman is suggesting no such thing. He simply seeks companionship on the long trek to the west."

"I can certainly understand that logic," Stuart said, tiring of a conversation that was going nowhere. Stuart turned to the stranger. "Join us tomorrow if you like. We must move swiftly to our destination. We have much to prepare before winter is upon us."

Major Stuart arose and retired to his bedroll stowed in the canoe upon the sandy beach. He wanted time to be alone with Sha-Na, but she gave no indication of following him away from the fire and her Iroquois friends. Stuart wanted her candid opinion of this new traveling companion. It was too much of a coincidence that Kor-Oh-Tin should want to travel with the French. Still, the stranger was only one man. Whatever his real motive for joining them, Stuart felt assured he could manage as long as he kept up his guard. As Stuart fell asleep gazing at the glittering constellations splattered across the dark velvet sky, he wondered why Sha-Na allowed the stranger to remain in her company the entire day. Stuart felt a small shudder bring a chill to his body as his inner conscious candidly suggested that he might be jealous. Stuart could sleep secure knowing that French sentries were alert to any mischief the Seneca might attempt.

As the brilliantly orange moon arose on the horizon much intrigue was happening that night. In fact, several contemplated or had performed a clandestine act. With the arrival of Kor-Oh-Tin the French missionaries now had three spies within the party. The master of each spy wished to use the travelers for their own sinister purpose. For instance, Monsieur Geoff's master, Bishop Colbert, hoped the missionaries would find wealth in the trackless interior continent of the New World. Geoff knew Colbert was, even now, impatient for some news that might suggest a treasure he could use to reestablish the power of the Catholic Church on continental Europe. Geoff was preparing a dispatch to be delivered to a Catholic priest back in Montreal. The dispatch would offer encouragement although Geoff himself felt there was little chance of finding an Aztec treasure in this northern climate.

Radisson, likewise, had sent a Huron back east to deliver a confidential message of encouragement to Frontenac. Unknown to anyone in this French party, Radisson was a Royalist completely loyal to King Louis. It had been his pleasure to volunteer as a spy to report upon the progress of the missionaries, Constance and Bertrand. At first, based upon the information provided by Frontenac, Radisson thought that the French party was treasure hunters employed by the wily Bishop Colbert. But now after weeks of travel Radisson was convinced the missionaries were sincere in their wish to convert the native population. Radisson also knew from his past journeys west that there was virtually no hope of stumbling upon any treasure either. Unless their avowed destination changed soon, neither the church nor the crown would become wealthy as a result of this mission.

Radisson reasoned that if there was another wealthy civilization in the New World to be plundered, it would be located much further west than Mere D'Osia. He had always believed there was a good chance of a water route through the interior of this continent to link up trade with Calay. Even without hope of finding a city of gold like the Spaniard's had found to the south, a trade route would surely give France a lucrative trade. Radisson chuckled as he thought this might earn him a tidy fortune as well. Perhaps he would explore a bit further west after he had delivered these simpleton missionaries to their heathen masses of humanity.

THE LESSONS 121

Finally, Kor-Oh-Tin had sent a brother Seneca back east to report the situation to his brother To-Ko-Wan. Kor-Oh-Tin wished his brother to know that he had befriended the missionaries and the heretic, Sha-Na. Once the mission was established in the land of the Peoria, Kor-Oh-Tin would relay their location and prepare for the arrival of the Iroquois war party. Kor-Oh-Tin, like his brother, believed that the menace of the Christian God must be stopped from infecting the Iroquois and their possessions. Likewise, the tribes inhabiting the western march of the Iroquois must feel their power. Too long had the Cahokia, Kaskaskia, Tamoroa, Sauk, and Fox tribes been allowed to escape Iroquois dominance. A mighty Iroquois raid would successfully serve this dual purpose. It was Kor-Oh-Tin's duty to see that his brother's vision was fulfilled.

The presence of Monsieur Geoff as a spy for the Cardinal was well known to Father Constance, Father Bertrand, and Major Stuart. Indeed, Geoff had accompanied them on other missions in the same capacity. Unfortunately, Geoff was bumbling and not a very clever man. Although Geoff was not aware that he had been exposed, the experience of Major Stuart had revealed his clandestine activities easily. Geoff did not plan ahead and was not very careful in whom he trusted to deliver his messages back to the Cardinal. Consequently, Geoff was not viewed as much of a threat. In fact, it was the Bishop's money that made their missions possible. If the Bishop had other motives than ministering to the poor and needy in the world, it was of little consequence to Father Bertrand and Constance. After all, without the funding of the Church, it would be impossible to do their good work.

On the other hand, the French missionaries were completely unaware of Radisson's capacity as spy for the King. They could not imagine why the King would be interested in a mission to heathens in the New World. Father Bertrand and Constance definitely did not possess an understanding of politics. While aware of the behind-the-scenes conflict between church and state in their native land, they were unaware that the existence of an inland treasure was even a remote possibility. Stuart recognized the political potential, but did not count it with much concern. At any rate, Stuart was unsure of Radisson's true loyalties. Radisson struck Stuart as the type of person who looked out for himself first and foremost. At any rate, Stuart could not imagine Radisson as much of a threat to anyone in the French party.

Of all the three spies, Kor-Oh-Tin was the best disguised and the one that presented the most danger to the missionaries. While Stuart and Sha-Na had reservations about placing any trust in the stranger, Stuart had dismissed the lone native as a serious threat to their mission. Whenever their Christian faith had conflicted with the local native culture on other missions, the conflict was direct and traumatic. Never had the native culture practiced subterfuge to meet the ideological threat. Without any experience in espionage, Father Constance or Bertrand could not imagine any link between their mission and Kateri Tekawetha, the Saint of the Iroquois. Soon this small French missionary party would be the focus of a military action craftily designed to both establish Iroquois dominance over a vast area of the New World and effectively block Catholic evangelism. While Stuart suspected Kor-Oh-Tin as having devious intentions, he had no idea what a serious threat the coming Iroquois raid posed to French colonization. Soon the will of God would surely be revealed even to the heathen in a very dramatic manner. These events would have an impact for centuries to come.

* * * *

The travelers only stayed in the Seneca village one night. Major Stuart recognized their luck at arriving when the potentially hostile natives were preoccupied with their own traditions. He didn't want to tempt fate by overstaying his welcome. Therefore, the Major woke early and pushed his charges to be ready to leave by dawn. Actually, this proved a simple task since none of his party got deeply involved in the Iroquois death feast. This was in part due to the unusual manner in which this culture treated death. The last canoe pushed from the sandy beach into the deep blue water with only a few dogs barking their good-byes. The Seneca village was sleeping off the effects of the feast of the previous night. Obviously, they viewed the French as no threat. The village did not even bother to post sentries. Indeed, Stuart had much to thank God for, especially when he remembered Sha-Na's earlier portrayal of the Seneca as warlike and menacing.

The remainder of the journey to Mere D'Osia would continue southwest on the Genesee River followed by a short portage to another great inland lake. Radisson had explained that they would travel the entire length of this lake called Erie before following a series of swift moving rivers that led generally to the west and their final destination. Although there were other great inland seas that would make their trip easier Radisson intentionally led them away from these lakes because he wanted to avoid some larger native settlements along their shores. Tribes like the Chippewa, Ottawa, and, particularly, the Huron had a reputation for war that rivaled the Iroquois. Years before these tribes had been pushed north and west from their homelands by constant Iroquois raids. Consequently, they held a deep hatred for the Iroquois. They did not hold the white man in high esteem either. Since Sha-Na and her maidens were Iroquois, the missionaries would be in jeopardy if discovered by warriors or hunting parties from these tribes. Early autumn storms on the inland seas also had a reputation of being very severe. Radisson believed that avoiding the remaining lakes would be the least dangerous and most direct course to follow. The leaders of the French party and Sha-Na concurred with his plan.

* * * *

By the time the French priest had reached this point in the story, it was late in the evening at the Bent home. John gave Ida a glance as if to suggest it was time for coffee and a stretch break. The fire was so comfortable especially in contrast to the snowstorm raging outside. On another night the Bent children would be upstairs asleep in their beds. John sensed that the story told by their foreign guest was special and he could not bring himself to deprive them of the opportunity to hear it. John was surprised that everyone was so wide-eyed and alert. This fact emphasized the importance of the moment. In fact, it was all John could do to get Ida to venture to the family kitchen to put on a pot of coffee. Only when he offered to help did Ida finally get up. Father Jacob finally took the hint and said that a break was in order. The good Father moved to the door and went out onto the open porch in the snow. The Bents could see him through the oval etched glass in their oaken front door gazing off into the dark oblivious to the noise of the surrounding storm.

"Why did you stop him in the middle of the story?" Ida exclaimed when she knew that their guest was out of range of their conversation.

"Honey, it's past eleven and he has been going on for hours," John replied slyly.

"Oh, you!" Ida shoved John playfully the way a loving married couple would while enjoying a private joke only they could understand.

"You were as interested as anyone, John Bent, and don't you try to deny it."

"I believe hypnotized is the appropriate term." John shrugged in amazement of the facts Father Jacob had provided about their small town and the meaning of their century-old church tradition. Both John and Ida sensed that they were being enlightened as to the true meaning of the ritual they knew as the "Rural Nativity." To most of the townsfolk in Meredosia, the Rural Nativity had become just a social function repeated annually for petty reasons. To be sure, the ritual collected both food and clothing that benefited the poor and downtrodden within the community. However, this goodness was overshadowed by the bickering of the performers in the play and the covetous vendors that turned out in droves to sell their wares to those who would attend the centuries old event. Like Christmas, the religious festival to which it paid homage, the Rural Nativity was nearly stripped of its meaning and its purpose.

"Ida, I have been praying for guidance in my duties as chairman of the festival committee. I believe that Divine Providence has answered my prayers in the person of Father Jacob."

"Everything and every act has its purpose in God's plan. I know that you are right, John."

"Then what are we waiting for? Grab the tray of drinks and cookies and let's get in the living room before Father Jacob decides to call it a night."

"Oh, Lord, don't let that happen," said Ida.

"He won't, dear. He won't," John said emphatically as Father Jacob came in from the open air porch smiling. The Father gave no hint of being cold as he graciously crossed the living room and took the tray of treats from Ida.

"Are you ready for me to continue?" Father Jacob inquired.

"Absolutely," said John. "I was afraid you would want to retire."

"It is written that there is a time and place for everything. I know that for you the time for this story has come. So let us continue!" Father Jacob easily returned to his role as an animated storyteller. The Bent family hung on his every word. For them their history had truly come alive and they could not wait to hear what was to come next.

*　　*　　*　　*

Like the coureurs de bois who had preceded them, Radisson with the counsel of Sha-Na led the French missionaries along rivers with future names like the Kankakee, the Wabash, the Des Plaines, and, eventually, the Illinois. This route took them deep into the heart of continental North America. While the time spent on these swift flowing waters was peaceful and relaxing, the portages, or treks overland from one waterway to the next, were extremely difficult. This was especially true since their birch-bark canoes were large and their provisions bulky. A portage would often be a distance of many miles up and down hills lushly covered by an interminable wilderness. Not only did the travelers have to carry their equipment, but they also had to push their way through dense foliage. By the time this monumental task was accomplished, everyone was ready for the rest and solace provided by the rivers. Major Stuart's military contingent found it extremely difficult to stay alert to danger given the peaceful lullaby of the rushing water.

After several days journey on a tributary flowing from the great lake which would be known to posterity as Erie, a most extraordinary event occurred. A war party that was later identified as Ottawa by Radisson had nearly surrounded a lone white man on the lakeshore. The man was devoid of companions and his back was protected only by the lapping, white-foamed waves. No one could guess how long the struggle had been in progress. Evidently the man was a fearless and skilled warrior for the beach was strewn by dead and wounded natives. Perhaps there were some white men mixed within the carnage for the distance of the canoes offshore made it hard to determine. While the skirmish was currently at a stalemate, it was inevitable that the white man would eventually succumb. Indeed, the natives seemed to be falling back regrouping for one final onslaught.

Major Stuart, acting in his capacity as commander in all military matters, had immediately directed the canoes to proceed to the white man's aid. Considering the size of the French contingent and their formidable armaments, they would easily be a match for the already battle weary Ottawa. Still, the distance the French canoes had to travel was great enough to leave the success of the rescue highly debatable. Luckily, the Ottawa were so involved with their lone victim that they were initially unaware of the approaching French. This fact provided precious moments in which to literally snatch the white man from the jaws of death.

The entire French party was extremely impressed by the military prowess of the white man fighting valiantly for his life. The man was definitely formidable in stature towering at least a head above the tallest native. A heavy beard and dark, probably Mediterranean, complexion obscured any recognizable facial features from a distance. He wore an armored breastplate and a skirt of chain mail that obviously protected his vital areas from the native weapons. The man was well dressed in embroidered cloth suggesting he was not a common trapper. His bearing and carriage indicated a gentleman as well as a veteran of several military engagements.

The most extraordinary part of the scene witnessed by the approaching French was the weapons employed by the lone swordsman. He could be termed a swordsman by the double-bladed rapier that he wielded in his right hand. The sword's razor sharp edges meted out death both on the forward and backward stroke. This made the man's sword a highly efficient instrument given his obvious propensity for maintaining immense strength in each blow. No native was a match for him head on. Even two or three attacking warriors were maimed at once by his arcing sword. But this fighting edge was not the secret to his ability to withstand such overwhelming numbers.

Stuart given his experience in hand-to-hand combat recognized immediately that the warrior's left hand held the secret to success upon the battlefield. Stuart himself was ambidextrous being able to efficiently wield both a cutlass and rapier. Although right handed, Stuart made most of his kills with his left hand. Surprisingly, most opponents concentrated upon the strong side of their enemy, paying little attention to the other. Stuart guessed that most warriors assumed their opponent would be as weak as they were with one hand. This gave Stuart the edge he needed to approach close combat confidently and end it to his advantage. Obviously, the lone white man on the beach recognized the necessity of using both hands effectively at close quarters as well.

As effective as the rapier was in the right hand of the stranger, this alone was not enough to hold the dreadful Ottawa onslaught at bay. Major Stuart knew that one lone warrior, no matter how skilled in close quarters combat, could never survive such a savage force for a seemingly interminable amount of time. Indeed, Stuart could discern that the stranger was imbued with nearly superhuman strength. This surely had insured his survival of the first few waves of screaming savages. But Stuart instinctively knew there must be more to explain the stranger's continued success in the face of such overwhelming odds. Courage and valor were evident, but Stuart knew the man had to have an "edge". This was the advantage that separated the supreme warrior from the mass of hideous carnage lying wounded or dead upon this field of valor. Blessed was the man who could fight next to a comrade with an "edge". Double blessed was he who possessed an "edge".

At this very moment, Stuart noted a sharp sparkle of sunlight reflected from the stranger's left hand. This glowed as the stranger struck a crushing blow against an unfortunate native skull. The continuing arc of this fist rendered an additional Ottawa unconscious before reversing in a deadly backhand motion. Stuart intuitively reasoned that no mortal hand of mere sinew, blood, and bone could possibly continue to inflict such damage. Any human hand would immediately be rendered useless pulp after several minutes of this severe abuse. Obviously, the stranger wielded some type of weapon. Yet, try as he might, Stuart could detect nothing more than what appeared to be a hand at the end of the stranger's long muscular arm. He guessed it must be some type of mailed glove.

Major Stuart, the veteran warrior of many Continental campaigns, knew that he had identified the stranger's "edge", or battlefield advantage. And Stuart was the one to quickly discern such a trait. The Major understood that his own ambidexterity had condemned many worthy, sometimes even superior, enemies. This skill coupled with his cold-blooded determination had assured his survival. Stuart prayed that the stranger's edge, whatever it might be, would sustain him until rescue was possible.

With a simple motion of his hand Stuart signaled his fusiliers to prepare a volley. Immediately the French soldiers rammed their charges home and prepared their flash pans. There was only grim determination on the faces of these men as the oars silently propelled the French canoes swiftly toward the beach. Stuart had accurately estimated the point where a fusillade would be most effective. His hand slowly rose to give the order to fire. Over forty muskets were prepared to release a deadly hail of lead into the oblivious Ottawa warriors. These natives were so intent upon the destruction of the stranger and his comrades that they ignored the approaching French. For them this would prove to be a deadly mistake.

As the Major's hand descended, he noted that the stranger was still standing as he proudly continued to cut down any approaching enemy. The stranger was also unaware of his impending rescue. Stuart silently prayed that a stray musket ball would not also spell the doom of the stranger at close quarters. The muskets roared in unison sounding more like a cannon than several individual weapons. The stranger obviously was startled at the sound as the canoes were enveloped in an acrid fog of burned gunpowder. The time to Stuart seemed interminable as he waited for this smoke to clear in order to determine the effectiveness of his first volley.

Every last man and woman, including the Huron oarsmen, crouched as low as possible in the canoes anticipating a retaliatory flight of arrows that might already be winging their way. The Iroquois maids and the Reverend Fathers were themselves protected by a human shield of French soldiers. Major Stuart himself personally made sure that Sha-Na was safely covered by his own body. Any airborne missile would first strike Stuart's back leaving the maid unharmed. Again the military man was torn between duty and emotion. Stuart knew he should be calculating his next battlefield move for experience taught that the difference between victory and defeat was often a swift response. Stuart feared that emotion was robbing him of another "edge" that had made him safe on other battlefields. For the sake of his charges he could not let his leadership be compromised.

However, when the smoke cleared it was easy to see that another volley would not be necessary. One solitary figure was left standing upon the sparkling white beach with weapons lowered. He gave the appearance of carrying the entire weight of the world upon his shoulders. The uneven sand about him was strewn with both the wounded and the dead. The effect of the fusillade had been so devastating that any Ottawa resistance was crushed.

"Hurrah!" The French soldiers shouted in unison at the sight of their complete victory. Although few smiled, all were relieved that more perilous hand-to-hand combat would be unnecessary to win this skirmish.

The French fusiliers quickly disembarked from the canoes as they were beached. The military contingent moved as one deploying in a strategic defensive position in anticipation of a possible counterattack. Major Stuart has taught his men well in the art of war. His unethical approach was undoubtedly the reason for his unparalleled success in warfare. While the true gentleman would bravely stand toe-to-toe with the enemy and exchange blows, Stuart reasoned that similar rules often compromised his chance of winning the battle. An equal proficiency with weapons on opposing sides usually resulted in only slaughter with no clear-cut victor. In contrast to other European military armies of the day, especially the British who stood squarely to meet an attack, Stuart had taught his Fusiliers to use unconventional tactics.

The French Fusiliers, whose name was derive from the weapons they carried, demonstrated their ungentlemanly approach to warfare as they worked to secure the beachhead. One line of riflemen kneeled near the canoes with weapons trained toward the forest in defense of their civilian companions. Another contingent fanned out in a semi-circle and advanced toward the brushy cover beyond the beach. These men carried unsheathed cold steel with their rifles slung over their shoulders. Stuart's experience with savages taught him that edged weapons were more effective in the face of a savage attack at a range of less than a musket ball. His men were well trained for close combat. This in tandem with well placed shots from the Fusiliers stationed guarding the canoes would prove a lethal combination to any enemy.

Fortunately the valor of the French Fusiliers was unnecessary on this particular day. Upon reaching the dense underbrush the French discovered that the Ottawa warriors had simply disappeared. Another line of defense was deployed at the forest edge while other soldiers aided the survivors of the fierce Ottawa attack. Sadly, very few had escaped the lethal blows of the savage war clubs. Several of these deadly war clubs laid about the sand in mute testimony of their effectiveness. Their sharp blade embedded in a balanced club with savage hieroglyphs was menacing even now.

Stuart approached the last standing combatant with extreme apprehension. The Major could tell the man was probably European even from the canoe, but he was unsure of the stranger's nationality. If the man was British the stranger might even now have some fight remaining for his mortal enemy, the French. Stuart hoped he would not be forced to face a valiant warrior in such an unequal situation. Fortunately, Stuart's misgiving proved unfounded for, as two Fusiliers approached the man, he began to collapse losing his grip on his weapons. The Fusiliers steadied the stranger as Stuart gave the order to evacuate the survivors to the canoes. The wounded would be tended to when they were relatively safe out on the water.

As Stuart surveyed the battlefield, he made a surprising discovery. The fallen colors of this unfortunate band were retrieved from the sand only to reveal the French Fleur-de-lis. Amazingly, these soldiers were actually French comrades-in-arms. Although Stuart was initially inclined to leave the dead where they fell in order to quickly retreat from danger, this information radically changed his plans. Stuart knew that he could not in good conscious leave valiant soldiers of his adopted country without administering the proper last rites. He ordered a detail to begin burying the dead Frenchmen while the advanced guard maintained their position just inside the tree line that crowded the beach. When all was finished over ten French soldiers had been given a dignified burial officiated by Father Bertrand and Father Constance. There were so few survivors that their purpose for being so far inland remained a puzzle.

In a surprisingly short time the piteous work had been accomplished. The Major gave a signal to embark on the canoes and his troops retired in a cautious and disciplined fashion. Stuart noted as he climbed into his canoe that this nearly annihilated squadron had accounted for themselves very well indeed. The bodies of the dead Ottawa were plentiful, by a quick count nearly five to one. Still success was extremely tentative to say the least. Stuart had made sure that the last man standing had been loaded into his canoe before departure. When this man regained consciousness, Stuart hoped to learn the true purpose of this armed French contingent.

As the French travelers and their entourage rowed steadily away from shore and out of immediate danger, Stuart had the luxury of scrutinizing the stranger he had rescued. The man had several cuts and bruises, but he was in unusually good condition considering the carnage of the battlefield. This man had no life threatening wound so he would live to fight another day. At this moment, Stuart remembered the man's ambidexterity that he used so effectively against the natives. Immediately, Stuart's gaze moved to the man's hands. The right hand was large and powerful, but not unusual in any way. Therefore, the stranger's left hand surely held the key to his battle "edge". Sure enough, protruding from the stranger's left tunic sleeve was a hand unlike anything Stuart had ever seen.

"Iron Hand!" Sha-Na cried with a gasp. Her gaze had come to rest upon the stranger's curious hand at exactly the same time as the Major's. Indeed, the man's hand appeared to be fashioned from some type of metal. Stuart reasoned that this must be the second weapon that the stranger employed so effectively against his enemies.

"Why have you given him this name?" Stuart retorted with a laugh.

"It is no joke Sir, rest assured!" Sha-Na detected sarcasm in the Major's voice and retaliated as if defending herself from attack.

"And none was intended, Mademoiselle." Stuart's voice softened as he detected Sha-Na's wide-eyed expression. For a second Stuart thought he saw a terrible fear cross Sha-Na's face. Stuart certainly did not understand this emotional outburst from the woman he was only beginning to know. He did not wish to risk this budding relationship over something he could not fathom.

"May our Lord protect me from this being." Sha-Na's voice trembled as she sought solace by moving as far from the stranger as possible. Within the confines of their canoe this proved to be extremely difficult. Stuart opened his arms to her and she immediately pressed her face against his chest.

"Iron Hand is a murderer of my people!" Sha-Na tried to muffle her sobs, ashamed at showing weakness so openly. The other natives in the canoe looked away, just as uncomfortable at seeing proud Iroquois cry.

"And how do you know this to be true?" Stuart was still mystified at this sudden emotional outburst.

"How can you in Christian conscience rescue a devil?" said Sha-Na, ignoring the Major's words.

"Has this stranger ever done you any harm?" Stuart decided to press for an answer. Obviously, he needed more information in order to determine how he should handle this situation before the stranger regained consciousness. While Sha-Na sobbed, Stuart noticed that Kor-Oh-Tin, the Iroquois who had mysteriously appeared upon their arrival at the Seneca village, was staring unblinking into his face.

"Sha-Na, you must explain how you know such things."

"Ask my brother, Kor-Oh-Tin, for I cannot continue."

Stuart looked questioningly at the Iroquois, but the man remained inscrutable.

"What must I do to get an explanation for your animosity toward my fellow countryman?" Stuart voice grew louder in frustration.

Kor-Oh-Tin merely turned his gaze to the rippling waves lapping off toward the distant horizon.

"Leave them alone and have pity, Sir!" came the voice of one Sha-Na's accompanying maidens.

"Sha-Na only recently learned of the death of her cousin at the hands of this wicked man. Though death is no stranger to my people, when it strikes close to home who can say how they will react?"

"And how do you know this?" Stuart shook his head in disbelief as he repeated his earlier question. He was trying hard to show empathy.

"For you have been traveling with us many days cut off from communication with your people." Stuart knew Kor-Oh-Tin had a hand in this and was determined to get a response.

"I received the news during the death feast at the village of my people. It had been relayed only recently from the East." Sha-Na reentered the conversation with determination and, possibly, a hint of venom in her voice.

Although Stuart was not acquainted with the stranger reclining in weary unconsciousness at the bow of the canoe, the man was, after all, a European just like himself. A man of such courage in the face of overwhelming odds should not be condemned prematurely and without hard evidence. Stuart found himself struggling not to take sides. Years of military command inclined the Major to dismiss this absurd circumstance as unreasonable emotion. Any other time he would comfort his obvious comrade-in-arms and move on. However, Stuart again found himself rebelling against his instinct. Subconsciously, Stuart was worried that feelings for a woman were compromising his ability to command. Instinct had saved his life many times before this. Stuart could not afford to lose that edge in a savage wilderness.

"Kor-Oh-Tin, please tell us what you know of this man," Stuart asked politely in an even voice that gave absolutely no hint of the turmoil he was holding within. Stuart knew very well that Sha-Na would never tell the source of her information. Stuart hoped he could redirect the conversation and, if not get the answers he required, at least diffuse the anger.

Rather than reply directly to the Major Kor-Oh-Tin simply mumbled something unintelligible in Iroquois dialect.

"Kor-Oh-Tin said all know Iron Hand for what he is." The Iroquois maid translated for the Major after a long silence.

"You have evidence then to prove such an accusation beyond a reasonable doubt?" Stuart calmly asked in a nonjudgmental tone. Again Kor-Oh-Tin mumbled with the hint of a sneer.

"Mademoiselle, tell your Iroquois brother to address me directly, or he may find himself traveling alone." Stuart knew from experience he must be firm in this matter. He grasped the hilt of his short saber and this gesture did not go unnoticed to the disrespectful Iroquois.

"I said I know you will believe the lies of a white man over my truth," Kor-Oh-Tin replied icily. He knew he could not afford to be insolent and risk being ostracized from the French. This would jeopardize his chance to spy for To-Ko-Wan, the Iroquois Shaman.

"Both of you are strangers to me. Since neither of you can nor will relate what you know, I must reserve judgment until later. Given the exhausted state of the stranger, I must provide assistance. I'm sure Mademoiselle Sha-Na, if her faith is true, will approve of such Christian charity. Never forget for a moment that it is my Christian charity that allows you to continue to travel with us."

Kor-Oh-Tin with his pride gave no indication that he had heard what Stuart had said. Therefore, Stuart was inclined to add.

"I am a warrior with a mission. I will protect this Jesuit mission even though they may travel to hell and back. I have no loyalty to any native, Iroquois or other. Do not impede my way!"

Thereafter, all was quiet until the canoes beached on an inviting shore for an evening of rest. Stuart knew his words might have jeopardized any possible relationship with Sha-Na. If this was the case then so be it. A warrior cannot afford emotion. The stranger the Iroquois called Iron Hand was carried to a place of warmth near the campfire where he spent a restful night. Stuart anxiously waited the time when he could hear the stranger's tale. Meanwhile, Stuart fell asleep to the spit and hiss of damp wood on a hot fire and muffled steps of the alert sentry.

Tonty's Identity Revealed

As the travelers continued along a southwest course on the rivers that lead to the heart of the North American continent, there was plenty of time for Major Stuart to unravel the mystery and intrigue that surrounded him. The late summer sun was hot especially when it reflected off the sparkling water as the oarsmen rowed each hard kilometer. The shade along the riverbanks was by contrast very cool and inviting. Stuart made it a point to stop at least twice each day to rest and do some foraging for the evening meal. Fish were abundant and easy to catch. Likewise, fowl and other wildlife offered a veritable smorgasbord of tasty food. The natives in their party were happy to join in the hunting and fishing. These same natives prepared exotic dishes that added variety to what might otherwise become a mundane journey. The subtle changes in foliage as they made the transition from deciduous forest to prairie lands assured there would be no boredom among the French.

Sha-Na reacted icily to Stuart's attempts to talk at length with the stranger Kor-Oh-Tin. Stuart's reluctance to prejudge the stranger had driven a wedge in their budding relationship. More and more, Sha-Na isolated herself from Stuart and his fusiliers. While she willingly served the needs of the Fathers, Sha-Na obviously tried to distance herself and her maidens from the rest of the party. Stuart found he could not talk in confidence with Sha-Na. She remained courteous and aloof. To Stuart's dismay, Sha-Na was more frequently in the company of Kor-Oh-Tin. Stuart frankly did not trust the Iroquois stranger. Brooding animosity between these two was evident to everyone. While Stuart suspected Kor-Oh-Tin of quietly promoting disunity among the travelers, Stuart could expect no answers from any of the Iroquois. Therefore, Stuart was forced to rely upon what information he could elicit from the man Sha-Na called Iron Hand.

At first the stranger slept many hours evidently from complete exhaustion. He only woke up to eat and was fast to fall back asleep. Stuart knew that the skirmish on the beach had been emotionally taxing for the stranger. As the last man standing, the stranger had been on the razor edge defining life and death. Only the unlikely good fortune of an improbable appearance by Stuart's Fusiliers had snatched him from the inevitable jaws of death. From experience, Stuart knew exactly how traumatic this could be; therefore, Stuart did not press the stranger with questions. The journey had turned peaceful and there was plenty of time to learn details. Within a day the jovial personality of the man the Iroquois called Iron Hand was revealed to all.

"What must a man do to get a taste wine?" Iron Hand's voice suddenly boomed followed by a hearty laugh. All were so astounded the days of silence had been broken that it took several minutes for anyone to reply. Stuart was glad that they could finally talk.

"And how are you so sure that we might have any to offer you?" Stuart spoke softly.

"I know firsthand that French troops do not travel without their ration of wine. You could surely spare some for a decrepit old soldier, could you not?" The stranger replied easily as if Stuart was an old comrade.

"We could probably manage a liter at our next rest stop. Meanwhile, you must grace us with the details of how a French force became surrounded on a remote beach in a savage wilderness."

"Monsieur, it is a long story."

"And we certainly have plenty of time," Stuart gestured at the sun that was now high in the sky.

"First I must know how many of my comrades survived the dreadful Ottawa." Iron Hand, like any successful leader of men, was obviously quite concerned.

"Only six and one of those has grievous wounds," Stuart slowly shook his head.

"Ah, non!" Tears appeared to cloud the stranger's eyes. "Over thirty courageous men had stood beside me shoulder to shoulder to meet the savage onslaught. They advanced so fast that we were only able to fire one musket volley before being forced to hand-to-hand combat!"

"Still, you can be secure in the knowledge that you fought with extreme valor. Many more Ottawa lay dead in the sand while their brothers beat a hasty retreat at our appearance." Stuart's words seem to reassure the stranger that his comrades had not died in futility.

"The Ottawa had obviously been following us for quite some time waiting for an opportune time to strike," the stranger continued without encouragement. "The Ottawa have not shown animosity toward us in the past. I do not know what we have done to deserve this fate."

"The Ottawa have been friendly to us as well. Indeed we have several in our group," Stuart agreed. "There must have been some personal vendetta causing the attack."

"Ah, the politics of these savages are far too difficult for a simple man to understand. Perhaps our commerce with their mortal enemies, the Iroquois, or some other clan to the south was perceived as a threat," the man called Iron Hand sighed.

"Or, they were covetous of your weapons and supplies," Stuart gave another plausible explanation.

"Ah, 'tis true, Mon ami!" The stranger exclaimed heartily as if trying to shake off his unhappiness. "In my limited experience with the savages, I have discovered many are deceitful thieves. They are like children without any sense of order."

The stranger paused for Stuart to affirm his observation. This did not come. Stuart had long since learned not to speak ill of anyone lest retribution come swiftly and abundantly. Major Stuart was tired of small talk and wanted answers, so he came to the point.

"What brings you to this remote wilderness, Monsieur?"

"I could ask you the same question," the stranger replied evasively. Stuart was wondering if this was the extent of the information that he would receive when the stranger began to talk.

"I am a captain in the force commanded by Robert Cavelier, Sieur de la Salle. I'm Italian by birth, but served France faithfully in the Sicilian Wars. You and I are much the same, are we not? You serve France, yet I detect an English birthright in your voice."

"You may serve a King, but my allegiance currently is to my employers. Please continue with your story." Stuart did not want to get involve in a lengthy political discussion at this point.

"Commander Cavelier has been instructed by our King Louis to explore these lands and claim them for France. My mission is to scout the area surrounding the inland seas and the region inland to the southwest that has come to be known as Illinois. This information will help to determine how best to proceed with colonization. The balance of power in Europe may well be determined by who controls this New World. Isn't it an apt name for a pristine wilderness yet unspoiled by our white politics?" The stranger's concentration on telling his story was again on a tangent.

"Oui, oui, now please continue! Must everything take so long in Italy?"

Stuart's impatience was beginning to show in his voice.

The stranger just laughed.

"You confirm my suspicions that you have been to Italy. From the way you fight you are probably a veteran of our recent wars as well."

This time before Stuart could speak the Italian went back to his story.

"Perhaps you are familiar with Louis Joliet and Father Marquette who preceded us to this land?"

"We are aware of the benevolent mission of these two men." Stuart replied tersely, hoping the stranger would continue. With all these questions, he was beginning to wonder who was getting more information. The Italian stranger was very clever as well as likeable.

"I see you have clergy in your entourage. Can I assume you are on a mission to the savages? Or, if I may be so bold, is their another purpose for your trek into this wilderness?" Both men knew this was in reference to the rumor throughout the French realm. The rumor suggested that the Church be in search of a treasure to rival that of the Incas and the Aztecs. Considering the expanse of land remaining unexplored, such a discovery was still in the realm of possibility. Stuart detested politics yet even here in a wilderness thousands of kilometers from Europe he was being forced to play the game of cat and mouse.

"You are correct in your first assumption, Monsieur. My military contingent is a mercenary force providing some means of protection to the good Fathers as they proceed with the work of God."

"Since our motivation is similar and we are both subjects of King Louis, we must make a pact to assist one another in our mutual endeavors." The stranger was now trying to form an alliance. With only few men, no supplies, and marooned in an inhospitable wilderness he had no other alternative. The stranger was at the mercy of the benevolence of a bunch of priests. This is the fortune of war.

"You must negotiate your pact with my employers, Father Bertrand and Father Constance. I only go where they tell me." Being a man of his word, Stuart did not want to commit his support prematurely.

"Then I will take the matter up with them at our next land fall, Monsieur." The stranger turned his gaze to the impenetrable forest passing by the starboard side of their canoe. He obviously wanted to be left alone.

"We still do not know your name, Monsieur." Stuart felt that he still did not know much about the stranger.

"Forgive me. My name is Henri Tonty. As I said, I serve Robert Cavelier, Sieur de la Salle."

"And your disability?" Stuart pointed to the metal hand.

"I do not consider it as such. I'm sure my enemies don't either." Tonty referred to the way he had used it on the battlefield.

"Do you not wish to speak of it?"

"Actually I'm quite proud of it. I lost it honorably in battle. It is now made of copper and very serviceable as a weapon," Tonty spoke with confidence.

"Obviously, since you already have a reputation among the natives of this continent," Stuart replied respectfully. He was happy that Henry Tonty was a friend rather than a foe.

"Why do you say that?"

"Our Iroquois friends call you Iron Hand. Given their fierce reputation for war, you surely must have done something to earn their respect."

"We have had our disagreements," Tonty chuckled evasively.

"Do you know any reason for the Iroquois to fear you?"

"Like it or not, alliances are the key to control of this vast wilderness, but I gathered from your previous comments that you did not wish to be bored with politics."

"From a practical security standpoint I must know. We have natives from several clans in our entourage. If you are to travel with us, I must foresee problems before they occur. If the Ottawa, the Huron, and the Iroquois all hate you and they are mortal enemies, your life in this wilderness is not worth a fig," Stuart said with finality.

"The Iroquois are being courted by the English to form a powerful alliance. Given the strength of the Iroquois nation in this New World the French cannot let this happen. I'm sure you have heard of the Iroquois reputation for war. Their very name kindles fears in everyone even Europeans. Commander Cavelier has been negotiating with the Iroquois and is intent on forming an alliance with them. It will be a delicate balance but I think we can keep the Huron in the French camp as well. Lord Frontenac has already laid a strong foundation for peace among the various clans within the lands controlled by France."

"No wonder the Ottawa were so intent on destroying you on the beach. I'm told by Radisson that the Ottawa have much in common with the Huron, especially their hatred for the Iroquois," Stuart said matter-of-factly.

"Me thinks that the attack was more motivated by thievery than revenge. After all, our possessions are very attractive to such poor bastards!" Tonty spoke assuredly.

"You don't have much respect for the natives, do you?" Stuart guessed from their conversation that Tonty was a man who lived, and would eventually die, by the sword. He had little of the milk of human kindness.

Tonty did not reply to Stuart's observation, nor did he give any indication that he took offense.

"My sources say that you do not have the love of the Iroquois either," Stuart continued probing for details.

"How so?" Tonty looked puzzled.

"An Iroquois member of our party immediately knew who you were when they first saw you on the beach. For one so recent to this new land, you are quite well known."

"So they see me as an enemy?"

"There was both fear and hatred in their tone," Stuart confirmed.

"I certainly hope that is not true, Mon Ami," Tonty shook his head. "It is vital that we secure Iroquois support against the English. Iroquois animosity could be very detrimental to our fortunes in this land."

"Then you have not used your famous Iron Hand in battle against the Iroquois?"

"On the contrary, I have met with the leaders of the Five Nations of the Iroquois to offer peace and an alliance. The deceitful Ottawa and Huron are the ones I relish meeting in battle. I understand why the Iroquois have only disdain for them. We are in agreement and the Iroquois should only have praise for French actions thus far."

"And you have not slain innocent Iroquois women and children?" Stuart was puzzled with the information so far.

"Non, non!" Tonty replied.

Regardless of what else this Italian might be Stuart was inclined to believe the man was not a liar.

"May I inquire who among your party is spreading lies about me? I may have to deal with this matter firsthand," Tonty was becoming excited. This suggested that Tonty wanted to maintain an impeccable if not entirely controversial reputation. Stuart respected Tonty for that.

"We recently spent a night at a Seneca village. This must have been where they heard the story."

"And what exactly was the story about me?"

"Only that a man known as Iron Hand had slain innocent Iroquois women and children."

"It is truly a lie, Monsieur. I must find out who would tell such a lie. It must be one of these bloody savages, a Huron perhaps. Non, non. I'll wager it was an Iroquois who supports the old ways. My mission to ally with the Iroquois cannot afford these lies to be told!" Tonty said with resolve.

"What do you mean by the old ways?" Stuart was beginning to understand the situation but he wanted Tonty to explain further.

"You of all people must realize the hatred held by many of these savages for the Catholic Church. The Church is in direct conflict with their so-called religion. Many would do anything to stop its missionaries among their people. You must know how many missionaries these stinking pigs have martyred. The Iroquois actually cooked and ate one priest on an Inland Sea not far from here only a few years ago. The English do not push their Protestant religion like we French Catholics. We must save the world from hell and damnation. Too bad that our missionary impetus puts us at a great disadvantage politically in this New World. This above all things may eventually doom our efforts to colonize this new land."

"I had never realized the politics of our action until now," Stuart said regretfully.

"Then realize now and return to France before it is too late. Your proselytizing puts the life of every Frenchman in jeopardy. These pigs can never be saved, nor do they want to be. Let them live blissful lives in squalor as God intended."

"You obviously have no regard for the salvation of mankind," Stuart was becoming defensive.

"And you, Monsieur, erroneously class these savages as men. They are but pawns to be used in the grand scheme of world politics. They only serve a purpose to extend white dominance as God intended."

"I'm not willing to debate you, Monsieur. However, you are a fine one to talk. You have successfully made mortal enemies, the Iroquois and Huron, agree on one thing. This would be a hatred for you."

"As I said, Major, I will find the one who spreads lies about me. When I do, I will resolve the situation. You must assist me in learning which savage I must kill," Tonty's anger was barely constrained.

"I will do what I can. Any threat to a Frenchman is a threat to me, but it may take some time and patience to unravel this mystery." Stuart had a suspect in mind but he did not wish to reveal this to Tonty so soon. Stuart wanted time to decide the proper course of action. Rash actions often cause regrettable results.

"Oui, Major Stuart, we have ample time to deal with this threat. It is a long trek to the interior of this savage land." Tonty ended the conversation this time by turning his complete attention to the scenery. Stuart was willing to allow this as he had acquired the information he needed. Stuart understood Tonty's subtle implication that they would be traveling companions. Stuart was inclined to let this happen. After all, Tonty was a dangerous man on a mission for a despotic king who wanted to rule the world. Tonty could do less damage within Stuart's sight than if he were allowed to go it alone.

"We will speak of this later, Monsieur." Stuart pulled the brim of his plumed hat down over his eyes to shade the glare of the midday sun reflecting upon the water. Like it or not, politics had become a problem within the Major's entourage. He must deal with these situations decisively.

The Iroquois in the French missionary party now shunned the company of Major Stuart and his men. Since Iron Hand had been offered comfort, the Iroquois apparently now viewed them as enemies. Sha-Na was torn between her affection for Major Stuart and the solace of her people. While one might expect her to cling to the French and her new religion, blood ties were exerting a strong influence. Kor-Oh-Tin was quickly becoming the undesignated leader of this political force.

Likewise, the Huron laborers who so faithfully served the French missionaries were distancing themselves from Stuart and his men. They had witnessed the battle between their Ottawa kinsmen and the French. Although the Huron serving the French could not personally know the slain Ottawa, they were obviously viewed as allies. Stuart shook his head at this sudden turn of events. The peaceful missionary band on an errand for God had turned into a hotbed of hate and discontent in only a few short days. Stuart would have to address the situation or face a major conflict between his traveling companions. Tension was in the air and building by the day.

Although Major Stuart was beginning to guess something was amiss, he would probably have been surprised to find that his group was now a mixture of spies. Each spy owed allegiance to a different master. There were the Royalists like Henri Tonty who were intent in expanding the French empire for their Sun King. Certainly, there were those including Monsieur Geoff who wished to further the Churches' temporal power here on earth by adding treasure and land to its coffers. Then there were those servants of the Church namely Constance and Bertrand with no other agenda than to minister to and convert the natives of this new land. Finally there was the native To-Ko-Wan who owed allegiance to his own clan and heathen gods. For added spice, there was a garnish of men like Radisson with a purely mercenary inclination to pillage the abundant resources of the wilderness. Stuart sensed it would surely take divine intervention for such a diverse group to survive in this savage uncharted wilderness.

* * * *

Under Radisson's experienced guidance, the French missionaries were soon off the large inland lake that would later be known as Erie and traveling in a southwesterly direction on a major tributary river. Soon the travelers would be faced with portages, traveling by foot overland from one major river to another. Each portage, despite the experience of Radisson and the strength of his Huron companions, would prove difficult given the number of women in the party and the large amount of supplies. Originally, they had discussed following a more northerly route recently traveled by Marquette and Joliet that led across upper Michigan. However, Tonty suggested and Radisson confirmed that a southwestern route led more directly to the location called Mere D'Osia. Both Father Bertrand and Father Constance were adamant that this would be the sight of their new mission because their predecessor Father Marquette had favored it.

The northern route along the Grand River to the inland sea to be called Lake Michigan also led directly through Ottawa territory. Presently, the Ottawa were engaged in protecting their homeland from the continuous encroachment of the Iroquois. While the Ottawa were not as fierce as the Iroquois, they still tenaciously defended themselves against any foreign power. It was best that the missionaries not place themselves between two powerful forces. War parties from both clans were constantly roaming this northern wilderness. The women and supplies traveling with the French would be a welcome prize. Tonty readily supported this route since he wanted to avoid any contact with the tribe that nearly annihilated his force on the Lake Erie beach.

Unfortunately, the southwestern route was not entirely safe for travel either. This easily negotiable river highway led through land claimed by both the Miami and the Kickapoo. While the Miami were known as being friendly to strangers, the Kickapoo had a reputation for being very disagreeable. Radisson recounted stories of comrades who had suffered extremely harsh treatment from the Kickapoo. Many Coeur de Bois, the French adventurers, had lost the work of several trapping seasons to these prairie natives. Traveling first upon the Kankakee River and then to the Illinois River should avoid a chance encounter with the Kickapoo. Still, a stray Kickapoo hunting party could conceivably venture to these waterways. Even though their southwesterly route was relatively uninhabited, Radisson knew they must be constantly on guard. The missionaries could not let the days of quiet river travel give them a false sense of security. The wilderness of 17th century America could be horribly unforgiving to the smallest mistake. Survival of the fittest was very real here. Radisson had vowed long ago never to endure native slavery again.

At the first opportunity, Henri Tonty discussed his tenuous status with Father Constance and Father Bertrand. Tonty had heard from his master La Salle's sources at the court in Versailles that Bishop Colbert had dispatched scouts to this New World in search of treasure. Quite possibly, this group was one such party disguised on a mission of mercy. The presence of the French Fusiliers seemed to confirm Tonty's suspicion. Most Jesuit priests had a well known disdain for the military. Consequently, Jesuit priests tended to travel alone and unguarded. If Tonty was correct in assuming that these travelers were on a mission to boost the fortunes of the Church, then any royalist would be viewed as an enemy. This made Tonty very uneasy due to his association with royalist forces bent on colonizing this New World and claiming its riches for the crown. However, Tonty's fear was somewhat assuaged when both Jesuit priests welcomed him with open arms. One evening over a steaming bowl of broth made from wild duck, Tonty and the Fathers had a long discussion about the trip before them.

"You are quite recovered from your ordeal, my son?" Father Constance asked with sincere concern. Father Bertrand also chimed in his sympathy while Major Stuart, Sha-Na, and Kor-Oh-Tin sat in quiet observation by the blazing campfire.

"Oui, Padre," Tonty nodded affirmation as his memory flashed back to his narrow escape from a savage war club.

"And your companions are recovering as well I am told," Father Bertrand stated expecting no reply.

"Oui, although my corporal is quite weak from extreme loss of blood. Even with constant attention by your people he remains very frail. I fear it will be many weeks before he can cope with the stress of wilderness travel on his own."

"Oh, I hope you are not contemplating leaving our company any time soon!" Father Constance exclaimed as if such a notion was entirely beyond contemplation.

"Our Christian concern for all God's children would not allow us to put you in this peril. You must travel with us inland, unless of course you plan on returning to Montreal," Father Bertrand added.

"From your guide, Monsieur Radisson, I have learned you are destined to establish a mission among the natives called Peoria," replied Tonty.

"This is our commission from God. There is already a French mission called Mere D'Osia situated along an interior river. The natives often come there to hear the word of our Lord. Father Marquette preceded us there and it was his hope to return one day. Unfortunately, that cannot happen." Father Constance hung his head in sadness.

"The news of his death was a tragedy," Tonty said.

"And for this reason we cannot knowingly allow other Frenchmen to place themselves in harms way. Please consider remaining with us at least until your men are completely recovered," Father Constance replied.

"Father, despite our brush with death, you cannot imagine how fortunate we were to have stumbled upon your party. It seems that we share the same destination."

"To Mere D'Osia?" Father Bertrand said inquisitively.

"Oui, bien sur," Tonty smiled.

"May I inquire for what purpose?" Stuart could not resist entering the conversation. "You cannot be concerned with the spiritual life of these, what did you call them, savages?"

"I will be only too happy to share the purpose for my trip to the interior, Monsieur," said Tonty suddenly in a jovial mood, for he sensed things going his way.

"Please proceed," Stuart said sarcastically.

"I was sent by my superior, Robert Cavelier, Sieur de la Salle, to locate a site for French colonists destined for this new land. Earlier exploration indicates that the climate near the Mere D'Osia mission is quite comparable to that of France. The land is fertile as well and you already know the abundance of wild game."

"Colonists can't be coming anytime soon!" Stuart replied with surprise on his face.

"As we speak, La Salle's emissaries are actively soliciting adventurous Frenchmen skilled in crafts necessary for communal life to join an expedition to the Illinois country. Quite a tidy sum of money has been offered by the King to those who will join and bring their family." Tonty spoke convincingly.

"Considering the continuing conflict among the various native clans as well as the English animosity, I wonder if the perils of such a trip are being fairly communicated to these potential colonists," Stuart said. He looked at the priests as if asking them to support him in this argument.

"The French army will protect its citizens from any such peril," Tonty replied.

"Like your soldiers were able to protect themselves from the Ottawa?" Stuart laughed. Tonty shrugged, not wanting to argue.

"At any rate," said Father Bertrand, "It is truly divine intervention that caused our paths to cross. Surely it is God's will that you accompany us to the interior."

"Now that I know I must contend with royalist soldiers in our midst, I wonder what I'm to do with a deceitful Iroquois," Stuart said inquisitively to the priests. He had learned long ago he could not argue with either Constance or Bertrand. Stuart knew the good Fathers would never expel anyone even an enemy from their presence. Stuart only wanted them to affirm that he must endure the devious stranger called Kor-Oh-Tin as well. Stuart sipped the steaming broth while awaiting a reply.

"Men of peace are always welcome among us, my son, regardless of their lineage," Father Constance responded. The Iroquois sat stoically listening to the conversation.

"Are they welcome even if they use lies to disrupt the tranquility of our party?" Stuart continued.

"To what are you referring, my son?" Father Constance asked.

"You know very well what I mean!" Stuart said. He had told the priests earlier about his suspicion that Kor-Oh-Tin had lied about Tonty's involvement with the massacre of Iroquois women and children. Stuart decided to bring to matter to resolution rather than letting it continue to be a divisive element among the travelers.

Sha-Na neither defended nor spoke against her Iroquois kinsman. She had come to trust Major Stuart. Sha-Na was willing to let the matter be resolved without her intervention. She watched the scene unfold with interest.

"Are you the one spreading the rumors about Monsieur Tonty?" Father Constance addressed Kor-Oh-Tin directly. The Iroquois stared with a smirk upon his face. For a moment Stuart thought the native might spit at the priest to show his contempt.

"If you do not deny this allegation, then we must assume it is true," Father Constance said demandingly.

"What good is the word of a savage against that of a Frenchman?" Kor-Oh-Tin venomously broke his silence.

"Ma Fille, you obviously have no appreciation for the Christian ethic." Father Constance said calmly and continued.

"What evidence do you have to prove this terrible claim?"

The Iroquois continued to stare into the fire that was becoming smoldering red coals.

"Ma Fille, I cannot fairly judge your motivation if you will not speak," Father Constance implored.

"Don't speak to me with your weak Christian words. I owe allegiance to the old spirits of the land. You cannot judge me."

"You are openly hostile to the people of Christ. Since spreading that word is our mission, you must accept this or be expelled from our group. Do you understand?" Father Bertrand spoke as if correcting a child.

Seeing no support from anyone gathered around the campfire, even his Iroquois kin, Kor-Oh-Tin ceremoniously stood up, rolled his blanket up, and strode away into the night. Everyone knew that he would not continue the journey with them the next day. Stuart breathed a sigh of relief that this divisive element was gone. However, in the back of his mind he wondered if Kor-Oh-Tin would be even more dangerous to them out of sight.

* * * *

Water was the preferred method of travel as it had been since man first trod this land. Innumerable rivers and streams offering easy travel to nearly all points of the compass intertwined interior North America. The French missionaries took advantage of this blessing and had only to endure minor portages across rough terrain. Soon the land was changing noticeably. Forests predominated by conifers gradually gave way to mixed deciduous trees. While these hardwoods shaded the river routes with a cathedral of green, one had only to venture a short distance away from the riverbank to encounter a vast terrain filled with tall broad stemmed grasses. Viewed from high promontories along the river this grassland actually resembled an ocean as the wind played upon its surface from horizon to horizon. Travel across this grassland would be extremely difficult if not impossible for the group. Everyone thanked God daily in their prayers for the rivers that made their travel easier.

The increasing distance from civilization seemed to increase the tranquility of the missionary group. A divided group of warring factions most feared by Major Stuart happily did not materialize. Sha-Na apparently trusted Jon Stuart so much that she accepted his judgment regarding Tonty and his companions. Given the benefit of the doubt regarding the story that he was a murderer of Iroquois, Tonty was able to win the friendship of everyone with his naturally jovial personality. Many evenings were passed quite enjoyably with his stories of the continental wars. The Iroquois maids were especially enamoured by the colorful description of places they could barely imagine. The quick departure of Kor-Oh-Tin seemed to remove a storm cloud that had once threatened the tranquility of the group. Stuart's job as escort was made easier since he could now concentrate on the external security of the travelers, rather than dealing with constant internal bickering. Spirits were high as the entire group anticipated a new adventure of providing Christian benevolence to the interior natives.

Likewise, Kor-Oh-Tin, the expelled Iroquois warrior, continued to travel west. He was never very far from the French travelers that had sent him packing. This crafty native had realized that traveling with the French would not facilitate his mission of scouting the interior and reporting to his brother To-Ko-Wan. Kor-Oh-Tin was a man of strong faith in the old ways. Even in silence, everyone knew his view of the new religion called Christianity. After all, a god that would allow himself to be nailed to a tree could not be a powerful and enduring force. The forest spirits would eventually take revenge upon everyone who worshipped this false god.

Kor-Oh-Tin also verified what his brother To-Ko-Wan had suspected. Sha-Na, the converted Iroquois maiden traveling with the French, was very close to Kateri Tekawetha. Kateri was a strong Iroquois voice for conversion to Christianity. If she could be silenced, a major blow would be struck against the new religion. Unfortunately, To-Ko-Wan had related the fact that Kateri was very well protected against assassins in the fortress of Montreal. The Iroquois shaman needed a way to make Kateri more vulnerable. From his conversations with Sha-Na, Kor-Oh-Tin had learned that Sha-Na and Kateri were blood sisters. In the Iroquois matriarchal tribe these women had a common grandmother making their relationship very close indeed. Therefore, Sha-Na might prove to be the key to the destruction of Christianity among the Iroquois people. Perhaps, Kor-Oh-Tin would eventually have the opportunity to kidnap Sha-Na and use her for this purpose. Kor-Oh-Tin could only imagine the prestige among his people if he could bring such a thing to pass. As the French moved inland so did their human shadow Kor-Oh-Tin. When they reached their destination, he would report back to To-Ko-Wan. Then a Mohawk war party from the most feared nation of the Iroquois would bring destruction upon these French Christians and the Iroquois vassals that had the audacity to listen to their false words. Stuart had guessed correctly that Kor-Oh-Tin would be more trouble out of his sight.

*   *   *   *

Eventually the travelers found their way to a wide river that flowed lazily in a southwestern direction through the heart of the prairie grassland. Confidently, Pierre Radisson said they were nearing their final destination of the French outpost known as Mere D'Osia. This was happy news since they would have little time to prepare to spend a winter on the prairie. The river bluffs were ablaze with sparkling autumn colors. As the cool wind blew among the tall cottonwoods along the river bundles of leaves fell into the calm pools along the riverbank. Each morning a blanket of glistening diamonds engulfed their sleeping encampment. Each afternoon the call of ducks and geese could be heard in the powder blue sky as these creatures made their way south for the coming winter. Father Bertrand and Father Constance feared there would barely be enough time to construct comfortable quarters to help them survive the cold winter blasts. Major Stuart wanted a chance to hunt game to meet their winter food requirements. Although they had adequate provisions of flour, meal and dried goods the meat would be a welcome and tasty addition. After many weeks of travel, all were ready for the long journey to end.

Given this state of mind you can easily imagine the joy as the travelers rounded a bend in the river to behold log houses with shake roofs reminiscent of those they had left back home. There on a promontory back from the river sat a French oasis amid the surrounding wilderness. Smoke curled in wispy spirals from red brick chimneys as manicured gardens filled with late blooming flowers seemed to cry welcome. A magnificent church steeple thrust its way to heaven. Dogs barked amid the sounds of laughter and conversation. A hint of fresh baked bread filled the air. At this sight more than one European had the passing emotion of homesickness and each briefly questioned whatever possessed them to wander so far from their beloved homeland.

On the periphery of this distinctly Old World encampment were the bonfires and huts of the natives. Like their European brethren, the natives were engaged in domestic chores as well. Women washed garments in a quiet pool along the riverbank. Children ran back and forth in the tall green grass playing games and laughing. Native men squatted near campfires talking quietly while they lashed bird points to arrow shafts or chipped blades from creamy smooth flint and chert. The entire scene was one of peace and tranquility. Obviously, this location would be a fine place to start a ministry. As the travelers beached their long birch-bark canoes in the sand a contingent from the village had already arrived to welcome them with open arms. Certainly, God had answered their prayers for a safe arrival.

The welcoming committee approaching from the settlement consisted of a black robed priest, men of fair skin dressed in flannel and buckskin, and native men bare above the waist with leather and moccasins beneath. Quite appropriately some native children carried a rough-hewn cross of green oak and other church relics. Obviously, the church was the main edifice in this wilderness village and churchmen were its designated leaders. An older man dressed in the plain black robe of a Jesuit and wearing a wide brimmed black hat to protect himself from the glare of the noonday sun stepped forward with arms widespread to greet the travelers. Everyone was smiling and laughing on this happy occasion. The arrival of visitors was a rare treat that must be savored.

"Brothers in Christ, it is indeed an honor to welcome you to our most humble outpost in the wilderness." The Jesuit Priest moved to shake hands with everyone even the native oarsmen.

"I am Father Bertrand and this is Father Constance." Everyone exchanged greetings as introductions were completed.

"My name is Father Osia." The priest continued in a jovial voice. "Please walk with us back to town and join us in a feast of thanksgiving for your safe journey across the continent. What act of Providence has guided you to this place?" Father Osia was evidently quite eager for conversation and news from the outside world.

"Like you we are on a mission of mercy." Father Bertrand responded for the travelers. "Bishop Colbert has directed us to minister to the natives of this continent who thirst for the word of God."

"It is good to know that our leaders continue to support our work throughout the world," Father Osia chuckled. "But, I must know how you happened to stumble upon our lonely outpost in this vast wilderness. The fame of Fathers Bertrand and Constance as evangelists to the world is well known to the Jesuit order. Have you succeeded in converting the entire Orient so that you now may turn your attention to the west?"

"Actually it was Father Marquette's last wish that a major effort be mounted to aid and convert the natives of this region. According to his companion Louis

Joliet, the good Father was quite fond of these particular natives." Father Bertrand answered.

"And Monsieur Joliet was enamored with the physical aspect of this region of many rivers. I'm told that it reminded him of his boyhood home in France, although it is said the winters here can be very taxing." Father Constance moved to join in the conversation.

"Oui, it is true the winters are freezing and the snow is unrelenting." Father Osia agreed. "But, if one knows how to prepare then even the winter season is a beautiful blessing to behold."

"Well, I'm sure we will know soon enough about this blessing of yours." Major Stuart remarked rather sarcastically while Sha-Na slapped his shoulder playfully.

"Then you plan to remain with us for awhile. I must confess that this is so overwhelming that I'm afraid to ask in so many words lest it be but a dream." Father Osia held his breath awaiting an answer.

"Dear Brother Osia, we are at your service for as long as we are required. Providence has guided our entire life work and it has led us to this point. God grant that we can continue to do his work in this world as long a breath remains in us," Father Constance said humbly.

"Our King has ambitious plans to colonize this region. We must make sure that our brothers who make the long and difficult journey from France are greeted with at least a little civilization." Father Constance added.

"It will take much labor to make this wilderness secure and hospitable to our French brothers used to the amenities of a civilized life." Father Osia commented matter-of-factly.

"I wholeheartedly concur!" said Major Stuart.

"Well, we have one of the King's best among us who is determined that colonization will succeed," Father Bertrand referred to Monsieur Tonty.

"The plan is already being implemented. Soon French settlers by the hundreds will be added to your flock. You may depend upon this for my master Robert Cavelier, Sieur de La Salle, has said it will happen. He is a man of determination." Tonty spoke with great confidence.

"Soon I will further explore this region and establish forts at key sites for the security of the colonists. In no time a New France will blossom before our eyes." The manner in which Tonty spoke suggested that such a dream might be possible.

"Well, we must first survive the fast approaching winter," said Major Stuart bringing the travelers back to reality. "The ice on the calm river inlets at night tells me that we have only a few weeks to build protection against the cold winter to come. Perhaps, Father Osia, you can provide some assistance with this. In turn, we have brought provisions that I'm sure you will find most welcome."

"Of course, Mon Fille. You have only to ask." Father Osia answered. "You need not be too concerned with the weather. We can make room for you quite comfortably I believe. Now let us move your things up to the town and we can discuss your future with us after supper tonight."

And so began the ministry of Father Bertrand and Father Constance in the region to become known as Illinois. Father Osia's encampment along one of the main tributaries of the mighty Mississippi River had already established a strong Christian presence among the natives of this area. A log church had been erected and services were held regularly. Other buildings such as a communal kitchen, bakery, and butcher shop had been built to meet the needs of a growing French contingent. While most of the French now were engaged in hunting and trapping, Father Osia's village provided the basis for a sedentary community. Both Father Constance and Father Bertrand knew that by contributing their labor French colonists unaccustomed to a harsh wilderness would have a chance to survive and flourish. With determination the newly arrived travelers put all their resources into establishing a strong base for Christianity in this wilderness. When the snows of winter finally arrived, there were more natives encamped around the French settlement that ever before. While the chance to trade had lured the natives here before, it was the Christian element that made their numbers endure and grow. A large oak-hewn cross over thirty feet in height was raised upon the banks of the river in memory of the love Father Marquette had for this region. It became a beacon of light for everyone, regardless of race, who desired peace and compassion.

Indeed, the traveler's first winter in the wilderness was frigid and harsh. Wood and mortar no matter how thick could not completely take the edge off the cold wind that blew harshly from the northwest. For weeks a blanket of snow was piled high upon the roofs and outside the walls of the French cabins. The only tolerable place to be was next to the huge fires that were continuously stoked in the red brick fireplaces. Frostbite was a common affliction and death by exposure was a constant threat to the new comers. The French were constantly amazed at how the natives could endure such extreme weather protected only by the mud and stick huts they erected along the periphery of the French settlement.

The French learned that modern equipment like their matchlock rifles were no substitute for the traditional methods employed by the natives. This was especially true of hunting techniques when it came to providing meat for a multitude of hungry people. Major Stuart, Henri Tonty, and Monsieur Geoff had the opportunity to learn this firsthand when the stores of meat got low as the deep drifted snow kept all but the most daring hunters around the cozy crackling campfire. Realizing the sad situation that Mere D'Osia would soon face without meat to supplement the diet of dried fruit, vegetables (squash and beans), and cornmeal, Major Stuart volunteered to lead a group of fusiliers on a mission to replenish the meat stores. Incidentally, Mere D'Osia was the new name coined by the missionaries for their settlement along the riverbank of this tributary to the mighty father of waters, known to the natives as the Mississippi. Unskilled in the ways of this wilderness, the hearty Frenchmen soon learned that it was impossible to wade the deep snows to get close to enough animals to harvest. At first thought this sounds implausible when one considers that the matchlocks carried by the French had a range of up to 300 meters. This was an advantage over the crude bows of the natives. Also, it was true that in deep drifted snows upon the prairie large cloven-hoofed animals like buffalo, elk, and deer tended to remain in a close knit herd until the weather improved. However, the French, unskilled in the stealth required to successfully hunt in this wilderness, found that they spooked the animals long before they could come into range with their matchlocks. It was indeed a sad and weary hunting party that returned to Mere D'Osia with only four white-tailed deer to assuage the hunger of the settlement.

Still, the French hunters were happily welcomed back into the bosom of Christian fellowship, especially by their native brothers who good-naturedly joked about the lack of success with the "fire sticks" as they had come to be called. These natives also asked if the French would be willing to help with a tribal method for taking meat during the winter that had been used successfully by the natives for centuries. Curious to discover exactly how large quantities of meat could be taken in inclement weather, the French jovially volunteered their services.

It was determined that elk would be the game to be pursued because these large animals would yield the most meat to satisfy the requirements of the settlement. While scouting the French had learned that elk tend to assemble in breaks of trees that give them both food from the bark and shelter from the heavy snow. Actually the elk trample paths into and out of these thickets and the snow drifts tend to be quite high on each side. These numerous paths provided easy escape routes for the elk that foiled the success of the French hunters.

The natives used these paths to their advantage. Large rawhide snares were prepared that could be set within the escape route of the elk. Where the snow was not deep enough to assure the elk would run into the snare, breaks of pine limbs and brush were assembled and placed along the elk paths. By running the elk through the rawhide traps the rawhide thongs would wrap around the neck of the beasts. Snared elk would then drag the poles of the trap until it became entangled in brush at the next thicket along the escape route. As the animal jerked and pulled to free itself, the rawhide knot would further constrict around the beast's neck and eventually result in death.

The whole assemblage of natives, even women and older children, would take part in the elk hunt. Scouts would locate the elk herds in the thickets. At night, despite the severe cold, the snares would be set along the elk route. The next morning everyone would descend upon the elk thicket screaming and yelling to force the animals to attempt escape. Some elk would be ambushed as they fled along their escape path. Others would become entangled in the snares and could easily be tracked down. It was quite amazing how much meat could be taken in just one night of hunting in this manner. The natives all pitched in to skin and prepare the meat. It was divided equally among the hunters and stored in caches for future use. Three or four nights of using this method to hunt elk yielded provisions for over one month. The practice of equal work and equal rewards seemed to work quite well in this primitive environment.

The French were so impressed with this method of hunting elk that they inquired about methods to hunt other beasts. Soon the local natives treated the French to a winter bison hunt that they would remember all their lives. To begin with, the newly arrived French travelers, except for Pierre Radisson, had never encountered a bison. Since the bison behaved much like cattle, there was usually a herd within one day walking distance in any direction from Mere D'Osia. Curious to actually see one of these beasts, all the French fusiliers, including Major Stuart, constantly asked the natives for an opportunity to scout and hunt this exotic animal.

Finally, one balmy day in mid-winter when the temperature hovered around freezing several natives guided a contingent of French hunters out on the prairie. Due to the warmth the top layer of soil was thawing. The combination of mud, melting snow, and tall prairie grasses made the trip quite taxing to the French who were unaccustomed to traveling long distances on foot. They found that the treat laid before their eyes was worth all the trouble. Ascending a rather steep hill covered with head high grass, the hunting party crawled quietly to the summit. Looking west along the slope of the hill, the hunting party saw a vast herd of bison basking in the warmth of the low winter sun. This herd had trampled the tall grass for miles in any direction. Off in the distant valley one could see the glistening water of a stream as it flowed leisurely southward among patches of ice and snow. Many bison were crowded around this stream to get their afternoon drink of water.

Mere description had not prepared the French for the animals that stood grazing on the plain before them. Like their guide Radisson had said earlier during their journey west, the bison looked like a cross between a bull and a camel. Although hard to imagine having never seen one, the comparison proved very accurate in hindsight. Everyone was quite surprised when first seeing these magnificent beasts in the flesh. Their immense heads with dangerous horns gave them a demonic look. However, the manner in which they continued to graze ignoring the hunters suggested a very docile beast. This was quite a contrast to be portrayed in one exotic beast.

It took at least an hour for the French in the hunting party to get over the initial shock of seeing this animal. The natives in the hunting party impressed upon the French the prudence of quietly stalking the bison. The natives had related how nervous a herd of bison could be when provoked. They said you definitely did not want to be within the path of a stampeding herd. Looking out across the prairie at this docile herd grazing peacefully, it was hard to imagine anything that could spook them. They would soon find out the effect of musket fire. It was decided to selectively take a few animals to be skinned, dressed, and carried back to Mere D'Osia. The natives said the bison skin was ideal for winter clothing while the meat from just one animal could feed a family for weeks. Soon the muskets were primed and four reports echoed across the grassland in the crisp winter air.

When the muskets were fired, the French had been prepared for anything but the ultimate result. Four huge bison literally dropped in their tracks like a cloth sack filled with grain. Other animals near these four continued grazing as if nothing had happened. There was certainly no stampede. While the other bison near their departed brothers did tend to move away, it seemed more like the naturally movement of the herd toward water than any actual peril that pushed them. Soon the hunters were on their prey with unsheathed knives. The natives who prized these parts as a delicacy quickly devoured the heart, liver, and kidneys of the beast. Even some French were encouraged to try this exotic food. The animals were bled, the meat quartered and neatly wrapped in skins for the trek back to the settlement. A huge red sun was hanging low on the winter horizon as the hunting party began their descent back down the eastern hillside. As the winter eve approached, the cold began to penetrate clothing damp from an afternoon's work. Looking over their shoulder as they passed out of sight, the last of the hunting party could see the bison still docilely chewing cud and munching grass. It was as if they had never been among the buffalo herd at all.

The native told the French that different tactics must be employed when more than a few hunted the bison. Although the beast had seemed quite docile, the native could not express how demoralizing a stampeding herd could be for an organized hunt. The size of the animals indicated that mere humans could not turn their charge. Something that the bison feared must be employed to keep them within range of the hunters for harvesting. Experience had shown that fire was the element that could turn the bison charge. The natives related that if the village wanted to harvest many bison to be cached for the winter then fires would be set in an enclosing circle around the herd upon the plain. Within this corral of fire, the bison were relatively easy prey for the arrows and spears launched by men on foot. However, the recent elk hunt had proved so successful that the natives saw no need to wantonly kill many bison. The rule impressed upon the French by the natives was to only take from nature what was a necessity. Excessive hunting and trapping would eventually result in a natural imbalance. The result would be that all mankind would pay for this indiscretion.

While the first winter at the mission was extremely cold, romance, on the other hand, proved to be quite warm. This was especially true for the relationship between Sha-Na and Jon Stuart. It was quite common for trappers to take a native mistress for a short time, but seldom was this enduring. However, the romance between Sha-Na and Jon Stuart was quite different. Sha-Na was obviously educated in the ways of the French and quite independent. Sha-Na took her conversion to Christianity very seriously. She had given her life to spreading peace and doing good works. This resulted in her being quite reserved in matters of a personal nature. Sha-Na was not seeking a concubine. In fact, that was initially not even a consideration. Sha-Na's sister, Kateri Tekawetha, had sent her with these French missionaries to guide them safely to the interior region and help establish a successful mission. Romance was a personal indiscretion that hindered her from reaching her goal. Although Sha-Na was attracted to the handsome military officer, her faith seemed to be guiding her in a different direction.

Likewise, Major Stuart was commissioned with a purpose that did not include romance. An officer and gentleman of the highest moral character, Jon Stuart could not entertain any activity that would distract him from his primary mission. The Major and his contingent fusiliers were essentially bodyguards charged with the security of the French missionaries. As long as everything was peaceful, there was plenty of time for personal distractions. Still, such relationships tended to dull the soldier's edge that would safely see him through perilous situations.

Unlike those he commanded Major Stuart held the life of many people in the palm of his hand. While adventurers like Radisson saw no problem in taking a native woman for their personal pleasure, Major Stuart held himself to a higher standard. In good conscious, he could not afford to jeopardize the mission by indulging in frivolous personal matters, nor would his respect for women in general allow Stuart to consider such indiscretion. Given the character and dedication of both Sha-Na and Stuart, the romance between them was destined to develop very slowly.

The months that followed the arrival of the French missionaries to Father Antoine D'Osia's settlement were marked with compassionate ministry to the surrounding native villages. The Jesuit priests, Father Antoine, Father Bertrand, and Father Constance, took turns holding weekly mass in the church along the banks of the river to be called in a future time Illinois. Indeed, the service was so well attended that the church, although quite spacious, could not accommodate so many converts. Services were forced to be held outside at least once per week which proved a hardship during the cold winter months. Plans were made to enlarge the Church as soon as the spring season returned. Major Stuart's fusiliers soon found themselves engaged as carpenters and bricklayers. Monsieur Geoff, the Royalist spy, in particular proved quite adept in the matters of construction. He had previously been employed as a head carpenter for maintenance of the King's properties in France prior to his sojourn to this wilderness. Considering the growing mission to the natives, the construction in progress, and the constant foraging for provisions there was little time for the personal indulgences of the inhabitants of Mere D'Osia.

Tonty Travels on to Creve-Coeur

With the advent of warmer weather in the spring of 1676 came scouts for future French colonization as foretold by Henri Tonty. By this time the survivors of Tonty's force had mended their wounds. Tonty being a man of adventure was bored with the mundane activities necessary to sustain a growing settlement in the wilderness. He was anxious to fulfill his commission to identify other sites in this region that might successfully sustain a newly transplanted group of colonists. Consequently, Tonty was quite pleased to find that none other than his Commander La Salle led the scouts.

The inhabitants of Mere D'Osia received Robert Cavelier, Sieur de la Salle, and his companions with great fanfare. It was learned that La Salle had wintered in Montreal and everyone was anxious to hear any news from civilization. La Salle was able to confirm that Kateri Tekawetha, the Iroquois Saint, was alive and continuing her successful mission in Montreal. This news very much relieved Sha-Na and confirmed Major Stuart's contention that Kor-Oh-Tin was a man of deceit. Lord Frontenac was having some success in pacifying the native tribes with his assurance that the French wanted only peaceful coexistence. La Salle explained that peace was vital to the safety and security of French colonists. Without this, La Salle's ventures in this wilderness were doomed for failure. Unfortunately, the Five Nations of the Iroquois seemed to be solidly aligned with the English. Since the Iroquois were the strongest native tribe, the animosity of the Iroquois could prove disastrous for French interests in this New World. Frontenac was actively sending gifts to the Iroquois to win their friendship, but it was said that the Iroquois had already signed a treaty with the English. If true, the Iroquois kept their sacred pledge. The fact that Kateri Tekawetha, the nominal head of the Iroquois Christian minority, was under the protection of the French at Montreal did not help the efforts of Frontenac to maintain peace with the Iroquois. La Salle, like Tonty, had discovered how dangerous it was to travel west from Montreal. If this trip was perilous for trained military men, how could prospective colonists unfamiliar with the savage wilderness have any hope of arriving safely let alone live in constant danger? Such was the good and bad news carried by the newly arrived French from Montreal.

While hospitable, the French missionaries remained reserved in their reception of La Salle and his entourage. Even in this interminable wilderness many thousands of kilometers from the European continent the long reach of politics could be felt. The Jesuits did not readily welcome colonization and the resulting civilization for fear of its impact upon their native converts. In their experience, the motives of colonists were often questionable. The ideal person to establish a successful colony was already a "pillar of society" so to speak at home. These people were happy and content with their current situation. Consequently, they were quite unwilling to be uprooted and face the harsh uncertainty of a wilderness with little hope of reward in their lifetime. Even when the King's men could find reliable people with the stability and skills to establish an enduring community, they were often religious dissidents that presented the Church with other unwelcome problems. Experience had proven that colonists were often people lured by promises of wealth and land. They usually had no intention of staying and were too naive to anticipate the dangers of the endeavor. In any event, the ones who did come became a liability for the Church, which must attend to their welfare. And worse, they would probably be a menace to the natives that the Church was trying to convert and educate.

For his part, La Salle never expected a sincere reception at any Jesuit settlement. La Salle recognized the political differences that existed between church and state. The long and short-term goals of the French Church and State were often not complimentary. The fact that they were both French in nationality was about the only thing they held in common. It was enough to assure mutual security when surrounded by enemies. From La Salle's royalist viewpoint, successful colonies meant a powerful France. Power in the world was its own reward. La Salle did not seek the blessing of these Jesuits at Mere D'Osia. He only wanted a brief respite from the rigors of wilderness travel. Soon he and his trusted lieutenant, Henri Tonty, would be on their way to fulfill his commission from King Louis. Then the Jesuits would be left to play nursemaid to these Godforsaken savages in this inhospitable wilderness.

Eventually the topic of conversation came around to a potential site for a successful French colony. La Salle hoped a fellow Frenchman who had lived in this region for some time could direct him in this matter. He had the opportunity to discuss this with Father Antoine after supper on the second night of his brief stay at the mission.

"Lieutenant Tonty tells me you have lived among these natives for quite some time now," La Salle said casually.

"For nearly two years actually," Father Antoine replied.

"Your advent to this region nearly parallels that of Louis Joliet and the good Father Marquette then?"

"Father Marquette and I were acquainted back in France although we pursued separate commissions in our travels to the New World."

"Then how did yours come to parallel Father Marquette's so closely?" La Salle questioned.

"Providence led me to the banks of this river and this fruitful mission among the natives. How can one explain God's ways?" Father Antoine was quite obtuse.

"You are aware of Father Marquette's death?"

"Oui, very tragic. But surely with a purpose. I like to think I'm carrying on where he left off."

"I'm sure you are very beneficial."

Father Antoine smiled and nodded as he gazed into the red embers of the dying fire in the large earthen fireplace. The night was getting on and the conversation was lagging.

"I'll come to the point," La Salle said in a friendly manner. "Are you aware of any site in this area that might be suitable to develop as a colony?"

"And what is wrong with our settlement here?" Father Antoine had assumed that this site would be chosen. After all, several buildings including a church had already been erected with immediate plans for more. The natives had come to trade here for years. It seemed a logical choice.

"What serves your purpose may not be the best site for a strong and enduring settlement." La Salle did not want to explain further.

"We have all the rudimentary amenities of a village and we are well situated on a river route," Father Antoine said defensively.

"You are not high enough to fortify and I'll wager that you are annually threatened by flooding. Is this not true?" La Salle snapped.

Father Antoine was forced to agree. His shoulders slumped as he realized his small settlement might not be so enduring after all.

"Considering there are many enemies of France that would threaten the peace of her colony, we must select a site very prudently. It is a very expensive proposition to bring settlers such a distance. We can not afford to needlessly place them in jeopardy," La Salle continued.

"But, we have not been threatened by the natives who have proven very friendly and receptive. The English and even the Spanish are no where near here. And we have such a good start!" Father Antoine replied defensively as if trying to convince himself.

"Although I cannot entirely rule out this location, I would be remiss if I did not investigate all possibilities," La Salle said encouragingly. He realized he was at risk of receiving no help from the priest.

"I have not ventured far from this place since I arrived. My brethren come to me," Father Antoine mumbled.

"Come, come, man," La Salle said. "Mon Dieu, surely you have heard talk."

"Well," Father Antoine said deep in thought, "up river several kilometers there is a native village inhabited by the Peoria that might meet your defensive requirements. I had the opportunity to spend a night there when I first journeyed to this region. The rocky precipice juts skyward from the river bank several hundred feet. It is quite imposing, I must say."

"Excellent, excellent!" La Salle exclaimed. "We shall explore that possibility on the morrow. I plan to explore both up and down this river. Can you suggest a reliable native guide to accompany us?"

"Of course, that should be no problem." Father Antoine was tired and wanted to get some sleep.

"Good night, Father." The two men rose from their crude bench and shook hands. La Salle was happy to conclude the conversation as well now that he had obtained the information he needed.

La Salle didn't waste any time in leaving the village called Mere D'Osia. He found the company quite stifling. Although the French Fusiliers were very intriguing, it was obvious that their loyalty was with the Jesuit priests. Military men were committed to do their duty. This was very commendable but of no use to a man involved in world politics and the balance of power. Men like the Fusiliers were merely pawns to be used on the great chessboard of the world.

Tonty, La Salle's trusted comrade-at-arms, was bored with the situation at the mission as well. He tried to entice some of the Fusiliers to join them in the exploration of the interior but they all remained loyal to Major Stuart. Indeed, several Fusiliers were unhappy that they were employed in what they considered menial labor. Fighting men should not be planting, cooking, and building. However, desertion was beyond the question. Desertion was dishonorable and could have undesirable consequences. La Salle, Tonty and the royalist force launched their birch bark canoes and left quietly in the red glow of early dawn. Life as missionaries at the tiny settlement on the river transecting the heart of North America resumed thereafter in all its monotony.

As for La Salle, the trip up river was uneventful. Nevertheless, his small force of musketeers was constantly on guard for unfriendly natives. La Salle, like most French adventurers traveling west from Montreal, was very nervous about any natives he met on the journey. Most had learned from experience that many tribes were openly hostile to the French. This was in part due to the alignment of the Five Nations of the Iroquois with the English. Since the Iroquois were the dominant native force throughout the northeast quadrant of the continent, even enemies of the Iroquois avoided trading with the French. They were afraid such negotiations might bring the savage wrath of the Iroquois down upon them. This was true to the extent that any Frenchman became open prey to many roving native bands. Even as far west as the Illinois territory, natives were careful not to extend much friendship. Many French trappers lost their treasure before they could get their pelts to market in the name of Iroquois appeasement. Real or imagined, the threat of the savage Iroquois war club was felt far into the interior of North America.

La Salle had determined that unless the balance of power changed drastically in the northeast no French colonist would ever be safe to travel to this beautiful interior land of swift flowing rivers and rustling prairie grass. Certainly, even if the colonists could somehow be transported safely to Illinois, there would always be a problem with maintaining the supply routes down the St. Lawrence River necessary to sustain a sedentary agrarian population. Governor Frontenac was currently engaged in an effort to win the Iroquois over to the French side, but La Salle feared this would never happen given the Iroquois penchant for loyalty to old allies. The Iroquois dealt honorably in all negotiations with foreigners. Perhaps they would never learn that such traits as loyalty and honor did not mix well with politics. In any event, La Salle recognized a need to fortify areas of potential French colonization in order to insure their security.

La Salle also had a plan that might resolve the problem of supplying and protecting French settlements. He had learned from previous French explorers like Marquette and Joliet that the large river just to the west flowed south into a great ocean later to be known as the Gulf of Mexico. La Salle wanted to explore the possibility of claiming the region along that river to the south in the name of his sovereign Louis XIV. While the Spanish currently laid claim to that area, La Salle felt it would be an easy matter to overrule that claim with French military and naval power. By opening up access to the ocean from the south, La Salle hoped that a more defensible supply route could be established to further French interests in this new continent. La Salle was anxious to pursue this course of action as soon as he could find and fortify a significant defensive position in the Illinois territory.

Rounding a bend in the river on their trip north, La Salle was treated to exactly the magnificent defensive position for which he had prayed. About two days travel up river from Mere D'Osia there raised a steep rocky landform resembling a mesa. Unlike the mesas encountered in other areas of the world, this high prominence was small, thereby lending to its defensive nature. Like Father Antoine said, there was a native encampment nestled next to the cliff at the waters' edge. Silently the French oars turned their bows toward the smoke that curled lazily up toward the overcast sky. An eagle's cry pierced the otherwise quiet landscape awakening several dogs in the encampment that finally recognized the approach of strangers. Before the canoes could be beached, a native entourage had gathered to greet La Salle and his fellow explorers.

Following the customary greetings that were always exchanged at the insistence of the local natives, La Salle distributed trinkets to win their friendship. Before long, the French were sitting around a native campfire enjoying exotic dishes prepared from nature's bounty gathered in the surrounding wilderness. Berries and nuts of several varieties were offered prior to the main course of extremely rare venison. While the Europeans preferred their meat more fully cooked, the rowing of the canoes upstream these past days had worked to build their ravenous appetite. Everyone ate heartily and soon smiles of contentment surrounded the campfire. No one in the French party seemed to notice that the majority of the camp in contrast dined in a rather meager fashion. The social mores of these natives dictated that they serve their best in abundance to guests even though there be nothing left for them. At any rate, given the aloofness in the demeanor of La Salle and his companions toward these human beings whom they viewed as savages, no compassion could be expected. The order of the day for the French was feasting and on to the business at hand.

Later that day, La Salle took the opportunity to inquire about the precipice that towered above his host's encampment and overlooked the river from a great height. He was told that the natives seldom ventured to the top of the hill due to a difficult access. Apparently, the heights were only accessible on one of four sides. Of course, this was music to the ears of an experienced military tactician. The native head of this clan known as the Peoria stated emphatically that there was no reason to venture up there since there was a lack of abundant wildlife necessary to sustain a village. Hearing this, La Salle inquired about the water supply in this area. He was happy to hear from the native headsman that natural springs abounded along the steep sides of the bluff. This gave encouragement to La Salle since he knew that a fresh source of drinking water would be vital to sustaining a fortress upon the bluff. La Salle asked if a native would be willing to guide him to the top of the bluff the following day. The council of the Peoria gathered around the campfire laughed heartily at this suggestion of wasting time for no useful purpose. Even the offer of some trade trinkets in return for a guide was barely enough to interest anyone in such a futile venture. Still, La Salle happily went to sleep in his threadbare woolen blanket next to a warm fire that evening. La Salle was almost sure that he had found a defensible position that could become a base to project French military power in this vast interior wilderness.

The following day, La Salle was treated to a wondrous view of the river valley from the top of the bluff. Although the ascent was quite tedious, La Salle and Tonty knew that this was exactly the type of landform required to establish an impregnable fortification. In essence, this location was a miniature Montreal. Three sides of the bluff would require no troops to defend while the fourth presented such a difficult trek that any aggressor would be hard pressed to effectively fight while climbing. La Salle recognized that a relatively small garrison could easily repulse a force many times their size. If the French could manage to place artillery upon this bluff, then the site would be virtually impregnable. Fresh water from the multitude of springs and wise storage of supplies could assure success from all but the lengthiest siege. Truly, La Salle's prayers had been answered. The

French quickly broke out their broadaxes and began felling trees to use for the battlements of the fortress they would build. Once complete, La Salle planned to leave a portion of his troops to defend the new fort while he continued his exploration to the South. If a less dangerous approach from the South could be found, he hoped to return to France very soon to organize French colonists to populate this promising region. It seemed fortune was now smiling upon his political venture.

* * * *

Meanwhile, back down the Illinois River at the trading post of Mere D'Osia the Jesuit mission was beginning to flourish. Word of the compassion of the missionaries passed swiftly among the tribes of the interior. It seemed that the arrival of Father Bertrand and Father Constance was exactly the impetus required to make the difference in spreading God's Word in this vast wilderness. Father Antoine alone was hard-pressed to mount a viable ministry, but the combined efforts of the three priests coupled with their extensive experience in missions around the world made all the difference. Natives of the Sauk, Fox, Shawnee, Omaha, and even the Miami tribes traveled many kilometers both overland and by interior waterway to hear about the Great Spirit of the white man. Of course, the trade goods offered by the French voyageurs were attractive to the natives as well. The metal ware including pots, pans, and knives were a prize for any native to own. The sparkling jewelry of bronze, copper, and silver and the colorful blankets and bolts of cloth also acted as a magnet to native hunters and trappers.

These goods were helpful, but the ingredient that made the mission at Mere D'Osia unique compared to other small Jesuit missions farther north was the charismatic oratory of Father Constance. A natural gift of verbal expression coupled with decades of practice had made Father Constance's preaching particularly mesmerizing. It was not uncommon for Sunday Mass to be attended by hundreds of natives from the surrounding area. Holy Communion bound this savage congregation with a feeling of family, regardless of the diversity of tribes represented. The presence of Major Stuart's mercenaries added a stabilizing effect that resulted in a feeling of peace and security within this sometimes-brutal wilderness. In a land where starvation or premature death was never far away, the mission at Mere D'Osia offered a type of contentment heretofore unknown to these natives. Mere D'Osia demonstrated to these people that a life of peace and harmony through the daily practice of the teachings of Christ might be possible for them after all. Travelers returning to Montreal carried news of the singular success of the Mere

D'Osia mission. This word was in turn passed overseas to the Catholic court in Paris.

Publicly, Bishop Colbert praised the work of his dedicated priests. Secretly, the Bishop chafed that God had not blessed him with a city of gold to match those found by the Spanish Conquistadors in Mexico and Peru over a century before. The agents sent by the Church with the missionaries to explore this possibility were not fulfilling their commission. Bishop Colbert would have to see what could be done about this unwelcome turn of events. On the other hand, King Louis' spies were also impatient that the possibility of finding wealth in the continental interior was not being pursued. While outwardly the mission at Mere D'Osia was a model of contentment, behind the scene there was turmoil for several of the French entourage.

This was the situation when Pierre Radisson and Monsieur Geoff finally had the opportunity to speak privately. It was late one evening when the tavern had finally become quiet. The patrons had either become too drunk or went back to their warm beds. Two men whose reasoning was not completely impaired by too much liquor began a conversation in the shadows of the small tavern.

"Monsieur Geoff, why do you always look so glum?" Radisson's voice boomed in the now quiet tavern. His large capacity for alcohol had left him bored while most around him were in a stupor.

"And, why are you always so happy?" Geoff retorted, shaking his head as he hunched his slouching shoulders over the half-empty mug of ale on the rough-hewn oak table. As usual, Geoff was worried and feeling sorry for himself. His sharp tongue did not stop to consider that Radisson could probably crush his skull with one blow.

"Come, come, Monsieur, things cannot be that bad!" Radisson laughed heartily. He liked to play cat-and-mouse to pass the time and he had found his mouse in Geoff.

"How can one person always be so optimistic?" The tavern keeper mumbled sarcastically as he cleaned up the mess on an adjacent table in preparation for closing.

"Mind your own business, my friend." Radisson's voice had a serious inflection.

"Pardon, pardon." The tavern keeper held up his hands in a surrendering gesture as he backed away. He picked up a roughly fashioned broom made of a hickory stick and prairie grass to begin sweeping a floor that would never be clean.

"I can't stand to stay in this burring backwuter hole while my en…nam…inies plot my demize." Geoff whined to no one in particular.

"You have enemies, Monsieur? That simply astounds me." Radisson joked as he recognized his folly in trying to talk to a paranoid drunkard.

"Ah, ah, ah. You'd be surr...prizz'd." Geoff waved his finger back and forth in a shaky manner.

"Do enlighten me, Monsieur." Bored as well, Radisson hoped to pass the time with some good gossip.

"My muster will surely mur...mur...kill me if I don't find him a treas...zure in this savage land." Geoff mumbled.

"Please go on." Radisson said encouragingly.

"Everyday I see strangers come into this village and wonder if they are here to kill me." Speaking of such a serious matter was beginning to sober Geoff up.

"You are such an imbecile," Radisson laughed. "Why would anyone waste precious time to journey into the wilderness to deal with such an unimportant person? You are delirious."

"My master does not accept failure and I have failed him miser...ab...ily." Geoff was nearly to tears.

"Surely your master, who ever that might be, didn't seriously expect to find a vast treasure in this savage land, did he? This folly has been tried by better men than you." Radisson patted the drunk on the shoulders.

"Oh, nooooo!" Geoff slurred the word. "I'm not supposed to say this." Geoff rubbed his finger clumsily across his lips as if to seal his companion to secrecy.

"Do go on Monsieur. You can trust me. Why I seldom get back to civilization," Radisson said encouragingly.

"Well............" Geoff squinted as he looked around the tavern for anyone that might be a threat.

"My masser......His Eminencezzz," Geoff brought his hand to his brow in a parody of a salute, "thought that, that...." His voice trailed off as he thought what might happen to him if he told his secret. Obviously, the liquor was making him more paranoid.

"Come, come, Monsieur. You can trust me and perhaps I can help you." Radisson was impatient since he believed Geoff's secret to be inconsequential and a waste of his time. "The mizzion you guided to this wilderness is only a dis...disquise for the Churches' true inten...shh...ions." Geoff nodded knowingly as he looked deep into Radisson's eyes.

"Mon Dieu, don't speak in riddles," Radisson said although he was beginning to get the true picture.

"Oui, oui," Geoff continued solemnly. "They noooooo. They know where the treasure is and will go and get it for the fine Bishop one of these days."

"You will be happy to know that you're secret is safe with me, Mon Ami," Radisson consoled. "It seems we are on the same side and didn't even know it."

"Huhhhhh?" This was all Geoff could muster as his liquor clouded mind tried to make sense of what was being said.

"My Lord Frontenac suspected the same ruse although I told him it could not be possible. At any rate, it was convenient for me to be Father Bertrand and Father Constance's guide. If the Church found a treasure, I would be on hand to claim it for King Louis."

"Nothing but savv…sav…a…ges." Geoff's head lolled as he tried to agree.

"Why, this terrain is not mountainous. Any imbecile knows that there are no resources here to support other than the most primitive civilization. The tools of these natives are made of stone. They have no time to do anything other than grub for a living. But no one will listen to me." Radisson raised both hands toward the tavern ceiling joists in futility.

"What to do, what to do?" Geoff said in despair.

"It is time to find a place that might be more conducive to sustaining a wealthy populace," Radisson waxed poetic. Geoff just nodded so Radisson continued.

"In the months since we have been here I have given this some consideration. The natives say the top of the world in farther west. That means mountains and, perhaps, gold and silver." Radisson slapped his friend on the back and lowered his voice.

"And I will tell you a secret as well." Geoff nodded soberly.

"I believe there may be a water passage through this continent to a vast western sea. The river that flows past Montreal and Quebec connects to several vast inland seas. The natives speak of this and I have seen three of them with my own eyes. Is it not reasonable to suspect that a similar river continues west to the Indies where Magellan died?" Radisson spoke passionately of his personal dream.

"Wealth comes in many forms, Monsieur," Radisson said solemnly. "Fame has its rewards as well. Imagine what our King will do for the man that can give France a direct route to the riches of the east."

"That will surely make France very powerful!" Geoff carefully put his words together.

"Therefore, it is time to make my dream come true. I propose that we," Radisson waved his thumb between them, "you and I, find this passage and a city of gold, if one truly exists."

"I'm with you," Geoff said shaking his new partner's hand. "I cannot return to France and if I stay here I believe I will die." "You may well speak the truth, Mon

Ami," said Radisson seriously. "The power of the Five Nations of the Iroquois has a long reach. Major Stuart and the one-handed man, Tonty, were not very civil to the Iroquois we picked up on our trip inland. I know firsthand how these savages can return a favor."

"Then let us depart. But when?" Geoff had sobered from the prospect of a new adventure.

"The sooner the better!" Radisson stood up from the table and headed for the crudely braced tavern door. He too was filled with the prospect of following his dream. "I'll the make arrangements. But, it is our secret!" Radisson raised his finger to his lips. The two men slipped out into the dark night. All was quiet except for the barking of a dog in the distance.

Unknown to the two conspirators a solitary figure watched this silent departure. This shadow stoically braved the coldest hours of the approaching day without fire or shelter. Actually Kor-Oh-Tin, the Iroquois warrior sent to spy on the French activities in this distant march of Iroquois power, had spent many similar nights in the past months. Kor-Oh-Tin knew plans were being finalized to reassert Iroquois power in this land of cowards. These river and prairie people had forgotten the strength of their Iroquois overlords. It was time to provide a lesson! Kor-Oh-Tin must be able to provide the logistic that would assure the success of the mission.

As Kor-Oh-Tin waited for Radisson and Geoff to pass in the darkness, he unfolded a cloth he had tucked in his belt. The sparklers from a dying campfire nearby provided just enough light for him to appraise the artifact that he held in his hands. The article gleamed so much even in this dismal light that the warrior had to be careful that its reflection did not attract the attention of the sentries that made their rounds regularly upon the hour. It was a beautiful piece crafted by artisans in the distant west. Made of some type of rock unknown to these eastern dwellers, the article was very unusual indeed. Slender by design, it was approximately 20 centimeters long. In reality, it was a meticulously fashioned blade crafted to exact specifications. The sharply angled double edge was honed for smooth cuts while the precisely defined point made it a formidable weapon. Yet the purpose of the blade was more ceremonial than functional.

Kor-Oh-Tin's visit to the French settlement called Mere D'Osia tonight was not to spy. Sha-Na, a sister of his clan, had requested a personal favor from him upon his arrival in the region many months before. She had provided him a picture of her necklace ornament meticulously drawn upon a soft piece of buckskin. Kor-Oh-Tin's kin as a child had seen a similar blade fashioned from an exotic rock only found far to the west. Sha-Na wished to present it as a gift of memorable significance. Kor-Oh-Tin was just the man to get such a piece since he had contacts with natives far to the west. He had made a promise to acquire the article and he was as good as his word. This was true even after he noticed the design to be that of a crucifix, the French term for the tree upon which their God was tortured. Even now, Kor-Oh-Tin was inclined to spit upon the symbol he held in his hand. Yet, he had respect for his Iroquois sister even though he believed in his soul that she was truly misguided.

"Halt! Who goes there?" A sentry who had rounded the corner of a crudely chinked cabin to spy the intruder in the flickering firelight shouted. Kor-Oh-Tin had been so engrossed in his inspection of the blade that he had temporarily let down his guard. It was an unaccustomed slip that almost cost him his life. Quickly rolling the blade back up in its cloth and tucking it into his belt, the warrior was off with the speed of a deer and the stealth of a bobcat. The report of a flintlock sounded the alarm but the lead ball only marked the place where the warrior had stood. His swift disappearance left the guard wondering if the shadow in the dark was only his imagination.

Kor-Oh-Tin let the familiar darkness envelop him as he moved to the safety of a large grove of cottonwoods directly north of the settlement. Unfortunately, his quick exit had not allowed him time to properly secure the artifact in this sparsely beaded knife belt. By the time Kor-Oh-Tin was at a safe distance from harm he realized that the blade was no longer in his possession. Since he had not fled along the well-worn footpaths in the forest Kor-Oh-Tin knew that he had little hope of retracing his route to find the artifact. There was no time to duplicate it for he must begin his trek back northeast to the Five Nations soon. He cursed the luck that had made him unable to fulfill his promise. Loyalty and honor were part of the very fiber of his soul. The French dogs would surely pay for their transgressions!

*   *   *   *

Meanwhile at Fort Creve-Coeur, the French garrison established along the interior river approximately 120 kilometers north of Mere D'Osia, rumors were circulating that would deal a tragic blow to La Salle's dreams of colonization. Two French sentries, pausing beneath a blazing torch that provided them a modicum of warmth against a cold, damp night, discussed news heard from the Peoria tribe that encamped on the riverbank below the seemingly impregnable French fortress.

"What do you make of the news that has so distressed le Colonel?" The one guard shivered as he rubbed his hands together trying to make some heat against the blustery night. His gold trimmed blue uniform was fashionable but far from functional in such adverse weather. Much to his regret he had left his great coat in the barracks.

"You mean the Iroquois rumor?" The other guard was likewise more intent upon keeping warm than making conversation. This soldier had been wise enough to wear his regimental overcoat, but the wind was cutting through the wool fabric. Fear has a sobering effect that can overcome the basic human instinct for warmth. The Iroquois reputation for savagery could easily make a man forget everything else.

"Oui!" One guard replied in evident disgust that the other could believe there was something else to discuss. "What are we to do if those bloody savages decide to pay us a visit? Even with our muskets, our small garrison could not hope to withstand an attack," he continued to whine.

"Le Colonel says that our position upon this river bluff is quite impregnable. Monsieur La Salle was quite impressed with this natural fortification. We should be as safe here as anywhere." The other guard tried to speak with confidence although the tone in his voice betrayed him.

"Our leaders, what do they know!" came the irritated reply. "You speak of safety, ha!" He spat upon the ground. "Ask Lieutenant Tonty's troops, the few that are left, if they would feel safe here. If it were not for the good fortune that brought Major Stuart's Fusiliers to their aid they would not be around to speak at all."

"But, I was told the savages that nearly annihilated those unfortunate soldiers were not Iroquois." This was only a half-hearted argument.

"Iroquois, Huron, who knows, or cares! If a lesser tribe can cause this much havoc, what does that say for the ferocity of the Iroquois, Mon Ami?"

"But, we are so far inland that the Iroquois surely could not bother us here?" The one guard was trying as much to convince himself as his compatriot. "In any event, we are stuck here on this desolate rock in an unfriendly land until La Salle decides to return."

"Are we now?" The other guard chuckled under his breath that fogged in the cold night air.

"Surely you are not contemplating desertion, Mon Ami. Alone you could not hope to survive in this wilderness. Better to stand together I say."

"Who said I would be alone?"

"Very well, even two of us could not hope to last for long in this savage land."

"I agree." The one guard was not willing to elaborate on such a serious matter. Even late at night someone might overhear and he well knew the penalty for desertion.

"You mean there are many who might join us?" The one sentry's voice trailed off as he was unable to voice the unspeakable. "To contemplate such action based upon only a rumor does not seem prudent?" Obviously, he wanted to be convinced.

"I spoke with the Corporal-of-the-Guard and he insists that he saw an Iroquois warrior lurking in the forest not more than a week ago. He was leading a group foraging for meat when they stumbled upon a native drinking from a spring in the rocks near the river."

"And how does he know this was an Iroquois?" The one guard replied wanting more evidence.

"That is precisely it, Mon Ami! It seems the Corporal has been with La Salle and Tonty many years. He was present when our Governor, General Frontenac and La Salle tried to negotiate a peace treaty with the Five Nations of the Iroquois. The headdress, deerskin leggings, and beadwork were unmistakable."

"And you believe this?"

"I am told the Corporal would not lie, especially considering the consequences."

"Even if it is true, how can one Iroquois pose so great a threat?" The one guard remained cynical.

"The Iroquois are noted for their camaraderie. Where there is one, many wait only to be called." The other guard spoke with finality. He had already made up his mind as to what he would do.

"So what are we to do?" Both guards were committed to a serious course. They had only to make plans.

"We have secretly taken a poll. Most of the garrison wants to leave. We have only to decide the time when we will take action," the one guard whispered.

"Desertion means death to us if we return to France," said the one.

"That is why there will be no witnesses. Our secret must be kept!" said the other with finality.

"I cannot become a murderer."

"Then one way or the other you will die."

"But, where are we to go if we leave here."

"Ah, that is the beauty," replied the one sentry. "As luck would have it a trapper from the mission just south of here has agreed to include us in his plans for exploration of the lands north and west of here."

"But he will know our secret as well." The one sentry appeared worried. "His word could put us before a firing squad."

"Don't worry. The man is a realist, which is another word for scoundrel. He needs us as much as we need him. You said yourself that alone one cannot hope to succeed in this wilderness."

"And what is to the northwest, more trees and savages I think."

"Gold, silver, and, perhaps a trade route to the Orient. We may become extremely wealthy men."

"Or dead men." The one guard shook his head, but he could see no other workable alternative. Within a day the plans for mutiny at Creve-Coeur were laid.

In less than a fortnight the complete destruction of La Salle's impregnable fortification was accomplished. The Peoria clan encamped at the foot of the cliff near the river first smelled the smoke early one morning. Little attention was given to this since prairie fires were quite common in this region. However, very soon the night sky above the river was ablaze as the orange flame spiked toward the Milky Way. The local natives could not imagine what was happening. There were no battle cries that would signal an attack of some sort. Neither did the flames engulf the shrieks of the sleeping suddenly. On the contrary, the disaster was accompanied by a strange silence that left the savages in wonder. While the fort indeed contained trade goods and gunpowder that the natives coveted, it was days before they mustered enough courage to explore the smoldering ruins. They were greeted with a smoldering pile of oaken poles and a rocky foundation that had survived the holocaust. Some charred bones were discovered within the ruins of the main command building. But there was no evidence to help determine whether these poor souls were murdered or victims of the flames. The grand fortification was completely and utterly destroyed. The inhabitants had disappeared. To the natives this suggested spirit intervention and the area became taboo to many future generations.

Word of the destruction at Creve-Coeur spread slowly. By word of mouth, the natives carried the news to Mere D'Osia and then on south. When La Salle heard the sorry news during his exploration to the south he was nearly crushed. This event coupled with his other trials upon the northern lakes seemed to indicate that God did not favor his work. Yet, La Salle was a man of great fortitude. He was able to shed misfortune much like a duck would shed water. La Salle resolved to rebuild the fort as soon as he verified that a trade route from the south could be established. A viable French colony must have the security of a fortification such as Creve-Coeur as well as a reliable line of supply. La Salle was determined to provide both.

Chapter 5

THE GOSPEL

By the time Father Jacob had arrived at this point in his interesting story, the Bent children were mostly asleep. Only the older boys hung on the priest's every word. Ida suggested that they all get a good night sleep and resume in the morning. Indeed, Father Jacob was somewhat exhausted from his travels and the excitement of the auction. The cold winter night coupled with the warm blazing fire was working to make everyone extremely drowsy. Both Jacob and John readily accepted Ida's suggestion and soon everyone was tucked away for a restful sleep. For his part, Father Jacob fell asleep very quickly. Usually his nervous tension at discovering the truth about the tradition of the wilderness nativity served him up many sleepless nights. However, the priest felt a contentment that he hadn't felt for years. Jacob was convinced that he was on the verge of solving the centuries old riddle. This reassurance coupled with the exhaustion of his travels blessed Jacob with a restful sleep. On the morrow, there were new facts to be discovered. Also, the priest knew that God's will was coming to pass and he was a main instrument. This was Jacob's calling and the promise to impending success made him feel very satisfied indeed.

Life on a family farm has many small blessings. One of these is awaking to the smell of breakfast cooking in the kitchen. Father Jacob had the opportunity to experience this blessing with the Bent household the following morning. Fresh coffee and frying bacon stimulated his appetite and made the ordeal of leaving a warm bed tolerable. As Jacob descended the steps the smiles of the entire Bent family made him thank God for being alive. It was evident to the priest that love was the foundation upon which this family was built. He basked in the warmth of that love as he accepted a fresh cup of coffee from Ida. Soon he tasted the homemade food that had filled the air with all those wonderful aromas. John gave a wonderful blessing for breakfast. It was with a feeling of anticipation that everyone gathered back in the living room for Father Jacob to continue his fascinating story of the night before. Father Jacob began again with the skill of an experienced storyteller.

The Great Iroquois Raid on the Interior

Kor-Oh-Tin personally made the trek back to upper New York to report on the activities of the French missionaries and the situation of the native clans of the interior. To-Ko-Wan, the Iroquois shaman, received the information with stoicism. The success of the French priests Constance and Bertrand came as no surprise to him. Christianity was a major threat to the old ways of all natives on the North American continent. The report merely reaffirmed what To-Ko-Wan already knew. Those who spread the foreign religion must be stopped. In order to do this, each successful mission must be destroyed.

Kateri Tekawetha, the converted Iroquois Saint, was the key to ending the Christian threat. Unfortunately, she continued to live and thrive under the close protection of General Frontenac, the French Governor of colonies in the New World. Despite many clever attempts to assassinate the native Saint, somehow she had miraculously survived. An Iroquois maid faithful to the old ways had even managed to infiltrate the kitchen staff of the French Governor that prepared food for Kateri. A natural poison had been dumped into the soup that was served to the Iroquois heretics. They had eaten this soup with relish and went on to the main course with no ill effects. Was it not for To-Ko-Wan's spirit journey that had shown the ultimate defeat of the French missions, the shaman might consider conversion himself.

Ko-Oh-Tin affirmed that the Iroquois maiden, Sha-Na, held the key to the destruction of Kateri Tekawetha. During his trek to the interior with the French missionaries, Kor-Oh-Tin had become well acquainted with Sha-Na. He had learned from Sha-Na that she and Kateri were like sisters. There was nothing that one would not do for the other. Sha-Na had even commissioned an obsidian blade to match the crucifix necklace that Kateri had given to her prior to the journey to the interior. Given such emotional attachment, To-Ko-Wan could easily imagine that Kateri would leave the security of the French to save her friend.

Therefore, it was imperative that Sha-Na be captured unscathed during the forthcoming raid on the interior region.

To-Ko-Wan was surprised and pleased that the Illinois clans still regarded the Iroquois with fear and respect. That fear was obviously not enough to counter the success of the French missions to the interior. There were a variety of reasons why a raid to the interior region must be mounted. The power of the Iroquois must be reasserted. The threat of a foreign religion must be ended. Finally, To-Ko-Wan's spirit journey had affirmed that the event would come to pass. These portents had great influence at the council fire of the Five Nations of the Iroquois. To-Ko-Wan brought his proposal with great confidence before the sachems and chiefs of the Five Nations gathered in council.

To-Ko-Wan was one of a group of Iroquois called Ho-nun-de'-unt, or "keepers of the faith". As the name implied, the Ho-nun-de'-unt protected the Iroquois way of life. To-Ko-Wan's proposal for war against the French was accepted. The Ho-nun-de'-unt presided over the festival during the council of Iroquois sachems and chiefs. This group performed the customary war dance and many volunteered from each Iroquois Nation. The war party numbered in the hundreds as a result in no small part of the reputation and prestige of To-Ko-Wan.

The power of the Iroquois Nations resided with its people. The Iroquois leaders directed the outcome of projects once the people had determined the course. This organization was unique to the natives of North America, resembling a democratic rather than a dictatorial form of government. The great numbers flocking to To-Ko-Wan's war party attested to the popularity of the mission. Obviously, the will of the Iroquois people had spoken. Therefore, the Iroquois' Leagues two hereditary war chiefs began immediate preparation. Since the Seneca tribe was the doorkeeper to the Iroquois League, these two chiefs were members of that tribe. One war chief called Ta-wan'-ne-ars, or needle breaker, gathered provisions and weapons. The other called So-no'-so-wa, or great oyster shell, organized and arranged transport. These two chiefs together with To-Ko-Wan planned the mission and the type of war strategy. Ta-wan'ne-ars and So-no'-so-wa were in charge of all military affairs of the Iroquois. They had the essential military experience required to successfully prosecute a war. To-Ko-Wan would be the battle field commander. Due to his popularity, To-Ko-Wan's leadership would be the crucial ingredient to assure success to a campaign that would be prosecuted many hundred kilometers from the home fires.

Soon the Ceremony of the White Dog was led by To-Ko-Wan for members of the war party. By ancient tradition this ceremony was held five days after the new moon following the winter solstice. First, a feast of dog meat was prepared and all ate heartily. Next, To-Ko-Wan recited his spirit vision in which he in the form of an eagle would descend upon the interior natives with a blade clasped in his talon and carry the Iroquois to victory. This vision alone was a great catalyst that gave great solemnity to the mission. The Ho-nun-de'-unt, or "keepers of the faith", each offered prayers for success.

"Ouiy! Ouiy!" shouted all assembled following each prayer.

By now the excitement of the war feast was at a fever pitch. In turn, each warrior who had killed an enemy in battle danced around the fire acting out the forthcoming battle and throwing embers in the fire. Each warrior also sang his own unique war chant that was his alone for it was an insult to sing another's song. Tobacco was solemnly offered by the Ho-nun-de'-unt to seal the pact for success. Finally, To-Ko-Wan and the two Seneca war chiefs stripped to the waist and blacked his own face, shoulders, and breast with coals from the dying fire.

As the horizon began to turn pink in the east each chief sat beside the fire and sang his death song. To-Ko-Wan, Ta-wan'ne-ars, and So-no'-so-wa would perform this same ritual at the break of camp each morning until the raid was complete and the war party out of danger. For his part, To-Ko-Wan took a hot rock from the campfire that resembled a crucifix and placed the glowing ember on his breast next to his heart. As his flesh scorched, To-Ko-Wan's facial features remained transfixed in grim determination. Daily this mark would remind him of what must be accomplished. Within a day, the Iroquois war party of nearly five-hundred warriors, one of the largest ever assembled, was moving in organized precision to the west and the rivers of the continental interior.

* * * *

A young Sauk sat motionless along a well-traveled north-south trail through the cool, shadowy, silent forest. The colorful leaves barely moved before a quiet breeze. The smell carried on the wind was damp and earthy. The young man looked across the creek branch where the stream dumped lazily into a wide, slowly flowing, green river. The water of the creek gurgled and rumbled over the rock where its fast pace was quickly slowed by the larger stream. This river was known to the Sauk as the "waters-flowing-from winter". The river was narrow and shallow at this point making it a natural ford for both the animals and the people of the forest. Likewise, it was the natural corridor for enemies to use if they intended to raid the local village.

His people called the young man Little Fox. Although the name suggested wisdom and cunning, it was a name bestowed upon a youth before becoming a man. It would take a dramatic event or intervention of a spirit guide to help him make that transition. Little Fox hoped this would be soon for, like all youth, he was impatient to grow up. Perhaps this vigil beside the river was part of his destiny and it would give him the opportunity to prove his manhood.

The late morning sun of autumn was unusually hot on his brow. Little Fox's lunch of mushrooms and tender roots was making him drowsy as well. It took all of his self-discipline to keep his eyes open and remain alert for any sign of an approaching war party. Each uneventful day made it all the more difficult for him to remain alert in the face of extreme boredom. Since many starry nights had already passed since he had been stationed as a sentry at this lonely outpost, Little Fox was beginning to think the rumors were untrue. He longed to be back at the Jesuit parish called Mere D'Osia. Life had been so placid since the missionaries had arrived to support Father Antoine. Oh, how he wished such peace could remain a blessing to his people.

Sitting completely camouflaged at the base of a towering white oak tree, Little Fox let his mind wander back to the mission and his new foreign friends. Little Fox was an altar boy and personal servant to the maid called Sha-Na. He was privy to much of the news and intrigue that remained transparent to most of his brethren. From this experience, Little Fox knew that most rumors were inaccurate and hardly worth repeating. However, the rumor of the advent of an Iroquois raiding party was something that could not be completely ignored given the reputation of this fierce tribe to the northeast.

In his capacity as assistant to Sha-Na, Little Fox had become a personal friend of Major Stuart. Many nights these three had sat around the campfire sharing stories. Major Stuart was eager to learn about the culture and traditions of the Sauk and Iroquois tribes. Both Sha-Na and Little Fox were fascinated by Stuart's accounts of Europe and his Scottish homeland. It was hard to imagine encampments with thousands of people. Still harder to comprehend were the description of stone paths that proceeded beyond the horizon and bridged rivers wider than the local river to be called in some future time Illinois. Little Fox was especially interested in the methods used by the white man to wage war. The Major had even taught Little Fox to fire the flintlock rifle and wield his long saber. How Little Fox wished that he had the magic-stick-that-makes-fire-to-kill in his possession this very moment. The presence of such a deadly weapon would make him feel more secure in his lonely vigil.

Since the arrival of Sha-Na and Major Stuart with the French missionary party, Little Fox could see that this man and woman of different cultures had grown very close. The romance had blossomed before his very eyes and he felt that in a small way he had become attached to them as well. Little Fox, like many of his tribe, had been quick to accept the new faith called Christianity. Although the message of peace had at first seemed foreign to people who were constantly fighting for survival, the presence of Major Stuart's Fusiliers and the close proximity of Mere D'Osia to the French fortress of Creve-Coeur made danger of attack seem a thing of the past. It was certainly distressing to have a rumor of an impending Iroquois raid shatter the tranquil lifestyle that had come to be accepted at the Mere D'Osia mission.

Indeed, no one quite knew where the rumor of an Iroquois raid had originated. Some had seen a native in the vicinity wearing a headdress and ceremonial belt that were certainly Iroquois in origin. However, Sha-Na being an Iroquois had confided that a fellow tribesman had made a clandestine visit to her on more than one occasion. She had said his purpose was to trade and perform a personal favor. Sha-Na would offer no more explanation and everyone left it at that. This could easily explain the sighting of Iroquois in the area.

The destruction and abandonment of the French fortress at Creve-Coeur up river was less easily justified. Several members of a Peoria clan on a trade mission to Mere D'Osia had confirmed they had seen the midnight conflagration with their own eyes. While they did not actually witness the attack that wrought this destruction, the Peoria were sure there were Iroquois warriors sighted near their village at the foot of the bluff where the fortress was located. Little Fox knew that the Peoria did not always tell the truth and the Peoria were no friends to the Sauk. Still, Little Fox could not fathom what it gained the Peoria to fabricate such a story. Given the well-known claim of the Iroquois to this region and their hatred for the French, Little Fox reasoned that it would not be prudent to dismiss the probability of an Iroquois raid out of hand. That was precisely why he willingly spent days at this lonely outpost in the forest separated from the communion of his home fire and new found friends.

The long, lonely vigil beside the animal path in this trackless forest was slowly dulling the senses of the Sauk youth. Little Fox found himself wishing that he might see the glint of sunlight on a flint lance or hear the light tread of a score of moccasin shod warriors on the plant strewn forest floor. How ferocious could these Iroquois be anyway he reasoned? Sha-Na was after all an Iroquois by birth and she did not seem to have a hateful bone in her body. From personal experience Little Fox knew how disagreeable the neighboring Kickapoo could be, yet the Sauk warriors in his clan could certainly match them. How much worse could the Iroquois be? The only disturbing stories he had heard were the manner in which the Iroquois tortured, murdered, and mutilated the French missionaries.

Could it really be true that the other foreigners called English offered trade goods for the hair of their enemies? Little Fox reasoned that if he were French he should probably be afraid. However, what amount of trade goods, or slaves, could possibly entice a warrior to travel so far for so little? With mixed emotions, Little Fox decided that his chance to prove his manhood in battle was remote at best.

Were it not for the sharp crack of a cottonwood branch that had sprawled upon the forest floor as a result of some recent thunderstorm, Little Fox might have missed the passage of one of the largest war parties to set foot in Illinois territory. This sudden snap on the far creek bank served to awaken him from his reverie. Little Fox's body tensed as he tuned all his senses to discovering the source of this specific sound against the background of the normal wilderness cacophony. The locust were singing a rasping late autumn concert. Insects hummed and buzzed. Reptiles and small animals rustled among the foliage. Was the cracking branch only the misstep of some larger mammal like a whitetail deer?

Suddenly, off to his left something glistened in the sun catching his attention. Was this the glint of a white flint lance blade in the afternoon sun? Little Fox's brow now broke out in a sweat as he had the sinking feeling that he had let the enemy discover him before he could warn his fellow tribesmen. Worse, had he let the enemy slip by his vantage post and on to his unsuspecting friends? So many questions remained unanswered. What could he do but remain hidden among the brush and try to verify what he feared had come to pass?

As the moments passed, the tension began to relax and Little Fox felt some relief. Seeing no more evidence of a war party, he began to rationalize that he was concerned over nothing. Maybe the flash of light had been a blue-jay wing as it rapidly ascended into the humid air, or a rock tumbling from its resting-place after being disturbed by a raccoon or rabbit. The piercing snap he had heard was surely the misstep of a grazing deer.

As Little Fox began to feel at ease, his vision came into clear focus upon what had been disguised heretofore. Suddenly, stealthy creeping men stripped to the waist with their bodies painted to gently blend with the landscape surrounded him. Each warrior moved quiet as a ghost. Their grim faces bespoke of their resolve. Several of this war party came so close that Little Fox could have reached out and touched them. The fact that these seasoned warriors did not detect his presence affirmed the woodland skill that the Sauk youth had already attained. Little Fox prayed to his Christian God that he could remain undetected and somehow alert his village and the French mission.

As soon as Little Fox guessed the last Iroquois warrior had passed his position he took a chance and bolted at a dead run onto the hard packed animal path that lead up over the bluff. Actually, Little Fox was running away from Mere D'Osia, but he reasoned that he must take a circuitous route to survive. Luckily, the Iroquois were moving slowly in order not to be discovered. They wanted to be silent in their approach to Mere D'Osia, which had been scouted the day before. Surprise coupled with the ferocity of the Iroquois attack would make their victory over the small mission easy. After burning the settlement, pillaging its stores, and killing all but the best prospects for slaves, they would move on to the next unfortunate village. Unfortunately for To-Ko-Wan and the Iroquois, Little Fox was a swift runner and he managed to alert the French and the Sauk warriors moments before the Iroquois arrived. While there was little time for preparation, Mere D'Osia was not engulfed in complete panic when the battle began in earnest.

While Major Stuart did not ascribe complete credibility to the rumors that a large band of Iroquois warriors were headed his way, his experience dictated that he always be prepared. For several weeks the French soldiers and many of the natives had worked to build a stone and earth palisade around the perimeter of the Mere D'Osia mission. Despite the grumbling complaints of his men about the foolishness of these preparations, Stuart had managed to build a very credible defensive position. The only tactical mistake that he could not correct was the insistence of the local natives in defending their settlement of sticks and mud huts beyond the mission perimeter. The natives adamantly refused to abandon their campfires and move their women behind bulwarks of the French palisade. To divide a defensive force in the face of unknown odds simply made no sense. It nearly resulted in complete disaster.

The ferocity of the Iroquois assault was only matched by the determination of the French defenders. With practiced military precision, the French fusiliers assembled the priests and the women in the safety of the mission church and closed ranks. By the time the first wave of screaming Iroquois broke through the dense foliage at the base of the river bluff French muskets were aimed to meet the onslaught. Major Stuart swung his saber in a short arc downward giving the signal to fire. The humid autumn air erupted with the flash and roar of ignited gunpowder. Within seconds all hell belched forth again as the front ranks knelt to reload and the rear rank laid a killing fire with deadly precision. Soon the fortifications were obscured by smoke coming from the repeating fire of five score guns, but no Iroquois blade had tasted enemy flesh.

As this great Iroquois war party had devastated one by one the villages on their path to the interior of the continent, they had become accustomed to quick and easy victories. While the Iroquois had learned in their skirmishes against armed foreigners to soften an enemy position with archers before a frontal assault, they had not expected Major Stuart's organized resistance. In this case, a tactical error accounted for the lives of many brave warriors. However, the war chief To-Ko-Wan's quick assessment of the situation and the large number of Iroquois served to nullify this short-term French advantage. Recognizing that the element of surprise would not carry the day, To-Ko-Wan held his warriors in reserve while his archers unleashed a devastating rain of arrows. While French chain mail provided marginal protection, the native Sauk warriors had little defense and their ranks were severely decimated. Before the Sauk could adequately recover, a detachment of Iroquois had broken through the Sauk defenses. In the subsequent hand-to-hand combat, the Sauk personally learned that the Iroquois reputation for warfare was well deserved. Being beyond musket range, Major Stuart and his French Fusiliers could only watch in anguish as many of their Sauk allies were killed. Only a few isolated bands of valiant Sauk warriors were able to withstand the Iroquois attack.

The French had little time to observe the fate of Sauk as the Iroquois turned their attention to the defensive position at the mission. Another hail of arrows served as a prelude to a two-pronged Iroquois attack. Before Major Stuart and his Fusiliers could totally recover, there were Iroquois warriors fighting hand-to-hand within their defensive perimeter. Stuart barely managed to direct another volley of musketry that temporarily stemmed the tide of the attacking Iroquois. The French knew that soon the temper of their cold steel blades would be tested in a life and death struggle. Considering the overwhelming number of Iroquois warriors Major Stuart gave his troops little chance of survival.

To-Ko-Wan prepared his personal squad to capture the French priests and heretic Iroquois maids alive. The priests would be publicly tortured to demonstrate the ineffectiveness of the Christian God to the local Iroquois vassals. Sha-Na, the Iroquois Christian convert, would be dragged back to Montreal and used to lure the Iroquois heretic Kateri Tekawetha from French protection. Then Kateri would be crucified upside-down and the threat of Christianity to the Five Nations of the Iroquois would end forever. To-Ko-Wan's spirit vision was surely coming to pass just as he had dreamed.

Suddenly, there was a rasping screech from above as a majestic, white-headed bird slowly circled above the battlefield. There was a glitter of flashing light as the rays of the late afternoon sun reflected from an object clutched in the bird's talons. Surprisingly, many of the combatants, including the Iroquois, paused from their feverish struggle to gaze above. Time was transfixed as recognition, like a bolt of lightning, flashed in To-Ko-Wan's brain. As the Iroquois war chief struggled to comprehend exactly what was happening to his best laid plans, the soaring eagle let the object loose from its grasp.

As fate, or perhaps Divine Guidance, would have it, a small band of Sauk warriors had managed to survive the initial Iroquois assault. Led by Little Fox, the youth that had first sounded the alarm, this band was actually holding its own to the point of actually going on the offensive. They had begun to advance toward the French redoubt that seemed to offer some limited protection from such overwhelming odds. Unlike many upon the field of battle, this small band of Sauk warriors did not have the luxury of pausing to observe the eagle in flight overhead. All of their energy was devoted to saving themselves from destruction. Consequently, the object dropped by the eagle landed within their midst nearly unnoticed. It was many minutes before a warrior retrieved the object and passed it to his leader.

At first Little Fox accepted the object with impatience at being bothered with such a small matter at this inopportune time. It took only a short time for Little Fox to grasp the real meaning of the divinely bestowed object. For upon closer inspection, Little Fox recognized a finely wrought battle lance of black obsidian. His quick wit grasped the monumental importance of the lance from heaven. Without stopping to question why, Little Fox lashed the lance to a nearby staff that had been discarded in the melee. Waving it in the air above the heads of his struggling, bloodstained kinsmen Little Fox shouted orders to continue the offensive. The immediate response was a resounding shout as the Sauk recognized their good fortune. Then came a roar from different sections of the battlefield as other Sauk warriors joined the song and redoubled their efforts. This mighty sound actually stopped the confident and determined Iroquois right in their tracks. After witnessing such an omen, the mighty Iroquois began to actually experience doubt about their own invincibility. This was all that was required to turn the tide.

To-Ko-Wan was the first to recognize that the attack of his Iroquois kinsmen was losing momentum. Realizing that he might have misinterpreted his spirit journey while he was in the French prison at Montreal, To-Ko-Wan was more determined to carry out his plans against Christianity regardless of divine intervention. To-Ko-Wan knew Kor-Oh-Tin and his other Iroquois friends would follow him anywhere and so he charged directly into the French line of muskets. He would capture Sha-Na and the French priests before the soldiers realized that was his true objective. Then To-Ko-Wan could put them under armed guard away from the battlefield and reorganize a counter-attack. The Iroquois war party numbered over five hundred before the assault and this superior force could still achieve victory.

It is important to understand the caliber of the Iroquois war party that was led into Illinois by To-Ko-Wan, Ta-wan'ne-ars, and So-no'-so-wa. Of all the North American tribes, few could match the skill, ferocity, and tenacity of the Iroquois. They are comparable to the present-day elite forces like the United States Marines or Rangers. Further, a significant portion of this Iroquois war party was taken from the Seneca tribe. Of the Five Nations of the Iroquois, the Seneca alone were bestowed the title of "keepers of the gate". In part this was due to their geographical position along the western march of Iroquois power. However none could deny that the Seneca held this sacred charge due to their skill in war. The Seneca were not only required to protect the Iroquois tribal fires from aggressors, but also to overrun and assimilate neighboring tribes. The Iroquois democratic vision of one united Indian tribe was focused in the Seneca tribe. It was the Seneca mission to spread this vision throughout North America. Indeed, this is the basis for the enduring Iroquois warlike reputation. Therefore, no isolated counterattack, even one like that mounted by the Sauk that seemed divinely inspired, could long deter the resolve of this Iroquois war party. In a relatively short time, To-Ko-Wan, Ta-wan'ne-ars, and So-no'-so-wa had again assumed the offensive.

The divine appearance of the eagle and the sacred lance allowed a tactical maneuver that saved the Sauk defenders from complete annihilation. Major Stuart knew that splitting his small force between the Mere D'Osia Church compound and the Sauk encampment by the river was a grave mistake. Even with an enemy force of comparable size, the division of a defensive force compromised a leader's chance of success. Given the superior Iroquois numbers and their resolve, it required divine intervention to save this day of battle from complete disaster.

Upon receipt of the lance from the sky, Little Fox, the only Sauk leader left standing, realized that his only chance to avoid complete annihilation was to join forces with the French. The inspiration of the lance coupled with the momentary disruption caused by the eagle's appearance gave Little Fox that chance. Instead of charging directly into the attacking Iroquois he led his force laterally toward the French redoubt. Likewise, Major Stuart seized the opportunity and directed his Fusiliers to concentrate fire upon that sector in order to soften the resistance to complete the maneuver. Soon the remaining Sauk warriors were fighting shoulder-to-shoulder to save Mere D'Osia from being completely overrun. As they all fought with renewed effort both the French and the Sauk realized that their very lives were at stake.

The death toll inflicted by the Fusiliers upon the initial Iroquois attack wave was incredible. While the Iroquois were familiar with the effectiveness of the foreign weapons due to past encounters with the French army, they did not expect such resistance from Jesuit priests with a few bodyguards. In truth, French missionaries were seldom accompanied with armed troops. After all, the message carried by the Jesuits was one of peace and coexistence. It seemed contrary to rational thought to believe the mission at Mere D'Osia could be any different. Yet Fathers Constance and Bertrand were Jesuits with vast experience in missionary work throughout the world. In order to be successful these good Fathers had learned early that they could not trust their security to the mercy of heathens and savages. Father Constance and Father Bertrand had placed their trust in Major Stuart and this had proved to be a wise decision.

Major Stuart had assembled one of the most effective fighting forces in the 17th century world of warfare. While primarily French, this force was truly multi-national. Stuart's subordinate officers were from France, England, Scotland, and the Low Countries. Each had years of experience in warfare ranging from continental wars to local rebellions. Above all, each officer was courageous and loyal beyond reproach. They knew military tactics and how to successfully overcome a superior force. These men would and had followed Major Stuart into the jaws of death. Likewise, each Fusilier was a veteran of many campaigns who knew how to survive and gain victory. While the Iroquois may have been the Marines of all Native American tribes, Major Stuart's Fusiliers were comparable to the Recon Rangers. The death and destruction that lay in front of the French fortification at Mere D'Osia was testament to the clash of these two elite forces.

Major Stuart's brief preoccupation with safely incorporating the remaining Sauk warriors within his defensive perimeter cost him the loss of something he held most dear. In the heat of battle, several French had been wounded. Likewise, many Iroquois who had succeeded in breaching the French battlement lay moaning from pitiful wounds. In the midst of all this carnage, the hearts of the Jesuit missionaries went out to all that suffered. Sha-Na and her sister missionaries quickly moved to give comfort to these wounded, both friend and foe. As a result, these angels of mercy left themselves unprotected and surrounded by fierce hand-to-hand combat. Before Major Stuart recognized the danger, To-Ko-Wan seized this opportunity to abduct Sha-Na, several other Christian Iroquois maids, and Father Bertrand. These prisoners were safely spirited to the rear and held under guard while To-Ko-Wan returned to finish the complete destruction of the mission called Mere D'Osia.

Indeed, it was quite sometime before Major Stuart realized the prize he had lost. In all his years as protector for Father Bertrand and Father Constance, Stuart had never allowed them to be placed in jeopardy. The fact that Stuart had probably never faced such experienced and determined enemies was not considered as an excuse. Likewise, Stuart was so engaged in saving the Sauk warriors that he barely survived the Iroquois offensive himself let alone provide security to others. While Stuart was truly lucky to be alive, the loss of those he had sworn to protect dealt a blow as savage as any Iroquois war club. However, the intensity of the renewed Iroquois onslaught left Stuart no time to find a way to correct the situation. Indeed, considering the sheer numbers of the enemy that pushed to break through his line of defense, Stuart knew that he would be lucky to see another sunset.

It seemed hours that the Mere D'Osia defenders stood strong to meet wave after wave of determined warriors although it was probably little more than one. At first, the precision volley of the battle-harden Fusiliers proved quite effective in demoralizing the enemy and discouraging frontal assault. Unfortunately, continued decimation of the French line and the brave determination of the Iroquois eventually wore down the defense. More and more Iroquois broke through the weakened lines to attack brave Frenchmen from behind. While continuing to successfully repulse these attacks, Major Stuart knew that soon the battle would be reduced to a hand-to-hand contest that he had no hope of winning. It was with much trepidation that Major Stuart walked his defensive lines shouting words of encouragement. The courageous French and Sauk defenders calmly awaited the final rush from the surrounding foliage that would spell their doom.

At that moment when everything seemed lost, salvation came marching along the riverbank to the south. At first, Major Stuart was barely aware of the flashing sunlight reflecting off armor and armaments. It was mistaken for the sun shining upon rippling waves stirred before a gusty wind. As another Iroquois wave, possibly the final one, broke cover there was no time to daydream about such things. The French released one final devastating volley before discarding their muskets and drawing their swords. Gunpowder smoke partially obscured the whooping warriors that were on a dead run to clash with the French defensive line. Cold steel would be their only hope of salvation in the face of the mighty Iroquois war clubs.

Few Iroquois in that final wave lived to meet the French standing grimly with drawn swords in front of the mission at Mere D'Osia. The mighty Iroquois were caught in a devastating crossfire that swept the no man's land leaving very few standing. Major Stuart and the French defenders could barely believe their eyes as their attackers were brought to the ground like ripe wheat stalks before a sharp scythe. Seizing the opportunity, Major Stuart ordered his troops across the body-strewn battlefield and into the trees. Since they could not withstand another concerted assault, Major Stuart had decided to take his chances with a counterattack. Fortunately, these final heroics proved unnecessary. To-Ko-Wan and the other Iroquois war chiefs had quickly assessed the situation. The remainder of the huge Iroquois war party disappeared into the forest like the wisps of musket smoke before the gusty wind. Recognizing the futility of another assault, the Iroquois began a swift and orderly retreat up river to the north.

As Major Stuart reached the tree line he was pleasantly surprised by what he found. There stood Henri Tonty directing a formidable force of La Salle's regulars. Tonty laughed heartily and spread his arms to embrace Stuart in a sincere bear hug.

"Mon Ami, now you know what it feels like to be snatched from complete despair, eh?" Tonty shouted over the hurrahs of both French forces as they met on the field of battle with unrestrained happiness.

"The Lord brought you to this place at a most opportune time!" Stuart said as he felt the weight of Tonty's iron fist slapping him on the back.

"I was looking forward to a delicious meal and some friendly conversation. Imagine my surprise when I found that I would have to earn it first," Tonty chuckled to himself.

"We are all most thankful for your fortunate return." Stuart spoke with evident fatigue in his voice. "If not for you, I am sure we would all be a feast for the crows."

"I could see that you were in desperate straits," Tonty replied seriously. "I was afraid to order a volley in close proximity to your position, but I could see no other alternative."

"Such peril also has its rewards. I'm afraid we had them in a crossfire. This amount of devastation always carries a price. I hope we did not likewise place your troops in jeopardy." Stuart spoke as a tactician rather than someone who had only minutes before faced death. He looked at his fallen comrades and shook his head.

"So goes the fortunes of war," Tonty said absentmindedly as he looked into Major Stuart's troubled eyes hoping to give some comfort.

"Now Mon Ami," Tonty continued, "please tell me how I can help you since you are evidently in distress. Are you wounded?" Tonty was referring to the damp spot of crimson on Stuart's tunic.

"No, no, it is nothing!" exclaimed Stuart. "I fear there is nothing I can do to correct my grievous mistake." Stuart's shoulders slumped and it seemed he would collapse to the ground. This was in contrast to the self-assured military officer Tonty and the other French troops had come to know.

"All is well," said Tonty grabbing Stuart around the waist to stop his fall. "I'm sure all is not so bleak."

"You cannot imagine," said Stuart dejectedly as if the weight of the world was resting squarely upon his shoulders. While a Fusilier began removing Stuart's chain mail to inspect a nasty wound to his left waist, a band of surviving Sauk warriors and several of Stuart's officers approached.

"Sir, is your wound serious?" asked one of the officers.

"Never mind me. Go and attend to what pitiful few of us remain." Stuart waved him off as he demonstrated sincere concern for his fellow troops that had suffered grievously.

"And how have you fared my young friend?" Stuart turned to address Little Fox, the leader of the Sauk band that had fought so courageously beside the French.

"I live and that is enough," Little Fox replied in a voice beyond his years. The heat of battle had sorely aged the young warrior.

"I see you still carry that special gift from God." Stuart referred to the sparkling obsidian lance that had mysteriously arrived on the wings of an eagle. The finely wrought black blade was even more magnificent up close.

"The Christian God protects much," said Little Fox reverently. He was obviously in awe of that defining moment. "His strong medicine saved us from death. We remember always." Little Fox spoke with halting French learned during his service at the mission of Mere D'Osia.

"It was more your courage than that rock that saved your life." Stuart paid homage to the bravery of his Sauk brothers who faced such overwhelming odds and managed to survive.

"No time talk," said Little Fox although he was obviously moved by this praise. "Must trail Iroquois so can save Mademoiselle Sha-Na and White Father."

Stuart looked deep into the eyes of Little Fox before replying. Stuart was obviously wrestling between duty and personal emotions just as he had these past several months. With all his heart Stuart wanted to rescue the woman he had come to love. But Stuart's sense of duty rejoined him to address his current responsibilities. The wounded must be attended to and the dead buried. Things must be put in order.

"How can you suggest such a thing with so much suffering around us?" The sound of Stuart's voice suggested that he was begging to be convinced otherwise.

"You mean these savages have taken that sweet maid Sha-Na and the good Father Bertrand captive?" Tonty interrupted. No one replied and only subdued nods answered his question.

"Then, by all that is holy, be on your way Major, and quickly!" Tonty shouted. "My troops will do what is necessary here. Your people are safe with us. Have no fear."

"But we have no experience with this savage land and we are not equipped to pursue an enemy across this wilderness." Stuart was rationally trying to weigh the odds of this mission.

"A few of us might just succeed where many would fail." Captain Reynard, one of Stuart's officers who had often served as scout, spoke with confidence. Reynard had spent much of his tour of duty at Mere D'Osia with the natives. He of all the French troops could speak from experience.

"I'm listening." Stuart's hope was rekindled.

"I venture to guess that the Iroquois force has split." Reynard drew his saber and drew a crude map in the bloodstained dirt. "The main Iroquois war party would retire up river. Even though decimated by this skirmish they are far from defeated and still a formidable force. They will maintain a rear guard and not be concern about pursuit considering the damage they have inflicted."

"How many do you estimate remain in this main force?" Tonty asked the obvious question.

"More than three hundred warriors," Reynard spoke in an even tone.

"No wonder they are not worried. They still outnumber us even in defeat," Tonty interjected.

"They are far from defeated, Captain Tonty," said Reynard. "Were it not for our musketry and their apparent mission to demonstrate their supremacy in this wilderness the Iroquois would not have given up until we were overrun. From the information received by Little Fox from surrounding tribal encampments, I believe the Iroquois will continue to pillage with little fear of retaliation."

"But what about the second Iroquois war party?" Stuart asked impatiently.

"That's the curious part. Sauk scouts dispatched to locate Mademoiselle Sha-Na report that a small party of approximately 20 or 30 Iroquois warriors have headed cross country in a northeasterly direction at a very fast pace." Reynard paused.

"What is your assessment of this development, Captain?" Stuart asked hopefully.

"It would appear this group is returning to the home fires of the Five Nations."

"But what of the captives? If they remain with the main Iroquois war party we have but little hope of rescuing them." Stuart hung on Captain Reynard's every word.

"There is hope. While the main war party continues to hold many prisoners, a few were sighted being force marched with the other war party on a trail up the bluff just east of here."

"And..................??"

"And we believe Sha-Na and Father Bertrand are with that group," Reynard replied confidently.

"Then, for whatever the reason, the Iroquois have given us a chance to rescue our friends. Do you have a plan?" Stuart could barely restrain himself.

"A small force traveling light has a chance to intercept this Iroquois war party. A few of the more hardy Fusiliers accompanied by Little Fox and several Sauk warriors might be able to save these prisoners from death on the trail or in captivity," said Reynard decisively.

"Then let us be off," said Major Stuart as he grabbed a musket and leather pack from another officer.

"But Major, you are wounded," Reynard started to object.

"Pay heed to your own resolve for I will not be an impediment to our success." Major Stuart was already ten paces ahead down the trail leading east across the river bottom before the other French and Sauk fell in behind him. Captain Reynard and Little Fox soon caught up with Stuart and Little Fox took the lead for he knew the last location of the Iroquois. The rescue party moved out at rout step. While the Sauk warriors whooped with enthusiasm, the French proceeded with grim resolve. They could have no rest until they encountered their quarry if they were to have any chance for success.

A thunderstorm rolled across the valley in a dark satin cloud against the bright autumn sun. Thunder rumbled and the gray sheet of torrential rain could be seen approaching in the distance. The warriors in Stuart's party welcomed the rain. It would disguise their pursuit to the departing Iroquois while making the fatigue of the cross-country trek more bearable. Their footing would become treacherous, but they could not afford to wait out the storm. They knew that each passing moment made the chance for a successful rescue more remote. Given the fatigue of the battle they had little hope of sustaining a long distance pursuit. Each face was grim with pain and determination as they pushed up the river bluff and into the woodlands beyond.

The Chase

To-Ko-Wan, Ta-wan'ne-ars, and So-no'-so-wa were indeed surprised to find themselves caught between two formidable French and Sauk forces. Each assumed that one final assault would secure the mission at Mere D'Osia. The Iroquois losses had been serious in the face of unexpected resistance, but certainly not debilitating. With the annihilation of the French force, the Iroquois would demonstrate their supremacy in the region. The Iroquois would then be free to plunder at will and take slaves back to their home fires. The appearance of a second French force made reassessment of the situation a necessity.

While To-Ko-Wan favored pressing the attack, Ta-wan'ne-ars and So-no'-so-wa showed reason and restraint. Ta-wan'ne-ars and So-no'-so-wa impressed upon To-Ko-Wan that they could not risk the security of the entire war party on a hurried attack against an unknown force. While victory would establish Iroquois dominance in this land once and for all, defeat would leave Iroquois warriors in a desperate situation many kilometers from home. This was a risk Ta-wan'ne-ars and So-no'-so-wa were unwilling to take. They reasoned it was better to regroup and continue raiding less defended villages in the area. Ta-wan'ne-ars and So-no'-so-wa knew that they had dealt a severe blow to the defending French force. They reasoned that for the weakened French pursuit was not an option.

When To-Ko-Wan realized that Ta-wan'ne-ars and So-no'-so-wa could not be persuaded to mount another assault on Mere D'Osia he begged them give him leave to return to Montreal. Ta-wan'ne-ars and So-no'-so-wa like To-Ko-Wan were convinced that Sha-Na was the key to ending the threat of Christianity to the Iroquois Nation. Kateri Tekawetha, the acknowledged leader of the Iroquois Christians, would likely leave Frontenac's protection to save her friends. To-Ko-Wan had little trouble convincing Ta-wan'ne-ars and So-no'-so-wa to let him choose a small party of warriors and proceed quickly to Montreal. Soon To-Ko-Wan, Kor-Oh-Tin and a score of seasoned Iroquois warriors were leading a group of French prisoners, including Sha-Na and Father Bertrand, single file along an ancient foot path that tracked to the northeast. They moved at a regular pace that was often slowed by prisoners who were tired from a long day of battle. Normally the Iroquois would dispatch those who could not keep pace, but To-Ko-Wan could not afford to harm Sha-Na and the French priest. After making little progress, To-Ko-Wan and his Iroquois brethren were forced to stop for the night. The Iroquois made campfires in a secluded creek valley nestled close to the river bluff to cook and provide warmth against the damp night. They took comfort in knowing that French pursuit was unlikely.

As evening approached, Little Fox took the lead of the determined rescuers. The late afternoon thunderstorm had broke to a crisp and clear autumn evening. A huge orange harvest moon made its appearance on the eastern horizon to light their way. As the evening shadows lengthened the moon lit the land in a surreal light. The beauty of this silver glaze somehow eased the painful muscles as the pursuers pressed on in their life-saving marathon. The cooling dampness of the impending frost quieted their passing. With an almost uncanny sense of direction Little Fox led them single file along ancient deer trails winding endlessly through the wilderness. Each warrior, both Sauk and Fusilier, knew that they must catch up to the Iroquois war party before the trail stretched beyond Little Fox's knowledge and everyone's endurance.

Little Fox stopped to kneel in the orange tinged sumac bordering the muddy animal path. Without a signal each warrior followed suit and peered ahead to identify the reason for the unforeseen hiatus. The white bark of several huge sycamores dotting the shallow, steep valley stood out starkly against the reflecting moonlight. Against the ghostly gray bark of a white oak tree flickered the red-orange light of a subdued campfire. Quickly Little Fox dispatched a scout to determine if they had been lucky enough to reach their elusive objective. Within minutes which seemed more like hours as fatigue began to dull the senses, Major Stuart received the welcome news that his prayers had been answered. The Iroquois raiding party was camped directly ahead.

That night Major Stuart, Little Fox, Captain Reynard and their companions struck the Iroquois encampment like a lightning bolt of the recently departed afternoon thunderstorm. The surprise was complete to the point that there was no initial organized resistance. While the Iroquois sentries were seasoned warriors they were fatigued from the stress of the recently fought battle. Further, the Ho-de-no-sau-nee enjoyed a false sense of security by believing that they would not be pursued. In stark contrast, the French and Sauk warriors fought like men possessed in the knowledge that failure in the rescue of their friends would be worse than death itself. With grim determination their blades flashed in the moonlight. Crimson pools sent sweet clouds of steam aloft as it contacted the early descending frost. The sentries were cut down quickly as the swift attack pierced to the heart of the Iroquois camp. In a moment less than ten Iroquois warriors stood between the rescuers and their captive friends.

Little Fox had been overzealous in his attempt to free the captives. All, including Major Stuart, had followed Little Fox's assault on the Iroquois encampment.

Indeed, one Iroquois sentry had succumbed so fast to the thrusts of Little Fox's lance, the very blade delivered by the eagle during the melee at Mere D'Osia, that he undoubtedly felt invincible. Still, To-Ko-Wan's mighty war club met this onslaught quite decisively. Somehow it was appropriate that these two inanimate objects, the war club and the blade, both descended from heaven, should meet in the conflict.

To-Ko-Wan's war club was the epitome of barbaric savagery. This war club was fashioned in the classic Iroquois manner. Resembling a gun stock, the club held a wicked iron blade embedded and lashed tightly to the wood. It was adorned with one eagle feather, the spirit guide of To-Ko-Wan. But the uniqueness of this particular war club lay in the variety of trinkets adorning the stock. For in his continuing crusade to stamp out Christianity among his people, To-Ko-Wan had used the club to savagely execute several Jesuit priests. The devotional cross of each priest adorned To-Ko-Wan's instrument of death. To-Ko-Wan had carved an inverted cross deeply into the handle to underscore his disdain for Christianity, the religion of the weak. This was the weapon that met the thrusts of Little Fox head on.

Undoubtedly Little Fox was beginning to feel the effects of the ordeal he had faced that day. Still his first thrust had nearly pierced To-Ko-Wan's black heart before the war club had deflected the blow away. Two more determined slashes by Little Fox succeed in keeping To-Ko-Wan on the defensive. It seemed for a moment that victory was within Little Fox's grasp. But, as Little Fox pressed the attack To-Ko-Wan sensed his opponent's strength was waning. One cunning side step and the evil war club was deeply embedded in Little Fox's side. Little Fox's lance was shattered and the blade that had delivered such a sweet victory earlier that day was cast off into the wilderness in defeat. As Little Fox's excruciating cry of pain echoed through the ghostly sycamores in the surrounding hollow, Major Stuart became aware of the life-and-death struggle too late to save his friend. But the outcome hardened his heart.

Like chaff against the wind Stuart dispatched the lone Iroquois warrior standing between him and his dying friend. Certainly, no solitary sole could stand between the Major's cold steel and this embodiment of evil. To-Ko-Wan barely had time to recover his balance to meet the onslaught. For a moment these two warriors glared at each other in the dying campfire light. Defeat and death never entered the mind of either opponent. One would surely taste these bitter pills.

Kor-Oh-Tin, To-Ko-Wan's faithful brother, sensed that Sha-Na and the priest held the keys to safe passage for the Iroquois. Kor-Oh-Tin moved quickly to claim them as hostages. While Kor-Oh-Tin knew that nothing could stop the impending conflict, he wished to have an option should the battle turn sour for his brother. However, Captain Reynard likewise sensed the importance of the captives and made his move to protect them. Immediately Reynard and Kor-Oh-Tin were involved in a deadly struggle.

Kor-Oh-Tin was swift and it seemed he would reach the captives first, thereby avoiding a fight. But Reynard was very resourceful. The Captain tossed a piece of firewood at Kor-Oh-Tin's feet that brought the Iroquois tumbling to the ground. By the time Kor-Oh-Tin regained his balance, Captain Reynard had positioned himself between the Iroquois and the prisoners. Kor-Oh-Tin knew he would have to cut down the Frenchman to retrieve his hostages. He swung his war club menacingly as he advanced. Reynard readied his long sword in one hand and a leather coverlet as a shield in the other.

In a split second this battle was at an end. Kor-Oh-Tin assumed the offensive but cunningly stopped short in his attack. This was intended to throw the Frenchman off balance as he lunged at empty air, but Reynard was an expert swordsman. As Reynard calmly stood his ground it was the Iroquois who became confused, as his opponent did not make the anticipated response. Reynard's downward blow with the hilt of his sword dislodged the war club from Kor-Oh-Tin's fist. A crashing blow from Reynard's leathered fist sent Kor-Oh-Tin sprawling and dazed to the frosty white speckled grass. Reynard's lightning sword thrust to Kor-Oh-Tin's heart was cut short by a restraining arm from behind. Reynard turned in surprise to see Sha-Na's piercing brown eyes silently imploring him to spare her tribal brother. In a moment, Kor-Oh-Tin was now a prisoner and everyone turned their attention to the gargantuan struggle unfolding by the blazing orange campfire.

Two ideals clashed that night in the silvery moonlight of the North American wilderness. Each opponent was instilled with the cumulative wisdom of their competitive civilization. Failure was not an option for defeat would somehow negate generations of collective thought. Such an idea had never and could never be contemplated. The heavy breathing of the fatigued opponents as they calmly sparred to gain an advantage only broke silence.

Perhaps physically Major Stuart was the weaker of the two combatants. After all, he had been wounded earlier in the day and had since expended much of his strength in a headlong rush through the primeval wilderness in pursuit of the captives. The natives of the New World, particularly the warlike Iroquois, tempered their strength by facing the constant hardships of daily survival. While both Stuart and To-Ko-Wan were seasoned veterans of war, the Iroquois had undoubtedly faced more extreme personal hardship. Further, To-Ko-Wan's heart burned with a perpetual desire to destroy the very roots of a foreign religion growing like a weed in his native land. In retrospect, one might wonder how Major Stuart had any chance of success at all.

But weighed against seemingly overwhelming physical odds were Stuart's sense of duty, his unswerving loyalty, and his survival in many previous life-and-death struggles. Stuart's numbed sense of deadly determination was further enhanced by the grisly death of his friend Little Fox at the hands of this demon incarnate. The reality of the sight had totally erased the idea of failure from Stuart's mind. The man facing the Iroquois in this deadly struggle was totally focused upon making death to his enemy a certainty. Had the Iroquois possessed the ability to realize the extremity of such determination, he might have been plague with a tinge of doubt.

As with his brother Kor-Oh-Tin, To-Ko-Wan was inclined to use cunning instead of brute force to win a battle. In most cases, a feint or unanticipated move brought To-Ko-Wan's opponents to their defeat in short order. But most seasoned warriors know this and compensate for it. Indeed, this was exactly how Captain Reynard was able to dispatch To-Ko-Wan's brother in such short order. Unfortunately, To-Ko-Wan in his disdain for all foreigners did not recognize the fact that anyone of them could be his equal as a warrior. Consequently, when To-Ko-Wan tumbled obliquely to trip up Stuart with a sweep of his war club, Stuart simply stepped to the side. In a split second, To-Ko-Wan paid for his disrespect as Stuart's rapier plunged deftly into the Iroquois' side. Surprise and disbelief painted the native's face as he retreated a few steps to regain his composure. Blood stained To-Ko-Wan's white deerskin leggings as he moved to attack again. This time blows were exchanged with little effect as both men realized that the outcome would not be decided quickly.

To-Ko-Wan had fought men that used two swords before. In each case he had learned to pay heed to their left side. Death would come to those who did not show respect. However, To-Ko-Wan had also learned that the strength was in the right side. Further, a warrior armed with two weapons usually compromised themselves as they tried to mount a concerted attack. Cunningly, To-Ko-Wan reasoned that Stuart would soon follow this rule and let down his guard.

Unfortunately for the Iroquois shaman, nothing could be further from the truth. While the strength might have been in Stuart's right-handed rapier, the left-handed short sword kept finding unprotected flesh with unerring accuracy. Soon To-Ko-Wan was bleeding from multiple cuts while the Frenchman remained nearly untouched. To-Ko-Wan found himself breaking his concentration as he tried to anticipate which hand would deal the next blow. To-Ko-Wan's early arrogance was eventually replaced with disbelief that a foreigner might be his equal. He found himself starting to rely more on brute force than cunning. To-Ko-Wan's lethal war club had never failed him before. He reasoned that it would soon prove the difference in this matter.

With methodical precision, Major Stuart began to wear down his opponent. Stuart fought like a man possessed. When he started the trek across country to catch up with the Iroquois war party, Stuart was determined to let nothing stand in the way of rescuing his friends and love. The death of several companions before his very eyes, especially his friend Little Fox, had endowed him with supernatural strength. Nothing could withstand his frenzied onslaught. Eventually, To-Ko-Wan came to realize this and for the first time in his life To-Ko-Wan came to know true fear. In desperation, To-Ko-Wan found himself blindly flaying at the determined Frenchman that countered his every attack. Exhaustion began to take its toll, as drops of crimson stained the ground from To-Ko-Wan's multiple wounds. Finally, a tragic miscalculation left To-Ko-Wan open to the Frenchman's skilled left-hand. One quick flash of the short sword and To-Ko-Wan was flat on his back as Stuart prepared to administer the coup-de-grace.

They say a man's life flashes before him at the moment of his death. This may have been the case for To-Ko-Wan for they say his gaze was that of a blind man as Stuart's rapier prepared to make its deadly descent. In any event, To-Ko-Wan made no attempt at defense as he stoically resigned to accept his fate. Time was truly suspended in space as the surrounding skirmishes, many likewise to the point of life-and-death, seemed to pause in anticipation of the outcome of this defining moment. Perhaps all the combatants realized the true impact of what was about to occur.

"Ayy-eeee, non, non!" The shrieking wail of a woman's voice broke the spell of silence.

As Stuart unconsciously turned his attention toward the source of the sound, To-Ko-Wan unexpectedly receive a chance to extricate himself and resume the fight. However, the Iroquois still remained transfixed numbly staring at the first stars twinkling in the twilight.

In a heartbeat Stuart realized his error and returned his attention to the business at hand. But it was too late to conclude this mortal struggle. Indeed, he was forced to drop the point of his rapier in response to what he beheld. The Iroquois maid Sha-Na had thrown herself between Stuart and To-Ko-Wan. She boldly shielded her tribal brother from his impending death.

At that precise moment Major Stuart realized two things. First, he was struck with the simple fact that had continued to evade him these many months in the North American wilderness. Stuart had found the love of his life. He had grappled with a shadowy foe that would not reveal itself. That shadow had made Stuart continually nervous and restless for he could not fight what he could not understand. Now he knew that the shadow that caused him so much turmoil was the fear of being committed to something he could not control. Total love was a new experience to Stuart. Being a military officer Stuart was comfortable in always knowing his options. Love placed him at the mercy of another. Stuart had always feared what he could not control. Until now he readily avoided the prospect of placing himself in such an uncomfortable position.

Second, Stuart realized that he might have just lost the most precious thing in his life. The Christian ideal of mercy had placed his newly found treasure in a most untenable position. Stuart knew that the Iroquois shaman had simply to draw his knife and take the maiden as hostage. Stuart's moment of victory was irretrievably transformed into a time of utter despair. No amount of cunning or fancy swordplay could retrieve Sha-Na from the hands of this devil incarnate.

Then fate stepped in to turn the table in a most astounding manner. To-Ko-Wan had been watching the events of the past few seconds as an observer cut off from the action. It was as if another person inhabited his body and he was totally removed from his impending death. As a spirit floating in the cool night breeze To-Ko-Wan was unconcerned about the things that preoccupy most humans. Hunger, thirst, pain, fear, happiness and all the other emotions that obsess us no longer held sway upon To-Ko-Wan's psyche. Rather, in this removed and peaceful state, To-Ko-Wan was able to reflect upon the passing of the events. He beheld his brother, Kor-Oh-Tin, lying wounded and bleeding in the ashes of the dim firelight. He watched as the priest, Father Bertrand, tried to staunch Kor-Oh-Tin's bleeding with shreds of linen from the shirt off his back. This was the same priest who To-Ko-Wan had dragged by a rawhide thong that chaffed his neck for many kilometers fearing death every step of the way.

Likewise, To-Ko-Wan saw Sha-Na, the self-proclaimed heretic of the old Iroquois ways, place her body between himself and the blade that would end his existence upon this earth. This was the same woman that To-Ko-Wan had told he would use to lure the Christian traitor, Kateri Tekawetha, to her death at Montreal. To-Ko-Wan struggled to fathom how his enemies, being so near to death themselves, could possibly show compassion for the Iroquois raiders. At that point, To-Ko-Wan heard the shrill shriek of his eagle spirit as it circled in his mind's eye in the vast blue sky above. Oblivious to worldly events around him,

To-Ko-Wan watched as the eagle released an object that descended to pierce his heathen heart. It was in the shape of a crucifix and when it struck To-Ko-Wan things were never to be the same. A blinding flash of light brought To-Ko-Wan back to reality with a strange sense of peace. No longer did he care about himself personally. To-Ko-Wan's life was transfigured as he realized the true meaning of the Christian doctrine. To-Ko-Wan collapsed in the welcoming arms of his blood sister Sha-Na content to accept his fate whatever that may be.

Major Stuart's mission to rescue the hostages and his beloved Sha-Na was a great success. The capitulation of To-Ko-Wan ended all Iroquois resistance that night. Mercy was shown to all the survivors and the dead was given a proper burial the following morning. In reality, too few warriors remained on either side. The Sauk allies had suffered grievously with the loss of their leader, Little Fox. Too few French would make the trek back to Mere D'Osia as well. As for the proud Iroquois, only four including To-Ko-Wan and Kor-Oh-Tin lived and each had sustained serious wounds. The sense of victory was tempered with extreme sadness as the very small band broke camp the following day to return to the mission on the Illinois River.

Devastated Mission

Tonty and the survivors at Mere D'Osia were extremely happy to see their friends return. The happy sight of Father Bertrand and Sha-Na alive provided welcome contrast to the death and destruction that surrounded the mission. News of the miraculous conversion of To-Ko-Wan and Kor-Oh-Tin further served to bolster the spirit of each newborn native Christian and provide hope for a brighter tomorrow. Father Bertrand spent many hours teaching the two new Iroquois Christians who were eager to learn all the mysteries of their new faith.

Although the presence of To-Ko-Wan and Kor-Oh-Tin at first tended to make everyone uncomfortable, the actions of these new Christian Iroquois soon won everyone over. Grateful for their salvation, To-Ko-Wan and Kor-Oh-Tin pitched in immediately to aid the wounded and comfort those who grieved. Even though their own wounds could be termed serious, they stoically proceeded to help others. Being a shaman trained in administering ancient remedies through the use of forest herbs, To-Ko-Wan proved invaluable in healing when French medical techniques failed. Many inhabitants of Mere D'Osia recovered, as a result of To-Ko-Wan's knowledge and determination to practice his new religion.

Unfortunately, the food stores of grain, fruits and vegetables harvested for the long winter had been devastated by the Iroquois raid on the mission. The inhabitants of Mere D'Osia would go into the desolate season of cold and snow with little to eat but what the hunters could harvest. Meat could be tasty but the health of the less hardy depended upon a well-rounded diet that would not be available. Likewise, the Iroquois raiding party had desolated many of the surrounding native villages. While many natives had died in battle, many more would die from hunger before the snow melted the following spring. Supplication was made daily to God to see them through this time of great hardship.

In the midst all this death and destruction, God continued to bless his people. The romance between Major Stuart and Sha-Na blossomed like a lily in springtime. This was in direct contrast to the bleakness of the approaching winter. Before the Iroquois raid, Jon Stuart had been totally committed to his mission as protector of the French missionaries. Now that had all been replaced by a total commitment to the love of a woman. While Stuart did not shirk his duties as leader of the French military contingent at Mere D'Osia, everyone understood that Sha-Na had now become his sole reason for living. The two were nearly inseparable. When Sha-Na offered her daily prayers Stuart could always be found kneeling beside her. Likewise, when Stuart inspected his troops, Sha-Na could be seen meekly observing the proceedings in an obscure position near the parade field. This mutual devotion compounded their effectiveness in all things. Consequently, the mission at Mere D'Osia was never better prepared to deal with adversity.

As the days grew shorter and the nights grew colder, Father Constance and Father Bertrand spent many weary nights in the sanctuary of the Mere D'Osia chapel praying for an answer to the suffering that had descended upon their flock of native Christians. Sha-Na would often enter the sanctuary of the mission church each morning to find both priests mumbling prayers in the flickering light of low burning tapers. Though nearing exhaustion both priest would refuse breakfast and remain at their lonely vigil. The chill of the descending winter mirrored the anguish in their hearts. Surely God would not desert his faithful flock.

At the time when hope was nearly gone an answer came from a most unexpected source. To-Ko-Wan had embraced the new religion with zeal unlike that of even the most committed converts. The ex-shaman wanted to know everything about his newly acquired Savior. Surprisingly, Major Stuart had become a steadfast friend of his recent mortal enemy. The Major spent many evenings reading from the Bible and relating the stories most of us have learned as children. To-Ko-Wan was especially taken with the idea that a God could so care for his people that he willingly suffered with them. The idea of Emmanuel, or "God With Us", being born in the lowliest of conditions simply amazed the Iroquois warrior. That an all-powerful being could be humbled in such a manner seemed a complete contradiction.

To-Ko-Wan especially liked the idea that only a few could really fathom God's will for his people. In his mind, To-Ko-Wan kept returning to the manner in which God through his spirit guide had brought him to this point in his life. To-Ko-Wan had been blind in his persecution of these Christians, but now he understood. He saw himself as a latter day Paul, chosen to perform a special mission to help fulfill God's plan. Nothing would ever be the same for him again. To-Ko-Wan sensed that God still had a purpose for him to fulfill in this world. Surely, To-Ko-Wan's attraction to the Christ in the stable had application to this current desperate situation. To-Ko-Wan began to practice prayer as a means to fathom how he could be of service to his new God.

Then it came to To-Ko-Wan just as the blade had descended from the sky piercing his heart and leading to his conversion. Like the wise-men from the land of light came bearing gifts for our God born in a stable, so should the people of the surrounding villages bring what little extra they had to feed and cloth the less fortunate. At first, Father Constance and Father Bertrand were negative about the whole idea arguing that with such devastation there would be nothing to give. But then To-Ko-Wan spoke of the few loaves and fish feeding the multitude and their hearts were swayed. They understood that God worked in strange ways, to perform his miracles. Who were they to question a revelation that was perhaps the answer to their own prayers as well?

All in the wilderness parish started preparing to observe the Festival of the Nativity. Joy began to replace the hopelessness and gloom. Man does not live by bread alone and even if there was not enough to eat, they could still make a joyous noise unto the Lord. Likewise, the many surrounding villages devastated by the recent warfare joined Mere D'Osia in this endeavor. What little of the food and clothing that remained could, at least, be shared to make life easier for awhile. The rest must be left to God. Faith and, perhaps, a miracle would see these newly converted Christians through this time of hardship.

Father Constance and Father Bertrand, for their part, took charge of organizing the Festival of the Nativity that would soon be celebrated for the first time in this wilderness outpost. A schedule of worship culminating with a feast at the winter solstice was outlined. While there was little food available to feed the body at least the spirits of the faithful could be sustained with the Holy Word. Actually, these preparations for a festival unlike any of these natives had ever known served to keep all from dwelling upon hunger, famine, and possible death.

Father Constance even devised an elaborate ritual that would culminate on the Feast Day of the Birth of Our Lord. To teach the lessons of giving and sharing with neighbors, Father Constance proposed that a type of play be devised and acted out. Of course, the scene would be the stable in which Our Lord was born. Key parts in this play, like Mary, Joseph, and the Wise men would be bestowed based upon selfless acts that the natives had performed for one another. The general native population could all participate by acting out the shepherds that came to adore our new born Savior on that singular night so long ago. Father Bertrand suggested that everyone bring gifts to lie before the King of Kings. While these poor people had little to spare as gifts, Father Bertrand was convinced that God would provide for his newly converted congregation. Certainly, these meager gifts left in adoration of the Lord might prove the difference between life and death for the starving. Soon it seemed the winter countryside was warming up with activity in preparation for the approaching festival.

Now Henri Tonty, the savior of Mere D'Osia, had been ordered by La Salle to meet the Griffin, a French frigate that sailed the vast lakes to the north, late that autumn season. In fact, Tonty had been returning from the south in route to fulfill La Salle's mission when he fortunately came to the rescue of Mere D'Osia. In his loyalty to La Salle's vision of a New France, Tonty had dutifully verified that the great river to the west flowed into a vast body of water many kilometers to the south. Tonty was convinced that this ocean could be accessed from the east and France. Since the native resistance amounted to only a few poorly armed savages, it seemed reasonable to assume that La Salle's interior continental French settlement could be supplied from the south using this great river. No longer would French colonists and adventurers have to suffer the terrors of a northerly trek through a wilderness claimed by their mortal enemy, the English, and fiercely guarded by the savage Iroquois. Tonty was sure that his master, La Salle, would be overjoyed to hear this good news.

The rescue of Major Stuart and his valiant Fusiliers had delayed Tonty in his march north to meet La Salle and his ship called the Griffin. Indeed, the devastation visited upon the French mission at Mere D'Osia was so great that Tonty could not bring himself to leave his friends to suffer. Many days passed before the wounded were bandaged and the dead buried. It took even more time to hunt and store meat for the fast approaching winter. Ice had formed upon all but the swiftest streams by the time Tonty felt comfortable enough to leave his comrades and journey north to link up with his commander, La Salle. It was with deep regret that Tonty moved out with his French troops one snowy morning.

Starvation would now be a constant predator stalking the Mere D'Osia mission. Being only primitive farmers, the local natives of the Illinois country relied heavily upon dried meat called pemmican. Unfortunately, the Iroquois warriors had generally destroyed the food stores of vegetables, fruit, and meat. To compound the distress, many of the hunters that daily provided fresh game throughout the long, cold winter had died in the battle. The local natives of the Mere D'Osia area barely had daily sustenance. Death began to visit the aged, infirm and the very young with distressing regularity by the time the ground turned white.

Sha-Na was able to get Major Stuart to concede in a matter that she likewise felt compelled to insist upon. Sha-Na's Iroquois brothers, Kor-Oh-Tin and To-Ko-Wan, had been miraculously converted to the Christian faith in the heat of mortal combat. Their evident sincerity had been so strong that all but the most vengeful inhabitant of Mere D'Osia had accepted them into the fold. The work of Kor-Oh-Tin and To-Ko-Wan eventually saved more lives than they had claimed. Therefore, through reverent prayer Sha-Na became convinced that both must accompany her beloved Stuart into the frozen north. She felt that God sent her Iroquois brothers for the salvation of this simple mission on the prairie. If something good was to come from the trek north, Kor-Oh-Tin and To-Ko-Wan would have to go with the travelers.

On a cold and blustery morning in early winter Major Stuart ventured forth with a small party in search of salvation for their suffering friends. Few word were spoken.

"Go in peace and may God Almighty bless your mission," said Father Constance. Father Bertrand offered a brief prayer.

"Farewell, my love," said Sha-Na. Her voice trembled from deep emotion even though the cold wind chilled everyone to the bone.

"I'll count the hours until I return." Jon Stuart took her in his arms for one last kiss.

"I had this vision of a great darkness enveloping the land. It ended in a blinding light. I awoke suddenly, but with a sense of peace. What can it all mean?" Sha-Na whimpered at the prospect of Jon leaving.

"Do not fear, my love. I have faith in my return and then we can be together." Jon gave her a final embrace and left with grim determination.

To accomplish his mission, Stuart handpicked a platoon from his crack Fusiliers. Several officers and twenty warriors from the Illini tribes that surrounded Mere D'Osia joined them. This basic war party was well armed but carried few provisions. The plan was to leave what little stores remained at the settlement.

The party would live on what wild game they could procure. Their hope was to meet La Salle's supply ship, the Griffin, on the great northern lake. Tonty had assured Stuart that La Salle would be generous with the supplies that had been brought to this distant land to support future colonization.

Despite the frigid temperatures and the drifting snow, Stuart's party proceeded north at a rapid pace. Soon they were camped along the river at the foot of the precipice where Fort Creve-Coeur lay above in charred ruins. The birch bark canoes were light with a shallow draft that slid easily upstream. Although rowing upstream was difficult, the men were accustomed to such work. The main problem encountered by the party was the thickening ice that had begun to choke off the flow of water along the riverbank. They camped only long enough to prepare a warm meal and rest overnight next to a blazing campfire. The warmth rekindled their spirits and these brave men were back on the river before daylight. Tonty encouraged haste for he feared that the ordeal at Mere D'Osia had already caused them to tarry to long. As the winter season made the vast northern sea more treacherous, La Salle would be less inclined to remain at the rendezvous. La Salle would retire to some safe harbor where he would await the spring thaw. Without an idea of that location, Stuart's band would be forced to return to Mere D'Osia empty-handed. Both Stuart and Tonty knew that was not an option.

The days of travel northward passed in rapid succession. The work of rowing the canoes kept them warm and the nights by a warm campfire were blessed relief. As warriors they were all used to forced marches with little rations. Their grim determination to accomplish this mission kept them from complaining. Only twice did they encamp for more than one day to hunt and prepare the meat for travel. On both occasions, their new God blessed them with bountiful game, which buoyed their spirits. Kor-Oh-Tin and To-Ko-Wan each set an example by praying dutifully for deliverance. Time was devoted to services rendering praise to God. Hope remained high as they approached the shoreline of the great northern sea. With a little guidance from above Tonty was sure that he could find the Griffin and return them all safely home.

The day was blustery and gunmetal gray clouds hung low off shore when the brave party finally reached the beach of the great Inland Sea. Sand whipped into the air and the scrubby brush bent before the cold, howling wind that blew from the northwest. Stuart's Fusiliers quickly established a base camp at the base of a cliff offering some respite from the wind. Tonty sent native scouts led by To-Ko-Wan and Kor-Oh-Tin to the southeast and northwest in search of La Salle's frigate. Tonty was sure that the ship would be near if they were not already too late. Anyone with spare time prayed diligently that God would not forsake their quest.

Kor-Oh-Tin and his scouts returned from the northwest as the frigid pink sun set in the west. They had traveled many kilometers without encountering a sign of life. Kor-Oh-Tin vowed to return at sunrise. Yet, the desolate beach that continued on toward the horizon offered little hope. Everyone hoped that To-Ko-Wan would return with better news, but night fell without any sign of these scouts. Still, God seemed to encourage them as the cold, wintry wind died down and the stars came out in magnificent splendor against a background of dark blue velvet. Another welcome sign was the speck of light that danced far off along the shoreline to the south. Had To-Ko-Wan decided to camp there for the night and continue scouting at first light, or was this something else? Stuart's party could only wait for news as they tried to remain warm when the temperature began to drop.

At about midnight Stuart's sentries noted movement along their defensive perimeter. Before long one of To-Ko-Wan's scouts was breathlessly crouched by the smoldering campfire drinking broth and relating his message to Stuart and Tonty. Kor-Oh-Tin acted as interpreter.

"Ask him where the rest of To-Ko-Wan's scouts are?" Tonty was impatient for news, barely able to contain his curiosity.

"Now, now, monsieur," Stuart gestured with his hand to slow down. "Give the man time to catch his breath."

Kor-Oh-Tin in the mean time had asked the question and nodded his head trying to understand the rather lengthy reply. As soon as the scout stopped to catch his breath, Kor-Oh-Tin began to speak.

"It seems that as the evening shadows began to lengthen, the scouting party became aware of a glowing light off in the distance along the shore. My brother, To-Ko-Wan, decided that they must not waste time to rendezvous with us and retrace their steps in the morning. If this happened to be a bonfire signaling the presence of La Salle's supply ship, they could not risk the chance that it might sail on the morrow."

Both Stuart and Tonty indicated their understanding and encouraged Kor-Oh-Tin to continue.

"Proceeding at a rapid pace toward the light nearly led to disaster for the scouts," said Kor-Oh-Tin abruptly. Before either Stuart or Tonty could ask why, Kor-Oh-Tin was again conversing with the scout. All were forced to await a reply while the interrogation continued. After several minutes, Kor-Oh-Tin was ready to relate the latest installment.

"For God's sake, monsieur, please continue." Tonty was beginning to pace nervously beside the dying embers of the campfire.

"To-Ko-Wan and his scouts arrived at a promontory overlooking the beach still nearly a kilometer from the bonfire. There anchored in a small inlet along the coast was this grand boat the likes of which the Fox scouts had never seen. Luckily, the Iroquois in the party had seen such things and were able to quickly assess the situation."

"Oui, oui. The situation was what?" Tonty wanted to speed up the story, but his impatience was only dragging the story out.

"The bonfire was actually a defensive perimeter of wood from the ship that apparently had been lighted to forestall a final assault on the ship and its crew. The beach was teeming with a band of Huron warriors. Fortunately for our friends, the Huron's attention was directed at the ship."

"And so To-Ko-Wan is safe for now?" Stuart wanted direct confirmation.

"Oui, but for how long we cannot guess. The Huron's are like our animal spirit the cougar. If they believe their prey is at their mercy, the Huron are inclined to play at the game. If this is so, they will not attack before sunrise." Kor-Oh-Tin seemed confident in his assessment.

"Bon!" Stuart exclaimed as he began barking orders to his men to break camp. "A forced march will put us with To-Ko-Wan's scouts before sunrise."

"But, will we be prepared to fight as we are already fatigued from the long march this day and the freezing cold? The scout indicated we will be sorely outnumbered." Tonty grabbed Stuart's tunic in an effort to forestall an impetuous decision.

"We have no choice, Mon Ami. The ship has the rations that will see Mere D'Osia through this extreme winter. If the ship is lost, we are lost as well. Failure is not an option, for if we fail, we have no reason to return to the mission!" Stuart looked his friend straight in the eye as he calmly replied. The balance of the Fusiliers heard this exchange and shouted a hearty "Hurrah" as they broke camp. Their leader had issued a challenge. They could not accept failure as an option.

The small band of French and Indians trudged off into the quiet starlit night. The wind had laid and the lake waves had seemed to calm. In spite of fatigue and the bone-chilling cold, their steps almost seemed light as they advanced into the unknown. Their goal was clear and ever present as the light of the Griffin's bonfire grew with each stride. Soon they would be able to test their mettal against another native war party. The Fusiliers had already gained the respect of the fierce Iroquois. How much of a threat could the lesser Huron be? Fear was in the back of everyone's mind, but these were professional soldiers and their experience proved that they knew their profession well. The hours passed quickly and soon they were linked with To-Ko-Wan's small band that were entrenched upon the promontory overlooking the battlefield. The horizon was turning pink with the first light of day as Tonty and Stuart split their forced to outflank the Huron. Surprise would be on their side and surprise alone has been known to win the field. As luck would have it, Tonty and Stuart were able to get into position without the Huron's detecting that anything was amiss. Indeed, the Huron were much too occupied with the anticipation of plundering a French supply ship to take other precautions. In the midst of their native wilderness, how could the Huron's suspect that they were not alone on that deserted beach?

Salvation!

A resounding Huron war cry split the interminable silence on the beach and several score of savages charged the smoldering wooden ramparts that had provided security to the ship's crew through the night. In quick response, the ship's defenders released a musket volley that fell many Huron in their tracks. Unfortunately, many more savages threw themselves upon the ramparts with a ferocity that the defenders alone could not hope to stop. The grim faces of the defenders demonstrated that they were ready to fight to the death.

At that very moment a concerted attacked was unleashed by Stuart' Fusiliers in a pincer movement upon each Huron flank. Suddenly appearing out of nowhere, the Fusiliers release a blistering musket volley that decimated the attacking Huron. In quick succession, native Fox and Sauk warriors led by To-Ko-Wan and Kor-Oh-Tin engaged the Huron in fierce hand-to-hand combat. Tonty could not constrain himself to remain with the Fusiliers, but rather joined his native companions in the melee. Tonty could be seen dispatching Huron to his left with his iron fist while his long cutlass carved a deadly swath to his right. The Huron observed firsthand the legendary warrior known as "Iron Hand" in action. Unfortunately for them, few would live to tell the tale.

The surprise attack of the Fusiliers was completely demoralizing for the Huron. By the time they could fathom what was happening it was too late to react. In fact, the greatest danger to Stuart's men was the defenders of the Griffin. Pushed to the point of annihilation, La Salle's troops were just as confused as the Huron as to what was exactly happening. Cutting through the Huron warriors like a hot knife through butter, Stuart's infantry led by Tonty, Kor-Oh-Tin, and To-Ko-Wan found themselves staring down the barrels of very desperate men. Since the rescue party included Sauk, Fox, and Iroquois warriors, it was indeed difficult to discern friend from foe in the heat of mortal combat. La Salle's men were on the verge of unleashing a final futile volley into the crowd when a booming shout rang out to save the day.

"Oh, Mon Dieu! It cannot be! Cease fire!" One or two muskets were discharged before the order was desperately repeated.

"Cease fire! I command you! It is our brother, Captain Tonty, come to succor us from these heathens." The order was delivered with such command that the battlefield fell silent for a moment. Even the poor Huron, the few that were still alive after being caught in the crossfire, paused to catch their breath.

"Must we do this dirty work by ourselves? Get out here and help if you're not too cowardly." Tonty recognized the voice and shouted back across the skirmish jokingly as he bashed another Huron upon the head with his iron fist. It was evident that war was truly a profession Tonty embraced with a fervent zeal.

Immediately, La Salle's troops jumped over their breastworks and met the remaining Huron head on. Swords flashed as the bloody work continued. Sensing a lost cause many Huron tried to run off into the safety of the underbrush. It was their misfortune that the beach along this lake did not offer much concealment. Stuart's sharp shooting Fusiliers made short work of these fugitives Huron. No Huron asked for quarter and none was given. In a very short time the battle was ended. Soon both the French and their allies were engaged in a victory dance.

After a rather brief celebration, the leaders of each unit began to tend to their casualties and count their loss. Stuart immediately dispatched two units of Fusiliers to the crest of the promontory overlooking the cove where the ship was anchored to establish a defensive perimeter. The seasoned soldier was worried that other natives might be lurking in the nearby forest. He didn't want any surprise to spoil their recent triumph.

When the mopping up operation was finally in full swing, Stuart and Tonty had the opportunity to turn their attention to the Griffin's defenders. They walked across the body strewn battlefield toward perhaps a score of soldiers gathered around a smoldering campfire tending to their wounds. As Stuart approached he noted the condition of both the men and their ship. The ship looked sea worthy but tattered. Obviously, parts of the ship's deck and fitting had been used to establish the breastworks behind which they had fought. To make matters worse it was evident that some of the wood had been used to stoke the campfires that provided comfort before the final Huron attack. The siege must have lasted several days. There could be no doubt from the appearance of the ship and men that rescue had come none too soon.

If the condition of the Griffin could be termed only marginal, the health of La Salle's men was much worse. The number of men nursing wounds attested to the fact that their Huron siege had taken a heavy toll. La Salle dispatched a burial detail to prepare graves to receive his valiant men who had died in this skirmish in the remote North American wilderness. After the survivors had briefly celebrated their fortuitous rescue, they attended to the post battle chores with a chilling numbness. Stuart noted that these brave souls had been so resigned to death that he wondered if they could ever feel the joy of living again. As Stuart and Tonty approached the officers of the Griffin's detachment, the man who had averted disaster earlier by yelling cease-fire moved toward them with outstretched arms.

"Mon comrades, you cannot imagine how thankful we are for your timely rescue." The man's voice and springing step were very familiar to Stuart. Another man broke away from La Salle's small group to follow. Suddenly, Stuart recognized the man that Tonty already knew. Stuart smiled broadly as Pierre Radisson gave him a great bear hug.

"Whatever are you doing here, Pierre? Have you found your city of gold so soon and returned to spend your ill-gotten gains?"

Tonty said as he slapped his old friend upon the back with his good hand.

"Ah-ha-hah!" Radisson laughed heartily. "You would not believe me if I told you and you know the lies I can tell. Oui!" Radisson looked jovial as ever, but frail and weak. The many years of perilous adventure in this wilderness had definitely taken its toll. Still, Radisson's friends could tell that he would have it no other way.

"Come, come my comrade and let us build a fire for warmth and a meal. While you regain your strength you can regale us with the details." Stuart and Tonty supported Radisson's weight between them as they moved him to a place protected from the harsh wind from the lake.

"But first, Major Stuart, you must meet my illustrious Lord who gave me refuge from these scoundrel savages." Radisson eyed Kor-Oh-Tin with malice as he waved the officers standing by the ship over to meet them. Stuart caught this subtle gesture and responded quickly.

"Likewise, Pierre, I must introduce you to two trusted comrades who have worked hard to save the mission at Mere D'Osia," Stuart waved his friends over.

"They look Iroquois to me, Jon. That would make them the devil's brood," Pierre whispered as he cast his eyes to the ground and spat with obvious disfavor. Both To-Ko-Wan and Kor-Oh-Tin stood stoically waiting to be acknowledged.

"Trust me in this my friend," Stuart's voice rang with sincerity as he continued. "They were once my mortal enemy as well. But their conversion has been miraculous and enduring. I have entrusted them with all I hold dear."

Pierre searched the faces of the two Iroquois warriors for an expression of reassurance, but they remained proud and resigned.

"Accept them, my friend, if only for the valiant attack they led to rescue you from the very jaws of death!" Remembering his recent predicament Tonty's comment was enough to sway Pierre. The animosity that had clouded this reunion was quickly gone. After embraces and slaps on the back the group turned to meet the entourage from the Griffin.

"Jon, may I introduce my friend and benefactor, Robert Cavelier, Sieur de la Salle." Major Stuart bowed gracefully with a courtly flourish that bespoke service in the renowned courts of Europe. Captain Tonty snapped to attention and saluted his superior. La Salle moved to embrace both their hands. This tacit gesture immediately won Stuart's favor and reaffirmed Tonty's respect.

"Mere words cannot express my gratitude for what you have done!" La Salle's expression conveyed gratitude, friendship, and respect all at once. He shook Jon Stuart's arm as one would move a pump handle to prime a pump.

"We are happy to be of service my Lord. Although, I must confess, we have an ulterior motive as well." A glimpse of a smile crossed Stuart's face.

"Well then, Major, let us break out some provisions and discuss this motive of yours over a hearty meal. Through Providence and your well timed appearance, we can at least dine well in this inhospitable wilderness." Eagerness to complete the grim business at hand was in La Salle's voice.

In an instant La Salle was ordering his men to remove stores hidden in the hold of the ship. A boiling kettle was quickly filled with both staples and small game including rabbit, quail and duck. Soon a savory aroma was enticing both soldier and native to finish the work and join the feast. A line formed as the ship's cook began ladling out bowls of the tasty concoction. Everyone ate their fill as the frigid weather made for hearty appetites. The balance of the day was spent recovering from the recent ordeal. While the day was clear and cold with a damp wind blowing from the northwest, the warmth of the camaraderie dispelled any discomfort.

"Sir, may I take this opportunity to report on my mission to the South." Tonty was anxious to relate the details of his successful mission to his master.

"By all means, Captain! Due to the lateness of your arrival, we feared that you had run afoul of savages and were lost. In a sense, it is lucky that these Huron laid siege, or we would have been already off this wintry sea and into a safe harbor," said La Salle.

"Hey, give me some credit, Mon General!" Radisson's voice boomed as he awoke from his contented reverie.

"It was I and Monsieur Geoff who insisted that Henri Tonty was a man of his word. We knew that he would let nothing stand in your way of this rendezvous. These Huron were merely a diversion, something to pass the time until your arrival," Radisson continued to joke while Geoff remained demure.

"Your so-called diversion nearly caused us to forfeit our lives," La Salle responded in kind.

"As you will, General, but pray tell us my friend what you discovered in this God-forsaken land to the south." Radisson redirected the conversation to the business at hand.

It took Tonty at least an hour to recount his adventure to the south along the mighty river that flowed through the middle of the continent. La Salle was indeed comforted to learn that a passage did exist to the south that might be used to supply the grand French colony he planned for this Illinois country. La Salle resolved to further explore this option as soon as the winter snow began to melt the following year.

Jon Stuart took his turn in describing the flourishing Jesuit Mission at Mere D'Osia. The Major recounted the devastating Iroquois raid in detail. He made it known that it was Tonty's timely return to Mere D'Osia on his passage north to rendezvous with La Salle that saved the settlement from destruction. Stuart also spoke of the ruins at Creve Coeur and the starvation that now stalked the people of Mere D'Osia.

"It seems we all owe a great debt of gratitude to Captain Tonty for saving both the mission and my ship, the Griffin." La Salle responded sincerely at the end of Stuart's account.

"It is time for us to pause to give thanks to God for delivering us through such tribulation," La Salle continued.

"Following a peaceful night of rest, Father Hennepin, recently arrived from France, will celebrate Mass. After worship we will arrange to transport some of our bountiful provisions back to Mere D'Osia."

"You have answered our prayers, My Lord." Emotion showed in Stuart's voice. "I was prepared to beg for the deliverance of my comrades, but you have saved my honor."

"No, no, Major, it is I who am indebted. Your courage has given France a steadfast foothold in this vast wilderness. You and your friends are helping to make my dream of a New France a reality. We will do what we can. I only hope it is enough to relieve your suffering." La Salle gestured for all to rise and he asked Father Hennepin to give a prayer of thanks. Soon the campfires were banked for the night. Sentries were dispatched and the weary warriors bedded down contented against a cold winter night.

Stuart was restless throughout that night. Experience had taught him something about the weather. Instinct told him that a winter storm was brewing. Ducks, geese and other fowl had been in a feeding frenzy all day and then activity had suddenly ceased. All was quiet and the brisk wind rustling through the dried prairie grass carried a dampness that chilled the bones. Stuart had heard voyageur tales of how devastating a prairie blizzard could be. Just as when he had left Mere D'Osia and his beloved Sha-Na to find La Salle, Stuart knew that failure was not an option. Failure would mean the slow, deadly starvation of those he loved. The sooner he began the trip south the closer he would be to saving his friends.

A hearty breakfast was cheerfully served as an ominous velvet blue bank of clouds approached from the west. Soon the warmth of the early morning sun was obscured and a chilly wind began to blow in earnest. To-Ko-Wan dutifully suggested that the provisions be quickly lashed to the makeshift canoe sleds and they begin the trek to the south. Given his deep abiding faith in divine providence, Major Stuart respectfully delayed their departure to observe Father Hennepin's Mass. By the time parting embraces were exchanged between La Salle and Stuart small pellets of sleet were descending from a foreboding sky. Within hours, Stuart knew the winter storm would descend upon them. They must attempt to cover as many kilometers as possible before the snow got deep and the travel tedious. The journey would take days, if it were possible at all. God would hear many prayers for their success in a very short time.

Meanwhile, back at Mere D'Osia preparation for the Celebration of the Nativity was continuing in earnest. Both Father Constance and Father Bertrand were determined to keep everyone's mind off of suffering and focused upon the greatest gift any person could ever receive. The priests searched their memories to resurrect any festive diversion. During their childhood in their native France they remembered gathering evergreen boughs to adorn community buildings and the Church. Many of the Mere D'Osia villagers were dispatched to the forest and soon the smell of pine added a pleasant aroma to the air. The bright green color of the pine boughs seemed to uplift the spirits of everyone.

Likewise, a huge pile of wood was assembled near the town commons to serve as a bonfire on Christmas Eve. A makeshift stable was constructed nearby to house the Holy Family. A Christmas pageant, perhaps the first of many in the New World, complete with the Three Magi and the shepherds was practiced in the days leading up to Christmas Day. Soon the time would arrive to gather and celebrate the eve of Our Lord's birth. The good Fathers were consoled to know that their preparations did make time pass quickly.

The weather had been cooperating to moderate their suffering from short provisions until a few days before Christmas. Destruction of many native long houses had left the survivors without protection from the elements. Moderate temperatures had alleviated some of the suffering of these unfortunate people. Small game was still abundant and a stew of this meat and roots dug in the woods became a staple to temper the hunger. Still there was precious little food to sustain the long lines of parishioners that descended upon the communal cooking pots. Hope was high that Major Stuart's mission to bring winter provisions from the north would be successful. Then dramatically the weather changed.

Natives of Illinois know how quickly weather can change in that region, especially in the winter. The inhabitants of Mere D'Osia experienced a severe weather change in these days leading up to Christmas 1676. From a balmy 60 degrees one afternoon the temperature dropped precipitously into the twenty-degree range by evening. Blustery winds from the northwest began howling and a sheet of snow could be seen advancing on the horizon. For the inhabitants of Mere D'Osia the days before Christmas Eve were spent huddling next to campfires shivering from the cold. Babies cried and those lingering with grievous wounds from the recent Iroquois raid died in the face of this wintry blast. Famine and death again stalked the land of the Illini. Only a strong faith in God and prayer could withstand such an onslaught.

As bad as conditions were at Mere D'Osia, it was even worse for Stuart's group on the trail from the Inland Sea. The portages between the streams and rivers were long and arduous. The heavens dumped billowy clouds of white, fluffy snow upon the woodland trails that deepened with each passing hour. It taxed everyone's strength to push the canoes on makeshift sleds through the woodland and along the buffalo trails across the prairie. Only brief respite was offered when a creek was finally encountered. The small streams were shallow and often solidly frozen. Additionally, their routes were so circuitous that no time could be gained by following them. It wasn't until a deeper river was reached that the travelers could get off their weary feet and into the relatively comfort of the canoes. Hours blurred into days and the icy northern blast did not slacken. The relative warmth of the evening campfire could not assuage the terrible weariness that began to overtake the travelers. Each night the group prayed to the Almighty that their efforts would not be in vain.

In the sanctuary of the little church at Mere D'Osia, Father Bertrand was rudely awakened from his restless slumbers by a booming noise. Or was it a voice? Bertrand had been kneeling in prayer the entire night before the eve of the Blessed Nativity. This had become common practice since the Iroquois raid that had devastated his congregation. As this noise echoed in his brain, Bertrand had managed to rise momentarily, only to stumble and fall upon the altar. Lying there half dazed with blood oozing from a cut on his forehead, the good Father tried to make sense of the noise he had heard. Finally, in the manner Bertrand always had imagined a revelation would be, he knew exactly what was required. Bertrand ran out of the church to find Father Constance and set in motion the final preparations for the Advent. He found Constance in a shelter near the edge of the settlement bent over a campfire and dispensing a stew made of wild game and sassafras roots to the hungry natives that had lined up for breakfast.

"Constance!" Bertrand yelled like a man possessed. "We must make haste or we will miss it!"

"Miss what? What on this earth are you referring to?" Constance grimaced at this early morning annoyance. After all, he had been out in the blowing snow preparing this meager meal while Bertrand slept in the sanctuary. "Can't you see I'm busy here?"

"Oh, but you don't understand! If we miss it we will be so wretched!" Bertrand still acted as if he was out of touch with reality.

"And you!" Bertrand pointed at Constance in distress. "What are you doing? Cooking on a day of fasting. The Advent fast cannot be ended until tonight's Midnight Mass. Our Lord would not approve."

"Look at these people, my brother," Constance responded quietly. "They have fasted too much already. Anymore and I fear for their lives." But Father Bertrand was back in his reverie of what he must do and did not answer. He began to direct preparation for the Fete de Noel that had been lagging in the face of the ominous weather. Bertrand knew there was so much to do and so little time if Mere D'Osia was to be saved from their present predicament. Luckily, our Lord was instructing Bertrand on exactly what must be done. The Pageant of the Wilderness Nativity, which the natives had been practicing for weeks, was set in motion to be performed at the Midnight Mass. Runners were dispatched to the neighboring Sauk, Fox, and Illini villages with word to bring what they could spare as a gift offering to those less fortunate. The young native Mary, Joseph, and the Baby were prepared for the performance. Still more wood was piled upon the already towering bonfire that would be ignited at the Mass to symbolize the light of the Christ coming into this world. Bertrand knew that, above all else, this bonfire must be magnificent. After all, Our Lord had commanded this in the sanctuary this very morning!

* * * *

Finally, Major Stuart and his weary party reached the wide and deep river that flowed back to Mere D'Osia. Due to the recent unseasonably warm weather, this river had only begun to freeze. Ice crystals zigzagged their frost way along the willow branches that overhung the riverbank, but the river current still ran deep and fast. With blessed relief, the travelers unlashed the makeshift sled runners from the canoes and embarked for the trip southward. Birch paddles dipped deeply into the frosty, free-flowing blue waters as the canoes began to gain speed. Despite the fluffy snow that billowed in mountainous puffs from the sky, the spirits of Stuart's party revived as the long trek began to seem less insurmountable. With a little luck, they all knew that there was a good chance they could celebrate Le R'eveillon, the French breakfast after midnight Mass, with their starving friends at Mere D'Osia.

Men attuned to nature like the Iroquois shaman To-Ko-Wan sensed they were in the midst of a true prairie blizzard. The falling snow seemed to be getting worse and the howling north wind was only increasing intensity. Even on the river, travel would become more difficult as the day progressed. Soon their ability to determine their exact location in relation to their intended destination would be compromised. At that time they might as well pull into the bank and seek shelter for they risked floating past Mere D'Osia. Their strength was already taxed beyond endurance. It would surely be the end of them if they had to paddle back upstream in their current frail condition. Major Stuart was determined to not let this happen. He asked that all say silent prayers for their deliverance. Several torches had been prepared in previous encampments to use as beacons to keep the party together when visibility was reduced. Major Stuart lit one of these and assumed a position at the bow of the lead canoe. The pellets of ice stung his face as he drew the collar of his woolen great coat close to protect from frostbite. He would remain there until they reached Mere D'Osia, or he fell overboard from sheer exhaustion. Everyone knew that the latter was a distinct possibility. Still, the weary travelers forged on through the prairie blizzard following the beacon of light.

Sha-Na had spent these many weeks since the Major's departure ministering to the suffering natives that descended upon the Parish of Mere D'Osia to spend the winter. While the weather cooperated, Sha-Na was optimistic that the wounds of the recent Iroquois raid would heal and starvation would be averted with the return of the party dispatched to the north. Indeed, wild game was still abundant as long as the weather remained warm and stable. While many of the hunters on whom the village depended for food had been maimed or killed in battle, the women and older children used ancient skills to trap rabbits and squirrels that took the edge off the hunger. The rifles of the French Fusiliers guarding the camp also provided larger game like deer and elk to fill the communal cooking pots that daily fed the natives. But the harsh reality of winter starvation arrived with the prairie blizzard that inundated them with mounds of chilling snow. Sha-Na could only offer bowls of diluted broth made from the meager supply of meat and words of comfort to encourage her native brethren. Death of the weak, aged, and infirm during the harsh prairie winter is an annual fact of life for her people, but this particular year might be worse. Although Fathers Antoine, Bertrand, and Constance preached about a better life provided by a new God, Sha-Na feared the harsh reality of their present situation.

It seemed only a miracle could save the people of Mere D'Osia from their present fate. But Sha-Na knew in her heart that her new God was the God of miracles. She had learned this much from her mentor, Kateri Tekawetha. Prayer was a powerful force and Sha-Na employed it regularly. Still, she knew that the good book also said that God helps those who help themselves. Sha-Na was determined to do all in her power to aid the poor village of Mere D'Osia. Despair threatened to descend with the blizzard to stifle all their puny efforts to survive. However, as the gloomy night began to envelope the faithful on that prairie Christmas Eve, the natives began arriving to pay homage to their new born master. Though these natives had little to see themselves past another day they willing brought offerings for those less fortunate. Sha-Na and Father Bertrand took heart at such a selfless demonstration. They ordered the bonfire to be lit!

At first the fire sputtered in the face of the blizzard's relentless onslaught. Mounds of billowy white snow sent many meager embers sizzling before they could spring to life. The native woodsmen struggled to give the bonfire its first foothold. Finally, a delightful crackling sound could be heard at the base of the huge pile of timber. As the roaring fire began to increase a joyful shout from the assembled populace echoed in the once foreboding night. Spirits soared with the spitting embers that began to dispel the darkness and warm the hearts of everyone. Sha-Na shivered despite the warmth emitted from the bonfire. She realized that the sensation came not from the cold, but rather from the anticipation of what was about to take place. Sha-Na silently asked the God's will be done, now and forever.

For hours, Henri Tonty had watched his friend, Jon Stuart, hold the lantern at the bow of the birch-bark canoe in the face of the relentless prairie blizzard. In the meager light he could see the whitecaps churned up by the gale upon the river. Tonty knew that Stuart was reaching the end of his endurance. When Tonty saw that Stuart began to buckle at the knees, he encircled his friend's waist with his one good arm. Although Tonty was near freezing himself, his strength allowed them to proceed several more miles down river in the ominous gloom. Luckily, the only paddling required was to keep the canoes in main stream. They were able to proceed southward at a rapid pace despite the weather. All at once Jon Stuart slumped and the lantern dropped into the churning waters of the river. The guiding light was extinguished and the travelers were plunged into the darkness of despair. Shout from behind urged them to make for the shore and find whatever refuge possible. And then the miracle happened!

A mighty blaze of fire erupted on the banks of the river several kilometers south of their location on the river. This beacon of light replaced the lantern that had been recently extinguished in the cold waters of the Illinois River. The travelers had a point of reference with which to navigate. With renewed vigor everyone put their stiff shoulders into the canoe paddles that increased their speed over the already fast flowing river. Soon Jon Stuart recognized the leafless willows that he knew surrounded the safe harbor of Mere D'Osia. The intertwined willow branches broke the wind and invited the travelers into a welcome refuge. In a moment the canoes were safely beached and their precious cargo secured. The travelers shouldered what they could carry and merrily began the short trek toward the huge bonfire that welcomed them home on such a treacherous night.

"Sha-Na! Mon ami, Sha-Na!" Jon Stuart spied his beloved though his words were stifled by the gusts of the roaring wind.

At first, Sha-Na thought she was dreaming as she thought she heard her name echoed on the wind. Sha-Na had been praying so devotedly for the return of her beloved that she was sure that her senses were deceiving her. Surely, only in a dream could she hope for Jon to appear out of the foreboding darkness? Yet, the gaiety of the roaring bonfire had lifted her spirits and the power of her new God made all things possible.

"Have you gone deaf, Mon ami?" Jon shouted at the top of his voice as he stumbled with renewed energy toward his beloved.

Sha-Na turned to see the answer to her prayers coming from out of the darkness. That initial embrace after weeks of separation rekindled the flame of a love that dwarfed the warmth of the Advent bonfire. In turn, Tonty, Kor-Oh-Tin, Tok-O-Wan, and all the travelers emerged from the darkness to link a circle of love that would not be broken.

Father Bertrand now knew why he had been obsessed with the need to light this tremendous fire on Christmas Eve. The Light of the World had come even to this wilderness. The Light had brought friends home from a perilous journey. It had brought bread to its starving people. More important, the Light brought salvation to all those who believe even unto these lowly natives in a vast, uncharted continent. Truly, this was a miracle!

This was indeed a night of firsts for the New World. Christmas Eve midnight mass was first celebrated on the prairie at Mere D'Osia. Surprisingly, the blizzard was dispelled with the advent of the travelers from the north. As the travelers and their friends warmed themselves by the huge bonfire, the wind calmed and the blustery clouds receded. Soon stars could be seen twinkling in the sky above like diamonds on velvet. If one looked closely, a particularly bright star seemed to take up residence above the Nativity that was being reenacted by the native children.

The French custom of Fete de Noel may have been first celebrated on the prairie of this new continent as well. The Advent fast at Mere D'Osia was ended by the traditional French Le R'eveillon, an enormous breakfast following Midnight Mass. Jon Stuart ordered the canoes to be unloaded and the supplies were stored in the Parish Hall. Flour was used to bake enormous loaves of bread. Great kettles of soup were prepared using both the native offerings to the Nativity and the staples donated by La Salle from the Griffin's hold. Everyone present was sustained by the bounty that the northern travelers delivered and the church services conducted in honor of the newborn King. Parties and revelry continued into the New Year of 1677. The feasting culminated with the Twelfth Night Ball on the eve of Epiphany, January 6. Although the dead of a prairie winter lay straight ahead, the inhabitants of Mere D'Osia approached this season with joy and anticipation. Surprisingly, this particular winter was one of the mildest in the memory of any of the old tribe members wintering at this French parish. Spring made an early appearance promising good fortune to La Salle's plans for colonization.

* * * *

Across the vast Atlantic Ocean in a splendid palace outside Paris a meeting occurred that was to change the course of history for an empire. Bishop Colbert, dressed magnificently in his flowing crimson robes of office and golden jewelry, held audience with a man of seemingly small stature. However, the result of their discussion would redirect the resources of France.

"Monsieur Geoff, what news do you bring from our western colonies?" The Bishop's voice boomed with authority and bespoke condescension.

"Unpalatable news at best, Your Grace," Geoff replied meekly. He was obviously fearful of the wrath his information might incur.

"Did you find me a treasure trove like those discovered by the Spanish dogs to pay for these interminable continental wars?" The Bishop sneered at his advisers gathered near his dais, as if his political problems were their fault alone. Geoff quickly got the impression that the Bishop was very unhappy. Geoff hoped he would not be the recipient of any displeasure. Heads have rolled for less!

"After many months of exploration with experienced Voyageurs I fear nothing of the sort exists. The natives live in huts of stick and mud. They can barely gather enough food to survive let alone have the time to dig for silver and gold. Please show mercy on me for being the bearer of such distressing news." Geoff kneeled with his left knee on the polished marble floor as if preparing for the headsman's axe.

"It is lucky for you that you are not the first to suggest such an outcome." Bishop Colbert kept his composure. He was the consummate politician and skilled at showing no emotion. This had served him well in the past as he negotiated to rule the European continent. The information presented by Monsieur Geoff was merely affirming his course of action that had already been decided.

"In your opinion is there any hope of finding the proverbial Northwest Passage to the spice islands of the East? Or, is this another myth that we must pragmatically dismiss and move on?"

"Your Eminence, I fear that is but another dream as well," Geoff paused to get his breath.

"And why do you think that is the case?" The Bishop seemed to be only amusing himself at this point. Geoff was relieved to sense no anger in the cleric's voice so he continued.

"I ventured down many interior waterways with men possessing more frontier skills than I could ever hope to possess. Like me, they had the dreams of finding gold or, at least, a passage to the East. After years of hardship and suffering in pursuit of this dream these men, at least those who remain alive, seem resigned to the fact that neither exists." Geoff did not remove his gaze from the floor as he spoke.

"And what of my misguided priests, Constance and Bertrand?" The Bishop chuckled. "Are they in good health?"

"Oui, and happy too! They are ministering to a poor rabble of natives on an interior river of that Godforsaken continent even as we speak."

"May Our Lord bless their poor misguided souls." The Bishop spoke as if repeating a benediction.

"Forgive me for saying, Your Grace, that you speak as if their fate is sealed," Geoff spoke meekly. Perhaps he would survive this audience after all, he thought.

"It is in God's hands now, my son." The Bishop was becoming distracted.

"Amuse me by giving your assessment of our fortunes in the so-called New World." Colbert listened attentively as did the Bishop's advisers.

"Forgive me if I cannot be optimistic, Father. Those Iroquois devils control the very access to the interior and they are firm allies of the English. It is true that Lord Frontenac has worked miracles in his attempt to pacify the native population. However, without hope of lucrative and immediate return, I would not waste precious resources. That is only my humble opinion." Geoff feared he had spoken too candidly and he fearfully awaited a reply.

"May God bless you, My Son." The Bishop arose and made the sign of the cross to indicate that the audience had ended.

"See that Monsieur Geoff is duly rewarded." Colbert snapped his finger and Geoff was quickly escorted from the palace reception room. The Bishop gestured for his advisers to gather around.

"My patience with our projects on that distant continent has come to an end. Geoff merely confirms what I have already decided. See that we redirect our resources here in Europe where they will pay the most dividends."

"But what is to become of La Salle. Even now he is exploring and claiming land in the name of France. Our Lord, King Louis, holds him in very high esteem." One of the advisers was bold enough to make such an assessment.

"La Salle is a dreamer. France needs realists. We can publicly support his dreams while privately redirecting our resources. Let him enjoy himself. But we must pay attention to the fortunes of France." The room was quiet as the Bishop continued.

"First, we must recall Frontenac and our experienced troops to protect France. I need my most skilled warrior beside me when we are surrounded by enemies."

"But who will protect our colonists?" One adviser remarked.

"God will protect his children as you well know." The Bishop's statement was more a pronouncement of sentence than a supplication to the Supreme Being.

"And what about your proselytizing priests, Bertrand and Constance?" Another adviser commented as an after thought.

"God will protect them as well, My Son. Now, I cannot be late for my audience with the King. I'm sure that will make for a fascinating afternoon." Colbert smirked as he arose to rapidly make his exit. His entourage scurried in pursuit.

* * * *

The next several months brought extreme pleasure to the inhabitants of Mere D'Osia, especially the French and the Iroquois brethren. With the help of Father Constance and Father Bertrand, Father Antoine spread the message of the Gospel through the region of the two mighty rivers. The many tribes, including the Illini, the Sauk, and the Fox, who had previously conducted war against each other, turned to peace. These natives learned to work together and the result was bounty for everyone. Each year when the tradition of the Wilderness Nativity was repeated the offering grew. Famine and starvation became relatively unknown in the region. While the fear of another Iroquois raid remained, all the native chiefs were sure that together they could face the worst. Luckily, the Iroquois were too preoccupied with the French in the northeast.

Likewise, the Iroquois missionaries and the French Fusiliers enjoyed a time of peace and tranquility. To-Ko-Wan, the fierce Iroquois shaman that led the attack on Mere D'Osia, continued to do penance for the suffering he had caused. True to his conversion, To-Ko-Wan used his woodland herbal skills to heal the sick and the wounded. The manner of his conversion was a favorite story around the winter campfires that was repeated without weariness. Like Saul on the road to Damascus, To-Ko-Wan grasped his new faith with a vigor that left an impression upon everyone who knew him. Kor-Oh-Tin, To-Ko-Wan's Iroquois brother, became an energetic Christian preacher as well. Since prior to the Great Iroquois Raid he served as an Iroquois spy, Kor-Oh-Tin knew this region and the vast lands to the west very well. He used this knowledge to carry the Christian message to many natives that had never before come into contact it. Kor-Oh-Tin guided Father Constance and Father Bertrand on many successful missions. The priests brought the comforting Word while the Iroquois maidens carried the healing touch. The Fusiliers provided security on these long satisfying journeys.

As for Jon Stuart and Sha-Na, their constant companionship blossomed into marriage. From that moment by the Christmas Eve bonfire the two were inseparable. The profound love they held for each other provided an example for everyone at Mere D'Osia. During the wedding ceremony held in the early spring, Father Antoine commented that he had never before known a couple so devoted to each other. Even though life on the prairie continued to be harsh and treacherous, together Jon and Sha-Na looked toward their future with blissful anticipation.

Unfortunately, this joy was short-lived in the face of reality beyond their control. In the next few months, events occurred in rapid succession to change the destiny of all living and loving in Mere D'Osia. First and foremost, Bishop Colbert tired of his game for dominance in the New World. Colbert knew he needed a large treasury if he hoped to challenge the English. The harsh reality was that there were no Cities of Gold on the wind swept prairies of the new continent. As was mentioned, Monsieur Geoff, Colbert's spy, reported that there was also little hope of finding a Northwest Passage to the riches of the Orient. Pierre Radisson continued to pursue his dream of a passage to the western ocean along the rivers and lakes that laced the northern prairies. Politically Bishop Colbert maintained an encouraging façade, but in reality his ambitions for the New World declined. Since Colbert wielded the power behind the French throne, the fortunes of many Frenchmen in the New World changed.

The fortunes of La Salle declined rather rapidly. While his ship, the Griffin, survived the winter, it soon met its doom. La Salle somehow got the reputation with the interior natives that he was a lover of the hated Iroquois. Needless to say the inhabitants of the region he sought to colonize constantly threatened his life. In one skirmish, La Salle was wounded and the Griffin destroyed. While he was able to make his way safely back to the garrison at Quebec and later to France, La Salle found little more that moral support for his colonization plans at the French court. He recognized that the southern route to the interior was the only way to successfully colonize the interior due to the opposition of the English and their Iroquois allies in the north. Indeed, La Salle was able to outfit another venture to the mouth of the Mississippi River. Unfortunately, in the face of extreme hardship La Salle's crew mutinied and murdered him.

Frontenac, the French Governor of the new continent, suffered a turn of fortune as well. As a wise leader, Frontenac recognized that he needed the goodwill of the native tribes if the French hoped to establish a foothold on the new continent. Unfortunately, the hatred of these natives for each other precluded them from being allies of one another and the French. Bishop Colbert was impatient with Frontenac's progress toward pacification of the continent. Indeed, Colbert had forced Frontenac to attack the Iroquois and other tribes hostile to the French. Similar ventures were of limited success and only served to increase the hatred of the native population for the French. Despite Frontenac's worthy reputation, Colbert succeeded in encouraging King Louis to recall Frontenac to France and appoint a new governor. This shortsightedness effectively ended all hope for French dominance in the New World.

* * * *

"So what happened to Sha-Na, Jon Stuart, and those two sweet priests?" Ida said as Father Jacob took a breath from his narrative.

"Yeh! If the French were falling apart I bet they had a devil of a time, didn't they Father?" George, the eldest of the Bent's, finally gave a sign of his interest.

"Watch you mouth!" Ida said playfully to her son secretly afraid her family would yet embarrass her in front of Father Jacob.

"Oh, Ma. I didn't say anything bad!" George replied now half embarrassed as well.

Father Jacob smiled at the loving interchange and answered Ida's question.

"Shortly after the inhabitants of Mere D'Osia learned about Frontenac's pending recall to France two letters arrived by special courier from Montreal. One was addressed to Major Stuart and the other to Sha-Na. Unfortunately, it would change their entire lives."

"Go on," said John Bent encouragingly.

* * * *

News from the east was always a particular treat since it was so rare on the faraway prairie of the Illini. Still more delightful was a letter from a friend or loved one. News was often just gossip and only worth passing time around an evening fire. News wasn't always true, but a letter was something to cherish. It reaffirmed that the recipient still had a bond with the outside world. The thought was indeed comforting in the face of trying to survive in the hostile wilderness. A letter was a comfort and a special blessing that wasn't taken lightly. In truth it was the envy of all those who didn't receive one. On this particular day, the community was doubly blessed for a brother and sister had special news to share with all. That evening both Sha-Na and Jon Stuart invited their close friends to share the news.

"Read yours first, my beloved." Sha-Na spoke with sparkling anticipation to Jon. Both Father Bertrand and Father Constance nodded in agreement.

"What if it is bad news?" Jon said half joking.

"Then we will have a second chance with mine?" Sha-Na laughed. All in attendance shared a laugh but they were all anxious at what they might learn.

Jon admired the precise penmanship of the address and broke the wax seal carefully so as not to tear the parchment. It was the seal of the French Governor and he let everyone know although it was not news to most. The letters had been a topic of speculation for several hours now. Jon held the letter next to the flickering candle and began reading.

"Speak up, Mon ami," Sha-Na said. Jon was so engrossed that he didn't realize he was whispering. With a look of distress on his face, Jon began speaking so all could hear. The letter read as follows.

In Anno Dominie 1678

To My Comrade-in-Arms
The Most Honorable Major Stuart
Commander of the French Continental Fusiliers

Greetings!

I truly hope this communication finds you in good health and eminently blessed by Our Father in Heaven, the Granter of all things worthy. A frontier officer in my service states that he has learned of your particular success in establishing a secure mission upon the banks of a major interior tributary. Your charges, the good Fathers Constance and Bertrand, have brought Catholicism to the heathen under your watchful protection. For that all Christendom can be thankful. Indeed, Monsieur La Salle could barely restrain his compliments for your courage and fortitude in the face of overwhelming odds on the interior prairie. Accept my praise and gratitude on the behalf of the reverent people of France. My sincere prayer is that you will continue to remain safe and secure in your endeavors.

Unfortunately, I must communicate some personal news that is distressing. Our most high King Louis has seen fit to relieve me of my duties as Governor of the continental colonies of France. From my point of view, I believe that I have been very successful in my mission to protect French citizens in this wilderness that some call the New World. The natives in close proximity to our colonies have been pacified and our mortal enemies, the English, have been met with strength. Indeed, the charge you left with me, Mademoiselle Kateri, has made significant progress in winning the benevolence of many of her Iroquois tribesmen and women. However, the King, and more likely

Bishop Colbert, remains unconvinced of my progress. Alas, I return to Paris within the month.

The consequences of this decision for you are simple. I have asked that all uniformed French forces on the frontier withdraw to the fortress of Montreal pending my replacement. As a result, I cannot guarantee the safety of any benevolent mission in the interim. I ask that you bring the Jesuit priest under your protection back to the fortress since I know you consider their safety of utmost importance. Further, I invite you to return with me to the continent as one of my staff officers. The clouds of war are again brewing and there is a perpetual need for warriors like us. The sons of France and Scotland must stand united against the English. It would be an honor to serve with a man of your stature, experience and courage.

Also, I must communicate that I can no longer guarantee the safety of Mademoiselle Kateri. She is most insistent that she returns to her people to begin a nunnery. In light of the recent developments, I find I can no longer in good conscience dissuade her. I do fear for her safety, but she is most committed. I'm positive that Our Lord will show her the way regardless of our wishes. If your decision is favorable, please do not tarry for we must leave for the continent very soon. At any rate, I pray for your continued welfare and success.

> **Bon jour, Mon Comrade,**
>
> **General Louis de Bade de Frontenac**
> **His Excellency**
> **Governor of Novae France**

Jon Stuart slowly refolded the letter and ran his finger over the wax seal of Frontenac. All was deadly silent even though the room was full of people listening to the news from civilization. A mongrel dog barked but Jon remained staring at the letter with his eyes cast toward the floor. Their idyllic life was about to come crashing down around their ears. Choices would have to be made and nothing would remain the same as before. Stunned by the news, Jon tried to review his options in a rational manner. He had never refused a call to arms before, but then he had never had a reason like Sha-Na. Jon was sure he could protect the Fathers regardless of Frontenac's recall. After all, the French garrison had done little to aid them so far save maintain a friendly presence. But an unfriendly Governor was certainly a factor to consider when weighing the safety of his charges. Jon could not guess what the reaction of Father Constance or Father Bertrand would be. With this thought, he raised his head to ascertain the reaction of either priest. At that moment, Sha-Na began to speak.

"Such awful news!" Sha-Na said. "Perhaps my letter will be more encouraging." She split the wax seal and unfolded the parchment. Her words sounded ominously in the quiet room.

"It is from my dear sister, Kateri Tekawetha." Her words came slowly.

My Beloved Sister in Christ:

Greetings and peace!

It is with both joy and sadness that I find myself writing to you. My days in confinement in Montreal are coming to an end. Our Lord has compelled me to go forth and redeem my people. For these many months I have struggled with the knowledge that our Iroquois brothers and sister live and die without salvation. My indifference condemns those who would heed the words of Our Lord to hell! I find that I am in constant distress and unable to rest. I minister daily to the poor and unfortunate here in the city yet I can find no peace. I inflict my body, God's temple, with severe penance but there is still no relief. My frail body wails when it can stand no more and I am more often in bed than industrious. The Lord bids me move or die! Therefore, for the salvation of my soul and despite the warnings of the good Fathers here in Montreal I have made a decision. I propose to return to the land of my people. Though not welcome, I will build an edifice unto my God and give comfort to my brothers and sisters. The decision is the easiest part and now to what is most difficult.

I cannot do this alone! You, dearest sister and personal confidant, know and have shared my dream of becoming a bride of Christ. Therefore, I implore you, if circumstances do allow, to join me in this quest. I will immediately return to the lake of our ancestors. There will I teach the words of our faith and minister to the infirm and unfortunate. I have heard of the miraculous

> conversion of our brothers To-Ko-Wan and Kor-Oh-Tin. It is said that their faith has worked wonders in the wilderness. Perhaps, you could persuade them to join in my work as well. However, please know that your decision must not be based upon my wishes. It is ultimately between you and Our Lord who will guide you along the path He wishes you to follow. It would be a great joy to see you once more. Regardless of your decision, remember that my love and prayers are always with you. We will be together, if not now, then in the long house Our Lord has prepared for us in heaven.
>
> **Your loving Sister in Christ,**
> **Kateri**

Sha-Na had barely finished reading when her body was racked with sobbing. She was torn between faith and love. God had surely led her to Mere D'Osia for some purpose. Until now Sha-Na had assumed it was to serve the natives of this remote mission and find her only true love. It had all turned out so perfect until this moment. Why was she being torn from this happiness? Did God expect her to turn her back on Jon? Sha-Na knew she must pray for an answer, but for now all she wanted to do was cry. Jon was immediately at her side holding her in his arms and trying to console her. Likewise, Father Constance rushed to her aid while Father Bertrand led the gathering in a heartfelt prayer. The inhabitants of the mission had gathered for a night of friendship and festivity. They returned silently through the dark night to their humble abodes with only sadness in their hearts. Truly Mere D'Osia would never be the same.

After great supplication to the Almighty God the devout travelers to Mere D'Osia soon made their decision about where Providence would lead them. Within days the preparations were complete and the contingent of Fusiliers led by their commander, Major Stuart, broke camp for the long trek back to Montreal. Father Constance and Father Bertrand felt compelled to return to France. They supported La Salle's efforts in bringing civilization to this remote wilderness and believed that they might use their meager influence to obtain funding from Bishop Colbert. Although they released Jon Stuart from his commitment as Security Officer-in-Charge, he felt he was honor bound to escort them safely back to France. Duty and honor was the soul of the Major that even the perfect love could not change. Of course, Jon wanted to take his new bride back to France, but it was not to be that simple.

At first, after much prayer Sha-Na was inclined to stay on at the mission of Mere D'Osia. God had called her to the wilderness and there was still much work to do. Her one true love was leaving but her faith dictated that God's will for her had to come first. Father Antoine needed the help of the Iroquois maids to minister to those who were recuperating from the Great Iroquois Raid. Indeed, Sha-Na's Iroquois brother, To-Ko-Wan, the shaman of the old ways recently converted to Christianity, had decided to remain in the interior wilderness by the great rivers. To-Ko-Wan's conversion was nothing less than a miracle and he could not bear to leave the sight of his transfiguration. God had made him see the suffering his actions had visited upon these poor natives. He felt guided to redress this great wrong. Several of Sha-Na's sisters had decided to make Mere D'Osia their life's work as well.

But Kor-Oh-Tin made his decision to accept the invitation of Kateri. He felt he was commissioned to bring his new religion to his Iroquois brethren. It would not be an easy task, but it had to be done. Sha-Na had always felt a spiritual connection to Kateri. Sha-Na realized that she could not turn down her friend's plea for assistance. She also reasoned that if she remained in Mere D'Osia she would now be forced to say good-bye to Jon. Sha-Na simply could not bear the thought. The trip back to her people would take some time. It was time she could spend with her new love. Perhaps, God would reveal a different path that would not force their separation.

"Father Antoine noted in his diary that a multitude gathered on the banks of the Illinois River one sunny day to see their benefactors off on their perilous journey back to Montreal. Antoine led the prayer as Jon and Sha-Na embarked on the large birch bark canoe. Both Jon and Sha-Na viewed the proceedings stoically as the oarsmen pushed off. Antoine noted that the two lovers clung to each other as if for dear life," Father Jacob sighed.

"I know little concerning the events beyond this point in time. Stuart's diary that was bequeathed to my parish is notably silent. It would seem Jon Stuart and Sha-Na sailed off into history. Anything I might say further would be extreme conjecture." Father Jacob realized it was time to bring his story to an end; for now, at any rate.

Chapter 6

THE SERMON

In the silence of the cozy living room Father Jacob noted the tranquility of the Bent family on this stormy prairie winter night. The children were nearly asleep as it was getting very late. John and Ida had been hanging on his every word. This spoke volumes about their interest in the French Priest's story concerning their Midwestern roots. It was well past midnight and Father Jacob feared he would wear out his welcome.

"I fear I have bored you with too much detail in my, how you say, long-winded account." Jacob smiled and a yawn passed his lips suggesting he was weary as well.

"Oh, no my friend!" John spoke emphatically. "I sense a personal connection regardless of how remote. I will not rest until you finish."

"Now John, at least let our guest take a break. We could all use a breather and I will put on a new pot of coffee. Please excuse me Father. I'll be right back." Ida patted John on the back and went to the kitchen. A couple of the children stirred on the living room couch as she got up. Shadows danced upon the wall from the flickering fire.

"A brief respite would suit me as well." Father Jacob rose from his chair and moved toward the main door. "I would like to see the weather conditions and get a breath of fresh air."

"Let me join you Father." John opened the door. Donning their coats both men stepped out on the expansive open porch attached to the front of the old white clapboard farmhouse.

The crisp air initially took their breath away, but soon they felt refreshed. It had stopped snowing but there was at least eight inches of the fluffy precipitation and it was starting to drift. Beyond the glowing yellow porch light the night held a fairy-like quality. Just like the Christmas Eve of that first wilderness Nativity so long ago, the storm front had moved through leaving a beautiful night of twinkling stars against a velvet blue sky. That old man moon seemed larger than usual and it gleamed as if it was trying to rival its brother the sun. The surrounding landscape assumed a special aura and it beckoned the two men to step from their sheltered refuge. This night was a natural wonderland where no artificial light would be required to navigate the rolling hills. Jacob waded through the snow to the barn lot and leaned against the fence to gaze at the mighty oaks in the woods beyond.

"Beautiful isn't it?" John felt his spirit soar at the sight of snowflakes twinkling on the trees in the moonlight.

"It has no rival on this earth, my friend," Jacob replied contentedly.

"At times like this I don't even notice the cold," John grinned.

"I'm glad you recognize this special blessing you have here in Illinois my son." The priest was reminded of similar winter nights at his home in France.

"Such a gift can make up for a lot of pain and hardship, I agree." John spoke solemnly remembering that today he had almost lost his beloved family farm. Jacob did not reply immediately. He paused momentarily as if carefully weighing what words he would speak next.

"It is good that we took a break from my story at this particular time."

"Yeah. We sure needed a breather," John laughed softly.

"It is not only that my son." Jacob was waxing philosophical. John wasn't sure he was ready for a sermon.

"Whatdaya mean?" John began to feel the cold now.

"The remainder of my story is more tragic than triumphant my son. The people I have come to love from the information I have been able to gather, including Jon Stuart, Sha-Na, Father Antoine, Bertrand, Constance, Kor-Oh-Tin and To-Ko-Wan, did not live happily ever after as your Hollywood movies would have us believe. They were real people living real life." Jacob cast his eyes downward as he continued.

"John, I know how much the money from the auction meant to you. As a counselor, I sense that the Bent family has been walking an emotional tightrope these past few months. I don't want the tragedy of my story to return you to despair, especially since I feel your deep frustration with your duties at your church."

"A story is a story, Father. They don't have to all be inspiring."

"Life by definition is good and bad as well, my brother. Life is full of both inspiration and desperation. It has both peaks and valleys. The trick is to minimize our plunges into the depth while maximizing the peaks." Jacob paused to see if there was a need to continue down this path.

"Go on." John was listening intently regardless of the brisk northwest breeze that was rivaling for their attention.

"Our humanity makes us by nature creatures of despair. This makes us as an individual our own worst enemy. No one can harm us any more that we allow them to do so. In the face of adversity we can dwell on either the good or the bad. It is our choice. Sadness is a part of living. We must accept it for what it is while not letting it get us down. Sadness and pain are merely the spice that colors our living."

"But it is so hard to get beyond the details of life, Father."

"I know my son."

"It is easy to say that I won't get depressed and enjoy my blessings that surround me everyday. But the sad reality is that I react before I can reason."

"Exactly!"

"I try," John spoke humbly.

"I know. No one can expect life to be easy. If it were easy it would not be life."

"What should I do?"

"You have to find that out for yourself. Personally, I try to remember the things that inspire me and forget the trivialities."

"Easy for you to say."

"I didn't say that I don't struggle with it daily."

"Getting nippy out here! How do you feel about a cup of hot coffee and then you can finish this story." John turned and walked quickly toward the light on the porch. Father Jacob only nodded and followed.

The smell of fresh brewed coffee attacked their senses and welcomed the two men back inside. Ida had carried a tray filled with a pitcher of hot coffee, cups, and delicious oatmeal cookies into the living room while they were out. She sat waiting patiently by the fire. Ida beamed as they removed their heavy coats, stomped snow on the colorful woven rug, and took their places. In a moment, Jacob was back to the story and the Bent family was again mesmerized.

After everyone was content with their late night refreshment, the Bent family settled in to listen to Jacob's story. They sensed that the tale was nearing an end and Father Jacob proved them correct.

"Both Sha-Na and Jon received correspondence that abruptly ended their idyllic existence at Mere D'Osia back in 1677. After all the hardships they had faced one knew that it simply could not last."

"What happened to them, Father?" Ida asked on the edge of her seat, obviously intrigued by the classic love story Father Jacob had told. John Bent was inclined to make some quip about a "chick flick" in reference to the genre of movies Ida adored, but he sensed the seriousness of the story so he remained silent.

"I really wish I knew," replied Father Jacob shaking his head and staring off into space as if he expected God to provide a revelation. "You see that my years of historical research and consuming passion for the subject have provided enough facts so that I may speculate with reasonable accuracy on my story up to this point. Following their departure from Mere D'Osia it becomes difficult to do more than guess."

"You mean it may have not happened like you said?" Ida seemed let down.

"On the contrary, much of what I told you up to now is true." Jacob smiled. Any other time he would have been defensive, but now he had proof. As yet the Bents did not know that the amulet Jacob had purchased at the Bent farm auction today was the link.

"You see, Major Stuart was a man of letters as well as a proficient mercenary. After his death in France, his estate became part of the library of our diocese since he had no immediate heirs. I also have documents by prominent historical figures like Frontenac and La Salle that helped me piece together the puzzle."

"But how can you know for certain about such things as the blade that saved Illinois from the mighty Iroquois raid? This happened such a long time ago." Elvin, one of the Bent boys, was showing his interest now.

"The answer is the artifact that you found in a meadow on your farm and I purchased at your auction just yesterday. Non?" Jacob held up the superbly crafted blade, seemingly waiting for them to ask him to explain.

"Although I agree that it is a native blade of unusual design, and believe me I have seen a ton, what is the link that proves that it is the Real McCoy?" John asked. Everyone listening was obviously skeptically of Jacob's answer even before they heard it.

"Did Father Bertrand or Constance draw you a picture of it?" John continued grasping for the answer.

"Better than that!" Father Jacob spoke triumphantly.

At that particular moment, Father Jacob produced a purple velvet pouch trimmed in gold. As he began to remove the artifact from inside the whole room became awe-struck. Jacob held up a tarnished chain with pewter silver trinket attached. This trinket was an exact miniature copy of the hand wrought flint stone from the auction. All were silent as the trinket reflected brilliantly in the fire light from the living room wood stove. Both the blade and the amulet were in the shape of a superbly fashioned cross obviously cut from the same pattern.

"You must have had that necklace made after a picture in some letter that survived these centuries?" Ida speculated.

"Non, Mademoiselle" said Jacob. "It is part of Jon Stuart's estate that has been in the possession of the Catholic Church these many years. Do you recall in my story that Kateri Tekawetha, the Iroquois Saint gave her sister, Sha-Na, a token for the trip west to Illinois?"

Jacob could see that his listeners were recalling the poignant meeting between the Iroquois women prior to beginning the canoe trip to the west.

"Well," Jacob continued, "Sha-Na must have given the necklace to her beloved Major Stuart because it was part of his estate that survived in France. Can you imagine my astonishment when I attended your auction and beheld an exact copy? A copy that was etched in stone and found in a meadow above the banks of the Illinois River?"

The Bent family just sat there speechless trying to comprehend what they had just heard.

"I never believed the part of the story about the eagle dropping a lance from the sky that led to the Iroquois defeat until now." Jacob's words came quickly now.

"It was only a legend repeated around Iroquois campfires for these many years. Most historians believed this to be merely a fabrication far removed from actual events. But it is hard to argue that most legends do not have, at least, some basis in fact. While I'm not saying that the blade is endowed with magical powers, I do believe that the legend somehow recounts a real event. Predatory birds like eagles, falcons, and hawks have been known to pick up shiny objects and deposit them in their nests. Perhaps, an eagle found the lost blade Sha-Na had crafted and somehow coincidentally released it at the appropriate moment during the attack. Fact can be stranger than fiction, you know. Your Monsieur Ripley amassed a fortune by capitalizing on this truth. Non?" Father Jacob passed the two artifacts around for all to compare.

"You see John, we are surrounded by miracles. Unfortunately, we don't always have the opportunity to see," Jacob smiled.

When Father Jacob received the two artifacts back he just sat there in the yellow glow of the lamplight staring at them. His lips moved in a silent prayer. God had led him to this miraculous discovery on the banks of the Illinois River a thousand miles from his home parish in France. It was the culmination of years of research and a personal quest, but Jacob was incisive enough to understand that God had led him to this small town called Meredosia for more than his own personal enlightenment. God's people were in distress. Perhaps he was meant as an instrument of aid and solace just like those French travelers from centuries past.

"Don't leave us hanging, Father. What about the rest of the story? Did Sha-Na and Jon Stuart live happily ever after?" Ida was anxious to continue.

"I cannot say for certain." Father Jacob replied. "From surviving documents I verified that Jon Stuart was recalled to Montreal by Frontenac. Jon's letters after that time are regarding continental battles in which he participated. Any information about the separation of these lovers is sadly lacking. Except for one instance, there is an absence of any mention of Sha-Na in Jon's later letters. This suggests that she did not accompany him to France."

"So there is no end to your tale?" Ida asked sadly.

"The letter provides evidence that Saint Kateri recalled Sha-Na to the Five Nations of the Iroquois to minister to her people. Sha-Na was a very devout Christian as I hope you gathered by my tale. She had pledged herself as a Bride of Christ, much like Catholic Nuns. When Major Stuart came along, he totally upset her world. Sha-Na must have been torn between her duty to God and the strength of her earthly love. I can speculate about what might have happened, but I can prove nothing." Jacob paused.

"Then, by all means, speculate away. You can't leave us up in the air! Did one of Major Stuart's surviving letters give you anything to go on?" Ida needed closure.

"This is just like one of your Sandra Bullock or Julia Roberts movies, but you get to make up the ending." John chuckled.

"Not quite, honey. I can already see what probably happened and I don't like it." Ida slapped John playfully on the shoulder.

"Well, the writings of Major Stuart indicate a man in despair. We know he was an adventurer who loved to travel the world. Being a mercenary allowed him to be able to do just that. I suspect he gloried in the danger of combat. Stuart could only feel truly alive by living on the edge of life and death. However, one of the Major's letters in particular indicated that he was in despair of living."

"Go on!" Ida was anxious.

"Major Stuart wrote to the effect that he had been unlucky enough to avoid all the blades and arrow thrust at him over the past few years. Love for living had departed and he was left in despair. I believe he literally meant that he had lost his one true love. He engaged in battle after battle in the hope that some adversary would do what it was a mortal sin for him to do himself."

"Truly unrequited love," Ida said. "For Pete sake go on!"

"I think Sha-Na's devotion to God forced her to stay with Kateri and minister to her people. It broke both her and Jon's heart to part. One can imagine the classic Hollywood scene where Jon is torn from Sha-Na's arms to board a ship back to Europe. Sha-Na is left behind weeping. Since the artifact that she had made as a gift is lost back on the banks of the Illinois River, Sha-Na gives Jon the precious necklace. The necklace is the symbol of their love and their link until they meet again in heaven."

"Wouldn't it have been a better ending if they had been able to share their life together?" Ida said emotionally. Tears glistened in her eyes.

"Happy endings are often fairy tales, my child. Life is reality and reality is God's Will. May we always strive to reflect God's Will for our own life." Jacob pronounced the benediction to the story. They all quietly departed the room with their thoughts. Each one was a little sadder and perhaps wiser.

*   *   *   *

The following morning was Sunday. It dawned bright, clear, and extremely cold. The intense snowstorm had moved on east leaving a wonderland of white over eight inches deep. But farmers have four-wheel drive trucks and John Bent was no exception. The early settlers on the Illinois prairie would have been paralyzed and homebound by a similar storm. But modern technology has its advantages. The snow would not keep the Bent family from their weekly devotions.

The Lutheran service in the river town of Meredosia, Illinois convened promptly at 11 a.m. The Bent family and Father Jacob arose, ate a hearty breakfast prepare by Ida, dressed in their Sunday best, and attended church. Of course, the staunch Lutherans were amazed to see a Roman Catholic Priest with his Roman collar sitting in the front pew of their church. Several asked Pastor Wilson, the Lutheran minister, if this was proper; for his sake more than theirs, they said. Anyway it was only for this Sunday so what could it hurt? Such rational thinking was a common Lutheran trait after all. Weren't they all surprised when it turned out different?

Advent was coming and the message was one of hope. Emmanuel, God with us, was coming and we must prepare. Father Jacob remained properly devout and silent. After the service, the congregation lined up toward the exit to be greeted by the Pastor. Pastor Wilson smiled heartily as he embraced each person, one by one. When he came to John, John accepted the proffered hug and proceeded to introduce Father Jacob.

"How is it that a French Priest ends up in a Midwestern Lutheran Church on Sunday?" Pastor Wilson joked making everyone feel comfortable.

"It's a long story, my brother," Jacob replied.

"And one that I would love to hear," Pastor Wilson said. "Are you in town long?"

"Oh, I don't........." Jacob began and John interrupted.

"Father Jacob is our guest for the next few days, longer if I can convince him to stay. He has the most uplifting story that should be shared with everyone."

"In that case, let's get together over coffee tomorrow?" Pastor Wilson was most accommodating. "I'll call to make arrangements this afternoon?"

"Fine, fine," John said as the rest of his family and Jacob moved out the red double doors of the century old church. Outside John turned to Ida.

"Take the car on home dear. Father Jacob and I will be home directly. I want to show him where we found the artifact."

Ida nodded and climbed in the car with everyone else. As they drove off, John and the priest moved toward the truck. Unfortunately, members of the congregation concerned with the upcoming pageant wanted to talk with John.

"I'm sure you will agree, John, that my daughter will make just the best little Mary of any Nativity." Before John could reply, the man continued, "And you can expect my check for five thousand dollars to the building fund tomorrow in the mail." The connection was obvious and not lost on Father Jacob. The man strolled off with a smirk on his ruddy face.

"Oh, John, when are we finally going to decide on the cast members for the pageant?" Another woman waved her church bulleting in the air. She was the Director and her theatrical training was evident. Even though it was cold and there was little room on the sidewalk between the huge piles of shoveled snow, several people began to form a line to talk with John about the pageant, or "Nativity" as the townspeople liked to refer to it. It was an important annual event not for the Church alone, but for the town itself.

John's heart began to pound and his face was turning red from more than just the crisp northwest wind. John simply did not know how he would be able to please everyone this year. Although John had organized the pageant for several years somehow this year seemed to be worse. John mentally asked himself how that could be.

Father Jacob sensed the distress in his friend and immediately came to the rescue.

"Please forgive me, my friends, if I speak out of turn." Jacob touched John's arm. He spoke with a definite French accent that had not been as pronounced before.

"Brother John is still trying to recover from the auction held yesterday. He needs only a little respite to complete his plans for the Nativity. John will communicate the final cast and schedule to you early next week. Bon jour." The surprise at being addressed by the Catholic Priest left the assemblage speechless. Father Jacob had John in the pickup in an instant. They were on the road before anyone could recover.

"Thanks, Father, for bailing me out. I don't know why this is all so stressful," John stated rhetorically.

"Don't trouble yourself, My Son. Even the People of God can be very callous. You are going through a life altering event and they cannot see beyond their own selfish motives." Jacob gazed at the snow drifting across the vast river bottom.

"We can only forgive them as Our Lord forgives us. Now, where are we going?" Father Jacob changed the subject.

"I'm going to show you where we found the obsidian blade. That may not be possible considering the amount of snow we got, but we can hope." John was in better spirits now.

"There is always hope, My Son." The priest never spoke truer words. They rode on in silence for awhile. There was little traffic due to the snow. They come up behind an orange tandem-axle highway department truck pushing snow. Huge billows of fluffy snow were being directed into the ditch. They spent several minutes discussing how the French addressed their own snow removal. It was an education in cultural diversity. Soon they were skirting the Illinois River bluff and John turned off on to a snow packed road that led up a steep hill. They passed a house where father and son were busy scooping out their driveway. Father Jacob noted the stately birch trees gleaming white with patches of black bark reflecting in the sunlight. It was hard to tell where the edge of the tree branches and the drifted snow met. Jacob recalled Jon Stuart's mention of the white birches glowing in the light of the full moon in a letter about the Iroquois

Raid. Somehow Jacob felt that he was being led home. What a strange feeling indeed to have history repeated.

"The gate leading to the meadow where we found the blade is just around the corner." John Bent broke into the priest's revere. "We may have to wait until some of this white stuff melts. Looks like you will have to be our guest for awhile."

"You are too kind, My Son." Father Jacob was too engrossed in the landscape and the details of his research. Just then John turned the truck into a patch of prairie grass in front of an open gate. The posts on each side of the entrance were gray from age and the wooden gate sagged on its hinges. The end of the ancient portal was buried in the dirt. Elm saplings sprouted between the cracks. The truck squeezed through the gap and into the meadow. The meadow was surprisingly devoid of snow since it was sheltered from the north wind by a towering bluff. This fact coupled with its south facing position relative to the sun actually made the meadow seem a few degrees warmer. No doubt this was a favorite winter encampment for the Native Americans over the past centuries. Before John could bring the vehicle to a complete stop Father Jacob was out on the ground and walking mesmerized toward a particularly huge sycamore tree. It was as if the priest was guided by an unseen hand. By the time John reached Jacob's side the priest was on his knees with hands clasped in prayer.

"Yeh, about there," John spoke even though he wasn't sure Jacob could hear. He raised his voice even though being out of the wind the area was surprisingly quiet. A blue jay squawked at the trespassers from a nearby white oak tree. The bird's blue wings reflected the sun as he moved grudgingly to another perch.

"In fact, my son George found the blade near to where you are kneeling. They had been taking soil for ditch fill and it was prime arrowhead hunting territory." John continued and then paused for a moment to collect his thoughts.

"But how could you guess the exact spot, Father?" John shook his head in amazement. The priest remained entranced and did not respond. John could see tears in Father Jacob's eyes. Knowing this to be a very private moment, John moved back to the pickup. He released the tailgate as quietly as possible and sat down in the warm sunlight. Soon the murmur of the half-frozen creek tumbling over the rocks lulled John to sleep. The long story told by the Priest had made for a very short night.

Father Jacob continued to kneel in the meadow oblivious to the world around for nearly an hour. He offered a prayer of thanks to God for bringing him to this spot in West Central Illinois. Jacob asked that God would continue to guide him along his way. Lastly, he asked that the burden of his new friend be lightened.

The warmth of the noonday sun even on this cold winter day seemed to refresh his soul and encourage him on with new vigor. Father Jacob arose renewed and ready to be of service to the people of God in this community. He found John Bent snoring in the bed of the pickup truck. Soon they were in the warm truck cab and headed back to the Bent farm.

"I can see that this pageant that you are organizing is causing you much anguish, My Son. Given the tragedy of nearly losing your farm, you should not have to deal with such things," Father Jacob said.

John only stared at the road ahead.

"Please let me help you in this matter. I'm sure that your Christmas Nativity has its roots in the original festival celebrated along this river so many years ago. It would be both a privilege and an honor to be part of such a noble endeavor."

"I'm sure you will change your tune when you get a load of those selfish parents who demand their child has the starring role." John could not disguise his frustration.

"Over the years my experience as a parish priest had allowed me to develop some skill in such matters. Allow me to assume part of the burden. The Lord will guide us through the rough spots." Jacob would not let his enthusiasm be diminished and John was beyond putting up a fight. The truth was that he needed help and he knew it. The only problem John could see was if his fellow parishioners would put aside denominational boundaries to work with a Catholic.

"Frankly, I'm not sure that you know how narrow-minded Lutherans can be when it comes to working with Catholics." John voiced his thoughts.

"Let me worry about that, My Son. I have been known to be very persuasive." Father Jacob smiled reassuringly.

"Then be my guest!" John said. In a few minutes they were back in a warm kitchen enjoying a Sunday feast of baked chicken and dumplings. By that evening Father Jacob had called all the members of the pageant committee and arranged a meeting for the next day. Pastor Wilson had been consulted and even invited Father Jacob to deliver the sermon on the following Sunday. John was able to sleep better that night knowing that his problem was in capable hands.

Surprisingly, the pageant casting went extremely well. Father Jacob was able to work miracles with the church committee. It was evident that he was sincere in his love of people. This warmth was reflected in the attitudes of all those he encountered. Jacob was even able to deal with those pushy parents who insisted that their children be given the key roles. Of course, the wealthy church members got their way, but somehow Father Jacob made John feel that it was all for the best. The first rehearsal on Thursday after school went very well. John was beginning to get the impression that everything would be all right. While John was correct in that assumption, he could not have imagined how it would all come about.

Father Jacob worked tirelessly all that week. He researched the local libraries for any information on the origins of this municipal tradition. He consulted church records and became convinced that the roots of the Wilderness Nativity could be traced to the early French explorers. Father Jacob also worked hard on his forthcoming sermon. He prayed often that God would let him be the divine instrument of the perfect message. Through his faith, Father Jacob knew that his words would be just right. While some parishioners dreaded the time that a Catholic priest could preach to them, most awaited that time with great anticipation. By the time Sunday rolled around, everyone knew the story of how this Frenchman came to be in their midst. The town of Meredosia was gossiping concerning the type of sermon he might deliver. In fact, the century old Lutheran church with the double red doors on the corner by the town square was filled to standing room only when Father Jacob mounted the pulpit. There was complete silence as the congregation hung on his every word.

"Greetings to you my brothers and sisters, I bring you peace from our Lord." Father Jacob began with a traditional salutation. He began reading from the Bible.

"Speaking to the Messiah in Isaiah 42: verses 6-7, God says 'I the Lord have called you to demonstrate my righteousness. I will guard and support you, for I have given you to my people as the personal confirmation of my covenant with them. You shall also be a LIGHT to guide the nations unto me. You will open the eyes of the blind, and release those who sit in prison darkness and despair.'" Father Jacob then murmured a soft prayer before he continued.

"God has sent the LIGHT of the world in his Son, Jesus Christ. It is the celebration of that coming that we observe each year during Advent. During the Advent season we are told to anticipate this great event and prepare. It is the best Christmas present that anyone of us has ever received. But I'm here to tell you today that we don't have to wait for that gift. It is already ours. We don't have to wait until Christmas morning to tear the paper and the ribbon off the package. We already know what we are getting and it is ours if we only are willing and know how to receive it!" The priest paused to let these words sink in. This was nothing that had not been said before. But, with God's help, Father Jacob hoped to give these words new meaning.

"The LIGHT is all around us if we will only open our minds and our hearts to see. The light is reflected in nature and our surroundings. It is in the pure white snow that covers the ground and the colorful snowbirds that flit from branch to branch. The light is in the ingenuity that created the steel bridge spanning the Illinois River and allowing us to travel freely to the other side. It is in the automobile that brought us to this place of worship. Most of all the light is in both you and me. It is in our history that molded us into the type of personalities that sit in these pews today. Our Lord is the light and he is shining in all things. We just need to remind ourselves to see the glow and let the glow in us shine forth. From that perspective all things are made new. In that light all things are possible." Father Jacob paused again to let the congregation consider his words.

"Let me propose to you that life is a miracle both individually and collectively. Our history is a miracle that got us to where we are today. Our short span of years that we have on this earth is a collection of miracles that make us who we are. We are but God's will reflected in the life we live. Unfortunately, we are often too blind to see what is going on around us. Our selfishness closes our eyes to exhilaration that we can feel both by witnessing and being a part of the light. Some of you already know about my collection of miracles and the light that guided me to this spot today. A few of these miracles we share and I will tell you how in a moment. One of these miracles is the tradition that you call the Wilderness Nativity. I ask that this afternoon you pause a few minutes to reflect upon my words and consider how they might apply to you."

"The collective miracle of this life is how history brought us to this point in time. As residents of Meredosia you have a unique history in which you can take much pride. Through Divine Providence I have the privilege of sharing some of this miracle with you. So let me tell you about my personal collective and individual miracles. By seeing my example, perhaps you can understand your own."

"As you have gathered, I'm a Frenchman. For many Americans that is the first strike against me. I have been told that we French are ungrateful for what you Americans have done for us. You are certainly entitled to your opinion and I'm not here to argue that point. But I hope that does not cloud your judgment when you consider what I'm about to say. With that let me begin with my collective historical miracles that helped bring me here."

"It was a miracle that brought Christianity from the shores of the Mediterranean to the barbarians of northern Europe. A miracle baptized Charlemagne and made him defender of Christendom. A miracle sent Charles Martel to southern France to stop the Moors in Spain from their invasion that would have destroyed Christ's Church in Europe. We are all familiar with Joan of Arc that saved France from British rule. God's miracle motivated the French Jesuits to come to the North American continent to minister to the natives. We all know how powerful the Iroquois were in the 17th century. It took another miracle to save the native inhabitants of Illinois from their savagery. Consider how improbable it was for the early colonists of this land to succeed in their rebellion against English rule. My native homeland had a small part in that miracle when France sent its warships to blockade Cornwallis from the sea. How many of you Americans that call us French ungrateful remember our hand in the founding of your nation?"

Father Jacob could not resist making this point. He was rewarded as a few people began to fidget in the pews. Knowing that this focus would detract from his central message, Father Jacob quickly moved on.

"It took miracles to preserve France from the destruction of our Revolution and the bloody guillotine, from the immense losses during the Napoleonic Wars, from the trenches of WWI, and the Nazi tyranny of WWII. Without those miracles, I may not have been able to speak with you today. That is my collective set of miracles. We share some of them and for that I'm grateful."

"Each of us has an individual set of miracles that define us as human beings. Although similar they are as different as the people on the face of this earth. Listen to my individual miracles and consider those miracles that have defined you as an individual child of God." Father Jacob paused to catch his breath. He hoped he was making God's message clear. Looking at the faces in the congregation Father Jacob could not be sure.

"I was born a Frenchman in the province of Alsace. My first personal miracle was involvement with the Church and being called to minister to God's people. I have always been intrigued by history, which led to my next miracle. It happens that my home parish possesses a body of letters and artifacts from the estate of a 17th century Scottish mercenary named Jon Stuart. This man provided protection for two Jesuit priests that were instrumental in the conversion of many natives throughout the world."

Father Jacob went on in detail to recount the main points revealed by his research concerning the link between these individuals and the annual Meredosia tradition known as the Wilderness Nativity. Like the Bent family did earlier, the members of the St. Johns congregation hung on Father Jacob's every word. Soon it came time to produce the evidence to support the story.

"Was it sheer coincidence or Divine Providence that brought me to this place? You all know this area to be rich in native artifacts. In fact, John Bent auctioned off several at his farm last week. This is a very unusual blade that I purchased at that sale." Father Jacob raised the gleaming obsidian point high in the air for all to see.

"Isn't it truly a miracle that a smaller copy of this artifact should be included in the estate of Jon Stuart in the museum of a church in distant France?" Father Jacob removed the chain from around his neck displaying the artifact in his other hand for all to see. Many stared in disbelief. Others were still trying to grasp the importance of what he was saying.

"Whether you believe my story or not is for you to personally decide. Whether you believe that Christ is the Son of God and Your Savior is another decision we have all had to make. Some things we must take on faith, others we are blessed with proof!" Father Jacob emphasized each and every word.

"This is my personal miracle, but we can share it collectively. We do share it collectively each year when you reenact the sharing of God's blessing with the poor and downhearted of this world. Those early French explorers had a huge bonfire to guide them back to the starving people of that early Mere D'Osia parish. Like these blessed people of old let us put aside our petty differences and work for the common good. As Isaiah said Our Lord 'shall also be a LIGHT to guide the nations unto me. You will open the eyes of the blind, and release those who sit in prison darkness and despair.'" Father Jacob was nearing the end of the sermon. He had done his best.

"The Great Light brought salvation across the prairie so many years ago. The same Light led my research to an auction on that same prairie. The Light encourages you to maintain that same spark each year in this small prairie town. Miracles are everywhere if we learn to recognize them. Miracles are a gift of the Light to his chosen people. God works in mysterious ways; his miracles to perform. God helps us each to be worthy to receive such a gift during this blessed Christmas season. Amen." Father Jacob pronounced the benediction as Pastor Wilson echoed his final Amen.

Most Lutherans do not commonly voice their enthusiasm in public, but there was a resounding Amen from the congregation that day. Of course there were more than just Lutherans in that standing room only crowd. The sermon of a Catholic priest from France no less was certainly an event. However, there was more to it than that. The pageant called the Wilderness Nativity was a tradition of the town. Somehow it expressed the compassion of the people of the Mid West and defined the personality of the town. Its success brought blessings to the region. Even though there was rumor of discontent no one could fathom that it might fail in its purpose. Perhaps Father Jacob's passionate sermon would reemphasize the pageant's real reason for existence. John Bent and his family left the Church that Sunday reassured that this would be the case.

Chapter 7

AN OFFERING

That particular year would see another Great Light on the prairie. Father Jacob certainly provided a great light in organizing the pageant. His skill with people stopped the public arguments, but a few in the congregation continued with their selfishness apparently untouched by the words of the French priest. Generally, their children had key roles and they were blatant in their performance of duty. John could hardly bear these slights and Father Jacob for all his experience was at wits end as to what to do. Father Jacob and the Bent family prayed devoutly that the great Light of our life would see fit to reveal another miracle. Then within a week of Christmas Eve their prayers were answered. The Church burned to the ground!

No one knew for sure how the fire started. The Fire Marshal was investigating, but the report would not be available for several weeks. It may have been some faulty wiring since the church was over one-hundred years old. A gas leak might be the cause since the building was heated by two older furnaces. Certainly, it did not appear to be vandalism. At least that was a blessing. Needless to say the destruction of the church pushed the tradition of the Wilderness Nativity to its very limits.

The Church Council met immediately to decide what to do. It was held in the high school gymnasium to provide room for all in the community that might wish to attend. Since this might be the year when the annual community tradition ended there were many interested people. The local media sent their correspondents and the meeting turned out to be quite an event.

"I will call this special meeting of the St. Johns Church Council to order." Pastor Wilson stated as President of the Council.

"I refer you to the short printed agenda you see before you." Seven council members scrutinized the list. Everyone was reluctant to speak given the huge turn out.

"The first item is to consider how to proceed with church services. Is there any discussion?" Pastor Wilson asked.

"What do you suggest, Pastor?" said one council person.

"Well, the Parish Hall suffered only minor damage. I think we can continue services there although we will certainly be a little cramped." Pastor Wilson spoke quickly wishing to move the meeting along.

"I move to continue regular services in the Parish Hall and for appropriation of funds to repair the Hall as necessary," said one member.

"I second." said another.

"I have a motion and a second. Is there any discussion?" Pastor Wilson paused.

"If not, all those in favor signify by saying aye?" A chorus of voices echoed in the large gym.

"Opposed?" All was quiet.

"The ayes have it. Let's move on to the second item." Obviously, Pastor Wilson wanted to make the meeting short and sweet.

"Wait a minute, Pastor." One council member said. "Do the services include the pageant? The items on the agenda don't specifically mention it and that is what everyone has come to hear about," said one member.

"I was wondering about that myself," said another council member. The crowd in the bleachers of the gym began to murmur.

"Given the circumstances, I assumed the pageant was out of the question." Pastor Wilson said with finality.

"But it's an outside event," the councilperson that brought up the question continued. "I can see no harm. It will be good for the community in the face of this tragedy." Most of those present seemed to agree but Pastor Wilson raised an objection.

"I hate to dampen your spirits but we must give consideration to our insurance liability. The Church property remains in a shambles following the fire fighting efforts. While the town park remains clear I'm sure that the large crowd that gathers each year for the pageant will probably come in contact with the ruins. We wouldn't want to chance anyone getting hurt. With the nails and the tin around it wouldn't be wise. Also, given the turn out tonight the crowd this year might be bigger than ever considering the publicity and all." Pastor Wilson lowered his gaze to the table before him.

"The ruin is roped off with barrier tape. That should warn everyone about the danger and remove out liability," said one council person. Affirmations were voiced from the crowd.

"Listen to yourself. Are you really willing to take that chance?" said Pastor Wilson. That seemed to silence any dissent and the council moved on to the next agenda item. The crowd began to disperse in silence. It seemed the tradition of the Wilderness Nativity had been ended at least for this year.

"And now for better news, if I dare say it," Pastor Wilson continued to guide the council meeting. "I have contacted our insurance agent and we will have more than enough money to replace the church with an even better structure. I only need your approval to file the proper forms."

After some more discussion concerning the details the appropriate motions were made and approved. The council meeting was completed in short order and Pastor Wilson asked if there was further business before they adjourned. He saw a small hand waving from the audience. Pastor Wilson thought about ignoring this but then thought better of it.

"Was there something you wished to bring to the Council before we adjourn, Madam?"

"My daughter has something to say," was the reply from the girl's mother. The mother was well dressed as was her daughter. They were from one of the wealthier families in the congregation.

"It's highly irregular since only council members are entitled to present business not on the agenda to the council." The Pastor looked at the faces of the members and they all seemed willing to listen. Politically, Pastor Wilson knew that he must give them time to speak.

"We won't be long, Pastor. Just let my daughter say her piece and then we will go," the mother said solemnly. She squeezed her child's hand and encouraged her to speak. Realizing the number of people assembled and that she was the focus of attention, the girl was suddenly afraid to speak. The child was no more than seven years old. She stood there in her fine blue velvet dress looking at the floor. Most knew that she was the child chosen to play the part of Mary in the pageant.

"Go ahead, Amy." The mother encouraged her child.

After a minute or so the girl worked up the courage to speak. Her voice quivered and she started off so softly no one could hear.

"Speak up, honey. They can't hear your," said the mother. This seemed to help and the girl began to speak with confidence.

"We've worked SO HARD on the play," Amy emphasized those two words, "and it's Christmas. It won't seem like Christmas without the play. Can't we do something to have it? We were all so happy and now it is so sad in town. My friends and I will do anything you ask?"

"From the mouths of babes," said Father Jacob in the audience.

The plea of this small girl melted the hearts of all present.

"I'm sorry dear but we just can't. You'll understand when you get a little older." Before anyone knew it, Pastor Wilson had adjourned the meeting and the gym was vacant. Amy and her mother slowly walked to the parking lot.

"Mommy, there's got to be something we can do?" Amy pleaded with tears in her eyes.

"Say your prayers when you go to bed tonight, honey," said her mother. "I'm sure God will make it all better." At first, Amy's mother had thought the reason the pageant was so important to her daughter was pure selfishness. After all, Amy had finally got the leading role and she had been bragging to her friends. Now she was not so sure. They drove home in the silence of a cold and clear December night. Somehow the canopy of glittering stars in the immense galaxy made these problems seem so petty.

Chapter 8

COMMUNION

Amy couldn't understand how the community could let the tradition die. She remembered the fun of the auditions and rehearsals even though she had argued with Jody about who would be Mary. It seemed a waste to let all the work go for nothing. The next day was Tuesday and the cancellation of the pageant was all that anyone at school could talk about. The social studies teachers said it was such a shame, but they weren't willing to do anything about it. One of Amy's classmates even asked their teacher in class if anything could be done. The response was merely sadness and regret.

It didn't take Amy long to decide that if the nativity was to come to Meredosia this year it was up to her and her alone. Christmas Eve was Saturday night. With some planning Amy thought she could make something happen. After all they had all practiced so hard. It wouldn't be the festive community celebration that they had come to know, but it would happen and that was enough. Amy began to talk with her friends and swear them to complete secrecy. There would be no more pageant practice or a dress rehearsal, but that didn't matter. One of the first kids Amy talked to was Jody and it was a hard sell.

At recess, Amy saw Jody over by the swings waiting her turn. Amy waited until their eyes made contact and she motioned Jody over to talk in private. At first it seemed Jody would not come over. They had different friends and seldom said more than hello. But with some perseverance Amy got her chance.

"What da ya want, girlie?" said Jody. "It's my turn to swing and recess will be over before ya know it."

"I've got something to ask you, but you've got to swear you won't tell a soul." Amy spoke very seriously. Jody could tell that something was up.

"I don't know. That's askin' a lot. You'd think someone is dyin' with that look on your face." Jody wasn't going to make it easy. Jody figured it must be really something if Miss Queen of the World was willing to speak with her in public. She couldn't help but push a little. Amy's rosy red cheeks grimaced as the winter wind blew her blond hair into her face. So that's how it's going to be, she thought. Still, Amy knew she needed help and so she swallowed her pride.

"Just hear me out, but you gotta promise to be quiet about what I'm gonna say." Amy put on her most sincere expression. It must have worked because Jody grinned.

"Okay. Whatta ya got?" Jody pulled up the zipper on her pink nylon coat trying to get warm on such a cold day.

"We gotta keep the pageant going! Right?" Amy wanted to find out what Jody thought before letting her in on the secret.

"You were at the meeting last night same as me. It ain't gonna happen." Jody was noncommittal.

"Just like that you're gonna let it go." Amy got a little huffy.

"Yeh. Just like that!" Jody was about ready to walk off and Amy knew it.

"Hey! I don't wanna fight. I just think we don't have to let it go." Amy was trying to compromise. Jody sensed her sincerity.

"I'm listening. Go on," said Jody.

"After all those years, it seems a shame to let it go just like that."

"Yah." Jody nodded.

"Well, I was thinkin'," said Amy. Jody thought here it comes.

"Hear me out. Without you I might as well give up," Amy said.

"Okay. What ya up to, girlfriend?" Jody could be a comic and she was trying to make it easier for Amy to talk. This was sure a switch that someone like Amy would need anything from her. Jody was beginning to get curious.

"We can do it."

"Do what?"

"The pageant, dummy." Amy bit her tongue after she said that, but Jody was still listening.

"You heard the church council same as me. The church is a pile of rubble and they don't wanna risk it," Jody said.

"I know, but we could do it ourselves. It doesn't have to be a big production. We don't have to do much. If we get together and do something it won't be like it died. Right?" Amy pleaded. Jody thought she was going to cry.

"Oh!" Jody exclaimed. "I see what you're doing."

"Whatdaya mean?" Amy sniffled and rubbed her eyes with her mitten.

"You just gotta be the big cheese, don't ya?" Jody said sarcastically.

"Huh?" Amy was getting red in the face now and it wasn't from the winter wind.

"It's your turn to be Mary and it ain't gonna happen. That's what it's all about, isn't it?" Jody mocked. Amy's first reaction was to stomp off in a huff, but then she knew she would have to swallow her pride.

"It ain't about that at all." Amy said with all the sincerity she could muster. It wasn't a lie and Jody sensed it.

"Like I'm supposed to believe that!" Jody still was going to make it difficult.

"After hear'n Father Jacob's story about the miracle we just can't forget it." Amy pleaded.

"But we'll get in trouble if we try. I don't want to get grounded, especially around Christmas. No way!" Jody smirked.

"Since when has that ever bothered you?" Amy spouted back. She could see she might have an ally.

"Right you are. Might be fun at that." Jody grinned. "So what's your plan?"

Amy and Jody spent the last few minutes of recess planning what they would do. First, they decided to get all the kids in the pageant that they could trust to help. Then Amy said that they would have a dress rehearsal in her father's barn on the edge of town. Some kids lived on farms so they couldn't make it, but it would have to do. Above all, they made a pact to keep this secret. They knew it would take some doing for a bunch of kids to sneak out of the house on Christmas Eve no less, but it was worth a try. Finally, they decided to stage the pageant on the school ground that was several blocks from the church. They reasoned this was a safe place and the church could not be held liable if something happened. Another miracle might happen after all.

Amy and Jody did a great job in organizing their impromptu pageant. In fact, the dress rehearsal in the barn came off without a hitch. Some of the children had no costumes. The costumes had either not been finished or were locked up in the church parish hall. But they made do with common articles of clothing and it didn't look half bad. Amy was worried that even though the pageant would be staged there would be no offering for the poor. She had come to realize that food and clothing for the poor was the whole purpose of the tradition. By doing this in secrecy, there seemed to be no way to help the needy. Still the children wanted to do something. They all decided to raid their parent's pantry and clothes closet. The kids reasoned that no one would miss a few cans of vegetables or fruit and some items of old clothes. Unfortunately, that was what let the cat out of the bag.

John Bent first got an idea that something was amiss when he couldn't locate an older chore coat. Discussions at the coffee shop one morning indicated that there seemed to be a rash of misplaced clothes. Generally, everyone laughed about it and moved on, but John decided to investigate further. When Ida sent John to the store for canned goods to make some favorite recipes John asked his son Bill to ride to the store with him. Bill had a part in the pageant and John suspected that he might know something. John knew his children wouldn't lie to him so he put Bill on the spot. Soon Bill told his father everything. Bill begged him not to say anything. Considering the decision of the church council John couldn't promise anything.

Immediately John talked with Father Jacob about what was going on. John was torn between his duty to the church and his inclination to let the pageant happen. Of course, Father Jacob was noncommittal, but secretly he prayed that God's will be done. Father Jacob suggested that John pray about it. Father Jacob reassured John that God would provide the answer. After praying and talking with Ida, John decided to let Pastor Wilson in on the secret. At first, Pastor Wilson was inclined to expose the plan. However, Pastor Wilson convened an emergency meeting of the church council in secrecy. After much discussion, the council voted to ignore John's information and let the children proceed. In fact, the adults carried this one step further. Just like the children, the adults of Meredosia would have a secret as well. By word of mouth, every adult in Meredosia was told that the children were planning something for Christmas. They were sworn to secrecy and asked to ignore anything suspicious that might involve their children during the next few days. The last few days before Christmas passed quickly with more anticipation than usual.

Christmas Eve came clear and cool with temperatures in the mid twenties. The snow was piled high but the roads were clear. Christmas Eve service was held at 7 p.m. and everyone went home in a festive mood. After midnight throughout Meredosia several children secretly donned their costumes under winter clothes, gathered their offerings, and made their way to the school playground. As in Clement Clarke Moore's poem, the golden moonlight "gave a luster of midday to objects" all around. Somehow a couple straw bales had been sequestered in a nearby garage. These were produced to form a manger. Amy and Jody directed everyone to take their places. Before giving the signal to start the procession, Amy pulled Jody to one side.

"Here, take the Baby Jesus." Amy offered the doll to Jody.

"What on earth are you doing?" Jody was anxious to start.

"I want you to be Mary this year," Amy said.

"You can't be serious." Jody was flabbergasted.

"Take it, I said!" Amy raised her voice.

"Would one of you take it for Pete sake!" exclaimed the child who had the part of Joseph. "The cops will be on us for sure."

"Are you sure?" Jody said meekly.

"Positive!" Amy had on a big grin that beamed even in the moonlight.

Amy gave the signal for the procession to begin. Although there was no earthly audience the children performed the parts they had learned for the pageant. The story of Christ's Birth was read from the Bible by the narrator. Traditional hymns were sung including "Oh Come All Ye Faithful" and "Angels We Have Heard on High." Shepherds gathered to adore the Christ. The Magi brought forth their gifts. The pageant was concluded by singing "Silent Night". It was a fitting ending to such an inspiring sight. The entire cast stood transfixed for several minutes as if a picture caught in time. Everyone could feel God's presence as the glittering stars twinkled in the heavens. The children departed for their homes in silence. The baby Jesus remained in the straw with the few items of canned goods and clothes strewn about. Soon the pageant participants were home all snug and asleep in their beds. Now it was the adult's turn.

The town police had been keeping a watchful eye on the proceedings unbeknownst to the participants. They passed the word to several townspeople that the coast was clear. Father Jacob, Pastor Wilson, and John Bent were the first to arrive. Soon people from around the area arrived one by one or in groups bringing their offering to the Christ Child. The poor and needy would be well taken care of from the bounty that was delivered that Christmas Eve. As God's People gathered for church services on Christmas Day they made it a point to drive by the school ground. All the children were amazed at the offering that had been given. Great mounds of food and clothing were stacked as high as the snowdrifts around the small manger that was nearly hidden in the golden straw. The children knew they had not left such a bounty. Where had it all come from?

CHAPTER 9

THE BENEDICITON

There was one particular gift found in the manger carefully tucked beside the Christ Child. It was a letter from the St. Johns Church Council dedicating most of the building insurance money to the town organization for the poor and needy called the ***Bread of Love***. The council had decided in their emergency meeting that they had lost sight of their true purpose in this world. The members realized that God's Church was more than a building. God had called them to minister to his people. They had been too obsessed with a building and an empty tradition with no meaning. For penance the council voted to build only a modest building and donate the balance of the insurance funds to the mission for the poor in the area. It had taken the example of their children to reveal the true Light. Wisdom had truly proceeded from the mouths of babes!

And so the tradition continues unbroken into the future. The miracle had come again to the prairie! Only the meek and the mild had witnessed it this Christmas Eve. Again God's gift had been given in silence. Like that first Nativity so many centuries ago, the Wilderness Nativity proved to be a gift from God that nothing could stop. May we all be humble enough to recognize this truth. If we can let the tradition be ever reflected in our lives, then we will all be truly blessed!

THE END

ABOUT THE AUTHOR

The author is well-versed in Illinois history holding a bachelor of arts degree in history from Western Illinois University. He is life long resident of Illinois and Meredosia. The book is dedicated to God, family, and the community he has come to love so much.

0-595-32137-2